Attractiv
Gorgeo
These passion
have a lot to offer…

Mediterranean Men:

Irresistible
Italians

Two fabulous, dramatic novels come from
international bestselling authors
Lynne Graham and Sarah Morgan

'Lynne Graham delights readers with a sexy, sensual
tale full of passionate characters, an intense premise
and volatile scenes.'
—*Romantic Times* on *The Italian's Wife*

'*The Italian's Passionate Proposal* is a charming romance
with two lovely characters.'
—*Romantic Times*

Mediterranean Men:

Irresistible Italians

featuring

THE ITALIAN'S WIFE
by
Lynne Graham

&

THE ITALIAN'S PASSIONATE PROPOSAL
by
Sarah Morgan

*M&B™ and M&B™ with the Rose Device
are trademarks of the publisher.
Harlequin Mills & Boon Limited, Eton House,
18-24 Paradise Road, Richmond, Surrey TW9 1SR*

MEDITERRANEAN MEN: IRRESISTIBLE ITALIANS
© by Harlequin Books SA 2007

The Italian's Wife and The Italian's Passionate Proposal were first
published in Great Britain in separate, single volumes.

The Italian's Wife © Lynne Graham 2001
The Italian's Passionate Proposal © Sarah Morgan 2003

ISBN: 978 0 263 85847 1

009-1007

*Printed and bound in Spain
by Litografía Rosés S.A., Barcelona*

The Italian's Wife

by
Lynne Graham

Lynne Graham was born in Northern Ireland and has been a keen Mills & Boon reader since her teens. She is very happily married with an understanding husband, who has learned to cook since she started to write! Her five children keep her on her toes. She has a very large dog, which knocks everything over, a very small terrier which barks a lot, and two cats. When time allows, Lynne is a keen gardener.

Don't miss Lynne Graham's new novels, *The Petrakos Bride* and *The Desert Sheikh's Captive Wife*, out in August and December 2007 from Mills & Boon® Modern™!

CHAPTER ONE

WHEN Rio Lombardi finally heard the apartment door open, his handsome mouth quirked and he sprang upright. Christabel was in for a surprise.

A breathless series of giggles and an urgent whisper which he didn't catch sounded from the hall, making him frown. Evidently, his fiancée had a friend in tow. That was the trouble with surprises, Rio acknowledged in exasperation: their very nature made them unreliable. He should've warned her that he might make it back to London a day early. Surrendering his fantasy of sweeping Christabel straight off to bed for a passionate reunion, Rio crossed the spacious lounge to announce his presence and make polite social chitchat instead.

But the hall was already empty. A pair of kitten-heeled turquoise shoes and a pair of diamanté-studded black satin mules lay abandoned on the carpet. Frowning a little at the suspicion that his fiancée might not be sober again, and now also wondering if he was about to break in on some cosy girly get-together, Rio strolled down the corridor to the bedroom. He'd intended to knock on the door but it was wide open and the sight which met his eyes was so shocking, so utterly unbelievable to him, that his lean hand froze in mid-air.

Halfway out of her dress, Christabel was kissing… another woman, also half out of her dress. Paralysed to the threshold, Rio stared, his dark-as-midnight eyes totally refusing to accept what he was seeing. They were drunk, fooling about, he started to tell himself; maybe they had realised he was in the apartment and were playing some stupid tasteless joke on him. But they were locked together, breast to breast, hip to hip, Christabel's glossy blonde hair mingling with the brunette's darker tresses as they touched each other with the unmistakable eagerness of lovers. He was so revolted by that acknowledgement that for an instant he felt physically ill. Christabel, *his* woman, *his* lover, *his* bride-to-be…

Christabel drew back with a husky, sexy laugh, her fabulous face flushed with excitement, and only then did the two women realise that they had an audience poised in the doorway. Rio recognised the brunette as one of Christabel's friends: Tammy something or other, another fashion model, also another man's wife.

For a split-second nobody moved or spoke. Aghast, Christabel and Tammy gaped at him, and then the brunette loosed a strangled moan of horror and fled into the connecting bathroom, noisily slamming and locking the door behind her.

'H-heavens…what a fright you gave me…' Christabel faltered, frantically yanking up her dress to cover her bare breasts, her face now pale and stiff as marble, her wonderful green eyes glittering with fearful anxiety. 'Please…you mustn't misunderstand what you just saw, Rio—'

'*Misunderstand?*' Rio could never recall it taking more effort to speak one word levelly. Initial shock and disbelief were giving way to rage and an unfamiliar sense of appalled bewilderment that only stoked the rage higher.

'We were just mucking around. Don't be old-fashioned about this…' Christabel urged in the charged silence as she moved closer and made a little pleading movement with her manicured hands.

Rio could not take his eyes off her. Christabel Kent, the world-famous supermodel and media darling who wore his engagement ring, her Nordic fairness and endless legs a legend in the fashion and beauty market. Perfect face, perfect body.

'OK...I'll come clean,' Christabel continued feverishly. 'So I was missing you dreadfully and I like a change occasionally—'

'A change? You make it sound like it's nothing—'

'It isn't...it's just *sex*!' his fiancée interrupted, reaching for the lean, powerful hands coiled into fierce fists of self-restraint by his sides. 'Nothing for you to worry about or even think about, because if you don't like it I swear it won't *ever* happen again!'

Rio backed out of her reach. In his mind's eye he could still only see one image: Christabel wrapped half-naked and excited round another woman. Just sex? He felt betrayed. He felt incredulous. He felt something he wasn't used to feeling: foolish.

'All right...you're shocked and furious and I understand and I'm really sorry!' Christabel was panicking at his lack of response. 'I'll make it up to you—'

'What with? An offer to *join* the two of you?' Rio derided between clenched white teeth.

Christabel looked up at him, green eyes gleaming with sudden relief lightened by a shard of seductive amusement. 'Would you like that, darling?'

Violence coursed through Rio in a molten wave and a shudder of angry revulsion passed through him. If she hadn't been a woman he would have knocked her through the wall and if that was an old-fashioned reaction, tough! Yet her stupidity in assuming that his contemptuous question might have been a serious hint that all would be forgiven if he got a piece of the same action freed him from that first binding shock.

'I'll give you time to move out of here,' Rio breathed

with raw clarity. 'I'll deal with cancelling the wedding arrangements—'

'You *can't* be serious!' Christabel gasped in stricken horror. 'We're perfect together!'

Rio swung on his heel and strode back down the corridor, Christabel pursuing him every step of the way, pleading with him to calm down and think again. In the hall, she shot between him and the front door to prevent his departure.

'If you tell people about this, my career will be ruined!'

Christabel's career had been built on her clean, wholesome image. No risqué lingerie assignments, no media coverage of Christabel whooping it up like a ladette in the clubs, no bad-ass boyfriends. Christabel liked to pose for off-the-record interviews with fluffy animals and talk about how mad she was about children, not to mention how crazy she was about the man she was to marry and how much she was looking forward to giving up work to be a full-time wife and mother…

Rio reached out and lifted her bodily out of his path. '*Dio mio*…I won't be talking—'

That fear overcome, Christabel cried in desperation. 'Then *why* can't you forgive me? Tammy means nothing to me. It's not like she was another man or I'm in love with her. I love *you*, Rio—'

She loved him? Had she *ever* loved him? Or had she loved his enormous wealth most of all? His sculpted mouth tightening, he recalled that Christabel had expensive tastes that far outran even her own healthy earning power. Within a week of his marriage proposal she had confessed to a string of outstanding bills and had told him how hopeless she was with money. Impressed by her honesty, he had felt hugely protective towards her and had cleared her debts without even thinking about what he was doing.

Yanking himself free of her clinging hands in growing disgust at what her every reckless word revealed about her character, Rio left the apartment and made it into the lift. He raised one of his hands and watched it shake in disbelieving outrage. Balling his fingers back into an aggressive fist, he punched the steel wall with the full force of the rage and the pain splintering through him, the savage pain he had been struggling to deny. He had loved her, he had *really* loved her and wanted to marry her.

Santo cielo, he might have given his children a mother who thought three-in-a-bed sex was a wonderful thrill! A woman who had contrived to hide her true nature from him so successfully that the sheer shock value of what he had witnessed and heard would linger with him for a very long time.

Just sex? Hadn't he been enough for her? Obviously not. As his bodyguards reared up from their seats in the ground-floor reception area, their surprise at his unexpected reappearance patent, Rio was blind to them, his darkly handsome features rigid and ashen pale. Outside, he drank in deep of the frosty night air before crossing the street to his limo. Had Christabel been lying back and thinking about other *women* in his bed? Had even her pleasure been faked? Had the eager desire she had shown for his lovemaking all been part of one giant con to ensnare a very rich husband? How could he have known so little about a woman he had been with for almost two years?

'Your hand's bleeding, boss. Are you OK?'

Rio angled a cursory glance down at his bruised and bleeding knuckles before meeting the troubled dark eyes of Ezio. The stockily built older man had been on his security team since Rio was a student and knew him too well.

'*Sì...*' But right at that moment Rio did not know when he was ever going to feel normal again. Like Saverio Lombardi, billionaire head of one of the proudest, oldest families in Italy and the driving force behind Lombardi Industries, one of the biggest, most successful companies in the world. He felt humiliated, sick and less than a man for the first time in twenty-nine years of existence.

How was he to explain this fiasco in acceptable terms to his vulnerable mother? Alice Lombardi was literally counting the days to her son's wedding and was pitifully eager to cradle her first grandchild in her arms. She was a sick woman, crippled by arthritis, further weakened by a series of debilitating illnesses. Every week she survived was a literal gift from God and her poor health permitted her precious few pleasures in life. Now there would be no wedding, no prospect of a baby to fill the empty nursery, no bright and chatty daughter-in-law to occasionally enliven her dull, pain-filled days...

He had never openly acknowledged the reality before but he *needed* a wife.

'Tammy means nothing to me...it's not like she was another man.' The insidious and seductive echo of Christabel's husky voice made Rio's hands clench into ferocious fists. No, he could not, would not forgive her, not for the sake of his own powerful libido, not even for the sake of the mother he adored. Christabel, the woman he had loved beyond belief, was a total sham. What did that say about *his* judgement? He had believed he knew his fiancée through and through, yet he had not even penetrated the surface of that calculating immoral mind of hers. He could not have chosen worse had he decided to marry a total stranger. He might as well stop and ask the first woman he met to be his bride...

With a harsh and bitter laugh at that insane idea, Rio Lombardi poured himself a large brandy from the bar in the back of the limo.

* * *

Holly was cold, hungry and scared.

It was barely one in the morning and the whole of the rest of the night hours still stretched ahead of her. For how long had she been walking? Her back and her legs ached and her vision was blurring with exhaustion but where could she possibly stop for the night that she would be safe? She had sat around in a train station for most of the day, moving seats every so often, striving not to attract the attention of anyone official, until the crude heckling of two youths had forced her to take refuge in the cloakroom. While she had been trying to freshen up there, her jacket, which had had her purse in the inside pocket, had been stolen. Her *own* fault for taking her jacket off, leaving it carelessly draped over Timmie's buggy and turning her attention away for a minute.

No point approaching a policeman, not when awkward questions would be asked and an address requested. Her purse, which had had her last few pounds in it, was gone and that was that. Like so much else that had happened to Holly since her arrival in London so full of naïve hopes seven months earlier, it was just one more kick when she was down, one more piece of bad luck in a run of bad luck that seemed endless.

As she paused to check that her eight-month-old son was still wrapped up snug against the chilly air, she shivered violently and fingered the two battered carrier bags that now contained all that she possessed in the world. She had to be the ultimate loser and failure, she decided wretchedly. Useless at everything, not even able to put the shabbiest roof over Timmie's head and look after him as he deserved. Here she was out walking the streets, homeless and penniless, next door to being a beggar…

Yet just twenty-four hours earlier she really had tried so hard to pick up her sagging courage and get a grip on her problems. She had gone to the Social Security office to report that her landlord had tried to break into her room twice during the night and that she was terrified of him.

'We've never had any complaints about him before,' the woman behind the protective barrier had said, coolly unimpressed, not even trying to hide her suspicion that Holly was simply trying to get her accommodation upgraded. 'If you don't return to the lodgings we arranged for you, you will be deemed to have made yourself intentionally homeless. I advise you to think long and hard before you make that mistake, as you have a young child to consider. I'll inform your social worker that you're having problems—'

'No...please don't do that,' Holly had begged, in terror of what such an interview might mean where Timmie was concerned. Her baby might be taken away from her and put into care. The last social worker she had spoken to had started out sympathetic but had lost patience when Holly refused to name the father of her child. But Jeff had said that if she dared to tell anyone that he was Timmie's dad he would make her sorry that she had *ever* been born...

Well, she was sorry enough herself about that fact, Holly conceded miserably. She had devastated the parents who loved her by giving birth to a baby outside marriage. When she had finally admitted that she was pregnant her father had cried. As long as Holly lived she knew she would never, ever forget the sight of her father crying...or her own sick sense of guilt and bitter shame.

Her eyes swimming with tears at that painful recollection, and lost as she was in her own thoughts, Holly did not even notice that she was approaching a junction. Staring blankly ahead of her, accustomed to the noisy flow of traffic down the main road as a background, she was equally unaware of the lights of a car coming from her right.

The sudden steep drop of the pavement down onto the

road took her by surprise and sent the overladen buggy lurching off-balance. As she made a frantic effort to right it, the scream of car tyres striving to brake to a halt alerted her to the danger that she and Timmie were in. In the split-second at her disposal Holly thrust Timmie's buggy away from her with all her might in the desperate hope that it would carry him out of the car's path to safety. But her own shaken attempt to make it back up onto the pavement was doomed as her heels hit the kerb and she lost her footing. Falling backwards, she felt a sickening explosion of pain at the base of her skull and then blackness folded in and she knew no more.

Rio Lombardi leapt out of the limousine. 'Did we hit her?' he demanded.

'No!' Ezio, who could move at the speed of light when required, was already retrieving the buggy and drawing it back from the other side of the road to a safer resting place.

'I didn't hit her...I *saw* her; I was already slowing down. But she walked out into the road without looking and just fell over!' Rio's chauffeur exclaimed over the top of the driver's door, his attention lodged in horror on the still figure lying in the path of the headlights.

'Call an ambulance...a private one from the foundation hospital; it'll be faster,' Rio instructed harshly, his tone of command pronounced to steady his companions.

He crouched down on the road and lifted a limp wrist to feel for a pulse, drawing in a slow deep breath of relief when he found what he sought. Although her skin felt frighteningly cold to his touch, she was alive. 'She's not dead...' Springing upright again, he peeled off his suit jacket and bent down to carefully drape it over her, surveying the face of the unconscious victim for the first time. '*Dio mio*...she's little more than a child!'

A very pretty child too, Rio found himself conceding,

scanning that delicate bone-structure and the mass of bronze-coloured ringlets rioting round her small head, their vibrant colour only serving to accentuate her pallor. 'What is she doing out with a baby at this hour? Did you see what she did for the baby? She was ready to sacrifice her own life to give it a chance—'

'She's probably its mother, boss,' Ezio suggested, lowering his mobile phone, having made the requested call for immediate medical attendance at the scene. 'It's depressing, but kids are giving birth to kids all the time these days.'

Rio found himself strangely reluctant to accept that opinion. After a second, lengthier appraisal, he was prepared to concede that the girl could possibly be seventeen or eighteen years old. But she looked so innocent and untouched, and he had already noticed that she wore no rings. Ezio stooped to retrieve his employer's jacket.

'What are you *doing*?' Rio demanded.

'I got your overcoat from the car, boss. It'll keep her warmer. There's no point you catching pneumonia.' Ezio had to pitch his voice higher to be heard above the noisy sobs now emanating from the depths of the covers heaped on the buggy.

'I'm OK. I wish we could risk moving her into the limo. Giovanni…you're a family man; comfort the child,' Rio urged his other bodyguard as he accepted the overcoat from Ezio but chose to lay it gently over the top of his suit jacket to provide an extra layer of warmth for the girl. 'She's frozen through.'

'Timmie…?' Her head pounding fit to burst, Holly surfaced and with a heroic effort raised her head, reacting to the sound of her son's cries. Not a pain cry though, only an anxious cry, she recognised in instant relief. 'My baby?'

Rio gazed down into huge anxious eyes as disconcertingly blue as a Tuscan midsummer sky. 'Your baby's fine. Lie still. An ambulance is on its way—'

'I can't go to hospital…I've got Timmie to take care of!' Initially bemused by that deep dark drawl with its unexpected liquid foreign accent larding every syllable, Holly was startled when the man dropped down on a level with her and pressed on her shoulder to prevent her from lifting herself higher.

Mouth running dry, she stared up at him just as he turned his arrogant dark head away, presenting her with his bold profile and the impossibly smooth, proud lines of a high cheekbone to address someone else out of her view. 'Have you contacted the police yet?'

'No police…*please*,' Holly broke in shakily. 'Are you the bloke that was in the car?'

In silent response, he turned back to nod in confirmation, regarding her with dramatic dark golden eyes which could have turned a saint into a sinner overnight.

Shaken by that abstracted thought, Holly said, 'We don't need the police or an ambulance. I'm all right. I tripped and knocked myself out for a second…that's all—'

'Have you any family…a boyfriend I can contact on your behalf?' he prompted, very much as if she hadn't spoken.

Even though it hurt, she turned her head away in self-protection. 'Nobody.'

'There's got to be somebody. A friend, a relative, surely?' he persisted.

'Well, maybe you're coming down with them but I've got nobody,' she muttered in a voice that wobbled in spite of all her efforts to control it.

Rio studied her in frustration. She wasn't a Londoner. She had a pronounced country brogue with rounded vowel sounds but he could not place it, although he had a vague recollection of once hearing an exaggerated version of a similar accent in a stage comedy. First things first, he reminded himself. 'What age are you?'

'Twenty. I don't want the police...do you *hear* me?' Fear made her strident and she began to sit up in spite of the sick whirling sensation that engulfed her the moment she moved. If she went into hospital, the police would call in the authorities to take charge of Timmie and he would be put in a foster home.

When she swayed backwards, Rio shot a supportive arm round her narrow spine. 'You must have medical attention. I promise you that you will not be parted from your child.'

'How? *How* can you promise that?' she gasped.

The ambulance pulled in, all flashing lights and efficiency, and the paramedics took over, forcing him into retreat.

'Timmie!' Holly exclaimed in panic as she was moved onto the stretcher.

Rio strode forward. 'I'll follow you to the hospital with him—'

Holly realised that he was asking her to trust him with her son. 'I don't *know* you—'

'But *we* know him.' For some reason, the paramedic who had spoken chuckled with decided amusement. 'Don't worry, love. Your kid will be safe as houses with this gentleman.'

Exhausted by the effort she had expended, and trembling, Holly mumbled her agreement.

As the ambulance drove off Ezio passed his employer his jacket and said, 'We've got the name and address of a witness and we should make a statement to the police just to be on the safe side.'

'*Per meraviglia...*' Somewhat bemused at the offer he had found himself making to placate the girl's fear on her child's behalf, Rio strode over to stare down into the buggy.

In the nest of bedding and beneath the bobble-topped woolly hat, all that could be seen was a pair of big, scared blue eyes full of tearful anxiety and a tiny upturned pink nose. 'You see to the statement. I'll take…Timmie the timid to the hospital—'

'I could take care of that and the statement,' the older man pointed out quietly. 'You haven't slept more than a hour since you left New York.'

Nor had he been planning to *sleep* for what remained of the night, Rio recalled, his strong jawline clenching hard as he registered that he had contrived to momentarily forget the climax of his unannounced visit to Christabel. Closing his mind to that grim awareness, he stooped to remove the baby from its concealing layers of bedding. Timmie emerged rigid as a stick of rock, if possible his fearful eyes growing even larger to encompass the tall, dark, powerful man cradling him with surprising dexterity.

'I'm a push-over for babies…especially scared ones.' Climbing into the limo, Rio watched as the rest of the baby's possessions were piled in, including the two worn carrier bags, one of which spilled over and let a feeding bottle roll out.

Timmie let out a squeal and stretched out a hopeful hand in the direction of the bottle, little feet kicking with eagerness.

'You're hungry…OK.' Rio rooted through the bags and discovered a packet of baby rusks but nothing of a liquid persuasion. Timmie wasn't picky. He had no manners either. He snatched at the rusk and lodged his two tiny front teeth into it, got them stuck and then let out a mournful wail.

Rio was kept fully occupied all the way to the hospital. He discovered that affectionately dandling one of his friend's babies while a fond mother hovered within reach to take care of all the necessities was a far different affair from actually trying to handle a real live squirming and complaining baby all on his own. With the aid of a glass tumbler and a bottle of mineral water from the built-in bar, however, he managed to quench Timmie's thirst—but not without soaking Timmie and himself into the bargain.

He emerged from the limo at the entrance to the hospital looking something less than his usual sartorially splendid self, with rusk crumbs scattered all over him and clinging to the damp patches. He was also for the first time feeling the effects of too little sleep on top of a severe attack of jet lag.

Ezio attempted to relieve his employer of his baby burden but Timmie wasn't impressed and lodged two frantic hands in Rio's hair and screamed in naked panic.

'If you don't smile at him, he doesn't like you,' Rio shared wearily, rearranging Timmie in a somewhat unconventional drape over one broad shoulder, where the baby hung like a limp but relaxed sack, one large masculine hand pinned to his spine. 'He's a real little bag of nerves.'

Greeted like visiting royalty by the receptionist, Rio was ushered into his friend's comfortable private office to wait and a nurse arrived at speed to remove Timmie.

'He needs to be fed…and other things,' Rio warned, wincing as Timmie tried to cling to his protector and then bawled blue murder at being detached from him. The high note of fear he could hear in the baby's cry was traumatic to listen to, Rio reflected, riven with discomfiture at the child's distress.

It was an hour before John Coulter, the senior physician at the hospital, came to join him and report back on his most recent patient.

'I think you just saved a life tonight, Rio,' the older man announced in his usual cheerful manner. 'That young woman is suffering from the early stages of hypothermia. Falling in front of your car was the best thing that could've happened to her. She and that child might have been dead by morning—'

'I noticed she had no coat on, but presumably she would've made it home before hypothermia got a grip on her,' Rio slotted in, his tone one of casual dismissal.

'But she was planning to spend the night walking round the streets...she's homeless, didn't you realise that?'

Rio frowned in surprise.

'I'll have to call in the duty social worker. I'll feel a heel doing it, though,' Dr Coulter confided ruefully. 'She's terrified that her baby will be put in care, and even though that is very unlikely, as Social Services work to keep mother and child together, I wasn't able to convince her of that.'

'How are they?'

'The baby's in fine fettle. But the mother's another matter...skin and bone, needs feeding up and looking after, but there's no sign of drug or alcohol abuse, which is something in her favour. That accent too...deepest Somerset,' the older man remarked with a wry smile.

'Somerset?'

'*Cider with Rosie* and all that,' John Coulter quipped, referring to the classic book set in a rural area. 'Although, come to think of it, that wasn't Somerset. I think it's based on Gloucestershire—'

'John,' Rio groaned. 'Never mind the book.'

The older man sighed. 'Holly's a country girl and hasn't a clue how to go on in a city like London. I imagine that's why she's in such a fix—'

'Holly? That's her name? Can I see her?'

'This *is* your hospital—'

'It belongs to the Lombardi Foundation, not to me personally,' Rio said drily.

Holly lay in her comfortable bed, scanning the elegant and luxurious layout of her private room and feeling as though she had dreamt it all up. But no, Timmie lay just feet away in the cot that had been provided. The kindly nurse had rustled up a proper feed for him, changed him and tucked him in. Her son was asleep now, snug and secure with a full tummy. Her eyes prickled with weak tears of shame over her own inadequacy. Timmie had a *right* to be snug and secure *all* the time.

The obvious solution to their predicament had been staring her in the face for many weeks now but she had been too much of a coward to confront it. She was not scared of social workers but she *was* scared of being made to look head-on at her own failings when set next to Timmie's needs. Timmie had to come first. She had been horribly selfish. What kind of mother love put a baby on the streets in the middle of the night? She was twenty years old, and she might have left school early but she was not stupid. She knew right from wrong and she was finally accepting that all along her mother had known exactly what she was talking about...

'If you give the baby up for adoption you can come home to us afterwards,' her mother had promised with red-rimmed eyes full of strain and regret. 'I won't let you put your father through any more pain, Holly. You did what you shouldn't have done and you're paying the cost of it now. If you try to keep the kiddy there'll be nothing but grief ahead of you.'

Over the past months Holly had learned the truth of words that had seemed so harsh to her at the time she had listened to them. Then she had still been foolish enough to hope that Jeff was making a home for them both in London, that he would want their child as much as she did and that he would go ahead and marry her just as he had promised. But Jeff had not made a home for them, had been outraged that she should've dared to give birth to a baby he did not want, and had never, ever had the smallest true intention of marrying her.

Timmie would be much better off adopted, Holly forced herself to concede. It would break her heart but it was cruel of her to keep him when she could not provide for him as he deserved. Her eyes stung with hot, prickling tears. There *was* no other choice available to her. She couldn't earn enough in the employment market to pay for childcare or a proper home. Even living off the state in recent weeks, as she had been forced to do after a spate of ill health had seen her sacked from her last job, she had managed no better. Everything she had once owned had either been sold for cash or stolen. She now literally owned only what she stood up in. It was time to do the right thing for Timmie. He would have two caring parents and a decent home. How could she stand in her son's way when she herself had so little to offer him?

The nurse bustled back in with a wide smile. 'Mr Lombardi is planning to come and see you...now, aren't you the lucky one?'

'Mr...*who*?'

'Saverio Lombardi. The man whose limousine you almost dented!'

'A limousine...Lombardi? Isn't that the same name as this hospital?' Holly queried in confusion. Had he been in a limousine? He had certainly been travelling with an awful lot of people, she recalled dimly.

'This hospital is run by the Lombardi Foundation. It's a charitable trust set up by Mr Lombardi. We only take in local patients on emergency,' the nurse explained. 'People come here from all over the world for surgery that they can't get in their home countries. The foundation covers the costs. Mr Lombardi is a very well-known philanthropist...surely you've heard of him?'

'No...I didn't notice the limo either.' The nurse was talking about underprivileged people from less developed countries, Holly gathered in some discomfiture, charity cases. Although she had been taken aback by her luxurious surroundings, she had not realised that the hospital was private. Indeed, she had assumed that the hospital was simply brand-new and that she had got her own room either by sheer good fortune or because Timmie's initial crying would have disturbed other patients. But now it was obvious that luck and Timmie's lungs had had nothing to do with it. *She* was a charity case too.

'Maybe you were too busy looking at those scorching tawny eyes of his,' the other woman teased. 'Not to mention the rest of him. Rio Lombardi is drop-dead gorgeous, and so fanciable you could kidnap him.'

On the other side of the ajar door, Rio hesitated in receipt of that unsought accolade and raised his brows in exasperation. Then, strong jawline squaring, he entered with a light warning knock on the door.

Holly jerked in dismay, her pale skin taking on instant discomfited colour as if she had been the one talking out of turn, while the night nurse scurried out with a bent head. But after just one look at the very tall, powerfully built dark male coming to a halt at the foot of her bed, Holly was challenged even to recall what had briefly embarrassed her. In all her life she had never seen a more breathtakingly handsome male and, no matter how hard she tried, she could not stop staring.

Drop-dead gorgeous had been no exaggeration. That lean, taut bone-structure, composed of flaring dark brows, proud cheekbones, wide narrow mouth and assertive jaw-line, was the very essence of raw masculinity. As she encountered his stunning dark golden eyes her mouth ran dry, and without any good reason at all she was suddenly very conscious that she was naked beneath the thin hospital gown she wore, suddenly hugely aware of her own female body. Her breasts seemed to ache and heat flickered deep in her pelvis, an oddly charged heat that drew her every muscle so taut that she could hardly breathe as he studied her.

Luxuriant black lashes screened his gaze as his attention lingered on her soft full mouth. In that quick upward glance he made to connect with her scrutiny again, she met the flashburn effect of those intense eyes of his and was appalled to find herself wondering how that beautiful male mouth would feel on her own.

'How are you feeling?' Rio Lombardi asked quietly.

'F-f-fine,' Holly stammered helplessly, aghast at a mind that could throw up such inappropriate thoughts, terrified that he might somehow suspect the effect he was having on her. 'But I've got concussion.'

'I know…' As Rio Lombardi strolled over to the cot to gaze down at her son, Holly, her face burning like a bonfire, struggled to get a grip on herself. But it was no use, for she could not drag her magnetised attention from him. He was well over six feet tall, his impressive physique lean and muscular, and in spite of his size he moved with extraordinary grace. 'Timmie looks happy, though.'

'Yeah…nice cosy cot,' Holly mumbled, feeling like an idiot as soon as the inane words escaped her.

Rio Lombardi glanced up from his scrutiny of Timmie's slumbering and peaceful little face, a faint smile still softening the hard line of his sculpted lips. 'You shouldn't have been on the streets with him,' he remarked with quiet assurance.

'I...I *know*,' Holly stressed jerkily, her dilated gaze clinging to the mesmeric tawny hold of his, her heart jumping as if she had just leapt off a cliff, pounding inside her so hard she could hardly squeeze the words out.

She was still blushing as fierily as a schoolgirl, Rio registered with reluctant amusement. He had switched his attention to Timmie to give her a moment in which to compose herself but his subtlety had been wasted. He turned her on and she couldn't hide it. Yet there was something strangely touching about her lack of artifice, her total inability to conceal what she was feeling and thinking. Those big blue eyes were like windows and that lush pink mouth betrayed her tension.

Her slight, slender body barely made a decent impression in the bed. She had the most amazing hair, though, Rio acknowledged. Released from whatever had held it in temporary subjection, her hair now cascaded in snaking corkscrew ringlets halfway to her waist, catching the light like rich, gleaming bronze. His attention strayed lower and momentarily lingered on the surprising fullness of the rounded swells pushing against the hospital-issue gown as she sat forward, the prominence of her taut nipples visible even through the barrier of starched cotton. Nice breasts, he found himself thinking, and he was startled when he felt himself hardening in urgent response, startled that even exhaustion and stress could not stifle his most basic urges.

'I'm going to sort me and Timmie out...I r-really am,' Holly swore earnestly in the charged silence, desperate to make him think better of her. 'When can I get out of here?'

'You need a couple of days of R & R,' Rio responded, recognising the naïvety of that question when she was free to walk out the door any time she wished. But he was relieved by it and did nothing to disabuse her of her notion that she had to pay heed to some superior authority.

'R & R?'

'Rest and recuperation. A lady is coming to see you tomorrow.' Recognising the flash of instant panic in her wide eyes, Rio gave her a bland smile of reassurance. 'Nobody is going to make any arrangements against your will, but I think you'll agree that you need some professional advice and support right now.'

Holly's tummy muscles contracted in a sickening spasm of alarm, her thin shoulders hunching as she lost colour. At last, she gained the strength to take her eyes from him, but only because fear and deep shame over her own failure to give her son a proper home made it impossible for her to continue meeting his level gaze.

'You'll both be fine,' Rio asserted in conclusion, strolling back to the door.

For an instant he hesitated as he remembered that crazy thought he had had only a few minutes before Holly fell in front of his limo. She was, indisputably, the very first woman he had met since walking out on Christabel.

Just as well he wasn't insane enough to marry a complete stranger, he told himself with grim amusement. After all, Holly Sansom might be green as grass but she was still an unmarried mother. While he was a male who prided himself on his open mind, his family background and traditional Italian upbringing had imbued him with certain values and expectations.

CHAPTER TWO

PALE as death, Holly flopped back against the pillows, feeling as weak as water and trembling.

She had gawped at Rio Lombardi like a bedazzled kid and had severely embarrassed herself. Since she had never felt that way around a man before, not even around Jeff, she could only put her behaviour down to the effects of concussion and total exhaustion. Fortunately a guy like Rio Lombardi, so rich and so important and so utterly above her in every way, wouldn't have noticed how awkward and silly she had been, she told herself. In any case, she had a lot more to worry about than the poor impression she had made on some bloke she was never likely to see again!

From her bed she stared at her sleeping son, tears stinging her strained eyes in a blinding surge. She adored Timmie; she could not begin to imagine her life without him. But tomorrow authority, with all its unlimited power, was coming in the guise of that lady Rio Lombardi had smoothly mentioned. Why hadn't she had the strength to get up and walk away after her fall in that street? Once officialdom became involved, the die would be cast.

Rio Lombardi had sworn that no arrangements would be made without her agreement. Did he really think that she was that stupid? She had had her baby out in the middle of the night. She had no home to go to and that doctor would confirm that she had been betraying signs of hypothermia. Those three facts were like three big extra nails being hammered into her coffin. The powers-that-be would

26

decide that she was an unfit mother and would lose no time in removing Timmie from such inadequate care.

Just half an hour ago she had been telling herself that it was her duty to give Timmie up for adoption, but when it came to the crunch she could feel herself tearing apart inside at the prospect of never, ever again having the right to hold his sweet, trusting weight in her arms. Surely she could do better? Surely she had enough backbone to pull herself up out of the mess she was in and provide for her own child?

Couldn't she allow herself one more chance? Was that so selfish? Tears streaming down her guilty face, she studied Timmie in despair. He was all she had, all the family she was ever likely to have. She would go to a shelter for the homeless, one of those places from which advice came without the price of remorseless, grinding officialdom. If it killed her, she would find them somewhere to live. Only if she was faced with another night on the streets would she acknowledge defeat and accept that adoption was the only solution. That was the pact she made with herself, the promise she knew she had to make for her son's sake.

But she had to get out of the hospital before that lady came to call in a few hours' time, she told herself frantically. However, Timmie needed his sleep and she still felt too dizzy to walk, so she had to be sensible and stay in her bed as long as possible.

On his way to a business meeting at eight that morning, Rio found the memory of Holly Sansom's frightened face continually flashing up between him and the figures he was scrutinising.

In one of the snap decisions that invariably threw his employees off-balance, Rio swept up the phone to communicate with his chauffeur and told him to head for the hospital instead of the Lombardi Industries building. Impatience tightening his sculpted mouth as he checked his watch, he questioned his sense of responsibility. He had done all that he could reasonably do. However, he should have kept quiet about the social worker's visit. Forewarning Holly had been careless, and he had only made that mistake because he had gone without sleep for too long.

The limo drew to a halt in the busy car park of the foundation hospital. Waiting with a sigh for his chauffeur to walk round the bonnet in his usual dignified fashion, which he knew was simply a ploy to ensure that his security team alighted from their car behind in advance of himself, Rio caught a glimpse of a bright bronze head moving behind the line of cars parked about forty feet away. In a sudden movement, a vicious swear word impelled from his lips, Rio thrust the door of his limo open for himself and sprang out to stride in the same direction.

'Holly!'

Hearing that shout just when she had believed she was free and clear of having attracted any adverse notice almost gave Holly a heart attack. Her blood literally chilling in her veins with fright, she spun round, her arms automatically tightening round her child.

Rio Lombardi stepped up onto the pavement ahead of her. 'Where the blazes do you think you're going?'

He was the very last person she had expected to see, and for the first time she was facing him upright and he was an incredibly intimidating figure. She was five feet four but he had to be almost twelve inches taller, and he had shoulders like a rugby player that even his fancy dark business suit could not conceal. He also looked...*livid*, shimmering dark golden eyes flaming over her, telegraphing anger and strong censure.

'I...I'm g-going to find a shelter for the homeless—'

'Like bloody hell you are!' Rio interrupted, lean strong face set in steely lines as he closed the distance between them in a couple of strides. 'Where's his pushchair?'

'I c-couldn't find it—'

Holly was trembling, her own guilty conflict over her decision to give herself one more chance intensified by the disapproval Rio Lombardi was emanating in powerful waves. Just twenty-four hours, only twenty-four hours, that was all she had wanted.

'Give Timmie to me...' he demanded.

And, so shaken and ashamed was Holly as she stood there with tears filling her anguished eyes, she found herself instinctively obeying that authoritarian note of absolute command. As Rio Lombardi reached out she let him take her son from her. A split-second later she could not credit what she had done and she stared up at Rio Lombardi in dismay, her distraught face pale as parchment. 'Give him back to me!'

'Not until you agree to go back inside and wait to see the social worker, who is going to *help* you,' Rio stressed, watching her begin to tremble and recognising her fear. Striving not to feel like a bully, he reminded himself that he was doing the best thing for both mother and child.

'I can't *do* that!' Holly suddenly sobbed.

As Rio removed his frustrated attention from her he caught a glimpse of Ezio's face. His security chief was positioned about twenty feet away, watching him in frank astonishment. Rio's high cheekbones fired with a slight rise of colour.

'You must be sensible about this...' Rio stated as the baby in his arms went all stiff and loosed an anxious little moan of fright at the sound of his mother's distress. Timmie was just about to blow. Indeed, any moment now, mass hysteria was going to break out and spread like a disease,

Rio recognised with a very male sense of discomfiture. *Dio mio*, they were in a public place and he didn't know what had got into him. He could only recall the savage jolt of pure rage he had felt at the sight of Holly trying to sneak away from the safety of the hospital.

'*Please*...give him back!' Holly cried.

An older man unlocking his car just yards away had now halted the activity to openly stare, his expression already that of someone thinking that perhaps he ought to intervene. Rio threw his proud head back and murmured in a tone calculated to soothe, 'My car's just over there. We'll discuss this calmly in private.'

Holly was totally disconcerted when Rio just strode away from her. But she raced after him in a panic. As the chauffeur yanked open the door of the gleaming silver limousine Rio broke the habit of a lifetime and, instead of standing back politely to allow Holly first access, climbed in ahead of her, thereby forestalling any possibility of further debate in public.

Holly shot in after him like a mouse in stricken pursuit of a cat. The passenger door closed on her. Rio Lombardi had her son clasped under one arm while he spoke to someone in his own language on the car phone.

In a daze of confusion, Holly absorbed the startling sight of Timmie smiling up at Rio. Timmie, who never smiled at anyone but her! Her head ached even more. She felt clammy and sick and scared. 'Please give him back to me...'

'Look, I haven't got time for this right now. I have a very important meeting to get to,' Rio imparted, leaning forward to make some curious adjustment to the rear of the leather seat facing them. Before her bemused eyes, a child's travelling seat complete with safety restraint folded down out of the once flat surface.

'Mr Lombardi—er—?'

'You can stay at my home for a few days until you feel stronger,' Rio cut in flatly. 'You're in no fit state to make decisions right now. It'll give you a breathing space.'

'Your...*home*?' Holly was so taken aback by that offer coming at her out of the blue that she could only stare at his bold bronzed profile with wide shaken eyes.

Rio settled Timmie into the baby seat. After tightening everything up, he snapped the harness into place with a definite air of satisfaction at his own efficiency.

'Your home?' Holly watched his manoeuvres in bewildered stillness, quite unable to react with any greater volubility. Her head was pounding fit to burst and her brain felt like mush, for she had had little sleep during what had remained of the night hours while she fretted and waited for an opportunity to steal out of the hospital without being noticed.

'Why not?' Suppressing the faint suspicion that once again he was reacting in an impulsive manner that was quite unlike him, Rio told himself that rescuing Holly would be his good deed for the year and he warmed to the concept at similar speed. He would soon get them sorted out. He might have given millions to humanitarian causes but when had he *ever* become personally involved in someone else's problems? But intervention was definitely required. Without a helping hand, there was an all too real possibility that Holly Sansom would end up selling her body for the price of her next meal. A pervert would spot her from a distance of a hundred yards, Rio reflected with distaste. She had victim written all over her. As for Timmie...well, Timmie was already measuring up to follow faithfully in his mother's footsteps.

'Why...not?' Holly echoed, pressing a weak hand to the bruising that still throbbed at the back of her skull. 'Because people don't do stuff like that for people they don't know.'

Rio settled brilliant, dark, deep-set eyes on her. 'Make your mind up.'

Holly tensed at that demand. He was offering them a lifeline. A roof, a bed, no worries about food or the future for a few days. He was an incredible guy. He was just so kind. She could not believe how kind he was being when he had been so furious with her only minutes earlier. 'OK.'

'I'll make the arrangements.' Rio swept up the phone and watched Ezio answer from the front seat. At one point during that conversation, Ezio twisted round to frown in amazement through the glass panel separating him from his employer. Rio ignored that pointed reaction.

That deep, dark, sexy drawl of his just seemed to shimmy down her spine, Holly thought absently. She *loved* his voice even though she hadn't a clue what he was saying. Catching herself up on that mortifying train of thought, Holly reddened fierily.

'As soon as I've been dropped off for my meeting, my security chief will take you to my town house. Any problems, speak to Ezio. He speaks English but most of my household staff don't,' Rio warned her.

Holly nodded uncertainly, momentarily attempting to picture the kind of world where a person had household staff, and then watching the gold in Rio's eyes reflect the light, her mouth running dry and her breath catching in her throat.

Rio sprang out of the limo outside Lombardi Industries.

Ezio cleared his throat. 'Miss Kent won't like another woman in the house, boss.'

Rio froze. 'The wedding's off, Ezio.'

Leaving the older man gazing after him in consternation, Rio strode on into the building, inclining his proud dark head in acknowledgement of the doorman's respectful greeting and concentrating his mind on the challenging business meeting ahead with considerable relief.

The limo nosed its way with all the arrogant assurance of its owner back into the flow of traffic. Holly breathed in slowly and deeply and then pinched the back of her hand. The stinging sensation of that small hurt convinced her that she was not dreaming. She was really and truly sitting in Rio Lombardi's fabulous limousine. For potentially the next forty-eight hours she could stop worrying. He had taken pity on her.

Inwardly, Holly squirmed, the self-esteem that had been battered to ground-level in recent months burning at the wretched awareness that she was just a charity case to a male like Rio Lombardi. Well, she had never let anyone do her favours for free. She would make herself useful round his house, repaying his generosity the only way she could. But at that moment the simple knowledge that she needed to worry neither about food nor shelter in the immediate future was like a giant weight rolling off her shoulders.

Just *how* had she contrived to sink so low that she was prepared to accept such charity? It had happened by degrees, she conceded. But undoubtedly her biggest and worst mistake had been getting involved with Jeff Danby...

Holly had grown up on a hill farm on Exmoor where her father was the tenant farmer. Her parents had married late in life and her mother had been forty when Holly was born. That her mother never conceived again had been a source of deep disappointment to her parents, for it had meant that there would be no son to help out when her father became too old to cope alone with the harsh winters and the lambing season and that eventually he would have to give up the tenancy.

She had had a happy childhood and she had enjoyed school. But possibly, as an only and much loved child, she had been a little spoilt, she conceded with pained hindsight. For, while her parents had urged her to aim at a college education, Holly had been more eager to find a job so that she could have her own money and spend more time with her friends who lived in the nearest town.

Working in a dead-end job that hadn't struck her as a dead-end job had been fine the first couple of years when all that had been in her head was buying the latest cheap fashions and finding a boyfriend. But, although boys had made her plenty of offers, they had all come with the price tag of casual sex attached. And, for all that she had liked to pretend to be as cool in her outlook as her peers, Holly had been raised in a home where that kind of behaviour was just not acceptable and had shrunk from doing anything likely to distress her parents.

And then Jeff had come along in her eighteenth year, Jeff, with his ancient sports car and cheeky grin and impressive aura of sophistication. He had been a pool attendant at the local leisure centre, much admired by all her friends and seven years older. So she had been thrilled when he had asked her out and infatuated by the end of the first week, but not so foolish as to jump into bed with him. In any case, if she was honest, the sex side of things had never appealed to her much, even with Jeff. She had liked the romantic stuff better, holding hands, just listening to him talk about his plans to become an instructor at some trendy fitness club in London and admiring the fact that he had a goal and ambition.

'He's too flash,' her mother had said when she'd finally met Jeff.

'He's a big-head,' her father had sighed. 'He's a lot older

than you are too. You'd be better off with a boy your own age.'

Jeff had ditched her a couple of times and gone off with other girls. Each time he'd come back to her, and she had been so grateful she'd repressed her hurt and forgiven him. Then he had got the job he had always wanted in London and, struggling to conceal her breaking heart, she had gone out with him and his friends for a last-night celebration. The drinks had been lined up in front of her and Jeff had kept on urging her not to be a killjoy and drink up. He had talked about how she was 'his' girl and how he would send for her once he got a place of his own. Hearing him talk like that, including her in his lofty plans, she had almost cried with relief.

'I really do care about you, Holly,' he had said fondly. 'You're the girl I want to marry, so surely you can come home with me tonight.'

And she had, and she had gritted her teeth in the darkness, tears running down her face at the roughness, embarrassment and pain of the experience. She had wanted to please him, had so wanted to prove that she was not the silly little girl still tied to parental dictums he had often accused her of being but a real adult woman capable of loving her man and being loved.

True to his word, Jeff had phoned her while city life was still strange to him. She had written great, long, adoring screeds to him and had been four months pregnant before she'd even realised that she had conceived. During his final phone call, she had begged him to visit for a weekend. She had needed to see him face-to-face to share her news. But he had complained that it would cost too much and he had not phoned again. Weeks afterwards, when she had been climbing the walls with panic over his silence and trying to conceal her changing shape from her parents, one of her many letters had been returned to her with 'Not known at this address' written across it. She had not seen Jeff again until she'd finally tracked him down in London many months later.

Emerging from those unwelcome memories, Holly felt cool air on her face and only then realised that the passenger door was open. The chauffeur was waiting for her to vacate the limo.

The most enormous house lay before her. It had a gravel turning circle in front and tall shaped evergreen trees in fancy metal troughs.

'Miss Sansom...I'm Ezio Farretti.'

Holly focused shyly on the heavily built older man with his steady dark eyes. 'Nice to meet you.'

Ezio engaged the employee positioned at the front door in a flood of foreign speech, and motioned Holly into the house. Feeling like a third wheel, Holly followed him inside and skimmed an intimidated glance round the huge hall, the fantastic staircase and the big pictures adorning the walls.

'Come this way, Miss Sansom,' Ezio urged.

'What's that language you speak?' she asked to fill the silence.

'Italian.'

He showed her into what appeared to be a drawing room. Well, she adjusted, what she would call a drawing room, because the opulent sofas and marble fireplace were way too grand to belong in a humble sitting room. A fire glowed in the iron grate. Holly had not seen a real fire since leaving home, and without warning her eyes smarted as she pictured the cosy farmhouse kitchen where her parents sat by the fire on cold nights.

Ezio extended a notepad and pen. 'Will you make a list of supplies for you and your son?'

'Supplies?'

'Anything you require.'

She reddened to the roots of her hair. 'I don't have any money.'

'That's not a problem.'

The waiting silence that followed embarrassed her into making up a list. Nappies, a feeding cup and baby juice were really all she *had* to have. She was down on her luck but she was not a freeloader, and she was sure to get the chance to wash their clothes.

'You should put down a few more things.' Ezio's voice was gruff.

Holly shook her head. Having to put down even the necessities had hurt. Rio Lombardi was putting them up and he would be feeding them as well. The very last thing she wanted to do was *cost* him money into the bargain.

Ezio led her up the imposing staircase. The magnificent landing was adorned with gilded furniture that looked as if it belonged in a palace. But then, Rio Lombardi's home *was* just like a palace, Holly conceded in a daze. She was shown into a fabulous guest room, complete with an adjoining bathroom, and then into the smaller room next door which contained a cot. The cot, which contained several very new-looking toys, surprised her. Belatedly it occurred to her that perhaps Rio Lombardi was or had been married and had children. Tensing, tummy suddenly feeling hollow, she asked Ezio right out.

'The boss is…single,' the older man stated after a slight hesitation. 'But he often has relatives with kiddies to stay. The Lombardis are a big family and very close.'

As Ezio departed Holly glimpsed her reflection in a mirror and a mortified gasp left her lips. The backside of her jeans was filthy, probably from the road the night before. Fetching a couple of the toys from the cot, she took Timmie into the bathroom, set him down with them on a bathtowel and then stripped down to her skin. Everything she wore went into the bath to steep in hot water. She stepped into the separate shower cubicle but could only run the water in bursts because she couldn't close the door properly while she watched over Timmie. Her son could not yet crawl but he could cover a surprising amount of distance by rolling.

It was such bliss, such *utter* bliss to feel truly scrubbed clean again. Making use of the luxury toiletries in the corner shower compartment, she shampooed her hair and then conditioned it for the first time in many months. Having pounded her clothes back to cleanliness with soap, she then realised in dismay that there were no radiators in which to dry them. At that point, a knock sounded on the bedroom door.

Wrapped in a towel, she peered round the edge of the door. It was Ezio Farretti and he had a large cotton sack in his arms.

'Where are the radiators?' she queried.

'There aren't any. The heating is under the floor.'

'Oh…'

'This bag is full of clothes left behind by other guests,' Ezio continued. 'There might be something which will fit you or Timmie.'

'I can't wear someone else's things…they'd be furious—'

'These are very rich people. They don't miss what they overlook; they just buy *more*,' the older man told her gently. 'I'll leave the bag outside the door.'

There was a horrid thickness in her throat. 'Thanks, Ezio.'

'No problem.' He cleared his throat. 'But, if you don't mind a spot of advice, give the boss a wide berth. Off the record, he's just not himself right now and you don't want to get your feelings hurt.'

Not just himself? Her feelings hurt? What on earth was that supposed to mean? Holly's face burned up scarlet. Oh, my goodness, had Ezio noticed her blushing and getting on like a teenybopper with a bad crush around Rio Lombardi? Was he warning her off? What else could he possibly be doing?

CHAPTER THREE

'HOLLY'S doing...*what*?' Rio ground out with rampant incredulity.

'Almost finished cleaning the kitchen floor, boss,' Ezio repeated with reluctance. 'She's been dusting and scrubbing and polishing all day and, short of physically restraining her, there was nothing I could do about it. She's got a lot of grit but she's on the brink of a collapse—'

'The kitchen floor...' Rio seethed, striding through the door that led down to the basement where all the household utilities were situated. His mood was not improved when he went through the wrong door on the lower floor and found himself in some sort of boiler room because it had been a very long time since he had visited the kitchen quarters.

When he finally located his own kitchen, the first sight that met his eyes was Timmie strapped into a high chair, slumped over fast asleep, curly dark head down on the tray, a feeding cup dangling from one tiny hand. He looked rather like a miniature drunken sailor, his little legs and feet clad in white...*tights*? And what was that frilly thing round his almost non-existent neck? *Dio mio*, Timmie was wearing a little girl's woollen dress with a lace collar! Rio was truly appalled by that discovery.

He strode round the protruding unit to gaze down the length of a kitchen that stretched more than forty feet in depth. He settled his outraged gaze on the female behind weaving from side to side as Holly knelt on the floor with her bucket and scrubbed like a Victorian housemaid. He stilled, attention entrapped by the wholly feminine fullness of that derrière, every line defined by the fine fabric shaping its delicious curves.

Without warning, an attack of such powerful lust assailed Rio that his every muscle clenched in shaken resistance. Four weeks without sex and he was turning into an animal, ready to jump anything female, he decided in even darker fury. His lean hands clenched into fists as he willed the throb of his aching sex to dwindle to manageable proportions.

'Get the hell up off that floor!' Rio launched with wrathful bite.

Dredged from her concentrated efforts to deny her exhaustion until she had completed her work, Holly swivelled round on her knees in fright, collided with the bucket and tipped it noisily over. Her soft mouth opening in dismay, she gasped strickenly, '*Now* look what you've made me do!'

'How *dare* you come here and start cleaning my floors?' Rio demanded with savage censure.

Very slowly, Holly picked herself up, the over-large green dress with its wide neckline lurching off one bare white shoulder. But that shade was incredible against that fair skin of hers, Rio noted before he registered that she was swaying and literally grey with pallor.

Holly focused on him, butterflies breaking loose in her tummy. Snatching in a stark breath, she met his stunning golden eyes and felt the burn of reaction deep down in her pelvis, an enervating sensation that made her weld her slender thighs together in fierce embarrassment. 'I'm sorry, I thought—'

Rio strode through the grimy flood that had spilled from the bucket and lifted her off her feet before she fainted in front of him. 'How could you be so foolish? Do you think I invited you here to slave for me?'

'I only wanted to make myself useful...' Holly drank in the scent of him that clung to the jacket beneath her cheekbone, her nostrils flaring with helpless eagerness on that fresh familiarity.

Holding her that close was doing nothing for Rio's rampant arousal. He was furious with himself, furious with her. Lack of control was not a sensation he was accustomed to suffering around a woman. But he was hugely tempted to tell her that if she wanted to make herself useful he had a whole catalogue of undomestic distractions to offer, not one of which, he was ashamed to admit, would have been thwarted by a wet floor, a child within hearing distance or even a fire alarm. He had seen her susceptibility in her eyes, in the way she held her slender, shapely body and in the mood he was in, a don't-give-a-damn-about-anything mood of intense bitterness, that awareness inflamed his libido even more.

Ezio was positioned by Timmie's sleeping form when Rio strode for the kitchen exit. 'Bring Timmie upstairs and get him out of that stupid dress,' he instructed the older man.

'I only put it on him to keep him warm until his own clothes dried. *He* doesn't know it's a dress,' Holly protested. 'It was all that was available—'

'You could be damaging his sexual identity for life!' Rio condemned fiercely.

'Do you think so?' she questioned, aghast, as Rio carried her into a lift that she had not known existed until that moment.

He set her down and hit the buttons, choosing not to wait for Ezio. The door buzzed shut. She slumped back against the cool wall. 'The floor's in a *real* mess now,' she lamented. 'I can't leave it like that.'

'Shut up.' Rio closed his eyes and breathed in deep and slow. He had had one hell of a day, barring calls from Christabel, putting his social secretary in charge of cancelling the elaborate wedding arrangements, watching the slow ripple of awareness pass round his personal staff one by one, recognising the amazed speculation in the eyes of those too stupid to hide their curiosity. Rio Lombardi and Christabel Kent, the *golden* couple, had broken up. All his life he had been a private individual, who hated others to breach his reserve. Now he was a mass of raw emotion and seething bitterness and, to crown his intense sense of raging humiliation at being *put* in such a position, all he could think about was the wild, savage oblivion of sex!

Holly shut up while the silence charged up. Rio opened eyes as bright as golden sunlight and dazzled her. The atmosphere was fraught, full of vibrations that skimmed along her nerve-endings, filling her with the strangest excitement in spite of her weary bewilderment. He was smouldering like a powder keg, she registered. She had no idea *why* but she had never been so aware of the potent magnetism of powerful masculinity.

In fact, she finally admitted, she was so hopelessly attracted to Rio Lombardi she could barely think straight, and that was a major shock to her system and her knowledge of herself. Jeff had never made her tremble just by looking at her. Jeff had never made her crave his touch. So, doubtless her ex-boyfriend had had good reason to call her a 'lousy lay'. That humiliating recollection from the past steadied her and cooled her as nothing else could have done and made her drop her eyes from Rio Lombardi's lean, strong face in shame.

'I'm sorry I spoke to you like that,' Rio murmured curtly as he stood back for her to precede him out of the lift.

She nodded with a bowed head.

'Go to bed and rest,' Rio advised harshly, stopping dead on the threshold of her bedroom but going not one step further. 'I'll have a supper tray sent up.'

'I'm not hungry,' Holly whispered shakily, no longer able to look at him. She listened to him walk away, feeling the loss of his vibrant energy and despising herself for that sensitised awareness.

A bloke like Rio Lombardi would never look twice at her, which was just as well, she conceded dully. She was useless in bed. *Frigid as a corpse.* She stilled a shiver of revulsion at that unforgettable description of her less than adequate performance: Jeff had spelt out exactly why he had lost interest in her. She might not have enjoyed that single session of physical intimacy that had none-the-less resulted in Timmie's conception, but Jeff had made it clear that he had enjoyed it even less. How could she have actually believed his drunken assertion that she was the girl he wanted to marry? That had just been a standard line to get her between the sheets.

'Why the hell didn't you get an abortion, you stupid cow?' Jeff had railed at her before he'd hit her smack in the face with his fist. He'd knocked her right off her feet in his rage almost five months back and had terrified her with his violence. 'If you think I'm forking out my hard-earned cash to keep you and your little bastard, you'd better think again! If you try to hang him round my neck, I'll make you sorry you were ever born...'

She was sorriest of all that she had been so unforgivably stupid as not to see through Jeff's superficial charm to the user and abuser of women that he was. He had slept with those girls he'd dumped her for twice over. He had lied about that, and in her heart of hearts she had always suspected that truth but had blindly refused to face the fact that a man who treated her that way could have no caring feelings for her. Jeff was the kind of creep whose ego could not bear female rejection. The instant he had taken her virginity, he had begun losing interest.

So she had got her punishment for being a silly, credulous doormat, dreaming of white dresses and the 'Bridal March'. What she could not stand was that her parents, and now Timmie, seemed to be sharing that ongoing punishment with her. For of course her parents would be missing her, but she could never go home as long as she had her son and no ring on her finger. Farming communities were not liberal. An unwed daughter and fatherless grandchild would shame and mortify her parents.

As Holly slumped down on the bed, slight shoulders sagging, Ezio appeared in the doorway, clutching Timmie. 'I got his clothes out of the drier but I'm afraid you'll have to change him.'

'Thanks…' she said chokily, getting up to reclaim her son.

Ezio hovered on the threshold. 'The boss is on a pretty short fuse at present. I did try to warn you.'

She was just no good at listening. Her stubborn pride had offended Rio Lombardi. She had slighted the one person who had tried to be kind to her in countless months of indifference. A rich, good-looking guy of Rio's calibre could not have any ulterior motive in helping her and she was ashamed of the reality that she wished that he *had*, ashamed that she reacted as she did around him.

The phone ringing by the bed woke her the next morning.

It was Rio. 'I'm taking you shopping and I don't want

to hear any arguments. The sight of you running round dressed like a bag lady embarrasses me.'

Holly was poleaxed. *'But—'*

'I've hired a nanny to take care of Timmie. You got to sleep in because she's already here. He's now getting his morning constitutional in the garden. As soon as you've had breakfast, I want you downstairs.'

Click went the phone as Rio cut the connection. Even as Holly replaced the receiver in sleepy, shell-shocked bewilderment, a manservant was knocking on the door and entering with the promised breakfast. A nanny had been hired just to take care of her Timmie? For goodness' sake, had Rio Lombardi gone mad? She could not possibly allow him to buy her clothes! It was out of the question.

However, hunger made her succumb first to the tempting dishes on the beautifully arranged bed tray. She explored the bruising at the base of her skull. The spot was still tender but she felt fine after a really good night of sleep. As soon as she had eaten she had a quick shower. Dressing in her clean jeans and shirt, she pulled on the man's sweater that she had found at the very foot of the pretty-much useless bag of clothing which Ezio had brought to her.

Her bronze ringlets fanning wildly round her narrow shoulders after a too vigorous and impatient brushing, she hurried down the stairs. Rio was pacing the hall floor and her first glimpse of him just took her breath away. His superb tailored suit in palest grey set off his exotic darkness and bronzed skin to perfection. His black hair gleamed in the light coming through the windows and was so temptingly touchable to her dilated gaze that her fingertips actually tingled.

'I can't let you take me shopping,' she told him unevenly.

A curious expression tensed Rio's darkly handsome features and his strong jawline hardened, his gorgeous dark golden eyes almost bleak. 'I need a distraction today. You're *it*. You'll be doing me a favour.'

So disconcerted was Holly by the roughened sincerity patent in that unexpected response that she was halfway into the limo before she recalled that she had not yet seen her son. 'Just two minutes, Rio.' She said his name for the first time and then reddened with self-consciousness.

The nanny was a really nice young woman and she even wore a uniform. She looked like the sort of nanny that might be hired by royalty and Timmie, propped up in an incredibly impractical but imposing coachbuilt pram, might even have aspired to being a little prince, had it not been for his shabby clothing.

'Satisfied, *cara*?' Rio asked as Holly got into the limo.

'Timmie seems happy enough—'

'You should ditch the Timmie and call him Timothy,' Rio informed her just as she glimpsed Ezio's unusually grim expression before the older man turned away to swing into the front passenger seat.

'Why?'

'He's timid. Give him a name he can grow into, not one that makes him sound like a pet pooch.'

Holly flushed but she said nothing. She was overwhelmed by the sensation that she was being carried away by a very forceful personality on a trip she did not understand. 'Is…is there something wrong today? I mean,' she muttered awkwardly, 'that you feel you need a distraction?'

His lean, powerful face tautened, brilliant eyes veiling. He had the most extraordinary long, inky dark lashes, Holly noted, studying his classic profile with helpless fascination.

'Everything's right. Everything is as it ought to be,' Rio

stated in a cold tone that contrived to chill her to the marrow.

The uneasy silence dragged.

Holly made a frantic effort to redress the apparent damage she had caused. 'So you're not working today?'

'No.'

'And you taking me out shopping is just a whim…the sort of thing rich people do when they're bored?'

The taut line of his sensual mouth eased and he flashed her a glittering glance that sent her heart racing like an express train. 'You could put it that way. Or maybe I want to spoil you because you don't *ask* for anything and I'm not used to that with a woman.'

'I'm not used to blokes buying me stuff,' Holly shared in a sudden rush of confidence. 'Jeff used to borrow money off me all the time. He was always running out. I've always paid my own way…well, until recently.'

'Jeff…Timothy's absent father? He sounds a treat,' Rio breathed with perceptible scorn. 'Where is he?'

Holly repressed a shiver and studied her tightly linked hands. 'Don't know…don't want to know,' she admitted shakily. 'He thumped me last time I saw him—'

'I beg your pardon?' Rio curved lean, strong fingers round her slight shoulder to turn her back to face him.

'Me and my big mouth,' Holly muttered, for she had never intended to tell anyone that.

Rio raked her strained face with flaring golden eyes. 'He *hit* you?'

'It was my own fault—'

'How *could* it have been?' Rio demanded.

'I came up to London with Timmie to find Jeff. It took time because he had changed jobs and moved on from his last address,' Holly explained heavily. 'I was stupid. After all, he *always* knew how to get in touch with me, but I couldn't accept that what we'd had had fizzled out—'

'You had a child. Naturally you didn't want to accept it. Did he *know* you were pregnant when he abandoned you?'

'Abandoned', she reflected, made what Jeff had done sound dramatically worse than it had been. All he had actually done was stop phoning, and had she had the wit to leave it at that she might never have sunk as low. Following Jeff up to London and searching for him had been her second biggest mistake, she conceded. With a child in tow she had found it impossible to make ends meet in so expensive a city, but she had had nowhere else to go and neither friends nor family to fall back on for support.

'No. I was a bit slow on the uptake when it came to realising that I was pregnant myself,' she confided in some discomfiture on that subject.

'So what happened when you traced him?'

'He was living in Notting Hill in a very smart flat,' she faltered, her mind taking her back to that ghastly day of awakening to the discovery that the father of her child was a creep of the lowest order and, worst of all, a *weak* one. 'I had Timmie with me because I had nowhere else to leave him. Jeff opened the door…'

'*And?*' Rio prompted impatiently.

'He said he had a friend visiting and he sort of yanked me into the kitchen,' Holly whispered shakily. 'I told him that he was a father and he just went berserk. Then his girlfriend came in…that was worse than being hit because she felt sorry for me.'

Rio expelled his breath in a slow, measured hiss.

'It was her flat and she threw him out to cool off. She was dead sophisticated, much older than me and not at all embarrassed by the situation,' Holly gulped. 'She even made me a cup of tea while she told me that chasing after

Jeff with a baby was really dumb. She said Jeff had lost his head because I had cornered him when she was home and he was desperate to get rid of me without her finding out that my baby was his.'

'Charming.'

'She was right.' Holly swallowed hard and raised her sleeve, intending to wipe her eyes. 'I was just too scared to face up to the fact that I was on my own, so I clung to this stupid dream that it would all work out once he saw...Timothy,' she pronounced with precision.

Releasing a groan, Rio Lombardi tilted up her chin to dry her damp eyes with a fine lawn handkerchief. 'Jeff was no loss. You're lucky that you and your son escaped a man so quick to use his fists in a crisis.'

Her drowning blue eyes gazed up into glittering gold and Jeff went out of her mind so fast he might never have existed. She tried and failed to swallow. Rio was so close that breathing was no longer an option. Lashes lowered, she focused on that wide, sensual mouth of his and the tip of her tongue snaked out to moisten her dry lower lip. Never in all her life had she been so desperate, so shamelessly eager to feel a man's mouth on hers. The craving was almost unbearably strong.

His fabulous bone-structure taut, proud cheekbones prominent beneath smooth bronzed skin, Rio murmured with a fracturing edge to his thickened drawl, 'It's not my fists you have to fear. I'm much more inventive but probably more dangerous.'

Please, please, kiss me, I don't care, was running through her mind as he set her back from him and turned to answer the car phone. She had not even heard it buzzing and she sank back into her corner again like a boneless doll, registering that she had just glanced into potent contact with a male far more sexually charged than Jeff had ever been.

It had been there in the atmosphere between them, an instant, surging awareness that shook her to her very depths.

Rio took her to an exclusive salon to get her hair done first.

'Cut it *short*?' Rio repeated on a rising note of disbelief when the retro-clad stylist made that laconic suggestion after poking through Holly's hair much as though it was beyond all human intervention. Closing one hand over hers, Rio dragged her back out of the leather chair and headed for the exit.

'What are you doing?' Holly gasped in embarrassment, horribly aware of every head in the place turning in their direction.

'I'm not leaving you at the mercy of a scissor-happy lunatic, *cara*—'

'*Rio!*' A female voice intervened.

Rio halted, his lean, strong features tensing.

A stunning brunette with cat-like eyes and vampish burgundy lips surged up to them, but, for all her elegant cool, she was exuding a definable air of panic. 'That stupid lump on the desk didn't recognise you, did she? You walking out of my salon with a big frown is very bad for business, Rio.'

'Your top stylist wants to chop off her crowning glory!' Rio delivered.

Cheeks burning, Holly stood there while the brunette's shrewd gaze flicked from Holly's cascading ringlets back to Rio. 'Obviously a guy with no imagination. I'll do it. She just needs some shaping round her face. One of your tribe of little cousins over from Italy?' she asked, as if Holly were mute.

'She speaks hardly any English,' Holly heard Rio state and, at that startling announcement, she shot him a wide-eyed glance of incredulity, barely able to credit her hearing.

'But I presume she has a name. I'm Sly.' The brunette extended a manicured hand to Holly. 'And *you're*—'

'Fiammetta,' Rio slotted in with a perfectly straight face. 'She's unbelievably shy. I'd like her made up as well—'

'What age is she?' Sly enquired of him with a cloying smile, both of them now talking over the top of Holly's head as if she were a very small child.

'Old enough to look like a woman,' Rio quipped huskily.

'Then I presume you're planning to do something about the clothes she's wearing as well,' the salon owner remarked with a speaking little giggle.

Fifteen minutes later, Holly was seated in front of a mirror while Sly cut her hair with exaggerated care. 'What Rio wants, Rio always gets...'

Since Holly had not one Italian word at her disposal and did not trust herself to emulate an accent, she compressed her lips and concealed her discomfiture. When she got her hands on Rio in private, she was going to scream at him for doing this to her. Why, though? Why deprive her of the ability to talk?

'I do wish I spoke Italian,' Sly sighed. 'I bet you have the inside track on the whole story, and I would *give* my right arm to hear every dirty detail on the fall of Christabel. The rumours are just *so* intriguing.'

Who was Christabel? Some ex-girlfriend of Rio's? Or possibly just a not very popular mutual acquaintance, Holly allowed, someone who had suffered some kind of disappointment. Gritting her teeth, she sat through the styling session and then through the incredibly tickly and painstaking experience of having cosmetics professionally applied. She wasn't able to see herself until the very last moment and then she simply stared in disbelief at her own transformed appearance.

'I'm the best in my field even though I say it myself,' Sly drawled with amusement.

Smoky shadow had been smoothed round Holly's eyes, giving them dramatic depth and enhancing their colour. She had cheekbones now like a model in a magazine and a mouth as ripe and pink and lush as a peach.

Rio was pacing the waiting area, talking in staccato Italian on his mobile phone, the cynosure of interest for every female in the vicinity. He lowered his phone, tawny eyes welding to her with gleaming intensity, a faint and wicked smile curling at the corners of his beautiful mouth. '*Bella*, Fiammetta…' he drawled with lazy amusement.

And in that same moment, Holly knew beyond all doubt that she had fallen passionately in love. Riveted to the spot by his unashamed appreciation, she could feel herself glowing inside like a megawatt light bulb suddenly connected to an electric current. *He* was the source of the current. He was redefining her in her own eyes, making her feel good about herself for the first time in almost two years.

Resting a casual hand on her spine, he urged her back out to the limo.

'Why did you tell Sly that crazy story about me being Italian?' Holly prompted, trying to muster her former fury but finding it strangely absent.

'She's the biggest gossip in town and not nicknamed ''Sly'' for nothing. She could have bared your soul for you in the first five minutes,' Rio mocked.

'I couldn't open my mouth! I don't know a single word of Italian!'

'I know. Class act, aren't I?' Rio teased. 'It was as good as gagging the two of you. Sly was seething with frustration.'

Holly mock-punched him in the ribs and then jerked her hand back, afraid that she had been too familiar. But he gave her a slanting grin of answering amusement that turned her heart inside-out. Nobody was ever going to accuse Rio Lombardi of being a charisma-free zone, Holly thought dizzily in receipt of that smile while she struggled to get mental feet back safely on the ground again. Only the ground had vanished. Every time he looked at her she felt as if she was flying.

The next stop on the shopping trip was a high-fashion outlet of such size and style that the deeper they got into it the more Holly tried to hide behind him, cringing at her own shabbiness.

'Who would you like to be here? Daughter of an eccentric billionaire?' Rio murmured, inclining his dark head down to hers, making her tremble at his proximity. 'Minor European royalty, travelling incognito?'

'I think I'll just be me, but you get to do all the talking,' Holly said apprehensively as a smiling, terrifyingly svelte female began to move in their direction.

'All these people care about is the colour of my money,' Rio breathed, his dark drawl hard-edged with what sounded remarkably like bitterness. 'And the richer you are, the more they grovel.'

'I wouldn't know a lot about that but I hope you're not going to be rude,' Holly whispered back worriedly.

Unexpectedly, he laughed.

He sent her off alone to the lingerie department. Ignoring the bountiful advice of a saleswoman keen to flog her a hundred of every item, not to mention undergarments that Holly had not until then known even existed, Holly settled for several sets of bras and briefs. No, she did not need nightwear. There had been a nightie in Ezio's sack that had done her fine the night before and she was no spendthrift. What she was doing was *wrong*, her conscience warned her. Letting Rio Lombardi spend his money on her could not be right. But it was making him smile, it was making him tease her. He could buy her a series of numbered fertiliser sacks if he liked.

'Now I get in on the act,' Rio announced when she was led back to him to find him seated on a tall stool at a mini-bar in a spacious room that contained a small stage and catwalk. 'Champagne?'

With difficulty, she made it up onto the stool beside him and accepted a moisture-beaded glass. 'What happens in here?'

'The models parade the product. We pick what we like. Then you try it on.'

'You've done this before.' The champagne bubbles tickled her nose but she didn't laugh. She did not like the idea that he had sat in that exact same spot with other women but he knew the form too well for her to doubt it.

'But never before without being asked or set up or cajoled,' Rio confided darkly.

'If you felt like that, you should just have said no,' Holly muttered uncomfortably, quite at a loss on how to comment on the behaviour of women capable of being that bold about their greed. 'I mean…this wasn't my idea and it doesn't seem to be amusing you any more, so let's just leave it here…*please*—'

Lean fingers tugged at a ringlet of her bronze hair, curving her heart-shaped face round to his. 'But I don't want to leave it. I want to see you look beautiful…'

Her breath feathered in her throat, her clear blue eyes betraying her confusion. 'I can't be what I'm not—'

'You can be whatever you want to be, *cara*.'

She gazed into lustrous eyes shaded with burning gold and her heart was racing. The sense of caution taught by the hard lessons of recent experience strove to keep her grounded, though. What he was doing for her was like a fairy tale but she knew fairy tales didn't happen in real life: there was always a catch. As she parted her lips to snatch in much needed oxygen to sustain her, Rio bent his head lower and let his tongue delve in a subtle flicker into the moist interior of her mouth. It lasted only a second, but in that second she was electrified by the instantaneous, stormy response of her own body, the surge of enervating heat that inflamed her every sense. Indeed, so great was the erotic hit of that sudden sexual foray she jerked, and if he hadn't shot a steadying arm round her she would have fallen off the stool.

'Relax,' Rio urged with husky clarity.

He lounged back from her again in perfect balance, the easy, indolent grace of his lean, muscular length in striking contrast to her trembling state of near-devastation.

Holly was in shock, mental shock, sensual, bodily shock. Maybe that had been a trifling bit of flirtation on his terms, but her quivering body was on fire with sensations it had never known before and she wanted to emulate his cool but found it impossible. What did he want from her? Surely not the obvious? Was he out trawling for a cut-price mistress or something? What did they have in common? Yes, *what* did they have in common? Well, they were both human.

'Sorry…I couldn't resist it,' Rio admitted in his smooth accented drawl.

'I bet you can resist me just fine,' Holly heard herself snap in her unease at not knowing what was likely to happen next. 'Don't play games with me!'

'Then stop giving me the green light,' Rio traded quick as a flash, plunging her into such mortified discomfiture that she went weak with relief when an older woman took up position at a speaker's stand. The curtains glided back and the first model strolled out, looking impossibly haughty and superior until she espied Rio and flashed up a seductive smile instead.

From that first moment Holly was entranced. She had never been to a fashion show before and the knowledge that the display was being put on for an audience of two just blew her mind. The descriptions of the various outfits were double Dutch to her, but every item struck her as the ultimate in colour and design. She was totally undiscriminating, for she could not imagine actually wearing such elaborate garments. She was learning what women who had pots of money and little to do but look good wore and it was an education.

'You enjoyed that…' Rio was watching her intently as the curtains finally glided shut.

'Yes…thanks,' she sighed, her slow smile breaking out like sudden sunlight.

'So now you go and try on all the selections I made.'

'But why? I'm never going to wear stuff like that in *my* life!' Holly protested in honest bemusement. 'I'm much more downmarket than that and quite happy to be. Where on earth would I wear suits and long dresses?'

Disregarding that argument, Rio lifted her down from the stool and sent her in the direction of the saleswoman awaiting her. She was taken into a room where she became the centre of a throng of eager helpers. A whole selection of shoes and handbags were already standing by. She was whisked into outfit after outfit and marched out onto the catwalk.

At first she was self-conscious and she stood there like a plum with Rio telling her to move about, but then someone put on background music with a dance beat and Holly got into the spirit of the occasion. She began to pose, eyes wide in a pretence of haughtiness, shoulders thrown back in what she hoped was a model-like manner. Every time he laughed she clowned a little more, answering amusement sparkling in her eyes, but her greatest pleasure derived from his.

'Put on the green dress,' Rio told her when her own personal show was at an end.

He could buy her *one* outfit. That was OK, Holly thought in considerable relief. He really wasn't a very practical bloke. A couple of skirts and tops and new trousers from a chain store would have been much more sensible, and heaven only knew what even just one designer 'ensemble', as the saleswomen called them, cost in such a fancy place!

The dress bared her shoulders and rejoiced in a fabulous boned velvet bodice and a flirty skirt that came to her knees. She absolutely loved it. In the mirror, she saw a fashionable stranger, a young woman who just might have been a high-society party girl without a care in the world. It was just an illusion, she *knew* that, but it had been so much fun and she would never, ever forget the experience. She walked out to rejoin him, conscious of the unfamiliar height of the heels on her shoes, and with her entire attention pinned as though magnetised to his darkly handsome face.

'You look gorgeous, *cara*.' Rio lifted something furry from a nearby chair and draped it round her shoulders. 'And now you look like a queen.'

There were mirrors everywhere. Now she studied their twinned reflection, the impossibly smooth and rich pale blonde fake-fur falling to mid-calf, the raised collar providing a glamorous contrast to the vivid fall of her hair. His proud head above her own, his tall, dark, powerful figure backing her slighter build. 'Do you flog dreams for a living?' she asked unsteadily, shaken by that view of them together, committing it to memory, knowing that dreams didn't last. 'You ought to.'

'The day's not over yet.'

But it was already evening. She had not realised how late it had got until they were ushered from the building and she saw the fading light. 'Does that place always stay open to this time?'

'They stayed open just for us,' Rio informed her lazily. 'We'll dine now.'

Ezio Farretti straightened from his lounging position against the bonnet of the limo. He stared at Holly and his whole face tightened and he turned away.

'Why did Ezio look at me like that?' she whispered in dismay.

'Ezio shouldn't be looking at you in any particular way,' Rio pronounced, a cool, hard edge to his dark, deep voice that made her tense.

He took her to a restaurant which appeared to be the very last word in exclusivity. The head waiter surged to greet Rio. He took the attention as his due and it was obvious that he was a regular customer. As Rio strolled between the tables the low buzz of conversation died and a kind of unearthly hush fell. Every head in the room seemed to be swivelling in their direction. Several people addressed Rio, but, with only a word of acknowledgement or a cool inclination of his dark head Rio kept on moving.

Holly dropped down into the seat spun out for her occupation by an attentive waiter. 'Why do I get the feeling that everyone's staring at us?'

Rio lifted one broad shoulder in a slight fluid shrug that was the very essence of supreme cool. 'They're staring at you—'

'*Me?*' Holly exclaimed in lively astonishment.

'Speculating on your identity. You *do* look incredible in that dress.'

Locked to the brilliance of his tawny appraisal, she felt her heart race like crazy behind her ribs and she smiled. She didn't believe that anybody had the slightest interest in her but she liked the compliment. However, she went on to study her enormous menu in growing dismay. At first glance the menu seemed to be in English, but what was a sorbet? A croustade? A coulis?

When the waiter reappeared, perspiration beaded Holly's short upper lip, because she was still looking frantically for a dish she could recognise.

'I'd recommend the sorbet,' Rio murmured.

'OK, yes...I'd like that,' Holly hastened to confirm with relief.

Rio was being a very entertaining companion when something that resembled a pudding in a tall glass was set in front of her. She tried not to seem surprised and just ignored it, because she couldn't work out which of the many items of cutlery she was supposed to use to eat it and Rio had confounded her by ordering soup. She would have loved soup but she hadn't seen it anywhere on the menu.

'I'm not really that hungry,' she said as the sorbet was borne off, but in truth her stomach was meeting her backbone and she felt on the brink of starvation.

'I love salad,' she dared when it came to the next course, and then inwardly cringed when it seemed that that was actually a special order and there was such a carry-on about what *kind* of salad she wanted. Just shove some lettuce on a plate, she wanted to scream.

She knew she used the wrong knife and fork for the salad because as she picked them up the waiter was trying to remove them, but she braved it out as if she hadn't noticed that. At least she got to eat and, although dining out with

Rio was an enervating challenge, he did not appear to notice her silent agonies of indecision.

She triumphed, or thought she did, when it came to the dessert course. *'Chocolat' had* to be chocolate. But the menu won all over again when her selection arrived. A sparkly cobweb thing covered a shell containing a mixture which she couldn't get at and a lot of leaves and tiny red berries were scattered round the edges. The latter tasted poisonously bad and put her right off the rest of it.

'You should be eating more,' Rio scolded, ignoring the greenery on his own plate and heading straight for his mouthwatering meringue concoction with a fork. A *fork*?

Suddenly, Holly was very grateful that she had pushed her own plate away. Hunger was better than public embarrassment, and as soon as everyone had gone to bed she would raid his kitchen fridge.

At the door, Rio draped the gorgeous coat round her shoulders. That personal attention made her feel ten feet tall. At the same hour just two nights back she had been walking the city streets, cold and scared, and already that seemed a lifetime ago, she conceded, sobered by that reflection. Yet the world she was now inhabiting felt far less real to her than the one she had so recently left behind. But then, it was Rio's world, not hers.

That fleeting kiss that had set her on fire earlier had only been a tease, Holly told herself. He was a very sexy guy and he had been flirting with her, that was all. Settling back into the limo, she thought about her son. Timmie, who was not high-class enough to aim at being Timothy, was *her* real world, along with bedsits, creepy landlords and dead-end, boring jobs, she reminded herself doggedly.

But still she found herself watching Rio, storing up images for the future. It wasn't just his sleek, dark good-looks, his innate elegance and grace; he had an incredible aura of self-assurance that made her feel safe. It was a challenge to credit that anything could go wrong while he was around. Was it possible to fall in love so fast? Well, whether it was or not, she would *have* to get over her silly notions. Cocooned in her glorious fake-fur, she took advantage of the shifting play of light and shadow as the limo travelled through the quiet streets to study him from all angles in search of a physical flaw. But he defeated her. He remained drop-dead gorgeous and no mistake.

'You don't need to restrict yourself to just looking. You can touch as well, *cara*,' Rio murmured in indolent invitation.

In sharp bewilderment, Holly froze. Agonised hot colour flooded her face. He might as well have stripped her naked and turned her out in front of an amused audience. Beneath the appraisal of those glittering golden eyes that saw far too much for her comfort she felt like a butterfly caught on a pin. He *knew* how he could make her feel but she had never made a physical advance to a man and she was not about to break that habit, she told herself fiercely, her small hands closing in on themselves. She had enough problems; she had made enough mistakes. Diving into bed for a casual one-night stand with Rio Lombardi would be the ultimate of mistakes. Not only would she fail to deliver what he expected, but she would also despise herself for being so cheap afterwards.

'Is that why you gave me the fairy-tale day out?' Holly heard herself accuse.

In the flickering lights, his lean, strong face clenched. 'Of course not.'

'But you got a kick out of dressing me up like some toy doll, trying to make me fit the blueprint of what presumably you like.' Holly was fighting so hard to keep the sob rising inside her from surfacing that her voice shook. 'But I'm still me, and I may not be anything that special, but if Jeff taught me anything he taught me that I need to have more respect for myself.'

'Right now, I do not want to hear about your abusive boyfriend,' Rio responded with sizzling bite. 'But, believe me, I've never had to bribe a woman into my bed!'

Holly did believe him, but she also knew that if she spoke again she would start crying and make an even bigger fool of herself. When the limo arrived at the house she jumped out, practically raced past Ezio and was indoors and up the stairs most probably before Rio had even made his own front step. Out of breath she went straight into Timmie's room and crept over to his cot. Her son was sound asleep, little face flushed and peaceful. Tomorrow she was going out to look for a job, and she would tackle the Social Security office again. Tomorrow was the beginning of another day.

Under the shower, she let her pent-up tears flow. How could she have been tempted? But then, how could she not have been? She was *mesmerised* by Rio Lombardi. It had been a magical day and she shouldn't have taken offence, for she had not objected to being kissed. Rio was no different from any other single oversexed male: he was programmed by his hormones to take advantage of willing women. If only she had had the wit to respond with a lighthearted negative, rather than getting upset and preaching and condemning. The memory of her own clumsy lack of tact made her cringe.

She slid into the silky white nightie she had worn the night before. Taken from the bag of clothing Ezio had given her, the garment was about a size too small in the bosom department, and rather revealing, but then she wasn't planning to walk down the street in it. She got into bed and tossed and turned for ages while telling herself that it was hunger that was keeping her awake. Then she heard a faint cry from Timmie's room and scrambled out of bed to check on him.

Timmie was still asleep. She straightened his bedding and assured herself that he was breathing normally and not too warm. Maybe he had had a bad dream. Slipping out of his room again, she stopped dead at the sight of Rio standing in the corridor, wearing only a pair of black boxer shorts.

CHAPTER FOUR

'I HEARD Timothy crying…is he OK?' Rio prompted.

'Yes, he's still asleep,' Holly told him in a rush.

His ebony hair was tousled, his strong jawline blue-shadowed and his eyes were bright in his lean, bronzed face. He looked like a very sexy buccaneer, all elemental male and rippling muscles. Welded to the spot, Holly gazed at him, her soft lips parting. If she had found it impossible not to stare when he was clothed, she was even more challenged to deny that temptation when he was half-naked. And, although she knew she should not be looking and she was embarrassed by her own fascination, she couldn't stop.

Her heartbeat felt as if it was thumping in her constricted throat. He was magnificent. Her dilated gaze ran from his wide, smooth brown shoulders down over the black curls liberally sprinkling his muscular torso to his tight, flat stomach, and about there, where the band of his boxer shorts encircled his lean hips and challenged all further curiosity, Holly stopped dead in horror at herself.

Eyes shimmering hot gold, Rio strolled closer and, barefoot as he was, he made hardly a sound. The quiet had become a silence that buzzed, a silence alive with dangerous vibrations. Rio dealt her a slow-burning smile of appreciation. Only then did it occur to Holly that her scanty nightdress was scarcely adequate covering in which to parade herself before any red-blooded male. Her cheeks burning fierily, she raised her arms and began to fold them protectively over herself.

65

'Equal rights, *cara*.' Rio snapped long fingers round her wrists and held her still for a lingering physical appraisal.

Her breath snarled up in her throat, for she knew what he was seeing, her full breasts shamelessly delineated by the sheer, tight bodice. She felt the burn of her own mortification right down to the soles of her feet and was duly punished.

Rio made a husky sound low and deep in his throat. He just reached for her, hauling her up to him, his lean hands curving round her hips to crush her feminine mound into connection with the full, hard force of his arousal as he lifted her up against him.

'I hope you're in the mood to satisfy one very hungry guy, *bella mia*,' Rio growled before he brought his mouth crashing down on hers with devouring heat.

It was their first true kiss and it blew Holly away. Crushed to the hard male strength of his big, powerful physique, she was conscious of his virility with every fibre of her being. His mouth was hard and hot and carnal and nobody had ever kissed her that way before. Prying her soft lips apart, he plundered the tender moist interior with his tongue in a very sexual onslaught. He made her want more, he made her want so *much* more that she trembled and gasped under the raw, forceful passion he unleashed on her.

His strong hands moulded her to him and he swept her right off her feet and up into his arms. Her shaken eyes opened just as he shouldered shut a door behind him. Tall lamps burned on each side of an enormous antique bed. The great carved headboard was topped by a fabulous canopy from which elaborate drapes fell to lie in opulent folds on the floor.

'I've been hot as hell for you all day,' Rio muttered harshly above her head.

'Honestly…?' Holly mumbled shyly into a sleek bare

brown shoulder, marvelling that she could have incited his desire, feeling his entire body flaming for need of his but terrified that she would be a disappointment. The option of saying no did not even occur to her.

'I'm as hard as a rock, or haven't you noticed that yet?'

That earthy assurance drenched her cheeks with colour.

Rio sank down on the edge of the bed with her still locked in his hold. One hand anchoring into a fistful of ringlets, he turned her hot face up to meet his searching scrutiny. 'How does an unmarried mother contrive to blush like a furnace every five minutes?'

'I don't know...' He hurt Holly with that question, for to her mind it suggested that he believed she'd slept around before she'd fallen pregnant, which was very far from being the truth. Yet he had only to settle those brilliant, beautiful eyes on her and she was lost without any hope of reclaim. This was the *only* way she would ever get even temporarily close to a male like him, a little voice whispered inside her head. This was not the start of a relationship. Blokes like Rio Lombardi didn't have relationships with ordinary girls like her. In fact she couldn't work out what miracle had occurred to make her seem attractive to him.

Rio set her down onto her own feet so that she stood between his spread thighs and reached up to the slender straps on her slight shoulders. 'I want to look at you,' he told her, and before she could even guess his intention he had tugged the straps down her arms and let the nightdress fall to her ankles.

'*Please...*' Naked in front of a man for the first time in her life, Holly trembled, the flush on her face now feeling as if it was enveloping her entire body, and it was with the greatest difficulty that she resisted the urge to try to cover herself. A coil of heat burned low in her pelvis as his intent gaze scorched over pert breasts crowned by prominent rosy peaks and the cluster of bronze curls at the apex of her slim thighs. She felt as if she was burning alive with shame on a slave block.

Rio scooped her back into his arms as if she was the size and weight of a toy. 'You're shaking…and I haven't even touched you yet.'

'Yes…' Her teeth were almost chattering together in the wake of an enervating wave of apprehension, shame at her own weakness and the most desperate physical longing.

He closed his hand into her tumbling bronze curls to tug her head back and arch her spine, so that he had better access to her shivering body. 'Your skin is so fair against mine,' he husked, letting his hand splay over her slender, taut ribcage, listening to her suck in a gasping breath before he finally let his lean fingers rise to the jutting swell of her breasts to play with her throbbing nipples. 'You have gorgeous breasts…'

Her head was falling back now of its own volition and she was gasping out loud, helplessly thrusting her aching flesh against his palms, white-hot heat snaking up from the very heart of her. He lowered his dark head and let his mouth engulf a distended bud and she cried out loud, shattered at the strength of her own response but helpless to control it.

His teeth teased at her tender flesh and then the tip of his tongue lashed the sensitised tips, sending tremors like lightning sizzling through her trembling length. She had not known that she could *feel* with such intensity, and the whole time he was touching her she was in shock at the twisting ache of sheer pleasure that jerked her every muscle tight.

Rio gathered her up and rose to bring her down across the bed. He leant over her, rearranging her to his own satisfaction, his control absolute. She connected with his burning golden eyes and felt herself melt like honey on the boil. Lying there so exposed, she had never been more conscious of her own body. Her nipples were swollen and glistening from his attentions and the private place between her thighs was embarrassingly moist. Her nails dug into the bedspread beneath her as she struggled to get a grip on herself, dredge herself from the unfamiliar world of what felt like an erotic fantasy, and as soon as she did she felt wildly out of her depth and as nervous as she had a mere second earlier been thrilled about what might be coming next.

'Could you put the lights out?' Holly whispered shakily.

'No…I want to *watch* you,' Rio asserted thickly, lean, strong face set with primal male determination, his sexual hunger unconcealed.

'W-watch me?' Holly stammered in dismay, utterly overpowered by that statement, that very concept.

'You don't hide anything. You *can't*,' Rio pronounced with almost grim satisfaction. 'I like that. I really get off on the fact that just about everything you feel you show me.'

'Do…I?' Holly dropped her eyes, gripped by intense mortification.

'Look at me…'

Holly shut her eyes tight.

'*Holly*…if you want me, look at me.'

For an instant she felt like a wind-up toy that he controlled. Her eyes smarted and opened and he came down on the bed on one knee, all domineering male but absolutely gorgeous, and she looked, of course she looked, was literally nailed to the spot by the sheer power of those scorching golden eyes holding hers.

With a roughened laugh of satisfaction, he let the tip of his tongue tease the tremulous line of her reddened lips and then slide between and delve in an erotic flicker that made her heart hammer and her pulses race.

Levering himself back, Rio stripped off his boxer shorts. Holly turned scarlet. Eyes widening, mouth running dry, surprise and dismay making her jerk. She had never seen a male in that state before, hadn't ever wanted to, but there he was, his sex fully aroused, and there was a great deal more of him than she had naïvely expected.

'What's wrong?' Rio noticed there was something wrong immediately.

'Nothing…' The denial emerged all shaky. She was already resigning herself to the prospect of pain but consoling herself with the thought that what she had once assumed would be the main event hardly lasted a minute.

Rio came over her with all the nerve-racking cool and grace of a predator. He toyed with her mouth again, let a knowing hand curve to a pouting breast and rolled the rigid pink peak straining for his attention between his fingers. All the breath that apprehension had made her hold in was driven from her on a long moaning sigh as her hips rose off the bed in an instinctive movement old as time itself.

'I want to torture you with pleasure, *bella mia*…'

He slid a fingertip between her parted lips and she sucked on it instinctively, the knot of hunger low in the pit of her stomach tightening.

'I want you begging,' Rio confided, shifting with fluid strength against her thigh to let her feel the hard, potent force of his arousal. 'Mindless…it's going to be a very long night.'

Shock gripped her at those words of sensual threat. She was melting again, she was enslaved by just the sound of his smoky drawl, the warm male scent of him and the incredibly seductive feel of that big, powerful, hair-roughened body in contact with hers. She lifted her hand

and touched one high, proud cheekbone, letting her fingers stroke down the side of his face, loving the feel of him, loving the right to touch him, totally hooked on her connection with his liquid dark golden eyes, and enthralled.

He turned his head and entrapped one of her fingers between his lips, and suddenly she was snatching away her hand and reaching up in desperation to find that taunting mouth again for herself. She buried her fingers deep in his black silky hair, a moan dredged from her as he ravished her mouth with hard, hungry heat. She was aching for him, aching where she had never ached before, wanting what she had never wanted before with the most wanton craving.

'Rio, *please*...' she gasped, twisting under him.

'You don't want me enough yet,' he assured her thickly, letting his hand splay against her quivering tummy muscles and then stilling to trace the fine scar he had discovered. 'What's that?'

Holly tensed at his reference to that imperfection. 'I had to have a Caesarean when Timmie was born.'

'It's OK. You're still beautiful.' Moving on, Rio let his fingertips flirt with the damp curls below and laughed with earthy satisfaction as she automatically parted her thighs.

Locating the tiny bud beneath her downy mound, he proceeded to slowly drive her wild. Excitement just exploded in her and she writhed as the throb of need centred at the very heart of her rose to unbearable proportions. And she was mindless, beyond thought, speech, everything, reduced to one gigantic, all too sensitive ache of screaming need. But when she thrashed about, instinctively reaching for a fulfilment she had never known before, he stilled and let her slide down again, withholding what she most craved. And every time it happened she became just a little bit more frantic, clinging to him, almost in tears of frustration, utterly at a loss as to what was happening to her own body.

'Please...I want you now,' she begged strickenly.

Rio traced the swollen moist cleft between her legs, let an expert finger penetrate her once, twice until she cried out, beyond all shame and control. 'You're hot and wet and gloriously tight, *amore*.'

He settled his hands beneath her squirming hips and thrust a pillow under her to raise her. Then there was a pause and she realised he was donning protection. But before she could even process that awareness Rio came over her like a Viking attack force, tipping her up to receive him at an angle that startled her, and then he drove into her in one long, deep thrust that put being startled right out of her mind. Indeed, *everything* went out of her mind. One moment she was almost sobbing with impatience, and the next she was plunged into the most wild physical excitement she had ever experienced.

'*Santo cielo...how* I want you,' he groaned. 'You feel *so* good...'

The intensity of her own excitement drove her crazy. He slammed into her with rhythmic force and she was on fire, gasping and sobbing for air, overwhelmed by the sheer raw pleasure of his every powerful plunge into her tender sheath. Blind and oblivious as she was to everything but the ongoing thunder of her own heartbeat and the plundering glory of his dominant possession, she was completely out of control. He sent her hurtling to the peak of ecstasy and a climax so strong that she felt as if she was shattering into a million pieces.

Letting her quivering weak body settle back down onto the support of the bed, Rio absorbed the shattered look of pleasure she wore. She collided dizzily with his searching gaze and her heart turned over at the sizzling smile of very male satisfaction he gave her. 'I never knew...' she mumbled in a total daze. 'I just never knew…I could feel like that—'

'Again…and again…and again, *bella mia*,' Rio husked, reaching down and lifting her to flip her over onto her stomach before she had the remotest idea of what he was doing. 'Let me show you.'

'*Rio?*' she cried in total bewilderment as he tugged her up onto her knees.

He slid into her again and she was so sensitised and so shaken by both sensation and shock at the position he had put her in, she let out a startled yelp.

'Am I hurting you?'

'No…' She shut her eyes in shame. I'm not doing this, I'm not. And she could not believe the pleasure that surged through her again, was seduced afresh within seconds, beyond caring about anything. She was a creature enslaved by sensation, totally wanton in her responses. Explosive excitement had her in a stranglehold and he controlled her, he controlled her so completely she was incapable of thought or reaction. And the second time that glorious joy racked her she didn't recognise the sobs and moans he dragged from her. The experience was all the more heightened by the feel of him shuddering over her and the groan of savage release he vented as he finally reached his own climax.

In the aftermath, Holly just collapsed, every piece of energy expended. Rio turned her over, flipped back the covers and brought her down on a cool linen sheet. Sprawling down beside her, he curved her back into his arms. He was hot and damp and the scent of him was so familiar now she pressed her lips against a smooth brown shoulder, glorying in that physical closeness. The silence didn't bother her. What she had just shared with him had been a revelation to her, and the languorous relaxation of her own satiation was so new to her she could not yet shake off the effects.

'You're not very experienced, are you?' Rio asked above her head, and for the first time she registered the tension in his lean, muscular length.

'No,' she whispered, suddenly wondering with a deep inner chill of fear if he had found her less than adequate.

Rio rolled her back against the pillows so that she could no longer evade his scrutiny. 'So when did you last indulge?'

Her wide, vulnerable eyes settled on his lean, dark features and the probing gold of his intent gaze and her eyes slewed from his in dismay. 'It's been a long time—'

'*How*...long?'

Feeling foolish, Holly worried at her lower lip before muttering with cast-down eyes, 'Not since the night I fell pregnant.'

'Not since the night you...?' Long fingers curved round her delicate jawbone and tugged her back beneath his searching appraisal.

'It was my first time,' Holly told him with mortified defensiveness.

'You got pregnant the *first* time you had sex?' Rio ground out in visible shock.

'It does happen, you know,' she mumbled, unable to work out quite what interest he could have in such a subject and embarrassed, but at the same time needing him to know that she was not promiscuous.

With a seemingly idle hand Rio brushed a stray corkscrew curl back from her brow and she noticed that there was a slight tremor in his fingers. His stunning dark golden eyes were trained to her with intensity, his blue-shadowed jawline clenched hard. 'Are you taking any current precautions against pregnancy?'

In surprise Holly shook her head.

'I didn't think you would be, *cara*.' His keen gaze screened by his luxuriant dark lashes, Rio released his breath in a long-drawn-out sigh. 'You were almost a virgin. No wonder my every move seemed to shock you so much. You hadn't a bloody clue—'

'No, I—'

'*Still* don't have a clue,' Rio contradicted with a raw edge to his deep, dark drawl, his accent very thick.

'I do!' Holly protested feverishly. 'Maybe I didn't before but I do *now*. I thought sex was awful until tonight…what did I do wrong?'

Above her, Rio closed his eyes, his expression pained, dark colour scoring his fabulous cheekbones. He threw himself back against the tumbled pillows with a very male groan. 'You didn't do anything wrong. I did it *all*. The condom broke…'

As those three words sank in Holly stilled, her face tightening in shock. As she processed that admission and registered the potential consequences her complexion paled to the colour of milk.

Springing off the bed with lithe ease, Rio strode in the direction of the bathroom. 'Come on,' he urged with wry mockery. 'Let's drown our sorrows in the shower!'

'In a minute…' As he vanished from her view she almost fell off the bed in her haste to vacate it. Struggling back into her nightie, she fled to her own room, driven by the kind of panic and shame that wanted no witnesses.

CHAPTER FIVE

EMERGING from a restive sleep, conscious that she had still been awake at dawn, Holly sat up in bed slowly. With every movement, a telling series of aches in certain private places reminded her of her abandoned behaviour with Rio the night before and her shadowed eyes filled with anguished regret.

Last night she had locked her bedroom door. Rio had followed her and, quiet though he had kept his demands that she open the door, she had sensed his angry impatience even through the solid thickness of wood separating them. When, minutes later, the bedside phone had rung she had rushed to unplug it from the socket.

She was *so* ashamed of how stupid and reckless she had been. It was her fault that the whole situation had developed in the first place. She fully believed that it had been her obvious attraction to Rio which had first incited *his* interest, was convinced that without that sexual spur and provocation it would not even have occurred to Rio to touch her. Her feelings, her weakness, her reactions had drawn him.

But at least Rio had thought of precautions. Such a sensible consideration had not crossed her mind once and he was hardly to be blamed for the reality that misfortune had struck. Misfortune was her middle name, Holly reflected, a shuddering sob hurtling up from her constricted lungs. Hadn't she learnt anything from Timothy's birth? Was she still irresponsible and naïve and foolish?

What on earth had got into her? Another sob quivered through her slender frame. She wiped at her eyes but the tears kept coming. How could she ever face Rio again? He had been so kind to her and she had had a magical time with him earlier in the day. Even last night, when she assumed other less well-bred males would have been cursing furiously over such an accident, Rio had maintained his cool courtesy. In fact he had proved himself a guy worthy of being loved.

But she had behaved like a slut, she told herself wretchedly; she deserved everything she had coming to her, but no baby deserved an inadequate mother. For the first time she glanced at the clock by the bed and her eyes flew wide in horror because it was already after ten and Timmie always woke up around seven!

Holly leapt out of the bed and unlocked the door. Pausing for an instant, she then stopped and grabbed up the luxurious fake-fur she had worn to the restaurant and dug her arms into the sleeves before hurtling into the room next door to check on her child. In an almost all-male household she needed to be careful to cover up and perhaps, had she been more sensible the night before, nothing would have happened between her and Rio.

In Timmie's room the nanny, Sarah, looked up with a smile. She was in the midst of dressing Timmie. Holly was startled, for she had assumed that the nanny had only been brought in to look after her son for just the one day.

'Good morning, Miss Sansom. Aren't these clothes beautiful?' Sarah said chattily as if there was nothing odd about Holly choosing to wear a fake-fur coat over her nightie. She held up a tiny navy reefer jacket embroidered with a Scottie dog motif and a pair of miniature checked trousers for Holly's inspection. 'Mr Lombardi had a whole selection of outfits for Timothy delivered this morning.'

The 'Timothy' tag had spread, Holly noted in a daze. Rio had had clothing purchased for her son? Was there no end to his generosity? Or her own indebtedness? Didn't he understand how hard it was to continually receive gifts when she was in no position to reciprocate? Although she was longing to hold her baby in her arms, she backed to the door again. 'I'll just go and get dressed.'

But her attempt to re-enter her own room was forestalled by the reality that there was a giant heap of boxes and bags now sitting on her bed and two manservants were engaged in opening them. A frown of bemusement on her brow, she stared. What was going on?

'I'm glad you put the coat on, *bella mia*,' a dark, deep drawl remarked from behind her. 'I wouldn't like anyone but me to see you in that nightdress.'

Holly whirled round. 'For goodness' sake, what are those blokes doing?'

'Unpacking your new wardrobe…what else?'

'Wh-what new wardrobe?' A band of tension was tightening like a vice round Holly's temples. It was as if she had woken up in another world where everything was slightly different from what it ought to have been. But she had still to look any higher than the level of Rio's gold silk tie.

'What we bought yesterday.'

'Are you telling me…there was *more* than that dress I wore out and the coat?' Holly gasped, appalled by that news.

'*Dio mio,* of course there was more. You had nothing but what you stood up in,' Rio pointed out rather drily.

'But I can't let—'

'Excuse me…' Striding past her, Rio snapped his fingers to alert his staff's attention and addressed them in Italian. The two men immediately abandoned their task and filed out. Closing his fingers over hers, Rio drew her into the bedroom and pushed the door closed. 'Right now we have something rather more important to worry about—'

Holly was gazing aghast at the huge heap of shopping strewn across the bed. 'You can't *do* this, Rio...it's not right, it's totally wrong—'

'Holly,' Rio slotted in grimly, 'in fifteen minutes a Miss Elliott will be calling to see us and you need to get dressed. I suggest you wear one of your new outfits.'

Her brow indented. 'Who's Miss Elliott?'

'The social worker whom you would have seen had you remained in hospital.'

Holly had turned a sickly shade. 'But how did she find out I was here in your house?'

Rio's wide, sensual mouth compressed. 'I informed Dr Coulter, who's a friend of mine, that I had brought you here—'

Holly was trying very hard not to burst into tears. 'Some friend...shopping me to the authorities!'

'*Per meraviglia!* Will you stop talking as though you are a criminal? You and Timothy are both all right now, but naturally enquiries have to be made to establish that fact.'

'They'll t-take him away from me...' Holly sobbed, backing away from him in her distress.

Rio gripped her by the shoulders, dark-as-midnight eyes level. 'Nobody is going to take him away from you. I promise you that. Now pull yourself together and come downstairs—'

'I *can't*—'

'You're talking like a child.' Rio dealt her a hard look of censure, lean, dark features set in impatient lines. 'This matter will be easily resolved. Once I inform the woman that I intend to marry you, she will see that neither you nor your son are in need of further support.'

As he released his hold on her Holly fell back from him,

thunderstruck by that statement. 'You're going to tell her that we're getting...*married*?'

'And the less you say on the subject the better...OK?' Rio breathed, striding back to the door and flipping it shut in his wake.

In a daze, Holly blinked as comprehension slowly sank in. Yet she was amazed that Rio was willing to tell such a whopping lie on her behalf. However, that fiction would indeed satisfy any concerns as to her son's future well-being. Rio Lombardi was rich, respectable and a noted phi-lanthropist, she reminded herself dizzily. He was the fake husband-to-be from heaven, only lacking an actual halo. He was also very clever. She was really touched that he was prepared to spout such a story purely for her benefit. Not that he was exactly looking forward to the prospect, she conceded, shame assailing her. Rio had had a bleak, grim aspect new to her experience of him. Most probably he wished he had never met her and never got involved.

But the least she could do to back up his story was look the part of a woman on the brink of marriage to a very wealthy man. She lifted a turquoise dress and jacket from the bed and rooted about until she found the toning shoes. Imagine him spending such a huge amount of money on her! So crazy too! He really and truly had no concept of the life she led or of her level in society compared with his own. Where the heck did he think she would wear designer suits and fancy evening outfits?

Neither Timmie nor his nanny were in his room when she emerged from her own. Holly descended the stairs, tak-ing careful steps in the high heels. Her heart was beating so fast with fear and nerves she felt sick. She dawdled in the hall, scanning her reflection, once again barely recog-nising herself. Who was that slender figure in the beauti-fully cut jacket that just screamed class and expense?

A door swung open off the hall. 'Holly…hurry up,' Rio urged with controlled exasperation.

Even talking like that, he was just so beautiful, Holly thought painfully. And fear was unknown to him. Of course, he could not understand or sympathise with her distress. Of course, her terror struck him as being exaggerated and illogical. He had probably never been in a situation he could not control. He did not know what it was to feel powerless and at the mercy of others. Good and well-meaning people those other parties might be, but sometimes they took terrifying and merciless decisions.

A blonde older woman with cool blue eyes and a distinct air of efficiency was seated in the drawing room and immediately addressed her. 'Miss Holly Sansom?' she queried, scanning Holly's appearance with dubious brows raised like question marks.

'Yes…I'm Holly.'

Timmie was sitting on the rug with some toys and he chortled and held out his arms when he saw his mother. In his fancy togs, he looked not only like a baby who had swallowed a silver spoon at birth but a baby who might well have swallowed an entire silver service. Scooping her son up, Holly sat down with him on her lap and hugged him tight, her chin resting on his sweet-smelling fluffy dark curls.

'Dr Coulter informed me that you're living here for the present, Miss Sansom,' the blonde woman commented. 'Is that true?'

'Holly and I are getting married,' Rio imparted with the utmost casualness.

And that was just about that, bar a few minor comments. The blonde was taken aback, but then she consulted the file in her lap and lifted her gaze to study Timmie. Last of all, she directed her attention in a discreet flicker at Rio and a faint smile flickered at the corner of her lips. 'I'm so pleased that the situation has been sorted out. Timmie looks very content.'

'I hope to adopt Timothy as my son,' Rio remarked.

The other woman nodded slowly but now looked slightly bemused before finally wishing them all well and rising to leave.

Leaving Rio to take care of the courtesies, Holly just flopped where she sat.

Rio strode back through the door again, lean, strong face taut. 'Miss Elliott just assumed that Timothy was *my* child.'

Holly flushed to the roots of her hair and sat up with a start, corkscrew curls bouncing. That possibility had not occurred to her, but as soon as Rio suggested it she recalled the way the social worker had behaved. 'Honestly? Did she say something on her way out?'

'She didn't need to. It was written all over her face. I suppose Timothy has quite dark hair and that possible explanation for our marital plans made the most sense to her. But I don't like anyone believing that I would treat the mother of my child as you were treated by your son's father. That's why I referred to my wish to adopt Timothy.' Having given her that frank assurance and made her stiffen with embarrassed discomfiture, Rio crossed the room to hunker down and survey her son, whose big blue eyes were drowsy. 'He's *amazing*. He spends half the morning getting fed and bathed and dressed and no sooner is he up and about than he's ready for his cot again!'

Grateful for that distraction, Holly burbled, 'He's always slept a lot. He's a good baby. You were really wonderful with Miss Elliott, Rio.' She nibbled awkwardly at her lower lip as she thanked him for his support. 'Very convincing. I know you couldn't have enjoyed saying *that* about you and me...but I'm very grateful and, no matter what happens, I'll never, ever take a risk like that with my son again.'

Rio surveyed her strained expression with narrowed dark, glittering eyes and frowned. 'I do believe we've been talking at cross purposes. We'll discuss that after you've taken Timothy up for his nap.'

Cross purposes? What cross purposes? And how come she was only now noticing how domineering his powerful personality could make Rio seem? He came off with commands as if to the manner born. But then, she supposed he *had* been born to that sort of stuff, she reflected forgivingly, feeling truly guilty and ungrateful for thinking on such lines after all he had done to help her.

What if you conceive again? a little voice sniped in the back of her mind. Are you going to think of that as help too? Her tummy churned. She adored her son but knew she could not in her present circumstances cope with a second child. But then Rio was already letting her know that he would not abandon her, wasn't he? How come she had not immediately recognised *why* he had made that speech about how he would not treat the mother of his child in the manner that her ex-boyfriend had treated her?

But there was so much tension between them now. He was no longer relaxed with her. That was what that reckless bout of lovemaking had done. It had spoilt things, she reflected wretchedly, and cringed at the intimate images teeming in her memory banks. Not once even yet had she managed to look Rio directly in the face. Last night she had sobbed and begged and pleaded for him to make love to her. There was no forgetting that. She had been out of control, totally out of control *and* out of her depth, but even she knew that men preferred a challenge to a push-over. Rio Lombardi was hardly the sort of male who needed an adoring slave to massage his ego. Women had to be falling in the aisles around him, so he would want and expect more.

Nervous as a cat walking over hot coals, Holly returned to the drawing room.

Rio swung round from the window, tall, dark and immaculate in his tailored business suit. 'When I said that we were getting married, it wasn't some crazy story, *cara*.'

Not understanding his meaning, Holly stilled with a frown of confusion. 'Then—er—what was it?'

'The truth of what we're going to do. I can't say that I feel flattered that you should assume that I would lie about something that important,' Rio continued with a level cool that only made her own astonishment feel all that more intense. 'We'll be married just as soon as I can get a special licence arranged.'

Her knees felt as if they were fashioned out of cotton wool and wobbled under her. She was finally looking at him for the first time that day and only because she was reeling with shock. Blue eyes very wide, she whispered unsteadily, 'You're not having me on?'

'I may have made you pregnant. I took advantage of you last night,' Rio breathed, aggressive jawline clenched hard. 'You were very vulnerable and I should have kept my distance. I took you to bed because I wanted—'

'That's OK. That's not taking advantage!' Holly protested with feverish relief at what she assumed he was about to tell her.

'Sex. I wanted sex. It was as primitive as that.' His superb bone-structure fiercely taut, Rio made an admission that slaughtered Holly where she stood, for she had believed when she interrupted him that he had been telling her that it was her, personally, that he had wanted. Only that was not the case, was it? The truth was much more painful. When a bloke said he had just wanted sex, it was like saying that she had only been a convenient body, Holly reflected in agony.

Deeply hurt by that confession, wishing he had thought enough of her feelings not to have voiced it, Holly dropped heavily down onto the nearest sofa, no longer trusting her weak legs to hold her upright. 'I wanted you...just you,' she heard herself mumble like a foolish child, digging herself into an even more embarrassing hole.

'I know...' That confirmation just splintered through her shrinking, shaking body like the cruellest of knives, tearing tender flesh wherever it touched. 'I must be honest with you, *cara*—'

'Don't call me that...whatever it means. You use it like it means something and it *doesn't*.' Holly squeezed out that condemnation in a voice that was far from level. 'So why are you talking about marrying me...feeling like you do?'

'I like you, Holly. I like Timothy too. I believe I could become fond of you.'

Holly wanted to die where she sat. Fond? She curved her arms round herself, appalled at the emotional hurt he was inflicting on her in the name of honesty. Even Jeff with his abuse had not wounded her as much as Rio wounded her at that moment. Rio was ripping apart everything, every naïve and harmless belief, every tiny inner hope. He *liked* her, well, whoopy-do! So she felt even more pathetic to be sitting there thinking that she loved him while he hammered the self-esteem he had rescued for her back into the ground again.

'Until relatively recently, I was engaged to another woman.'

That startling admission hung there like another giant slap in the face just waiting for her to lift her cheek to receive it. But something stronger than she was, the most powerful curiosity, forced Holly to lift her head again. The brilliant flare of anger lightening his gaze in the aftermath of that acknowledgement did not match her expectations. There was none of the regret or emotion that she had feared that she would see. In fact, his darkly handsome features were set hard in stone.

'Engaged?' she prompted uneasily.

'I finished it. That's over and done with and in the past.' Beautifully shaped mouth curling, glittering golden eyes resting on her, Rio murmured, 'I only mentioned it because while I was engaged I got used to the idea of being married, and I do still need a wife.'

'What for?' It sounded inane but Holly couldn't help it. But then, she was weak with relief at the finality with which he had pronounced that his engagement was over. It must have ended quite some time back, Holly assumed, or he would hardly have been saying that it was in the past.

Rio spread his lean brown hands in a fluid expressive movement. 'Some day I want a family of my own.'

'Oh...'

'I also need a wife to oversee my domestic arrangements and entertain friends and family. A wife who will try to be a daughter to my mother, who suffers a lot of ill-health,' Rio enumerated, very much more relaxed now that he was getting to talk practicalities. 'A wife to make *me* more comfortable, for I have got beyond the stage where I enjoy spending my time, indeed, often *wasting* my time with a variety of different women.'

And he wanted superwoman as a wife. He had huge expectations, Holly thought heavily, knowing she could never, ever measure up to such requirements, and marvelling that he had not immediately realised that fact.

'You could *learn* to be the wife that I want,' Rio informed her confidently.

But it sounded as if lifelong training would be necessary.

She had been stymied by one trip to a fancy restaurant. A near-hysterical giggle bubbled in her aching throat but she had never been further from laughter.

'You need to know that I've good reason *other* than the risk that you may already be pregnant to talk of marriage,' he continued in his dark, deep drawl that flowed like honey even now down her sensitive spine.

'But we're probably worrying about nothing—'

'Are we? You're young and fertile and I would prefer not to wait for proof one way or the other.' Rio expelled his breath in a measured hiss. 'If we wait and a child is eventually born there will be those who believe that I was *forced* to marry you. That would be humiliating for you.'

He really did expect the worst. He really did believe that there was a very strong chance that he might have impregnated her. His certainty scared her. But how could she marry a man who felt nothing for her? Did that mean that she was considering his offer? Of course she was. Dredging her attention from his lean, strong face, she knew she did not even have to take her own feelings for him into account to make that decision. She had nothing to offer Timmie, who would no doubt thrive as Timothy. If she married Rio her baby would want for nothing. He would have a home, love and security and a bloke who was willing to be his adoptive father. Rio liked kids. He liked her son already. In fact she had pretty much hit the equivalent of the jackpot falling in front of his limo, she acknowledged guiltily, feeling that *she* would very much be taking advantage of *him*.

She linked her trembling hands together, hugely worked up but trying so hard to emulate his calm and logical approach. 'When did you start thinking of all this?'

'Ten minutes after you fled from my room last night,' Rio admitted, bringing her bright head up again. 'I have never felt so guilty in my whole life.'

'Thanks…' Her voice wobbled again and she pushed her lips together hard, striving to will back the tears threatening behind her eyes.

'I'll look after you and your son. You need me. I like to be needed. I'm *used* to being needed,' Rio completed with a shrug of Latin acceptance.

He was so volatile. So very, very volatile and until now she had not even recognised that reality. He had seemed so controlled and reserved at their first proper meeting at the hospital, only to overturn that impression with his angry, intimidating reaction when he had found her trying to sneak away from the Lombardi hospital. Ever since then he had alternated between fiery heat and indolent cool. He could switch from one mood to the other within seconds. He fascinated her.

'You might go and fall madly in love with someone else…' she heard herself say, although it was an effort to make herself say that.

'You must be joking,' Rio said in a tone of icy derision.

He was so sure of himself, so sure he knew everything there was to know. Recalling all the awful anxiety she had suffered just struggling to survive, she felt reassured by that infinite confidence of his. So how could she hold his patent belief that she would *snatch* at his offer of marriage against him?

After all, here she was, dead keen on him and incapable of hiding it, not to mention homeless and broke. Had he pretended a little uncertainty as to his reception it wouldn't really have been convincing, she told herself. He was incredibly good-looking and sexy and a huge catch for someone like her. But he was also feeling guilty as hell over taking her to bed, she reminded herself reluctantly. She really *ought* to be turning him down flat. Wasn't it wrong to let him make such a massive mistake? He didn't love her, he hardly knew her, and in time he might even come to despise her for the mistakes she would make trying to fit into his world. But he was right, she could learn, and a part of her that she wasn't very proud of desperately wanted that chance.

'I shouldn't say yes to this,' Holly breathed unevenly.

'But you will.' Rio leant down and closed his hands round hers to pull her up to him. His sudden flashing smile as her cheeks blossomed with self-conscious colour made her tummy somersault with excitement. The warm, intrinsically familiar scent of him made her ache. The mere fact that he was only inches away reduced her to quivering, melting compliancy and, guilty as hell aside, she could see that he liked that, he *liked* that very much. That she did not mistake.

He gave her the kind of brief kiss that he excelled at, provocative, intimate, intensely erotic. Then he set her free again when she was desperate to cling and every nerve-ending craved the heat of his passion.

'We'll be very uncool and wait for our wedding night,' Rio decreed, soft and husky and boundlessly sure, it seemed, of his welcome.

And for the very first time Holly realised that she could crave him like an addict and still want to scream at him.

CHAPTER SIX

THREE days later Holly climbed into the limousine that would ferry her to the wedding that had been arranged and the ceremony that would make her Rio Lombardi's wife.

Ezio Farretti beamed at her in flattering admiration of her bridal regalia but it felt so very strange to be alone, with neither friends nor family for support, indeed none of the more personal trappings Holly had once naïvely assumed would be part and parcel of such an event.

She had thought of phoning her parents and telling them that she was getting married but had given up on the idea when it occurred to her that naturally her parents would want to know all about her relationship with Rio. How on earth could she admit that she was marrying a man she had known for less than a week? She would have to wait until her marriage was already an established fact before meeting up with her parents again.

For three solid days she had done little but shop, first for her gown and then for clothes for both her and Timothy that would suit a warmer climate. That last instruction from Rio had actually caused a panic when it had emerged that he was planning to take them abroad after the wedding and she had confided that neither she nor her son had a passport. Fortunately it had proved possible to redress that oversight, but Rio's incredulity that anybody should be without a passport had reminded her all over again of how different her world was from his, for her parents had never been abroad in their entire lives.

Emerging from that recollection, Holly rearranged the

skirt of her dress, fearful of creasing the delicate folds before she arrived at the church, desperately wanting to look the very best she could for Rio. She had fallen in love with her ivory and gold wedding gown at first sight, but Rio had told her to pick something traditional and a dress strongly reminiscent of a medieval bride might not fit the bill, she reflected anxiously.

Long pointed sleeves ornamented the boned V-shaped silk bodice which was decorated with exquisite gold embroidery and laced tight at her tiny waist, and the skirt was long and elegant. A fabulous sapphire and diamond tiara was lodged in her bronze curls and she wore a matching and equally impressive necklace and drop earrings. The set was Lombardi family jewellery sent from Tuscany by special courier and Rio had requested that she wear the items. She had had to tie on the earrings with thread because her ears were not pierced and, terrified of losing the earrings, she checked that they were still in place every few minutes.

In fact, nerves were eating Holly alive, for Rio had been abroad and she had only spoken to him on the phone in recent days. Indeed, at one stage she had honestly believed that the wedding might have to be cancelled. The same day that she had agreed to marry him Rio had flown out to Stockholm on business before travelling on to Florence to call on his mother. Rio had hoped to bring the older woman back to London with him to attend their wedding but Alice Lombardi had felt too weak to make the trip.

'I *was* going to fly you out for the day so that you could meet,' Rio had informed Holly on the phone twenty-four hours earlier before he explained why he could not return that evening as he had hoped. 'But she had palpitations and I had to call her doctor in. He prescribed complete bedrest.'

Holly had repressed the troubled suspicion that her future mother-in-law might have been felled by sheer horror that her only son was about to wed a stranger who was not only an unmarried mother but also a young woman from a background that in no way matched their own. Since that possibility did not appear to have occurred to Rio, she had not liked to mention it.

'What's Mrs Lombardi like?' she had asked Ezio.

'A fine woman,' he had responded. 'But a martyr to ill-health.'

'Maybe the wedding will have to be put off.' Holly had felt horribly guilty at the dismay which had filled her at that prospect.

'Mrs Lombardi has a remarkable ability to pull back from death's door,' Ezio had asserted bracingly. 'In fact, I wouldn't be surprised if the lady outlives all of us.'

As the limousine turned off the road Holly was amazed to see that the church appeared to be buried in a sea of parked cars and that there were a lot of people standing outside the iron railings bounding the car park. Had there been a wedding booked before their own and had it run on late? Or was she arriving too early?

Leaning forward, she lifted the car phone to ask Ezio.

'They're all here for *your* wedding,' the older man informed her, his astonishment at her question audible.

All those cars? Holly was aghast. She had assumed that there would be no guests, had believed that their wedding would be a very quiet and private affair. True, Rio had not said that, but he *had* told her to leave Timothy at home with Sarah, and in the time frame concerned and with him out of the country who on earth could have made arrangements for so many people to attend?

As she emerged shakily from the car a seething crowd seemed to come out of nowhere at her. Security guards held back the crush while aggressive men with cameras shouted and urged her to look up. In the midst of that fracas, she

was seized by a shock and fear so profound that had Ezio
not seized her elbow and hurried her on into the church she
would have shot back into the limousine and screamed at
the chauffeur to drive off again.

In the church porch, she shivered and stared at Ezio in
incomprehension. 'What's going on? Who *are* those people?'

'The press.'

'But why would they be interested in our wedding?'

'Rio getting married is news,' the older man advanced.
'Nobody knows who you are either, and that was sure to
whip up a storm.'

At that point the double doors near by were opened wide
from the other side and organ music flooded out from the
main body of the church.

Holly gazed in horror at the packed pews she could now
see, the swivelling heads of those keen to see the bride,
and she backed out of sight again at speed. 'I can't *do* this!'
she gasped in genuine panic. 'Not walk down that aisle on
my own without my dad or any bridesmaids. Why didn't
Rio *warn* me it would be like this?'

'He probably didn't think. You'll be fine,' Ezio Farretti
soothed.

Holly liked and trusted the older man. She scanned his
smart appearance in his well-cut suit and mustered the courage to make a special request. '*You* could give me away…'
A note of entreaty underlined her strained voice. 'That way
I wouldn't look so odd and I wouldn't be alone.'

Ezio dealt her a startled look and then absorbed the fact
that she was still backing in the direction of the exit. With
a slow smile, he straightened his shoulders and extended
his arm. 'I would be honoured. But remember that this was
your idea, not mine,' he warned her gently.

However, if Rio was taken aback to see her approach the

altar in tandem with his security chief, Holly was too enervated to notice. No sooner had she arrived than the priest
began to speak, and as she looked at Rio and met his brilliant dark eyes her heartbeat just went haywire. The instant
the ring went on her finger was so precious to her but it
also made her regret that she had not thought to ask him if
he would have liked to receive a ring too.

But then, he would have had to buy that for himself as
well, Holly realised with a stab of mortification. She wondered how it was that when life had been normal she had
never worried quite so much about money nor felt so much
of a pauper. It hurt her pride that not a shred she wore even
on her own wedding day had been paid for with her own
money, for she had nothing that he had not given her.

'You look really stunning in that gown.' Rio flashed her
an appreciative smile while they stood on the church steps
being filmed and photographed.

His smile filled her with warmth and security. Without
him by her side, Holly knew she would have bolted for
cover. Never before had she been the target of so many
speculative stares and she had never dreamt even in her
wildest fantasies that she would ever marry a male likely
to attract such enormous attention from the media. She fingered the slender band of gold on her wedding finger as if
it was a talisman that might yet make her feel that she was
really and truly Rio Lombardi's bride. But just then, regardless of the winging sense of happiness strengthening
her, it still felt like a crazy daydream.

As a limousine whisked them away from the church she
turned to him, her lovely face betraying her continuing
strain. 'Why didn't you tell me that there would be so many
people coming?'

Rio elevated a smooth ebony brow and responded with

his own question. 'Why would you have thought otherwise?'

'You told me to leave Timothy at home—'

'I thought that that would be more relaxing for you,' Rio slotted in smoothly. 'Nor would Timothy enjoy being deprived of his mother and surrounded by strangers.'

Both statements were indisputably correct but Holly could not help wondering if her son's exclusion might also have been linked to a certain unwillingness on Rio's part to brandish the fact that his bride was already a parent, and to a child who was not his.

Rio rested knowing dark golden eyes on her. 'You're *wrong*.'

Holly flushed. 'I didn't say anything!'

'You don't need to. I also once sat through a wedding during which a baby screamed continuously. It left a lasting impression on me,' Rio mocked, reaching for the taut fingers coiled on her lap and closing his hand over hers in reassurance. 'I will look on Timothy as my son and treat him accordingly. Didn't I promise you that?'

'*Yes…*' Holly's throat had thickened with tears because she was ashamed that her own insecurity had made her doubt him.

'If I kiss you now I'll wreck your make-up,' Rio teased.

'To heck with that…' she muttered in a wobbly undertone.

With a husky masculine laugh, Rio laced indolent fingers into the bright fall of her hair and crushed her soft mouth under his own with a hunger that sent miniature lightning bolts stabbing to every sensitive spot in her quivering body. 'Enough,' he groaned, setting her back from him. 'We still have a reception to get through, although I'm not planning on a lengthy stay.'

Holly tensed. 'A reception?'

'Feeding one's guests is an inescapable duty,' Rio quipped. 'Sometimes I wonder if we grew up on the same planet, *cara*.'

At that crack, Holly paled and said defensively, 'I just didn't know we were going to have a proper wedding.'

'What else could we have had?' Rio regarded her in polite bewilderment. 'What did you expect?'

'Just us.'

'Just *us*?' Rio stressed in patent astonishment at the idea. 'Don't you think that would have looked very odd? In the circumstances, the very last thing I would wish is the suggestion that there is anything odd about our marriage.'

'So who arranged all this stuff, then?'

'My staff. I have an extensive staff,' Rio pointed out gently.

Her mouth still tingling from the smouldering contact of his, Holly nodded hurriedly in receipt of that information and strove not to look as if her own ignorance was embarrassing her when indeed it was.

In the grand and exclusive hotel where the reception was staged, she shook hands with a countless number of people and later recalled not a single face or name. Rio's relations, his business connections and personal friends got all mixed up inside her buzzing head. During the superb meal that was served, a lot of the conversation around her kept on switching from English into Italian and she tried not to feel excluded and tried not to seem conscious of the enormous curiosity behind the lingering appraisals she received. Obviously learning to speak Italian was going to be one of her first challenges, she told herself, but it was something of a shock to meet with that language barrier and to sit there feeling like the quietest bride that had ever existed.

She angled her head closer to Rio's and whispered, 'I'm just going to find a phone to ring Timothy.'

Rio interrupted his conversation to turn questioning eyes on her. 'Ring...Timothy?'

Holly reddened. 'Yes. Sarah can hold the phone to his ear so that I can talk to him.'

Rio eased a hand into his pocket and withdrew his cell-phone. 'Be my guest.'

'I wouldn't know how to use it—'

'It's *simple*.'

Accepting the phone, Holly slipped away from the table to find a quiet spot in the foyer, but no matter how many buttons she stabbed she couldn't work out how to use the darned thing and got nothing but words coming up on the tiny screen. Peering down at it in frustration, she only then noticed that the same words seemed to be going round and round: 'I love u. Call me.'

A chill ran down her sensitive spine. As she stood there by the wall, two women engaged in animated conversation strolled out of the crowded function room. 'Well, all I can say is...if the *baby* bride stole Rio from Christabel, there's hope for all of us!'

'Did you hear that hilarious accent of hers? I almost burst out laughing! She talks like a hayseed—'

'I could practically see Rio wincing. He is *so* refined. And she obviously doesn't have a single presentable relative because I know *everyone* here.'

'Poor Christabel,' the first woman said with mocking sympathy. 'Just imagine the agony of being that beautiful and being replaced by a creature with red hair like an electrified ragdoll! What did you think of her wedding dress?'

'If you're that skinny, you should hide it, not flaunt it!'

'It was so cheap-and-nasty-looking too. Bargain basement. You could tell *he* hadn't paid for it.'

Her back pinned to the wall, her tummy churning at those comments, and trembling, Holly waited until the women had moved out of sight before setting off without even knowing where she was going. She just wanted to hide somewhere. Rio was getting love messages on his phone and everybody was laughing at her. In an archway, she stumbled as her gown caught on her heel and she had to pause to free the hem. When she looked up she realised that she was in a bar and that people were looking at her. Espying a cloakroom at the far end, she began to walk fast towards it, head held as high as she could manage.

'I'm *telling* you…' a loud, very upper-class male voice proclaimed full of amusement just as she moved past the bar. 'I'll lay you a grand that I'm right. Rio's bride is preggers. He's been playing away behind Christabel's back and then *bang*…his perfect life just went up in smoke!'

Holly stopped dead behind the tall blond man in full flood. 'If that's what you think, why did you come to our wedding? Guests are supposed to want to wish the bridal couple well…fat chance!' Holly snapped with stinging disgust, her charged voice falling into a deathly silence that she was quite beyond noticing. 'The likes of you are too nasty to wish anybody well!'

The young blond man swung round. Warm colour flooding his fair, open face, he stared down at her with appalled blue eyes. 'Oh, no…I am *so* sorry!'

Holly only dimly recalled him from the long procession of guests she had been forced to greet. But, without another word, she headed on into the cloakroom. She wondered dismally if she could brick herself up in one of the cubicles and stay there for ever undiscovered. She studied her 'electrified ragdoll' hair and her 'cheap' dress, which she had believed was so lovely, and tears started streaming down her face. On her terms the gown had been quite expensive enough for something that would only be worn once, but probably by rich people's standards it *had* been bargain basement.

Yet all she could really think about at that moment was the woman sending 'I love you' text messages to Rio on his phone. A woman called Christabel, the same name that the beauty-salon owner, Sly, had mentioned that day she trimmed Holly's hair. Christabel, who was so obviously Rio's former fiancée. *Beautiful* Christabel, whom Rio had evidently dumped and yet nobody seemed to have the slightest idea why. Unless it was because he had got Holly pregnant behind Christabel's back.

But only time would take care of that kind of spite and, knowing her own luck in the fertility stakes, time might yet convince people that their suspicions had been entirely correct. Furthermore, Rio had married her but he didn't love her and she had better get used to that reality. How could she demand the same boundaries as any other new bride? It was not a normal marriage. Mopping her damp face dry, powdering her shiny nose and repairing her lipstick, Holly headed back into the fray.

As she recrossed the bar, looking to neither left nor right, the young blond man fell into step beside her. 'Go away,' she spat out of the corner of her mouth.

'I don't think you even know who I am. I'm Jeremy, from the English side of the Lombardi clan—'

'Didn't know there *was* an English side—'

'But Rio's mother, Alice, is English…she's also my mother's sister,' Jeremy remarked, his surprise at her ignorance unconcealed.

Holly walked away from him. Unable to face returning to the function room until she had got a better grip on her overtaxed emotions, she picked one of the sofas in the seating area just off the main foyer. Her unwanted companion infuriated her by throwing himself down beside her and reaching for her hand.

'Look, I'm willing to grovel. What I said was utterly indefensible but I was sounding off for a laugh,' Jeremy asserted earnestly. 'I would sooner have cut off my right arm than hurt you like that—'

'It's not too late. Go ahead,' Holly told him.

Amused respect flared in Jeremy's eyes. 'All right, so I was laying on the syrup a bit thick.'

Without the smallest warning, Rio strode into the alcove. His sudden appearance made Holly jerk in dismay, and Jeremy hurriedly removed his hand from hers. His devastatingly handsome features set like steel, Rio flashed scorching golden eyes over the two of them and then settled his hard gaze on Holly with intimidating force. 'Where have you been all this time? Sitting out here flirting with my layabout cousin?'

Jeremy shot upright, visibly disconcerted by the speed with which that accusation had emerged from the bridegroom. 'I was trying to make a grovelling apology to Holly—'

'What were you apologising *for*?' Rio demanded of the younger man.

'Oh, leave it, for goodness' sake!' Attempting to reclaim some dignity, Holly got up. 'I still have to ring Timothy.'

Jeremy had already started to speak to Rio in a low-pitched flood of Italian. It was just as though she wasn't there, and she had had enough of that throughout that endless meal. She had married an Italian, she reminded herself ruefully. Had she really thought that his family would talk in English just for her benefit? What was she…stupid or something?

She located the public phones and called the town house. However, Timothy was having a nap. Sarah offered to wake him but Holly told her not to be daft and just to leave him sleeping. Even so, denied even the small comfort of talking to her baby, Holly felt tears sting her eyes afresh. She had never felt so alone in her life.

'Holly…Jeremy told me what happened.'

It was Rio's dark, rich drawl, his hand coming to rest on her taut shoulder, and Holly gulped, fighting for composure before she could turn round. 'It doesn't matter—'

'It *does* matter—'

Holly spun round. 'Just before that, I heard another couple of your charming guests talking about my cheap dress, my hilarious accent and my *electrified* ragdoll hair—'

'Who the hell—?' Rio growled after a shaken pause at that outburst of confidence.

'They're all the same…horrible!' Holly was feeling so alienated from him that she was in no mood to accept sympathy. 'You know, *my* friends, had they been invited, might have drunk too much and laughed a lot louder, but they wouldn't have attended only to pull the bride or the groom to shreds. Where I come from, weddings are *happy* occasions. I've had more fun at a wake than I've had today!'

'Really?' Rio breathed glacially.

Finally, Holly thrust his phone back at him. 'I don't know how to get rid of that stupid message going round and round,' she framed jaggedly. 'But either you're making a mug of me or you're being too *refined* to tell her where to get off!'

His dense black lashes screened his gaze as he studied his phone. With a fingertip he jabbed a button and the screen went blank. Even the ease with which he did that annoyed her, for she had hit every tiny button on that even tinier panel in her frustration and got nowhere. She stared up at him, saw the faint rise of dark blood scoring his cheekbones.

'You shouldn't have accessed my messages,' Rio drawled with freezing cool.

Holly could not credit the level of sheer rage that blasted through her at that facetious response, that unjust attempt to turn the blame back on her. 'Well, your simple phone wasn't *simple* enough and I couldn't get rid of the blasted thing. And what's more,' Holly snapped, truly lathered up into a steaming temper, 'you're just trying to sidestep the whole subject and I'm not so stupid that I can't see that!'

'If you raise your voice once more, I'm going to cart you out to the limo like a sack of coal,' Rio murmured with a smouldering smile full of threat.

Holly sucked in a deep, charged breath. She felt as though the top of her head might fly off with the force of unvented anger still blazing up inside her.

'So go upstairs now and get changed and we will say our goodbyes,' Rio completed in full command mode.

'Get changed into…what?' Holly queried helplessly.

'Into your going-away outfit—'

'I haven't got one,' Holly told him. 'You told me we weren't going abroad until tomorrow. It's about the only thing you *did* tell me. I mean, you didn't mention the two hundred guests, the press or the hotel reception either.'

'I can't believe you didn't pack anything.' Rio was impervious to that blatant invitation to take their argument into a new and fresh dimension. 'But I presume you want to throw your bouquet.'

'You must be joking. Waste my lovely flowers on this crowd?' Holly shrugged a rigid shoulder not very successfully and stuck her nose in the air.

Fifteen minutes later they were in the limousine and seated in silence. Indeed, the silence went on and on and on until it seemed to howl in her ears like a gathering storm, clawing at her nerves.

'You have gorgeous hair,' Rio murmured in a gritty tone. 'If you heard anyone comparing that glorious mane of yours to a ragdoll's, it was pure bitchiness. As for your gown, it looks wonderful, and if it was cheap it was the find of the century. Your accent's cute, it's you. I can't imagine you without it.'

Holly snatched in a shuddering breath but said nothing.

'Jeremy was drunk and he is very sorry but, let's face it, he wasn't to know the bride would be in the public bar. I don't like what he said and I'm angry that you should've been hurt but I really don't give a damn what people say!'

'Like Rhett Butler...?' she squeezed out shakily.

'He walked away. I'm not about to...*not* on my wedding night,' Rio purred like a predatory tiger on the prowl, his earthy intonation sending a quiver of helpless awareness down her sensitive spine. 'As for the text message you saw. It was an old message. I wasn't aware it was still stored and it's now been deleted.'

'People think you got me pregnant and that that's why you broke up with your fiancée. I don't like being stuck with the blame.'

'It's a five-day wonder, not worth worrying about.'

'Was...*she*?'

The silence hummed as if she had turned on a turbo switch. She could literally feel his rising tension.

'At one time I thought so, and then I realised that she wasn't.'

'I'd kind of like to know what went wrong,' Holly admitted, but only after a long pause to see if he added anything more.

'I don't want to discuss that. It happened before I met you and has nothing to do with you,' Rio countered with cool emphasis.

In receipt of that snub, Holly felt flags of pink mortification unfurl in her cheeks. Well, he hadn't missed and hit the wall there, had he? Christabel was not to be talked about. Only at that point did Holly notice that they appeared to be leaving the city behind them. 'Where are we going?'

'We're spending the night at my country house and flying out to the Maldives tomorrow.'

She had never even heard of the Maldives and once again felt crucified by her own ignorance. All those hazy schooldays she had sat daydreaming and looking out of windows, giggling at notes passed between her friends, never, ever appreciating that some day she might regret not taking school seriously. *He* probably had a university degree, she thought with a sinking heart. Every time she opened her mouth she was at risk of dropping herself into a big black hole of embarrassment.

'I've asked for your cases to be sent down to the Priory. I assume you can get by without Timothy until tomorrow when we all meet up at the airport.'

Holly swallowed hard and nodded in reluctant silence. It had not been a great wedding. She had been too nervous and her self-esteem was still too low for her to feel confident in such exalted company. She so much wanted their marriage to work but she could not feel she had made much of a start.

'Are you *still* in love with her?' Holly hadn't even known that she was about to ask that question, but even as the anxious words escaped her lips she saw that that was what she most feared: that every moment he spent with her he might be fighting the desire to be with the unknown Christabel.

Rio did not pretend to misunderstand. 'No.'

Slowly she breathed again and her tension eased. Obviously something pretty serious must have happened for him to break off his engagement to Christabel. She did not feel he was a here today, gone tomorrow sort of bloke. So she had nothing to worry about and it would be very foolish of her to risk spoiling the early days of their marriage with pointless regret and envy that *she* did not have his love. She would just have to make herself lovable, which meant finding out where the Maldives were and learning Italian and trying to put him first rather than Timothy.

Some time later, at the end of the long, winding, wooded drive that the limo had traversed, an enormous Gothic pile in mellow stone met Holly's stunned gaze. Against a backdrop of mature trees and smooth green lawns, the house looked magnificent.

'How old is it?' Holly's attention lingered on the innumerable diamond-paned windows and turrets and the hotpotch of different roof levels.

'The earliest part of the building has been dated to the twelfth century but the main building works took place four hundred years later, although, of course, it has been altered in many ways since then. Marchmont Priory was my mother's family home.' Rio assisted her out of the limo. 'She stays here in the warmer months of the year.'

Old words were carved into the weathered stone lintel above the heavy oak door. Elizabethan English, welcoming all to the Priory, Rio explained before sweeping his curious bride up into his arms and carrying her in traditional style over the threshold. There was no sign even of who had opened the door and she commented on that.

'The staff are engaged in tactful invisibility,' Rio informed her.

Laughing at that explanation, Holly let her admiring gaze roam over the worn flagstone floor and the inviting fire burning in the giant stone fireplace. There was a wonderful atmosphere of peace and comfort.

'It's just beautiful,' she told him.

Rio set her down and tugged her face up so that he could gaze down into her eyes. 'So you don't think it's a little shabby and outdated?'

'No, it's glorious…it feels like a proper home, you know, not all perfect and fancy like the town house.'

Rio sent her an appreciative smile that made her heart lurch inside her. 'I confess that I've always loved it just as it is. As a kid, I used to run wild here with my English cousins.'

'What were you like as a kid?' Holly was smiling, happiness enclosing her in a protective cocoon, all her earlier uncertainties set behind her and forgotten. She loved him. It might kind of embarrass her that she felt that strongly after so short a time but just then she felt that there was absolutely nothing that she would not do to make him happy.

'Spoilt rotten. Only-child syndrome. Got everything I ever wanted and more, *cara mia*…ah, forgot, terms of endearment are on the forbidden list,' Rio mocked.

'Not now we're married,' Holly hastened to assure him as his hand settled on her spine to draw her closer and her pulses began racing.

'Makes a difference, does it?'

Holly nodded.

He let caressing fingers toy with her ringlets, watched her arch towards him in instinctive response, seeking out the hard heat of his lean, strong body. His stunning dark golden eyes flamed and he bent his head and brought his mouth swooping down on hers with an irresistible passion that she felt right down to her curling toes.

When Holly emerged from that scorching first move she was being carried up the big carved staircase and she was weak with the strength of her own longing.

Shouldering open a door, Rio glanced down at her with a look of amusement. 'I'll close the curtains for you if you like...'

It was only early evening and she blushed and shook her bright head, taking the opportunity to scan the big wood-panelled room and the oak four-poster bed, resplendent in dark red brocade drapes that glowed in the fading light. A beautiful arrangement of white lilies adorned a table near the burning fire. A fire in a bedroom. She could hardly believe the luxury of it.

Rio lowered her to the floor and began removing her jewellery piece by piece. When he realised that her earrings were tied on, he surveyed her in wonderment.

'I need to get my ears pierced...it's just I'm a bit squeamish about that sort of thing,' Holly admitted ruefully.

She followed him to the doorway of the most incredible Victorian bathroom that also rejoiced in its own fire and watched him locate a pair of scissors. He was so beautiful, she thought with an inner ache of possessiveness that seemed to squeeze at her very heart. Daylight picked up the blue-black tint of his luxuriant hair, already ruffled by her disrespectful fingertips. She studied that bold, vibrant profile with consuming fascination that he was *her* husband. That against all the odds someone like her should have ended up with someone like him. He cut the thread with which she had attached the earrings and smoothed a finger over the tiny red score marks left behind.

'Why did you hurt yourself like that?'

'I didn't want to lose them.' That he had asked her to wear them went unspoken.

He removed his tie, undid his collar and tossed his jacket down onto a chair. Suddenly she felt shy, shy as she had been before the revelation of that first experience with him. But now there was a wicked burn beneath the shyness, a tingling expectation she could not repress. She just looked at him and she wanted him. It was that simple and it had been that way from the first moment for her.

'I'm glad you couldn't get changed, *bella mia*,' Rio confided lazily, scorching golden eyes flaring over her slender figure. 'I spent half the day fantasising about undoing those very provocative laces.'

'Did you?' Beneath the tight bodice, her breasts were stirring and lifting, the tender peaks straining to taut points. Momentarily she was embarrassed by her own susceptibility to a certain look, a certain tone in that dark, deep drawl. He just generated the most impossible level of excitement inside her and he did it without even trying.

'I love the way you watch me. Like there is no other guy in the world for you.'

Well, there wasn't for her, but it was no longer a sentiment she wanted to brandish, not for the benefit of a male who had informed her that he thought he could get *fond* of her. If he had to think about it too much, the likelihood was that he would never get beyond lust and liking. And she wanted a lot more, knew it in that instant, saw it as clear as day. She wanted him to love her, *really* love her, the way he must have loved his ex-girlfriend.

'You're all warmth and promise and desire...' Rio drew her back against him, brushed her bronze-coloured hair out of his path and let his mouth press against a taut, slim shoulder. 'And it fires me up every time I look at you.'

'Oh...' A slight sound was wrenched from Holly as she trembled in reaction to the heat of his knowing mouth against her cooler skin. He knew exactly where to touch her. Her head tipped back against his muscular chest, throat extending as she struggled to breathe again, eyes sliding languorously shut. She felt as if the very blood in her veins was turning liquid with longing.

'You match this room. I ought to be wearing a Tudor doublet and a plumed hat,' Rio teased thickly, his proud dark head bent over hers as she opened her eyes and saw them etched together in the carved mirror adorning the table set in front of the tall windows. She watched long brown fingers pluck loose the laces with studied slowness and her heart raced. She pushed helplessly back against him, already aroused beyond belief just by the contact of his big, powerful body against hers.

'The Tudor bridegroom was probably a pig,' Holly mumbled, recalling that much from her history lessons on the subservient role of women through the ages.

'Not necessarily. There are love letters and diaries stored in the library downstairs that tell a very different story.' Rio loosened the laces level by level until her anticipation was at such screaming pitch that she was ashamed of herself.

He released his breath in a soft, sexy hiss as he discovered that she was not wearing a bra. Embarrassed, she mumbled, 'My bra showed through the silk at the back and I took it off again—'

'Don't apologise for what I like, *cara*.' He eased down the dress from her shoulders and shimmied the soft fabric down her arms so that it fell to her hips, baring her full breasts to his view and attention. Her breath caught audibly in her throat as he let his expert fingers roam over her achingly sensitive nipples, catching the swollen buds between thumb and forefinger.

He might as well have set a torch to kindling inside her, for the strength in her lower limbs just dissolved, legs shaking under her as she fell back against him, the whole of her consumed by the power of her own almost agonised response. With a husky laugh he gathered her up with easy strength and laid her down on the big bed.

Rio gazed down at her, lean, strong face intent. 'Your response to me is the biggest erotic buzz I have ever had.'

Odd how that assurance seemed to both reassure and undermine, she reflected as the wave of weakness lessened while he plucked off her shoes and began to tug her gown from beneath her hips. On the one hand, it did not say much for his intimate experiences with other women, which delighted her, but on the other hand, it suggested all over again that it was her longing for him which was her strongest attraction, and that was humiliating.

'*Dio mio…*' Rio backed off a step, the better to appreciate the sheer stockings, diminutive briefs and the blue garter his bride wore. His shimmering scrutiny lit on her hot self-conscious face and he flashed her a wolfish smile. 'Full marks for surprising me.'

'What do I have to do to get a ten?' she heard herself whisper.

'Just lie there. I'm in a very uncritical mood,' Rio murmured with considerable amusement. 'And during the next couple of weeks I intend to teach you everything I want you to know, *bella mia*.'

She watched him peel off his shirt with scant ceremony and dispense with his well-cut trousers. Watching him thrilled her, she decided, so she could hardly blame him for enjoying her visual attention. He was all bronzed, hair-roughened skin and taut, strong muscles with not an ounce of superfluous flesh on his athletic frame. She couldn't tear her gaze from him or unlock herself from the mesmeric hold of those dark golden eyes. It had barely been four days since he had first made love to her but her body was behaving as if it had been denied for months.

He came down over her, teasing fingers flirting with the garter. 'An old-fashioned girl?'

'Yeah…'

'So what was old?'

'That jewellery you loaned me.'

'It's not on loan and that set is only a small part of it,' Rio informed her, running an unsettling hand in an exploring motion down over a slim stockinged thigh as he stared down at her. 'It's all yours. I'm the head of my family and you are my wife.'

And then he kissed her and it was different from the last time in a way she could not identify. Then within seconds she lost the ability to discriminate and to think. A kind of slow, drugging heat began to warm her in secret places and she speared her fingers into his thick, silky hair, raising herself to him, unable to restrain her own hungry impatience.

Rio settled her hands back to the bed and lifted his head, heavily lidded eyes narrowed to a glint of hot, determined gold. 'We've got all night...I want this to last—'

'I don't want to beg...' she mumbled shakily before she could think better of that admission, for every time she remembered how she had behaved the last time not even a recollection of the ecstasy could wipe out the sense that she had demeaned herself and been something less than she should have been.

Slight colour burnished the sudden taut angle of his fabulous cheekbones. 'It won't *be* like that again.'

He framed her face with his hands and claimed her lips again, and it was so sweet but so intense that she could feel the burst of heat low in her stomach, the quivering readiness of her own wretched body, and it crossed her mind then that he did not need to *make* her beg. He turned her on so much she might well end up begging all on her own. He eased himself down over her and found her swollen nipples with his mouth, suckling her tender flesh, sending arrows of arousal right to the very heart of her so that her hips shifted and squirmed against the mattress. He drifted on down, skimming her panties away in a motion so smooth that she only noticed the cool of the air hitting her where she was warm and damp.

'Relax…' Rio urged thickly as she tensed instinctively.

She could not comprehend such an instruction when he was doing things to her that made relaxation a total impossibility. She shut her eyes, panting for breath and restraint, striving to be what he wanted without even knowing quite what that was but dimly suspecting that greater control was what it was all about. But keeping still, preventing her hands from rising to his broad shoulders and clinging, was the most dreadful challenge when she was trembling and hot and far too eager for his every move.

He let his lips travel down over her flexing tummy and her spine arched of its own volition, the burning tingle in her pelvis already starting to torment her. 'Stop it…' he told her raggedly.

And then he roved in a direction that was entirely unexpected and her startled eyes flew wide. 'What are you *doing*?' she gasped in dismay.

'What do you think?' Rio angled a dark, wicked smile up at her and eased her thighs apart, his intent unhidden.

Her face burned. She wrestled with fierce embarrassment, curiosity and secret craving, and while she was engaged in that massive inner struggle he splayed his hands beneath her slim hips and just did what he wanted to do. And the chorus of urgent complaint she'd believed to be on her lips remained unspoken, because the instant that he made contact with the most sensitive spot in her whole shivering body was the same moment that any idea of her staying in control was vanquished.

Never had she ever imagined that level of sensation, so it was like one glorious shock piled onto another, so that she lurched mindless and wordless from one splintering wave of excitement into the next, and all the time the tormenting hunger was notching up higher inside her. She moaned, she sobbed and she jerked in a wild response beyond any denial, and when she was within what felt like touching distance of the satisfaction she craved with every sense he settled himself between her thighs and surged into her with measured force and cool.

And suddenly she was snatched up into the eye of the storm. The feel of his hot, hard fullness stretching the slick, wet centre of her inner heat just exploded through her in a cascade of multicoloured, blinding sensation and she hit a peak of ecstasy that burned through her in an explosive flood of pleasure.

'Good?' Rio tugged her head up and kissed her breathless in the aftermath, male satisfaction and fire in his smouldering gaze as he looked down at her and started to move again, slowly, almost teasingly, allowing her shaken still trembling body a little time for recovery.

'Unbelievable...' Holly muttered shakily.

'Oh, you can believe, *bella mia*,' Rio asserted in ragged promise, sending a reawakening surge of excitement through her with a subtle encircling motion of his lean hips. 'We're going to have an incredible honeymoon.'

Getting out of bed the next morning was something of a challenge for Holly and she was pretty much shell-shocked by the amount of raw energy Rio had and his ability to spring out of bed as though he had had a full eight hours' sleep.

Yet the urgency with which she longed to hold Timothy in her arms again would have sent her to the airport at dawn, had that been an option. As Rio had promised, her cases had been brought down to the Priory. She dressed at speed but had to sit through a long breakfast while Rio behaved as though they had all the time in the world.

Her baby was not *his* baby, Holly reminded herself. They were only having one night away from Timothy, which was very, very reasonable of him. How many blokes wanted to drag a nanny and a baby off on their honeymoon? But he had not even mentioned the option of leaving Timothy behind.

At the airport, the minute Timothy laid anxious eyes on his mother he went frantic, waving his arms and legs in excitement and relief. Sarah confided that Holly's son had had a rather unsettled night. Holly's eyes stung with tears and she got Timothy out of his seat restraint so fast there might have been a fire alarm howling. Clasping his warm, cuddly little body to her, she hugged him tight, only becoming conscious of her husband's scrutiny some minutes later.

Rio looked grim. 'Don't you ever let me *do* that to you again,' he breathed in a driven undertone of reproof.

Holly turned pale. 'Do…what?'

'Timothy spent the night fretting for you and you couldn't get here fast enough this morning because you missed him so much,' he spelt out flatly. 'I didn't know I was doing that to you. Why didn't you say something?'

Too many frank words hovered on her lips. Timothy was not his son and there had to be limits to even his tolerance at this stage of their marriage, she thought fearfully. The very last thing she wanted was to turn him off with the downside of parenting. He was used to complete freedom of choice and he was not used to the restrictions of being with a woman with a child either.

'It was only one night. I just didn't want to spoil things—'

'You just *did*,' Rio drawled ruefully. 'Sarah told me he

was inconsolable and she called the doctor out to check him just in case there was something else wrong. Timothy isn't secure enough to do without you for very long.'

Holly was ashamed of that truth.

'But I couldn't have done without you last night either, *bella mia*.' Rio slanted her a sudden flashing smile of forgiveness that turned her heart over inside her tight chest. 'Maybe we're going to have to work out some way of dividing you in two.'

CHAPTER SEVEN

Two days later, lying on the sun-deck that overhung the lagoon, Holly trailed idle fingertips in the crystal-clear water below. She could see every rise and dip of the soft sand below, each tiny multicoloured fish darting beneath the sparkling sunlit surface.

She thought the Maldives were a paradise on earth. The lagoon was ringed by lush green palms and vegetation. The sky was a deep, dense cloudless blue and the white sand on the beach merged with a sea the colour of turquoise. Their magnificent villa was set on its own tiny island where privacy was assured, but Rio had informed her that more populated places lay only a short boat trip away on one of the thousand-plus coral islands that made up the Maldives nation.

'What's so fascinating?' Rio crouched down beside her to ask.

'The lagoon is like a giant rock pool,' Holly confided. 'It takes me back to when I was a kid and my aunt used to take me to the seaside.'

'Not your parents?'

Holly levered back on to her knees and collided with stunning eyes that reflected the golden sunlight. Three days into their honeymoon, her heartbeat was still hitting earthquake mode every time he got close—and that seemed to be *most* of the time.

'Dad could never get away from the farm,' she explained.

'You must miss your parents a great deal.' Rio made that observation with quiet understanding.

Holly nodded agreement. 'But hopefully not for much longer.'

His ebony brows drew together. 'I don't follow.'

'Once we've been married a couple of months, I'm going to tell Mum and Dad about us and then we can go and visit,' Holly outlined with a slight flush. 'That way there won't be so many awkward questions about how long we've known each other and so on.'

Rio dealt her an incredulous scrutiny. 'Are you telling me that your parents are still *alive*?'

It was her turn to look confused. 'What else would they be?'

'I thought they were dead. When we first met you told me that you had *nobody*,' Rio reminded her.

'I didn't mean they were dead!'

'But you didn't even mention the possibility of inviting your parents to our wedding! Of course I assumed they were gone. What else was I to think?'

Biting her lip with discomfiture, Holly averted her eyes from the level probe of his and released a rueful sigh. 'Mum and Dad were very upset when I got pregnant. They sent me to live with my aunt in Manchester. I was supposed to give Timothy up for adoption and then go back home again. But once he was born I couldn't do it, so that was that... I was on my own.'

'When did you last speak to your parents?'

'A week after Timothy was born,' Holly admitted half under her breath. 'But I've written to them a few times to let them know that I was all right—'

'But you *weren't* all right!' Rio cut in drily.

Holly ignored that reminder. 'I didn't give them an address, though, because I didn't want them feeling they had to get involved. It wouldn't have been fair. I made my choice,' she completed gruffly.

Rio closed his hand over the taut fingers clenching on her slim thigh. 'You made the right choice.'

'Well, until now it didn't seem like it…it seemed like I was the most useless mother ever,' Holly admitted, her throat thickening with sudden tears.

Curving a strong arm round her downbent shoulders, Rio raised her up. 'You had a lot of bad luck.'

Holly looked up into the beautiful tawny-gold eyes set in that lean, dark, devastating face. Suddenly, he was claiming her lips with devouring hunger, crushing her softer curves into his hard, muscular frame, giving her all the reassurance she needed. Her heart pounded like crazy beneath that surprise onslaught and she clung to his broad shoulders to stay upright.

Rio lifted his dark head again with a ragged laugh. 'I should be cooling the wild passion. You might be pregnant, *bella mia*.'

'I don't think so.' She had had a headache earlier and only a minute ago she had almost succumbed to tears, both of which were familiar signs to her of PMT.

'Why?'

'I just know—'

'But you didn't *know* when it came to Timothy, did you?'

Holly reddened. 'I don't think I wanted to know—'

Rio stared down at her, shimmering eyes intense above his hard cheekbones. 'I hope that isn't the case with *my* baby.'

'How could you think that?' Holly was taken aback by that undercurrent of dark suspicion in his response. 'But it would be better all round if I wasn't pregnant this soon…people will talk if I have a baby short of the nine-month mark.'

Rio gave a fluid shrug that signified his supreme indifference to such gossip.

'Well, maybe it doesn't matter to you,' Holly conceded tautly. 'But I wasn't exactly happy when I was carrying Timothy, and if I have another baby I'd like it to be different. I'd like to feel proud that I'm pregnant and not feel that people are judging me or sneering at me behind my back.'

In receipt of that frank speech, Rio groaned out loud and eased her close again. '*Dio mio*…of course you want it to be different, but believe me, whatever happens, it will be.'

Did Rio actually *want* her to have conceived his child? Holly wondered anxiously. As she was almost certain that she had not, she could not help worrying that perhaps his certainty that she would so easily fall pregnant again had thrust him into a marriage that he might just as quickly regret. That very evening, her period arrived. She was putting Timothy to bed when she chose to tell Rio that there was not going to be a baby.

Rio tensed, strong bone-structure tightening, and then he gave her the heartbreaking smile that always made her feel as if she was the only woman in the world for him. 'It's too soon for you anyway, *tesoro mio*. We should wait until Timothy is a little older.'

'Yes…' But, perverse as human nature was, Holly then found herself wishing that she *had* conceived, for she sensed that with Rio a baby would be a major and welcome event. Timothy was undeniably enthralled by the tall, dark male who had become part of his life, and Rio was so good to him.

However, the world Holly was living in still did not feel quite real to her. Although she worked hard at hiding those stabs of insecurity from Rio, she could not help being scared that suddenly it would all be snatched away again. Had she been pregnant with his child, perhaps she would have felt safer, she acknowledged uneasily, ashamed of that lowering reality.

Holly watched while Rio tasted.

'This is sensational,' he breathed appreciatively. 'What is it called?'

'Somerset apple cake.'

'You're an incredible cook.'

'I started learning when I was four. Baking skills are a matter of pride in a farming community,' Holly told him with a rueful grin, light playing on her animated face as she sat cross-legged on the bed, clad in a colourful silk sarong. 'But to tell you the truth, Mum was really grooming me for the neighbour's son. She thought Robert was wonderful but I just didn't fancy him—'

'Did he *fancy* you?' His beautiful mouth slanted with vibrant amusement at the term.

'Well, just then I think he fancied anything female,' Holly confided, heart lurching predictably in receipt of that glorious smile of his. 'He was dating one of my mates when I left home and his parents didn't approve because she was a real townie.'

The phone by the bed buzzed and Rio answered it. She listened to him talk in Italian and just watched him while she melted into a hopeless puddle of love and longing. They had been married for exactly twenty-one days and already she could not imagine existing without him, could not even accept that she could have lived for twenty years on the same planet without being aware that the love of her life was breathing the same air. For that was what he was:

Rio, this male who had become so impossibly precious and important to her every waking hour.

He was just...*perfect*. Entertaining, clever, caring. He spoilt her like mad. He was always buying her loads of stuff she didn't need, introducing her to fantastic new experiences and somehow making every single day seem special. She had learned to water-ski, snorkel and sail. He was also fantastic with kids. Timothy was enslaved, and adoring Rio seemed to be good for Timothy because her son was much more confident. And a restaurant menu would never terrify her again because they ate out most evenings and she was familiar with most of the terms now and quite happy to ask if she came across anything she didn't understand. She had also finally had her ears pierced, but her nerve had almost failed her at the last minute and only a fear of embarrassing Rio had got her through it.

Nobody was perfect, her more sane self cautioned, so she worked hard at coming up with a flaw or two. Rio didn't need much sleep. He was incredibly active, but good diet and lots of exercise had increased her own energy. He was naturally dominant, but when he had been teaching her to water-ski that had been welcome because the first time she sank below the waves she would have given up if he hadn't bullied her into repeated efforts. She had ended up having a fabulous time, she reflected forgivingly.

Indeed, every morning she woke up in Rio's arms she felt as if she had won the jackpot. All her insecurity had evaporated. No man had ever treated her so well and no man had ever wanted her to the degree that Rio appeared to want her. Face warming, she scanned his bold, bronzed profile and the long, sexy, indolent slump of his lean, hard, muscular frame. There was something very reassuring about a bloke who could not keep his hands off her for longer than a couple of hours, she thought with a secretive smile. Obviously, he was pretty highly sexed, but he made her feel as though she was irresistible. The strong attraction between them was anything but one-sided. Was it any wonder that she was blissfully happy and more madly in love than ever?

So what if he didn't love her? There was time enough for that to come. He did do romantic stuff. He gave her surprise presents and held her hand and seemed truly fascinated by every mundane aspect of her previous existence. And in three long weeks they had not had a single argument. She didn't count screaming at him when he told her to get back on the water-skis and not act like a baby. Or that time he had dragged her out of bed before dawn to go fishing and cheerfully told her that she ought to stand up for herself more often. And when she had done so five minutes later he hadn't liked it at all.

'You're coming with me,' he had delivered in full command mode.

And much later, when she had been even more bored out of her mind than she had expected to be on that stupid boat, she had asked him why it had been so important that she join him.

'I just like you around,' Rio had murmured in some surprise that she should need to ask.

Only then had it occurred to her that a bloke who had been twenty-four hours a day in her company but who could still demand the twenty-fifth hour, figuratively speaking, was paying her quite a compliment.

Rio slung the phone aside with an impatient sigh. 'Business is intruding even before we fly home tomorrow. My mother's at the Priory and expecting to meet you but I'm afraid that I have to head for New York more or less immediately.'

'Oh…' Her heart sank at the prospect of the parting

ahead, and then she scolded herself for being too posses-sive.

'I know it's far from ideal but I really don't think another raincheck would be acceptable. Do you think you could handle meeting her on your own?' Rio reached for her with the unquestioning self-assurance of a male aware that his attentions were always welcome, his question clearly rhe-torical.

Seated on the edge of the bed, he set Holly down on her feet between his long, hair-roughened thighs while he pro-ceeded to ease loose the knot on her sarong. At that mo-ment, with her heart racing, he could have asked her to walk into a fire and she would have gone in blind faith. She trembled, reacting to the tiny flame already igniting deep in her pelvis, the delicious wave of anticipation al-ready currenting through her. No matter how often he made love to her, it was always the same.

'I ache just looking at you...' Rio confided thickly as the sarong dropped to the floor and his appreciative ap-praisal settled on pouting breasts crowned by straining pink nipples.

'Me too...' She felt wanton, breathless, entirely in the grip of quivering excitement.

He touched her, toyed with her aching flesh and stripped off her bikini briefs to run a seeking hand down to the damp welcome already awaiting him. By the time he tipped her back on the bed she was a willing sacrifice. Straightening, he peeled off his T-shirt and shed his chinos, revealing the awesome thrust of his virile shaft. Liquid longing filled her and she pushed away an instinctive shame at her own pow-erful response to his bold masculinity. He laced long, in-dolent fingers into her hair, drawing her up, encouraging her to caress him with her mouth, an exercise that she had been stunned to discover raised her own level of arousal to an almost embarrassing degree.

'You're so incredibly sensual...' Rio breathed in a roughened growl of male satisfaction. 'I'll have to drag myself away from you tomorrow. You're turning me into a sex addict, *cara*.'

Certainly it wasn't very long before he tumbled her back on the bed with a groan of raw impatience and sank into her hard and fast and without ceremony, sending her excitement racing to such a peak that a strangled cry of joy was wrenched from her. And then there was nothing for her but the relentless rhythm of his lean, hard body over and inside hers and the intense pleasure that sent her rocketing to an ecstatic height with his name on her lips.

'Sex with you *is*...' Rio mused reflectively in the aftermath, making her tense a little, for she would have much preferred him to use a less earthy term and she was unsettled by the rather disconcerted light in his dark-as-midnight eyes, '...absolutely sensational, *bella mia*.'

'Good,' Holly mumbled, both arms wrapped round him tight as she revelled in the lean finger stroking her cheekbone and the kiss he dropped on her brow. She was far too sensitive, she told herself. So Rio didn't talk about his emotions, but could she consider that unusual? Even the day her own father had cried over her being pregnant the older man had uttered few words. Her male schoolmates had been more given to off-colour jokes and clumsy flirtation, and Jeff had never really talked about anything but himself.

'Go to sleep...' Rio urged lazily. 'We have a very early start in the morning.'

During the flight the next day, Rio was fully occupied with his laptop. Bored with watching the films on offer, Holly went to check on Timothy, but he was sound asleep and their nanny was catnapping too. With a smile at the picture they made, Holly returned to the main cabin and decided to entertain herself with the pile of glossy magazines which she had seen Sarah absorbed in earlier.

She leafed through the pages, pausing to admire the fabulous fashion, only to be bemused by the belated acknowledgement that she could now probably afford to buy anything she liked, courtesy of her incredibly generous husband. Shooting his darkly handsome profile at the other end of the cabin a tender lingering scrutiny, she settled down to read.

A full-page shot of a vaguely familiar beautiful blonde wearing the ultimate in country casuals caught her attention and she scanned the name below. Of course, she had known that face! It was Chrissie Kent, the model who had become a household name after doing an entertaining series of luxury car advertisements on television a couple of years earlier. Holly admired the handsome pair of springer spaniels seated at Chrissie's feet and thought that the model must be a genuinely nice person if she made time for pets in her jet-set existence. She then turned to the opposite page, only to be confronted by a far more familiar face.

Billionaire Italian tycoon, Saverio Lombardi, escorting his fiancée at the Cannes Film Festival.

A fevered pulse beginning to thump like mad at what felt like the foot of her convulsing throat, Holly read and re-read that single line and then fixedly studied the picture of Rio and Chrissie Kent together. Perspiration beaded Holly's short upper lip. She was in shock, so much shock that she just sat there for a long time. Rio had been engaged to Chrissie Kent?

Christabel...of course, Christabel. The woman was incredibly beautiful, pale blonde hair falling waterfall-straight either side of her stunning face. Her fantastic figure was sheathed in a daring cerise-pin satin gown slit to the thigh and so tight that only one in a million women could have got away with it. She even had legs that went on and on and on to the most abnormal but flattering length.

Tummy unsettled by the revelation that had burst like a bombshell upon her, Holly began to read the article and turned the page, only to see Christabel seated on a silk-upholstered sofa in the town house where she herself had once dared to sit. Without warning, Holly also remembered how she had posed and clowned for Rio while she paraded designer fashion and pretended to *be* a model. Instantly she wanted to jump out of his jet without a parachute. Instantly she felt humiliated beyond belief.

But what shook her most of all was that the magazine was not that old an issue. Only six weeks ago Rio had *still* been engaged and had *still* been committed to a summer wedding with another woman. Like a bloodhound on the scent, Holly began to leaf frantically through the remaining magazines in search of further information. But when she found the facts that she had believed she wanted in a weekly magazine of much more humble origin, she wished that she had missed seeing it.

The issue which announced the sudden 'shock' break-up of Rio and Christabel had come on sale only a week after Holly had first met Rio, and indeed also featured a small grainy photo of her own wedding and much speculation about her identity. There she was, posed on the church steps with huge scared eyes, hanging on to Rio with an extreme lack of cool. Wild curly hair was blowing round her in a messy tangle. She looked a total fright. She looked like the bride of Frankenstein…

CHAPTER EIGHT

'YOU'VE been very quiet,' Rio told Holly in the limo that collected them from the airport to ferry them home to the town house. 'Are you feeling all right?'

'I'm fine.' Even to Holly's own ears, her voice sounded strained, but a more expansive response was impossible with Sarah and Timothy seated beside them.

In any case, Holly still had no idea what she planned to say to Rio when she did finally get him alone. She was still mentally reeling, her mind awash with a crazy cascade of ever more confused thoughts. The anger surging higher and higher inside her was no help to her concentration. Behind the anger lurked pain and fear and a terrifying sense of betrayal. Without the smallest warning, her confidence in what she had believed to be a happy marriage had been smashed to pieces. It seemed that their relationship was built on the proverbial shifting sands rather than on firm foundations.

Faced with such unpalatable and humiliating facts, what else *was* she to think? Rio had bedded her within days of breaking up with one of the most beautiful women in the world. Christabel Kent was an icon, every male fantasy combined, but, worst of all, she was ten times closer to being Rio's equal in looks, sophistication and importance than Holly could ever hope to be. Indeed, Christabel was exactly the kind of female that men like Rio Lombardi *did* marry: a trophy wife, famous in her own right.

Common sense told Holly that Rio had married her on the rebound, and that was *very* bad news, she thought wretchedly. Rio could not have been thinking straight when he swept her off to bed on a passionate impulse. Nor could he have seriously considered what he was doing when he then insisted that he wanted her to marry him.

Only now was Holly recalling Ezio Farretti's prophetic warnings. 'He's just not himself right now and you don't want to get your feelings hurt.' Older and wiser, and knowing the situation as Holly had not, Ezio had recognised the high risk factors at play. Holly's vulnerability, Rio's volatile temperament and simple proximity had been a dangerous combination.

After all, Rio must have been with Christabel for quite some time and breaking up with her must have been traumatic, Holly reasoned painfully. Hence Rio's short temper, his need for a distraction, his sudden startling susceptibility to a youthful redhead incapable of concealing her starry-eyed admiration. In the normal way of things, Holly reckoned that Rio would barely have noticed that she was alive.

'I'll be heading back to the airport in a couple of hours,' Rio reminded her as they entered the town house. 'I'm going for a shower.'

Before she could follow him she was held back by their nanny, who needed to discuss arrangements for the weekend off she was about to take. Agreeing that Sarah could depart that afternoon, Holly then hurried off in Rio's wake.

He was in their bedroom, already half-undressed, his shirt hanging loose, a bronzed, energising slice of muscular, hair-roughened chest on view, his potent and entirely natural sex appeal pronounced. Holly came to a halt just inside the door, her heartbeat accelerating, her mouth running dry, no matter how hard she tried not to react to him. He was so gorgeous, from the crown of his proud, dark head to the soles of his bare brown feet, and she loved him as she had never known she could love anybody. But what she had learnt from those wretched magazines had ripped her apart, not least because she knew that she *should* have received that same information from him. And the very fact that Rio had *not* told her only made her feel that her every worst fear was justified.

Rio surveyed her with level dark golden eyes. 'There is no point throwing a three-act tragedy, *cara*. It won't change anything.'

Totally disconcerted by that statement, Holly stared at him. 'What are you talking about?'

Unimpressed, Rio slanted a dark brow. 'You've been in a hellish sulk ever since it dawned on you that I'm leaving you to your own devices for the next week,' he informed her drily. 'But you'll have to get used to the idea of getting by without me when I'm away on business.'

'Will I?' Something close to a hysterical giggle feathered in Holly's tight throat as she realised how he had interpreted her silence and how he had put his own rather demeaning spin on what lay behind her behaviour.

'It'll be a challenge for you at first because you haven't made friends yet. But by this time next year you won't be dependent on me for company,' Rio asserted with confidence, strolling closer and reaching for her hands. 'You'll learn to lead your own life while I'm abroad. My mother will support you. She knows a lot of people and you can get involved in the charities we support through the foundation or, indeed, in whatever else interests you.'

Her hands jerked in the warm hold of his. Her husband knew how besotted she was with him and he thought that her poor little heart was just breaking at the prospect of surviving an entire seven days without him. And the way he was talking about a future in which they led separate lives chilled her to the marrow.

As Holly yanked her fingers free of his hectic colour fired over her cheekbones. 'Is that what Christabel would have done?'

Rio's sculpted mouth tightened, eyes hardening at what he clearly translated as an ungenerous and potentially catty response. 'What *she* might have done hardly concerns us.'

'Are you going to tell me why I had to read a flippin' magazine just to find out that your ex-girlfriend is the world-famous model Chrissie Kent?' Holly demanded half an octave higher.

Rio went very still, golden eyes gleaming from below luxuriant black lashes. 'I don't quite understand the relevance of Christabel's public profile.'

'Like heck you don't!' Holly snapped, her temper provoked by that cool, snubbing response. 'You knew I had no idea. Couldn't you at least have told me that much about her?'

Rio expelled his breath in an impatient hiss. 'I knew you'd be intimidated. I knew you would beat yourself up making stupid comparisons. So, *no*, I wasn't in a hurry to ram that fact down your throat.'

At that disconcertingly honest response, Holly lost every scrap of her feverish colour. She felt as if she was standing there naked and as see-through as clear glass. She felt humiliated that he should understand her that well and face her with her own insecurity. 'Yes, it would be a very stupid comparison to even try to attempt...wouldn't it?'

'*Santo cielo*...that's *not* what I meant!' Now anger brightened Rio's gaze, tautened his lean, strong face. 'I just felt that you'd be better equipped to deal with all that after we'd been married for a while.'

Holly's hands coiled into hurting fists. 'Oh, you know me so well, do you? You think you can predict how I'm likely to react to everything?'

'It seems that on that particular score I was accurate.'

Holly refused to be squashed. 'But then your ex-girlfriend's public profile, as you called it, was only the tip of the iceberg, wasn't it? Like when were you planning to tell me just how little time passed between you breaking up with *her* and getting involved with *me*?'

Perceptibly, Rio's big, powerful frame tensed.

'I want a date,' Holly told him feverishly. 'I want to know how much of a time lag there was.'

'Believe me, *bella mia*…you don't,' Rio countered flatly.

'It was barely even a couple of weeks…I'm right, aren't I?' Holly persisted, determined to get the truth out of him. 'Going by the date on that magazine article, it couldn't have been much longer than a couple of weeks since you'd broken up. Why else was Ezio warning me that you weren't yourself when I first met you?'

His darkly handsome features froze. 'Thank you, Ezio. Tell me, do you make a habit of discussing me with my employees?'

'Oh, I'll be sure to make a habit of it from here on in. It seems to me I've got more chance of getting an honest answer from *other* people than from you!' Holly condemned, refusing to be embarrassed by his freezing disapproval and defending herself. 'I still remember what you said when you asked me to marry you. You said you had been engaged "until relatively recently". Which hardly suggests a gap of less than a month—'

'Leave it,' Rio cut in with ruthless bite. 'I'm going for that shower before this ridiculous argument escalates any more—'

In incredulous, seething frustration, Holly watched him resume stripping off his clothes. Clad only in his Calvin Kleins, he headed for the bathroom.

'I could ask Ezio,' Holly threatened between gritted

teeth, although she knew that now that they were married she would never ever go behind Rio's back like that, or indeed place the older man in such an awkward position.

'I parted from Christabel an hour before you walked out in front of my limo.'

Holly blinked. Those words hit her as though they were in a foreign language she could not fathom, for in a self-protective act her brain seemed to throw up barriers to her understanding. And then, without warning, she grasped what he had said and there was no hiding from it, no avoiding the reality that what he had just admitted was a hundred times more devastating than she had expected.

Rio swung round, scanned her pale, shattered face and swore in roughened Italian, but as he moved back towards her she backed away.

Holly parted dry lips. 'An...*hour*?'

Strong jawline clenching, he studied her with grim golden eyes. 'I don't see that the precise amount of time is material in this particular case...'

An uneven laugh was dragged from Holly as she collapsed down on the side of the bed, fearful her knees were about to give way under her. An hour. Only an hour had passed between him leaving Christabel and first meeting *her*, and forty-eight hours later he had hauled her off to bed. And he expected her to accept that there was nothing relevant in that super-shrunken timeline?

'You couldn't possibly have known what you were doing,' she said sickly.

No way did she need huge experience of men to make that statement. An hour. It was laughable, terrifying, outrageous. And only two days later Rio had proven that reality to her beyond all possible doubt by doing something that she knew in her heart had been quite out of character for him: taking her to bed.

He wasn't the sort of bloke who went in for one-night stands. He wasn't the sort of bloke who got a kick out of going to bed with some woman he hardly knew just for the sheer hell of it. There were men like that but Rio wasn't one of them. Rio had a real good-taste threshold. Rio had a conscience. Rio was not an oversexed teenager with out-of-control hormones.

But Rio had one quirk which had betrayed both her and him: it would take torture to make him talk about his own feelings. He would probably sooner slow-roast over a hot fire than admit that he had been upset and off-balance after breaking off his engagement. In fact, that was an under-statement, she recognised, and hadn't she seen the evidence of how he was feeling for herself? His emotions had been seething, but more than anything she had sensed anger…anger and bitterness. Anger against himself, anger presumably against Christabel, bitterness that their relation-ship hadn't worked out?

'I *always* know what I'm doing.' Rio made that claim as though it was etched in stone on his soul, a credo through which he lived his entire life.

But Holly wasn't convinced. She had often thought that she knew what she was doing and then later looked back and marvelled at how persuasive other promptings could be in overruling all caution and common sense.

'What did you do? Decide to turn round and marry the very first woman you met?' Holly demanded shakily, striving for an ironic note with that question, for she was not serious in asking it.

'Believe it or not, that thought did cross my mind,' Rio ground out fiercely.

Holly just stopped breathing altogether and gazed back at him in horror.

'Only to be just as quickly set aside because I am *not* a lunatic!' Rio continued with raw force.

'But that's just what you did. You married the first woman you met. Dear heaven…I could've been anybody!' Holly gasped.

'Don't be ridiculous. Do you think I would marry just anybody?' Rio roared back at her, visibly outraged by that suggestion.

Holly lowered her head and studied her tightly linked hands. She was more or less just anybody on her own terms. She was young, female and reasonably presentable but that was that. She was trembling. 'Maybe you would if you were angry enough. Tell me, did Christabel dump *you*?'

'*Per amor di Dio*… I could snap my fingers and get her back right now if I wanted her!' Rio slammed back at her.

The silence sparked like hay threatening to whoosh into flame.

'I didn't say that…' Rio groaned out loud. 'OK…I said it but I shouldn't have.'

So now she knew who had done the dumping. But now she also knew something she would have been happier *not* to know: that Christabel wanted Rio back and that he was well aware of the fact. That news was like a cold wind chilling her sensitive skin.

'Just tell me why you broke up with her,' Holly prompted dry-mouthed, her tummy churning at the terrible tension in the room.

'We wanted different things,' Rio said flatly.

'What kind of different things?'

'I think that's my business and hers.'

Holly paled as if he had slapped her. Then she got up and began to walk towards the door but Rio was ahead of her. He leant back against the door and trained smouldering golden eyes on her, his angry frustration unconcealed. 'This is *crazy*—'

'Get out of my way,' Holly demanded.

Instead, Rio closed strong brown arms round her and jerked her up against him. 'No,' he said, soft and succinct. 'I won't let you make Christabel a bone of contention between us.'

'You're the one doing that…' Holly condemned chokily, tears of stress and agonised confusion clogging up her vocal cords.

Long fingers swept up to frame her cheekbones. Her bright blue eyes evaded his. She was rigid, refusing to give an inch, but then he took her by surprise. He lowered his dark head and drove her lips hungrily apart with his own, his tongue delving deep into the moist interior. Angry, unhappy, confused, she fought her own response for the first time.

She shivered against him, insanely conscious of every hot, taut angle of his lean, muscular body, and she thrust her hand against his shoulder to push him away. But her enervated state of mind made her all too vulnerable and the sudden excitement burning like a betraying flame inside her was her undoing. Just as quickly, she was kissing him back with the same breathless fervour.

He lifted her up, brought her down on the bed, came down over her. He lifted her skirt and brought up her knees to deprive her of her briefs and tights. And all the time he was taking her mouth time after time with the same drugging, demanding heat and her heart was racing like an express train, every fibre of her being madly aware of him and on fire.

By the time he slid between her parted thighs and entered her she was more out of control than she had ever been, overwhelmed by a wild, desperate craving which left room for nothing else. The excitement of release threw her to the heights and then dropped her down again lower than ever before.

'Now you can join me for a shower,' Rio murmured huskily, gazing down at her with a scorching satisfaction as he leant down to kiss her.

Sick at her own weakness, but outraged by his manipulation, Holly took him by surprise by twisting her head away and jack-knifing out from beneath him to roll off the bed. Clawing down her skirt, her face feverishly flushed and her eyes glittering like blue sapphires, Holly shot him a look of furious mortification.

'Do you think that's likely to solve anything?' she snapped in a voice that shook with the force of her disturbed emotions.

A wolfish and irreverent smile slashed Rio's darkly handsome features. 'There's nothing *to* solve, *bella mia*.'

The anger went out of her then, leaving her feeling hollow and miserable. The craven part of her wished she had not forced him to tell her even part of the truth. One hour, she kept on thinking, one hour between leaving Christabel and meeting her. *Of course* he had been on the rebound. How could their marriage have a hope of surviving? He would eventually wake up and feel trapped with her and Timothy, marvel at his own impulsiveness, his own failure to take a long-term view. Why would he stay with her when he didn't love her? Why would he settle for her when he could have Christabel Kent or her equivalent as a wife? Off with the old, on with the new...but life wasn't that simple. Sooner or later, Rio would regret marrying her.

As the door thudded shut on the bathroom Holly sagged. He wouldn't discuss Christabel. Why not? Loyalty? Or lingering feelings? And did he even care how she felt, knowing that Christabel would still take him back? A relationship that had lasted almost two years when she herself had only been with him for a month wouldn't be easily forgotten. Was she making herself unhappy over nothing? What, after all, had changed? Just twelve hours ago, she had been so happy.

Timothy was having a nap when she went into the nursery. She was chatting to Sarah when Ezio phoned to tell her that she had a visitor waiting downstairs. A Mr Danby. Holly paled. Jeff? Jeff had come to see her? How on earth had he known where she was and what could he possibly want?

Jeff was in the drawing room. Slim and dark, he was more smartly dressed than she had ever seen him, but he had grown a goatee beard and a tiny clipped moustache that struck her as affected. And somehow he seemed much smaller than she recalled him being.

'Well, don't you look good?' Jeff remarked, studying the fashionable skirt and cashmere twin-set that fitted her slim figure like a glove. 'But then, why not? I suppose you have a whole string of credit cards now—'

'How did you find out where I was living?' Holly interrupted, hating the familiar way he had eyed her up and carefully keeping her distance.

'After seeing your wedding photos splashed all over the newspapers, I didn't need to hire a detective. You've fairly landed on your feet here, haven't you?' He glanced round the beautifully furnished drawing room and his full mouth twisted in acknowledgement of the staggering change in her circumstances. 'Well, more power to you. It's great that you've done so well for yourself—'

'What are you doing here?' Holly pressed unevenly, for every time she looked at him she remembered the shock of that fist coming into her face, the speed with which he had lost his head and attacked her.

'Obviously, I want to see my son,' Jeff informed her.

What colour remained in Holly's face drained away. 'Why would you suddenly want to do that?'

'A boy ought to know his father.' Jeff gave her a smug and pious smile, relishing her bewilderment and dismay.

Nausea stirred inside Holly. 'You said you'd make me sorry I was ever born if I told anyone that Timothy was your child. And when we needed you, where were you? You didn't want to know—'

'Things were awkward that day—'

'Awkward? Timothy and I ended up on the streets with nowhere to go! You didn't give two hoots about either of us. If you want to see the child you have the nerve to call your son, when are you planning to start paying towards his keep?' Holly demanded, her strained voice rising in volume. 'Do you think that you can just walk in here and—?'

An arm curved round her taut spine from behind, startling her, for she had not heard the door open, and then Rio murmured, 'It's OK, *cara.* I'll deal with this.'

'I'm afraid Holly and I didn't part best friends.' Jeff grimaced, moving forward with an insincere smile and extending his hand to Rio. 'I'm Jeff, Timothy's father.'

'Saverio Lombardi…'

Holly was appalled when Rio shook hands with her ex-boyfriend. It felt like a betrayal. She was equally appalled at the threat of being forced to trust a man with Jeff's temper around Timothy. She could not even bear to have Jeff inside their home. He brought back nothing but bad memories and regrets.

'I've seen a solicitor. Just so that I could check out my

position,' Jeff hastened to explain. 'I'm going to ask for access visits and apply for joint custody of my son.'

Holly's heart sank right down to her toes.

'Of course. That's your right,' Rio responded equably.

'But Rio—' Holly began, not comprehending his failure even to proffer an argument or indeed understanding why Jeff, given that easy agreement, should look more startled than pleased.

'At the same time, however, any access visits would have to be supervised,' Rio continued.

Jeff frowned at Rio. 'Supervised? Why?'

'You assaulted Holly.'

'That was an accident!' Jeff protested vehemently, but even Holly could see that that reminder coming from Rio had severely disconcerted the younger man.

'My lawyers already have a statement from the woman whom you were living with at the time,' Rio told him with complete cool. 'She's quite prepared to testify that she saw you not only attack but also threaten Holly with further violence should she ever name you as her child's father.'

It was now Holly's turn to stare at her husband with shaken eyes, for only then did she recall the seemingly idle questions he had asked her in the Maldives about where she had found Jeff living when she had finally traced him to his girlfriend's apartment.

'You've got a statement from Liza?' Jeff was flushed with incredulous rage.

'Naturally you can still apply for access to Timothy and whatever else you like,' Rio pointed out. 'But it is only fair to tell you that I hope to adopt Timothy and that I will fight to do so, whether you have access or not.'

Jeff gave him a furious look of frustration. 'But I'm quite happy for you to adopt the kid! I'm here ready to discuss a friendly arrangement with you—'

'Any arrangements or agreements required will be reached through the usual legal channels,' Rio asserted levelly.

'I've had enough of this!' Jeff stormed off to the door.

'You're still Timothy's father,' Rio said quietly. 'If you want to get to know your son I won't stand in your way.'

'Forget it!' Jeff yanked open the door, his eagerness to leave unconcealed. 'You're welcome to the yappy little brat!'

As her ex-boyfriend departed Holly was so ashamed of the way he had exposed his true nature that she could not meet Rio's gaze. 'Why did you keep on telling him he could see Timothy?'

'I won't let Danby use your son to threaten you or as a bargaining chip in some sleazy attempt to profit from the connection. But I needed to be sure that Jeff genuinely doesn't have any interest in Timothy.'

'What you said about Jeff's girlfriend, Liza…was that a bluff?' Holly mumbled.

'No. My lawyers do hold her statement. I felt that it was necessary to have proof of Jeff's violence to protect you and Timothy.'

'Has Liza broken up with Jeff?' Holly was still in shock at what she had learnt.

'Yes. I gather she caught him fooling around with one of her friends and she was more than willing to speak up on your behalf.'

Hell hath no fury, Holly reflected in a daze.

Level dark golden eyes scanned her pale, strained face and he caught her hands in his. 'I have to leave…I'm already running late. You look exhausted. You should lie down for a while, *cara*.'

'Thanks…for sorting out Jeff,' Holly said jerkily.

'I'd have liked to do it with my fists,' Rio confided with

unashamed male regret. 'But that could have put paid to any hope of adopting Timothy, and at the end of day Danby's not worth that risk.'

For a long time after Rio had gone Holly just sat beside Timothy's cot, watching over her son while he slept. Rio had spiked Jeff's guns with ease and she was very grateful, but she could not help thinking that he had not been half so successful at quieting her fears about the future. She was married to a bloke who truly believed that a rousing bout of sex answered all ills. And why did Rio imagine that? She had let him make love to her. And a sufficiently angry and alienated woman would have said no.

So why *hadn't* she said no? What she had learnt about Rio and Christabel had filled her with sheer panic. She loved him. She loved him so much. Wanting to kill him only went so far when she had felt that her whole world was under imminent danger of collapsing round her. She had started out all right when she first confronted him but then she had got too emotional and lost the plot.

When Rio came home she would make a more tactful and calm approach, and, one way or another, he was going to talk about Christabel whether he liked it or not, she swore to herself.

CHAPTER NINE

Two days later, the limousine in which Holly was travelling drew up outside Marchmont Priory. The picturesque house was bathed in afternoon sunshine. Climbing out of the car, Holly breathed in deep and straightened her shoulders.

Holly had thought about calling Mrs Lombardi in advance but she had been afraid that her offer to visit would somehow be put off. Although Rio seemed determined to cheerfully ignore all the signs that his parent was anything but happy at his sudden marriage to a stranger, Holly was not that insensitive. Naturally, Alice Lombardi would be concerned, but she was hoping that once Rio's mother actually met her she would realise that her new daughter-in-law was not as bad as she had feared.

She was ushered into the sunlit panelled sitting room, where a slim, still attractive blonde in her early sixties awaited her in an upright armchair. A closer and lengthier appraisal revealed the fine lines on Alice Lombardi's worn features and the pained stiffness of her movements.

'Please excuse me for not standing up to greet you,' she murmured in her well-bred voice. 'My arthritis is particularly troublesome today.'

'I'm sorry. I should have phoned first—'

'Did Rio send you here?'

Holly reddened.

'I thought so,' Alice said ruefully. 'Rio can be very ruthless.'

'He wanted us to meet and I was glad of the excuse,'

Holly responded awkwardly, backing down into the seat that was indicated.

'I may as well admit that Christabel is staying here this week,' the older woman replied. 'I shan't apologise for that. I can hardly turn my back on her simply because my son changed his mind about marrying her. She often visits me.'

'That's really none of my business.' But the news that Rio's ex-fiancée was on the premises was daunting and made Holly feel very much as though she had foolishly strayed into the enemy camp.

'If you say so…' Alice's gaze was as keen as her son's. 'How honest may I be?'

'As honest as you like.' Holly lifted her chin.

'Is your son, Timothy, my grandchild?'

Holly flushed. 'No.'

'And are you expecting a child now?'

'No, I'm not.' Holly supposed that those were fairly obvious questions to ask in the circumstances but she felt horribly like a little kid being questioned by a stern headmistress for unacceptable behaviour.

'I'm sorry if I've embarrassed you but I had to know.' The older woman now looked weary and defeated.

In the hiatus, a maid knocked and entered with a tray of tea. At a leisurely pace, fragile bone-china cups of heirloom quality were filled and delicate cakes were offered. Holly could not get a morsel past her tight throat and even to moisten her lips was a challenge.

'I don't know what has got into Rio,' Alice admitted tightly, tears glimmering in her strained gaze. 'Perhaps I am better not knowing, but if you have somehow contrived to trap him into marriage and your motivation was his wealth I will be your enemy and a most bitter one.'

Holly paled at that unhesitating assurance. 'I—'

'You have no career. You're penniless. How could my

son even have *met* you?' Alice made no attempt to conceal her bewilderment. 'You're not from our world. Of course I'm suspicious of you. Rio won't tell me anything about you.'

Reminded of how poor she had been before her marriage, Holly was mortified. The smart outfit which had helped her confidence suddenly felt like finery she had no entitlement to be wearing. 'I really don't know why Rio sent me here—'

'Don't you? You're supposed to be ingratiating yourself. He's a typical man and he's planning to stay well out of the way until I've come to terms with you,' the older woman informed her drily. 'What age are you, for goodness' sake?'

'Twenty.'

'So now Rio's cradle-snatching.' Alice Lombardi was openly taken aback by the news that Holly was that young. 'I can only assume that my son is madly in love with you. There is no other possible explanation for his behaviour.'

Holly remained silent, unable to lie.

'Have you nothing to say?' Alice demanded in frustration.

'I love *him*,' Holly muttered fiercely and, setting down her untouched tea, she stood up, truly desperate to escape. 'I don't think there's much point me sitting here because I'm only upsetting you and I don't have the answers you want.'

'If Rio loves you, I don't need any answers.' The older woman studied Holly's troubled face with belated discomfiture. 'Nor will I interfere.'

'He doesn't love me,' Holly said bluntly. 'He likes me. He said he thought he could get fond of me but I'm not holding my breath.'

And with that confession, which appeared to startle her

hostess, Holly slipped back out to the flagstoned hall and
heaved a huge, craven sigh of relief. Only then did she see
another woman poised by the massive stone fireplace.

'So you're Holly,' Christabel drawled with a scornful
head-to-toe appraisal that would have left Holly squirming
had Holly not been so intent on staring herself.

Sheathed in a fake-fur coat, a short dress the colour of
cranberry and knee-length black leather boots, the blonde
was so incredibly tall that Holly actually had to step back
to receive the full effect. And the full effect of Christabel
in the flesh was nothing short of spectacular. The shining
fall of pale blonde hair, the startling green eyes, the volup-
tuous pink mouth. Then the lithe, shapely figure, the hand
on the hip angled forward, the endless length of gleaming
thigh presented by her taunting, aggressive stance.

'You look even better than your pictures,' Holly conceded helplessly.

'Are you trying to be funny with me?' Christabel spat,
lips drawing back from her perfect teeth in a venomous
flash. 'You've got some neck, coming here to visit Alice.
This is my turf. Don't you kid yourself that you've stolen
my man. You only have him on loan!'

'*Extended* loan.' Holly threw her bright head back,
bronze ringlets tumbling back from her pale heart-shaped
face, clear blue eyes as steady as she could make them. 'If
you were careless enough to lose a bloke like Rio that's
your problem, not mine. But he's my husband now—'

'And how long do you think that's going to last?'
Christabel loosed a shrill derisive laugh.

'As long as he wants it to. I don't want this bad feeling
with you,' Holly admitted tautly. 'I'd nothing to do with
you and Rio splitting up—'

'But if you hadn't come along we'd have got back together,' Christabel condemned. 'I'll break up your marriage if it's the last thing I do!'

'Christabel...*no*!' another voice interrupted, charged with censure.

Both young women spun. Leaning heavily on a stick, Alice Lombardi was several feet away, her thin features rigid with shocked disapproval as she stared at her house-guest.

All the way back to London, Holly thought of Christabel. Beautiful, angry, vindictive Christabel. She tried to tell herself that she wasn't worried. But a woman so flawless she barely looked human was hard to downsize in her memory bank. And if the gorgeous Christabel still hoped to get Rio back, even though he was now married, what did that tell her? Well, for one thing, it blew a large hole in Holly's dim assumption that something very serious had broken up their engagement. Now she was no longer so sure. Christabel's declaration of war suggested that although Rio and the blonde might have had a major row when they had split up there had still been hope of a reconciliation.

And that new angle on the situation scared Holly, *really* scared her. For the first time Holly was afraid that Rio might have used her just to strike back at Christabel. Not deliberately, but reacting to a subconscious very male urge to level the score, might not Rio have turned to Holly and their marriage as a weapon? By nature, Rio was shockingly stubborn. He was also volatile and deep. What was going to happen if Rio woke up one day and realised that he still cared about Christabel? Already painfully aware that Rio had married her on the rebound, Holly could not see that as a far-fetched fear. Rio didn't love her. Their marriage would not survive if he still had feelings for another woman, all too willing to take him back.

Forcing her thoughts to a halt at that point, Holly told

herself that she was overreacting. Even so, after the afternoon she had endured it was impossible to feel good about either herself or her marriage. She needed to find a job, she decided in desperation, show some independence. Alice Lombardi thought that she might be a gold-digger who'd trapped Rio into marriage. Rio had also talked about the need for her to lead her *own* life. Maybe that was why he had hired a nanny to take care of Timothy. And, if their marriage did fall apart, she would be better off if she was already employed.

Rio phoned her every day, often twice a day. She lived for his calls, woke up every time she turned over in bed and found him missing and just counted the hours until he was due back. But, wanting to surprise him with actual results, she told him nothing about the Italian lessons she was already taking and kept her plans to find a job to herself. After signing up with a couple of office recruitment agencies, she devoted the remainder of the week to Timothy.

The evening of Rio's return, Holly went to the airport to meet him off his flight. It was a last-minute decision and the limousine had already left to pick him up, so she had to call a cab. The cab got caught up in traffic and, fearing that she had missed him, Holly had a frantic rush through the airport. Her heart leapt at first sight of Rio's lean, dark, devastating features as he strode into view with Ezio in his wake, and then, out of nowhere, it seemed, came Christabel.

Holly fell to a stricken halt as the beautiful blonde surged forward to intercept Rio and engage his attention. Holly stood there unnoticed, shattered by Christabel's sudden appearance and the suspicion that such an encounter could only have been prearranged.

With equal abruptness, Holly turned and walked away

again. Still in shock, she went into a café, bought herself a cup of coffee and sat over it, determined not to go home until she had calmed down. Why had Christabel come to meet Rio off his flight? How had the other woman known where he would be? Furious anger welled up in Holly and festered into a rage like nothing she had ever known. Who was the wife? Who was the 'other woman'? All Holly knew as she finally set off home again was that throughout the week she had been made to feel more like Rio's mistress than his wife!

By the time that Holly finally arrived back at the town house it was getting late. As she crossed the hall Rio appeared in the doorway of the library. Shorn of his jacket and tie, his black hair tousled, he looked rather less smooth and self-assured than he had when she had seen him earlier that evening. His lean, strong face was taut. His dark golden eyes scorched over her like a flame thrower's.

'Where the hell have you been all evening?' Rio's opening demand disconcerted her, for she had lost track of time while she had seethed at the airport.

'Out...' Awarding him the most minimal glance, Holly threw her head high, her gaze feverishly bright.

'Sarah told me that you went to meet me at the airport.'

'Well, I won't be making that mistake again,' Holly informed him from between gritted teeth. 'Tell me, is this house a Christabel-free zone or can I expect to trip over her here as well? After all, she appears to be welcome everywhere else, certainly more welcome than I am!'

Rio tensed. 'So you *did* see Christabel with me at the airport.'

'My goodness...you are *so* quick on the uptake!' Holly fired back at him.

Rio straightened to his full commanding height, narrowed golden eyes pinned to her furious and flushed face.

'Do you realise how worried I've been about you?' he condemned, sidestepping the issue of Christabel with infuriating dexterity. 'I got in at seven. It's now eleven!'

'You're lucky I came home at all!' Frustrated rage was climbing so high inside Holly that she could hardly get the words out.

'Am I? I'm not going to stand here and argue with you in the hall,' Rio breathed glacially, throwing wide the door of the library in invitation.

'Is the room soundproof?' Holly enquired sarcastically.

As Rio thrust the door closed he reached for her hand. 'What on earth has got into you?'

Holly yanked her fingers free. 'I've had about all I can take for one week. At your request I went to visit your mother, and do you know who she had staying with her?'

'I haven't a clue.' Winged ebony brows pleated as he lounged in an attitude of outrageous cool against the edge of his desk, Rio surveyed her in expectation of receiving the answer.

'Your ex-fiancée, although there's not a lot of the "ex" about her this week!' Holly snapped angrily. 'I don't feel like your wife. Your mother's been entertaining Christabel as an honoured guest but I got the frozen mitt, not to mention a lot of embarrassing questions that *you* should have foreseen—'

'*Dio mio*…Christabel was down at the Priory?' Rio queried in surprise.

'I want to know what she was doing at the airport tonight!' Holly informed him.

'It was *my* fault that Christabel had to ambush me like that,' Rio stated with flat emphasis, his beautiful mouth compressing. 'I refused to accept her calls. But certain matters did have to be resolved.'

'Like what?' Holly could have done without knowing

that Christabel had been bombarding him with phone calls as well.

'She's living in an apartment I own and hasn't yet found other accommodation—'

'She's living in an apartment you own...?' Holly was aghast at that news. 'But you broke up with her weeks ago. She's famous. She must earn a fortune as a model and you're trying to tell me she *can't* find somewhere to rent?'

'She hasn't had the time. She's been in Paris.'

'She should have been out flat-hunting, then, not sucking up to your mother for sympathy! I'll be in one of your guest rooms until you've thought up a better story!' Holly told him fierily, wrenching the door open. 'And you still haven't explained how she knew where and when to find you to-night.'

Rio released his breath in a long-suffering masculine hiss that set her teeth on edge even more. 'It's common knowledge that I was in New York this week...and I usually fly home on Fridays at that hour.'

Holly's usually generous mouth closed tight as a coffin lid and she set off upstairs regardless, her slender back rigid. Of course, Christabel would know his movements better than *she* did. The blonde had been in Rio's life a lot longer. But Holly was fed up with being wrongfooted by Christabel, first with Rio's mother, who had made it quite clear where her loyalty lay, and then with Rio himself. Rio was acting as if she was being unreasonable, but worst of all he had taken the blame for that encounter at the airport himself. Holly would have been much happier had he bestowed blame on his former girlfriend.

When Rio strode into their bedroom Holly was slamming through drawers in search of a nightdress.

'You're not sleeping apart from me,' Rio told her.

'Watch me,' Holly advised.

'Do you have any idea how much I was looking forward to coming home to you tonight?' Rio demanded in a roughened undertone.

Her eyes stung with sudden tears and she closed them tight. *Could* she believe that? She had devoted the entire afternoon to beautifying herself and getting all dressed up for his benefit. And then she had seen Christabel, gorgeous blonde mane trailing and legs as long as a racetrack on display, and she had known she could not compete. But also that she should not *have* to compete.

'Everywhere I turn she's there where she shouldn't be—'

'I'm amazed that Christabel had the nerve to visit my mother,' Rio confessed, his anger audible. 'That shouldn't have happened and, believe me, now that I know it has, it won't happen again, *bella mia*.'

Holly gulped. 'I don't know *what* to believe any more—'

Slowly Rio eased her round to face him and scanned her shuttered face. He ran caressing fingers down the taut line of her cheekbone, laced them gently into her hair and turned her strained gaze up to his. 'You have to learn to trust me. Christabel's in the past. I've started a new life with you and Timothy.'

Denying herself closer contact with the heat and strength of that hard, muscular frame of his, Holly drew in a slow, sustaining breath. 'I can only accept that if you promise me that you won't have anything more to do with her.'

'No problem…' Appraising her with smouldering golden eyes, sculpted mouth in a sensual curve, Rio backed her over to the bed with predatory determination and an innate sense of good timing. 'Why would I want another woman when I've got everything I want and need at home?'

Holly wondered why, if that was true, he still wouldn't talk about *why* he had broken off his engagement. But then, perhaps from Rio's point of view there had been no great drama involved and he genuinely had nothing more to say on the subject. Possibly he had known for some time that the relationship wasn't working out and giving up on it had not been a sudden decision on his part. Why hadn't that possibility occurred to her before?

Having dealt with her own anxiety and triumphed, Holly concentrated instead on the hammering acceleration of her own heartbeat and the knot of enervating anticipation tightening low in her pelvis. She only had to look at Rio to want him.

Rio laughed with vibrant amusement when she practically tore his shirt getting it off him. 'You missed me,' he told her with immense satisfaction.

'Maybe…'

'I want to hear you admit it…' He took her readily parted lips in a passionate demonstration of hunger and her senses leapt and her wanton body flowed and surged under the powerful masculine demand of his. 'Well?'

'Can't talk right now…better things to do,' she confided, running a provocative hand down over a taut, muscular male thigh, feeling him jerk with a satisfaction as old as time itself and a knowledge of her own feminine power.

'Who taught you to do that?' Rio groaned, straining against her with unconcealed sexual need and extracting her from her dress with more haste than cool.

'You did…'

Hours later, in the dawn light, she watched him sleep. Jet lag had felled him where nothing else could. Jet lag, added to a couple hours of insatiable lovemaking. Yes, he had definitely missed her. *In bed.* She squashed the snipey little voice that came up with that unnecessary addition. Instead she contemplated Rio, lying with one long bronzed, hair-roughened thigh clear of the crumpled sheet, six feet four inches of golden masculinity so gorgeous that she still could not quite credit that he was her husband. She kissed a smooth brown shoulder, rubbed her cheek there with sensuous pleasure, revelling in the familiar musky scent and feel of his skin.

Her own body ached and she smiled with sleepy pride in that reality. Christabel was history. He had convinced her. If seeing his ex-fiancée after so long had not upset him, what was she worrying about? He might not love her but he certainly seemed happy with her, and in the early hours he had *still* been demanding to know what she had been doing at the airport to get back to the house so late. He had been worried about her, worried that she had seen him with Christabel, worried that she, Holly, might be upset. He always liked to know exactly where she was. Why hadn't she noticed how possessive he could be, how protective?

When she woke up again Timothy was nestled up against her, fast asleep. Fully dressed in tight-fitting black jeans and a husky sweater, Rio absorbed her surprise at her son's presence from his stance at the foot of the bed.

'I heard him crying and he stopped the minute he saw me. Sarah had already fed him, so I brought him in here. I played with him for a while and then I took him into the bathroom while I went for a shower. Never again,' Rio groaned feelingly.

'What happened?'

'First, he yanked a towel down over himself and screamed the place down, then he pulled a drawer out and got his hand stuck in it...and, when I took a peek out of the shower because I thought he was being *too* quiet, he was trying to eat the box of plasters he must've sneaked out of the drawer!'

Unconcerned by the furore he had caused, Timothy slept on, looking angelic.

Rio came down on the side of the bed, lean, powerful face taut. 'He really scared me. Suppose he had got his hands on something dangerous or choked on the plasters?'

'But he *didn't*,' Holly soothed, touched that he had missed Timothy enough after a week's absence to bring her son back to their room to play with him. 'He's just at an age where he needs a lot of watching.'

'I'll be a lot more cautious in the future, *cara mia*,' Rio swore. 'But it's just as well for him that nature made him cute and appealing because I almost shouted at him.'

Holly killed a guilty smile at that assurance. She definitely would have shouted out of sheer relief that Timothy had not got hold of anything more dangerous.

Five days later, an hour after Rio had left for a meeting in the City, Holly received a call from one of the recruitment agencies she had signed up with. An insurance company was willing to interview her for a receptionist's position. As the first agency Holly had approached had pointed out the paucity of her qualifications, the implication being that she was aspiring too high, Holly was thrilled just to be in line for consideration.

The interview was set up for noon that day. But at a quarter to eleven when Holly was coming downstairs, elegant in a fitted black suit, Rio breezed through the door. 'How do you fancy going to the races, *bella mia*?' he enquired.

Holly sighed. 'If you mean right now, I've got an appointment.'

'Reschedule it,' Rio told her carelessly.

'I can't—'

'Oh, yes, you can. You haven't learned how to be a Lombardi wife yet.' Rio gave her a breathtaking smile of amusement that made her heart skip a beat. 'With the sole exception of Timothy, I expect you to drop everything to be with me when I'm free.'

Holly worried at her lower lip for a second or two and hardened her heart to the sheer vibrant appeal of him. 'So what was all that about me needing to lead my own life when you're away on business?'

'I don't always practise what I preach. And you may not have noticed, Mrs Lombardi, but I am *not* away. What are you fussing about?' Rio mocked. 'A hair appointment?'

'I wasn't going to mention it yet but I have a job interview...that's not something I can rearrange.' Holly gave him an apologetic smile.

Rio stilled. In fact, not only did he still, he also stared, dark golden eyes fixing to her as if she had announced an intention of going bungee-jumping with a frayed rope. 'An interview for a...*job*? If this is a joke, where's the punchline?'

Holly stiffened. 'Why would it be a joke?'

Rio regarded her levelly. 'I don't want you to work. Why would you look for a job? It's not just a question of what I want either. What about Timothy?'

'Most women work,' Holly replied defensively. 'Anyway, the position is only part-time.'

'"Most women" are not my wife. What is this job?'

'Receptionist.'

'Are you even remotely aware of how wealthy we are?' Rio prompted in a charged and incredulous undertone.

'I'm not wealthy...*you* are.'

'It would be quite inappropriate for you to take an employment opportunity from someone else who really needs it, and that's my last word on the subject.'

'Well, it's not mine.' Holly's temper fired. 'I got the interview on my own merits and I'm proud of that and I intend to show up—'

His lean, dark, devastating face set hard. 'But I said no.'

Holly smoothed an unsteady hand down over her skirt but kept her chin high. 'Don't I have the right to disagree with you?'

'Not when I know better. You're not making the Lombardi name a laughing stock by chasing after some menial job,' Rio decreed with cutting emphasis.

Holly paled. 'So let's get this straight…if I was a brain surgeon or something snobby or important you would have a different attitude. But, as I'm only capable of work that you consider *menial*, I have to stay home to conserve your dignity.'

'As you're not a brain surgeon, I don't think we need discuss that angle. Come on,' Rio urged ruefully. 'Go and change into something livelier for the races.'

'No.'

'In a minute you're going to be chaining yourself to the railings outside the house like a suffragette fighting for the vote,' Rio countered very drily. 'Be sensible. I work very long hours. When I'm around, I want you around too—'

'Did anyone ever tell you that you can be very domineering? And the sort of bloke who has to control everything around him?' Holly paused and then went on, 'If I want to work, I will work.'

'Is that your last word?'

Holly nodded without hesitation.

Rio surveyed her with a level of brooding dissatisfaction that would once have filled her with instant wholehearted panic. Then, swinging on his heel, he mounted the stairs and left her standing there.

An hour later, while Holly waited her turn with the other applicants called for interview, she began to wonder exactly what she was doing there. Was she happy to leave Timothy solely to Sarah's care for half of every week? Hadn't she neglected to take into account the other demands on her time? Was she going to drop out of her Italian lessons? Shouldn't she be taking a more hands-on interest in the running of her own home?

In addition, Rio led a busy social life. They had already dined out once that week, with the directors of the Lombardi Foundation, an occasion that had not been half so intimidating as she had feared. And that very evening they had a big private party to attend. As Rio's wife she had to look good at such events and that meant more than running a last-minute brush through her hair and wearing the first thing that came out of her wardrobe.

Suppressing a rueful sigh, Holly decided that there was no point whatsoever in putting herself through an interview for a job she did not even want. Only pride and the suggestion that she might be a gold-digger had sent her off in search of a job in the first place. Indeed, she had stood up to Rio purely on principle and she knew that her stubborn refusal to give way had shocked him.

Evidently, the husband who had told her that she would have to lead her own life hadn't really meant it. She started to smile then. Just as he had once carelessly admitted, Rio was spoilt. Alice adored her only son. Holly imagined others of her sex had added to that spoiling even by the time Rio became a teenager. He was drop-dead gorgeous and rich and absolutely charming…as long as he got what he wanted. Which, most of the time, he did. And why not, when he made her so happy?

Arriving back home, she was disappointed to learn that Rio had returned to his office at Lombardi Industries. Around three she went to get her hair done. Sly, the owner of the salon, who had long since grasped the fact that Holly was not Rio's imaginary cousin, Fiammetta, and had done so with very good grace, always gave Holly her personal attention.

'I hear Christabel didn't get that big cosmetics contract she was up for,' Sly remarked when she began trimming Holly's hair. 'But then, let's face it, she's not getting any younger...'

After telling herself that she was about to do the decent thing and change the subject, Holly heard herself saying instead, 'What age is she?'

'She's got to be over thirty...' Sly lowered her head to continue more confidentially, 'She's supposed to be pretty difficult to work with. A lot of people in the business don't like her. It makes you think that some of the juiciest rumours about her *have* to be true.'

'Rumours?' Holly was ashamed of herself, deeply ashamed, but she was as hooked as a fish on a line to the other woman's every word.

'The big cosmetics companies are very careful of their image and they expect the model they select as a figurehead to have a *clean* reputation...and Christabel, well, I've heard that she does— Oh, excuse me.'

As a stylist interrupted Sly with a query the brunette broke off what she had been saying and left Holly seething with curiosity. But the minute of reflection that followed sobered Holly and made her face burn. It was truly awful of her to be listening to gossip about Christabel. Rio would kill her. Rio would expect better of her. For goodness' sake, didn't she expect better of herself?

'Can we change the subject?' Holly asked when Sly returned to her.

'But we were having so much fun doing down Christabel,' Sly pointed out in amazement.

'I'm sorry...I know I encouraged you, but talking about her makes me feel bad.'

'That's what I keep on *telling* people about you. Sweet sincerity shines out of you. I bet Rio was blinded by the comparison between you and that female we're not going to mention again. My final word on the subject? Rio had an incredibly lucky escape.'

On the drive home Holly gathered her courage and stopped off at the same designer outlet where Rio had once taken her shopping. She wanted to buy an outfit that Rio hadn't seen before, something that he hadn't chosen for her. And she found it: a strappy short dress that was wholly feminine in design and made of glorious fabric that shone like pure, opulent gold beneath the lights.

Clad in her new lingerie, a daring combination of gossamer-thin lace-topped stockings, oyster silk panties and a matching strapless bra, she was putting the finishing touches to her make-up, which she had laboured long and hard over, when a knock sounded on the bathroom door.

She opened it, focused on a silk tie and automatically tipped back her head to connect with the dark golden eyes she loved, saying, 'Be honest…does this eyeshadow make me look like a panda with a hangover?'

'*Santo cielo…*' Rio murmured huskily.

'That bad?' Holly groaned in frustration. 'I've wiped it all off once already and I'll die if I have to do it again!'

'You look totally fantastic just as you are, *bella mia*,' Rio said very slowly.

Comprehension sinking in, Holly watched her husband literally trail his hotly appreciative gaze over her scantily clad body and she reddened and threw the mascara wand in her hand at him. 'My *eyes*, Rio!'

He caught the wand in one lean brown hand and threw back his arrogant dark head, raw amusement dancing in his dark-lashed gaze, a slashing smile of shameless acknowledgement on his mouth. 'Gorgeous…all of you, absolutely gorgeous. How long do we have before we have to leave?'

'Rio…' Her breath caught in her throat at the smouldering glitter in his scrutiny. His effect on her was instantaneous. A slow simmer of heat rose inside her, spread at wanton speed to sensitive places. Her nipples tingled and tightened and pushed against the cups of her bra and a tiny tightening sensation pulled deep in the pit of her stomach and made her press her thighs together.

'We have more important things to think about,' Rio imparted rather raggedly.

'Have we?'

'I was a real bastard earlier. How did the interview go?'

'The…interview?' Holly coloured, averted her gaze, not yet ready to admit that she had dropped out in advance of it. 'OK…fine.'

Rio spread his hands in an expressive motion. 'I personally feel that the wisest solution is for you to work somewhere in the Lombardi empire. Now, before you start saying that's nepotism, listen to the pros and cons…'

'Pros and cons…' Holly parroted, hugely taken aback by his suggestion.

'Your hours would be negotiable. So if I want us to take off somewhere for a break at short notice, or even have you accompany me on a business trip, there won't be a problem.'

'I see…'

'Of course, you will *have* to do some business courses first, and some of our company courses are quite demanding. But, when you're so keen to have a career, I can't see that being a problem. You just haven't had the opportunities before but now you do,' Rio informed her with satisfaction.

The silence lay, a silence of expectancy.

Holly was aghast. She was seeing demanding business courses stretching interminably into her future and cringing from the prospect. But after all the noise she had made about working, how was she supposed to turn round and tell him she had changed her mind? Especially when he had made such an effort to alter his own outlook on her behalf. Why were men so obtuse sometimes?

'Holly?' Rio prompted.

Holly swallowed hard and forced a weak smile. 'You're being really supportive. I'll think the idea over.'

'I have a surprise for you, *cara*. Put out your hand and close your eyes,' Rio urged.

Her mascaraed lashes clogged together. She felt him slide something onto her left hand and she untangled her lashes to look.

'Six-week anniversary present,' Rio imparted.

A fabulous sapphire and diamond ring now sat next to her wedding ring. Her throat closed over. When he went on a guilt trip, he really worked hard at it, she reflected, tears stinging her eyes. 'It's just gorgeous…' she said in a wobbly voice.

'What are you crying for?'

'I'm not crying,' she swore chokily. 'Look, I'd better get dressed.'

'Spoilsport,' he murmured huskily.

She had had to fall like a ton of bricks for him to discover that sometimes she loved him so much it literally hurt to think about it.

The party was held in a huge town house by a very fashionable middle-aged couple. The decor seemed to have a gothic theme, or maybe it was just the party theme, Holly thought, but there was a giant mural of dragons adorning one end of the vast main room and the lights were dim and the air heavy with the scent of incense. Huge mirrors hung on the walls and veiled marble statues lurked in dim corners.

'You've got some strange friends,' Holly told Rio.

'Frank and Lily are very conventional but they slavishly follow every fashion trend,' Rio informed her with amusement. 'The next time you visit it will all have changed.'

Holly saw Christabel make her entrance, could not really have missed it even had she tried. Wearing a shimmering, extremely short white dress that caressed every curve of her perfect body, Christabel turned every head in the room, both male and female.

As Holly sat there frozen by dismay and an instant sense of being under threat, Rio drawled softly, 'I'm afraid that on some occasions you will have to get used to seeing her around.'

'Did you *know* she was going to be here?'

'I didn't even think about it,' Rio countered in a decided tone of exasperation.

Holly then noticed that Christabel had a very presentable male companion in tow and the sight soothed her. She knew what Rio was telling her and wished she hadn't commented. Christabel had a perfect right to go where she liked.

An hour later she watched Rio's ex-fiancée putting on a stunning exhibition of salsa dancing and generally becoming the life and soul of the party. By her side, Rio got quieter and quieter. When he had asked her to dance she had said no. She didn't know how to do salsa but now everyone was doing it and doing it with real style.

While Rio was at the other end of the room chatting to their host his cousin, Jeremy strolled up. 'Would you like to dance?'

'No, thanks.'

'You shouldn't let Christabel get you down,' Jeremy said bluntly.

'Oh, is she here? I hadn't noticed.' Holly knew she was sulking and feeling sorry for herself but she was unable to stop. She felt so plain, so colourless in comparison to Christabel. Why had Rio become so silent? Maybe he was jealous. Maybe seeing Christabel with another man annoyed him. How could it not annoy him, for goodness' sake? Christabel was just so unbelievably gorgeous, she conceded miserably.

Jeremy drifted off again and Holly watched Christabel giggle in company with their hostess, Lily. And then something happened. The older woman's face froze and she turned on her heel and stalked over to her husband and Rio. Christabel returned to her table and lifted her handbag to rifle through it. Then the dancers screened her from view.

But when Holly glanced back at Rio for the first time she saw him looking in Christabel's direction, lean, strong face taut, his tension unmistakable. Suddenly Holly's heart felt as if it was thundering at the base of her throat and threatening to choke her. As if in a dream, she watched Rio cut a path across the crowded floor, making a beeline for Christabel. Then she saw her husband standing with his ex-fiancée in the circle of his arms and she couldn't believe it. Her very worst nightmare was coming true before her eyes but she could *not* believe it.

But Christabel's head was down on his shoulder, her hair trailing across his dark jacket like a blonde banner. Some people had even stopped dancing to stare. The taste of bile in her dry mouth, Holly watched sickly as Rio, with a supportive arm wrapped round Christabel, walked her out of the room.

Holly sat very still, just staring into space, eyes burning

in her sockets, tummy cramping with nausea. She was horribly conscious of the surge of comment washing round the room in a tidal wave. She couldn't hear it because of the music but she could see and feel it: the heads moving together, the clumping up of couples into bigger groups, the agonising moment when she accidentally collided with a speculative glance.

Jeremy appeared in front of her. 'Rio called me on my mobile. He asked me to keep you company.'

Rio had phoned Jeremy? Rio had actually *left* the party with Christabel? Her husband had just walked out and left her stranded in front of an audience? Well, where did you *think* he was going with her? she asked herself numbly.

'I want to go home.' Holly got up, legs trembling, wanting some magic process to transport her outside, away from the watching eyes and the clattering tongues. Never in her life had she felt more humiliated. Never had she dreamt that Rio would do such a thing to her.

There was no sign of their host and hostess, which was a relief. Jeremy tucked Holly into a cab as if she might shatter into pieces if he wasn't careful. He climbed in beside her.

'There's no need for you to come with me,' Holly said woodenly.

Jeremy's phone started playing some ludicrously upbeat tune. He handed it to her. 'It's Rio...'

'Holly, I'm really sorry but I honestly didn't have a choice,' Rio breathed in bleak undertone. 'Look, we'll talk later.'

Later? *Never*, Holly told herself, returning the phone to Jeremy, blanking out his questioning appraisal. What was there to talk about? Rio had said he hadn't had a choice, but in actuality he had made his choice. Of course he was sorry. He had a conscience. But when push came to shove he just hadn't been able to resist the woman he really cared about.

'Rio's a very decent guy,' Jeremy asserted forcefully. 'He's my cousin. I know him. OK...I didn't see what actually happened but I'm certain there's nothing for you to get upset about.'

'Are you?' Holly held back an hysterical laugh at that plea on Rio's behalf. Decent guys don't walk out on their wives at parties. Only besotted ones did.

'There has to be some explanation. Christabel was acting weird and her antics were embarrassing Frank and Lily. Her date didn't stay long.' Jeremy lowered his voice to a constrained mutter. 'You know, she wasn't wearing anything under that dress.'

Slut, Holly thought, aghast and shocked, tears welling up in her aching eyes. Christabel had got to him with sex. Real brazen-hussy stuff. She was going to burn her stupid lace-topped stockings. Waste of time. She should have known better than to try to appeal to a bloke on that level. Especially when it was now painfully obvious that she was literally still in the nursery league in that department.

An hour later Holly wrote the ubiquitous note.

It was really great while it lasted but now it's over.

Dry-eyed, she packed her plainer clothes and then called a taxi. Hadn't she always known it wouldn't last? It *had* been wonderful while it *had* lasted, she reminded herself doggedly. And he had never said he loved her and she had never said she loved him. But he had given her a wedding ring and only hours ago he had given her a second ring that looked very much like an engagement ring. And suddenly she hated him with a hatred that tore her apart and she was sobbing into her suitcase, stabbed to the heart at the image of him with Christabel. It took her a good ten minutes to plaster herself back together again.

Striving not to waken their nanny in her room next door, Holly crept about her son's room, gathering up essentials. Timothy was going to miss Rio so much, she reflected wretchedly. But what could she do about that? Why was it that at the most awful moments of her life she always felt powerless and guilty, as if everything that went wrong was her fault?

No, she caught herself up on that thought. She was making her own decisions, *not* waiting on him. She was leaving him. She was going to divorce him for adultery too. If he was expecting civilised forgiveness, he had no hope. She might even make him wait the full three years before she agreed to a divorce. Not that a hussy like Christabel was likely to be put off by the prospect of living in sin. Stop it, *stop it*, her saner self intervened. Let him go, let him have her if he loves her, and to behave as he had he *had* to love her...

CHAPTER TEN

'WHAT have you done to that pastry?' Mary Sansom demanded in dismay. 'It looks like you've been torturing it!'

Holly stared down at the shredded pastry and then glanced across the kitchen at her mother, a sturdy little woman with iron-grey hair, wrapped in a floral apron. 'I'll make some more.'

'I'll see to it.' The concern in her parent's steady blue eyes filled Holly with guilt.

She had been trying so hard to be cheerful, but putting a happy face on her misery was a challenge she had yet to meet. It had been almost three weeks since she had left London. By the end of her first day home she had been hoarse from making a clean breast of everything that had happened to her since Timothy had been born. And there had been tears, rebukes and regrets, but a lot of love too. That her parents could forgive her for all the grief she had caused had been a tremendous comfort to Holly, as was her mother and father's loving acceptance of their baby grandson. So she felt that they deserved more than the continual sight of her drooping like a wet weekend.

Yet, as the days dragged by, her mother or her father would often come up with some statement that unsettled Holly. 'Is this bloke you married a fool, then?' her father had asked, infuriating her with that mere suggestion. 'I reckon only a right fool would wed one woman when he still fancied his chances with another.'

'You just never think before you act,' her mother had lamented. 'But marriages have to be worked at and you should have talked to your husband. He was good to you. Why would he suddenly take off with this other shameless piece? I can tell you, your father would have no truck with a female like that,' her mother had told her with staunch and touching pride. 'No decent man would want a woman who carried on that way.'

Holly went up to bed that night and feared that the generation gap was yawning. She lay in her pine bed and felt the tears trickling again. She felt as if half of her had been brutally ripped away. She missed him with every breath she drew. She turned a dozen times a day to tell him something before she remembered that he wasn't there any more. She ached for him and despised herself and kept on wanting to phone him but could not begin to imagine what she could possibly say.

Two days later Mary Sansom announced over breakfast that the house needed 'a good going-over'. Knowing well that a thorough cleaning session was intended, Holly suppressed a groan. By teatime even the battered kitchen range shone from industrious polishing. Her parents were attending a church social that evening and Holly noticed that her mother seemed unusually quiet and anxious.

'You know, Dad and I...we always want what's best for you,' the older woman remarked without warning as Holly carried cake tins out to the car for her. 'It's not as though you've done so well on your own.'

Hurt by a comment that she was none the less well aware her mother had grounds to make, Holly retreated back indoors and got on with putting Timothy to bed. 'Da...Da?' he asked in a small mournful voice, from which hope had pretty much gone.

Eyes overflowing with tears of regret, Holly was on the stairs when she heard the back-door knocker sound.

Assuming that her mother had overlooked something in her rather flustered departure, she hurried to answer it.

It was Rio. Stunned, Holly gaped at him, her tear-streaked face pale as a ghost between the tangled bronze ringlets tumbling round her shoulders. He gazed down at her with dark golden eyes that glittered below the heavy fringe of his black lashes and it was as if he had yanked a panic button in her heart, setting off a chain reaction that went right through her slender body in a stormy wave.

She parted dry lips. 'How...how did you find me?'

'Finding you down here was easy. Unfortunately I wasted over two weeks on the assumption that you'd taken some job and stayed on in London,' Rio admitted. 'Are you planning to invite me indoors?'

At that pointed question, Holly coloured and stepped back. Clad in fitted black jeans, a cream sweater and a loose-cut black fleece-lined jacket, Rio cut a powerful figure, dominating the homely kitchen, his dark head reaching within a couple of inches of the overhanging rafters.

'Watch out for the doorways,' she said automatically. 'They're lower.'

Poised with his back to the low-burning fire, Rio was staring at her. As his incisive gaze wandered intently over her she realised what a mess she must look, for her hair needed to be tidied and she was wearing ancient jeans and an even more ancient sweatshirt.

'You look about sixteen...' Rio murmured huskily.

Picturing Christabel's glittering sophistication, Holly paled and tore her gaze away. She stared out instead at the sleek red Ferrari parked in the yard. 'How did you get that car up the lane?'

'Slowly.'

She could feel his tension as much as her own. It was as if he didn't know how to talk to her any more. She marvelled that she had ever convinced herself that she could avoid a final meeting with him. But, oh, how she wished that that had been possible when he stood only feet away and she was aware of his presence with every screaming fibre of her being. She was a mess of conflict: hurting and hating and hungering all at once.

'How could you just walk out of our home with Timothy?' Rio asked with raw-edged abruptness.

'It wasn't difficult after what you did at the party,' Holly replied tightly.

'You don't trust me at all...'

Holly said nothing. Her experience of his sex had not taught her trust. When she had first given her trust Jeff had broken it, and more than once. With Rio, she had lived each day as it came, protecting herself by trying not to look too far ahead but secretly always expecting disappointment and heartbreak. That the worst had ultimately happened had come as no surprise. It was as if she had been waiting for it all along.

'You want me to talk about Christabel...'

The nasty bit of her wanted to tell him not to bother, as it was a bit late in the day for explanations. But common sense told her that, no matter how much hearing the truth might hurt, some day in the future she would be grateful that she had heard him out.

'OK...' Rio conceded, but the silence still dragged on like a hangman's rope threatening to snap tight at any moment.

Is it the sex? That was what *she* wanted to ask, what she was forcing herself to hold back because it would reveal too much. Only a woman eaten up with jealousy would even consider asking such a thing. A woman in love, desperate to reduce the breakdown to the lowest common denominator in the hope that it would somehow make it more bearable.

'Where do you want me to start?'

Holly spun right round in frustration. Rio was raking a not quite steady hand through his luxuriant black hair, pallor spread below his usually vibrant complexion and accentuated round the tight line of his sensual mouth. For the first time she noticed that his dark, devastating features had harder angles, as if he had lost weight. She was delighted that he looked so downright miserable and strained. Evidently life with Christabel was not one of unalloyed joy and frolics.

'*Dio mio*...maybe I should have rehearsed this first,' Rio breathed, his jawline clenching hard. 'Christabel and I had a long-distance relationship. Sometimes a month or more would go by without us seeing each other. Her career took her all over the world and I had similar commitments. I may well have spent more actual time alone with you than I ever spent with her.'

Surprise assailed Holly, for she had not expected to hear that.

'When we were together we usually had company. The less I saw of her, the more I thought I loved her.' Faint dark colour burnished his spectacular cheekbones. 'It's taken me a long time to work that out.'

'Work what out?'

'That, when the chips were down, I didn't know Christabel at all. What we had was superficial but I would've married her without ever appreciating that,' Rio admitted grudgingly.

'So what changed?' Holly almost whispered.

A faint sheen of perspiration overlaid his bronzed skin and he turned pale again right before her eyes. 'The night

I met you, I let myself into her apartment to wait for her coming home. She wasn't expecting me...surprise, surprise,' Rio framed grittily, his dark, deep drawl slowing and tautening. 'When she came back she wasn't alone...'

Comprehension came to Holly in a surge. 'She had another man with her?'

'I need a drink,' Rio said hollowly.

Holly was ready to poison him. He had *forgiven* Christabel for carrying on with some other man? Incandescent rage at such injustice flamed through Holly. Her parents were virtually teetotal but brandy was always kept for emergencies. She poured him a glass and set it on the table so that he would have to reach for it. Rio drained the measure in one gulp.

The silence came back then, thicker and heavier than ever.

Rio threw back his proud dark head. 'I should've told you weeks ago but I didn't want to talk about it. She wasn't with a man...she was with a woman.'

Holly's lips parted company and stayed parted while she attempted to compute that rather more shocking slant to her inner picture of infidelity and betrayal, but no matter how hard she tried she could not fit Christabel into that context. 'Are you serious?'

Rio dealt her bemused face a sudden exasperated appraisal. 'They were making love.'

'Oh...' Holly had no ready response to make.

'I promised her that I wouldn't talk about it...' Rio hesitated, intense eyes darker than she had ever seen them. 'But, let's face it, that's not why I kept quiet. I was shattered. I felt humiliated...sexually and in every other way,' he admitted in a raw undertone.

Holly could see what it was costing him to confess to

that vulnerability and it hurt her even to listen. But her own thoughts were in turmoil as she tried to make sense of what he was telling her and make it fit more recent events. Unfortunately that attempt only left her more confused than ever.

Rio snatched in a deep, charged breath and gave her a bleak glance. 'Most guys like to think of themselves as studs. When you walk in on a scene like that with the woman you're planning to marry it's annihilating. I doubt that Christabel was ever faithful to me.'

'Then what do you still see in her?' Holly demanded in bewilderment. 'I mean…you're describing a situation most men couldn't forgive.'

'Christabel is so screwed up right now, I'd have to be a real bastard to walk by on the other side,' Rio countered grimly. 'Didn't you register what was happening at that party? Lily begged me to get her out of their house—'

'Our hostess, Lily…Frank's wife? *Begged* you?''

'By that stage, Christabel's escort had done a timely vanishing act, probably out of embarrassment. She was out of her head on drugs—'

'Drugs?' Holly was totally disconcerted.

'Lily caught her in the act with cocaine and asked her to leave. Christabel refused,' Rio explained ruefully. 'Frank and Lily lost their eldest son to heroin a couple of years ago and Lily was very distressed. I agreed to help, not just for their benefit but also for Christabel's. She was out of control and making a total ass of herself.'

'But if you'd come and spoken to me first, *explained*—'

'You wouldn't have listened. You'd have lost your temper and I had to get Christabel out of there fast and without a scene.' Dark golden eyes rested on her in level challenge.

Holly swallowed hard, for there was a lot of truth in his

forecast of how she would have reacted had he approached her first to warn her.

'The circumstances were exceptional.' His lean, strong face hardened. 'But I made the mistake of assuming that you'd understand that there was something really serious happening.'

'Yes…' Face burning, Holly gazed into the fire, no longer able to meet his scrutiny. 'Were you aware that she did drugs?'

'Before that party I'd no idea Christabel had a problem, but then she was too clever to take them around me. And that night I didn't want the responsibility, but she was part of my life for a long time and I felt that I *had* to help her,' Rio stated harshly.

'So what did you do with her?'

'I took her to the foundation hospital and contacted her family. Two days after that Christabel signed herself into a rehabilitation clinic. She's still there.'

Recalling all the nasty thoughts she had had about the other woman, Holly felt sincerely ashamed. Christabel had genuine problems that she needed help to cope with and Rio had done the right thing in giving her his support.

'Did she go off the rails because you ditched her?' Holly mumbled uneasily.

'No. Her sister, Gwen, was able to tell me that her drug and alcohol abuse had begun well before she met me.' His darkly handsome features serious, Rio released his breath slowly. 'I did think she drank too much sometimes but I'm afraid I didn't recognise it as a problem and she didn't confide in me. However, her sister was very frank…'

'Did she blame you for Christabel's problems?'

'No, far from it. Apparently, Christabel was confused about her sexual orientation when she was a teenager. More recently, she was terrified that she was losing her looks and struggling to keep an increasingly heavy drug habit hidden,' Rio revealed.

'So where did you fit into her life?'

'According to Gwen, Christabel saw me as a financial security blanket for her future.' Rio grimaced at that tag. 'My defection faced her with realities she had refused to deal with and now she's *having* to deal with them. Her sister's a psychologist and she says that's much more healthy.'

'I heard that she had recently lost out on some big modelling contract as well,' Holly remarked uncomfortably.

'Gwen mentioned that too. Said there'd been rumours about Christabel's lifestyle. Naturally. People talk.'

Holly stood there several feet from him, struggling to face her own reality, but it was a daunting one. She had judged Rio without even giving him the chance to defend himself and she was ashamed that she had had so little faith in him.

'I'm sorry...I'm *so* sorry I just walked out the way I did,' Holly muttered shakily. 'I was really jealous of Christabel and what I thought you must've had with her. I felt like second-best, and then when I met her down at the Priory—'

'I *wish* you'd told me about that encounter—'

'She said she wanted you back and that I'd come between you, and that really upset me—'

'Of course it did because you don't think enough of yourself,' Rio breathed not quite steadily, reaching out for her hands and drawing her closer. 'And that's my fault—'

'No, it's not,' Holly sighed, her hands quivering in his. 'If I'd mentioned Christabel's threats then maybe you would've understood why I was so sensitive about her—'

'There was never any chance of a reconciliation. But if I'd been more honest with you you'd have found that easier to accept.' Brilliant dark eyes scanning her troubled face, his hands tightened their grip on hers. 'The truth is...I didn't know what hit me when I met you. I couldn't think of anything else *but* you and I told myself I was unsettled after what had happened with Christabel—'

'Naturally you were...I mean, that's OK,' Holly hastened to reassure him because she was so grateful he was holding her hands and still talking to her after the manner in which she had left their home.

'No, it wasn't OK, *cara*. I wasn't giving you what *you* deserved. I don't know when or how I fell in love with you but I was in deep very fast. You must've noticed that I couldn't let you out of my sight...did you think that was normal?'

'Normal? I felt the same way.' And all the time her mind was reaching back to what he had said just before that. 'I fell in love with you'. Had he really said that or had she imagined that he had said that?

'There was the most explosive attraction between us right from the start and the lust I could handle,' Rio asserted wryly. 'But I couldn't acknowledge that I was seriously involved because that would've meant admitting that I was this pretty stupid and potentially shallow guy who almost married a woman he didn't really love—'

'You didn't really love Christabel?'

'I believed I loved her but we were never close, not the way you and I are, but I didn't know what that closeness was until I found it with you, *cara*.' Rio confessed, dark golden eyes troubled. 'I got over Christabel too quickly. And it might seem strange to you but I was ashamed of that...and it made me very wary about what I was feeling for you.'

'Yeah...you told me you *liked* me—'

'But the cool-guy act went out the window when you

disappeared,' Rio broke in feelingly. 'I was tearing my hair out. I was desperate. I couldn't work. I couldn't sleep. I was haunting homeless shelters...you just have *no* idea what I went through the first two weeks you were missing!'

But, gazing up into the over-bright shimmer of those speaking dark eyes resting with such loving intensity on her face, she did have an idea and she ached for him even as the first stirrings of joy began to wing through her.

'*Dio mio*...I went to hell and back. I was worried sick. I thought I might never find you or Timothy again—'

'Eventually I would've gone to see a solicitor, but doing that and talking about a divorce...it would have been so final and I couldn't face it yet,' Holly confided chokily, her voice breaking up on her as she realised how near she had come to losing everything she cared about.

Rio wrapped his arms tightly round her and held her so close that she could hardly breathe, but at that instant it was what she needed more than anything else. 'I'd have fought a divorce. There's *nothing* I wouldn't have done to get you and Timothy back,' he swore above her head. 'I'd have begged you to come home. Don't you realise how happy I've been with you? Couldn't you feel that...*see* it?'

And she had felt it, seen it so often, she recognised with a shamed stirring of regret. He had been so caring, so tender and romantic, but without the words of love she had been afraid to simply trust in his behaviour. 'You said you liked me...and that bit about getting fond of me,' she reminded him. 'It was so unemotional and it was like you saying that you could never, ever fall in love with someone like me.'

Rio winced and looked down at her with more than a hint of embarrassment. 'I just didn't know what else to say to you. It wasn't meant the way you took it. I was very wary of that word "love" that soon after breaking up with Christabel—'

'And you deliberately misled me about that—'

'Yes, because I sensed you'd say no otherwise. Didn't you start wondering what planet I was from when I asked you to marry me only a few days after I had met you?' Rio muttered with rueful self-mockery. 'I jumped on the first excuse I got to hang on to you and Timothy. Where is he, by the way?'

'In bed...you can see him if you want.' Holly looked up at him, her heart in her eyes, for she was so happy with what he was telling her about his feelings. He wasn't trying to hide anything now. He was admitting that he had been confused and acting out of character but letting her know that his most driving motivation had been to keep her in his life. 'I love you so much.'

'I love you too, *tesoro mio*.'

Holly took him upstairs to see Timothy, who was still awake. His lashes lifted on sleepy eyes and he stared at them. Then her son sat up and with sudden startling energy tried to claw his way up the side of the cot into standing position. What was more, what he had often tried but never yet succeeded at, actually worked on this occasion.

'When did he learn to do that?' Rio demanded.

'That's the first time he's managed it.'

Clasping the cot bars, big blue eyes very wide, looking as surprised as a baby could be at finding himself fully vertical, Timothy gave them a huge grin. But then he made the strategic error of letting go of the top bar and he fell back onto his bottom with a howl of disappointment.

With a husky laugh of amusement, Rio lifted Timothy up into his arms. 'You were brilliant...Mum and I were really impressed!'

After that excitement, it took a while to persuade Timothy back into the notion of going to sleep but eventually tiredness won the day.

'Mum and Dad will be home soon,' Holly told Rio at the top of the stairs.

'No, they won't be. They're spending the night in a local hotel—'

Holly blinked in confusion. 'I beg your pardon?'

'I made my first visit here yesterday afternoon while you were out shopping with Timothy,' Rio confided rather tautly. 'Your parents invited me in and gave me the third degree. They suggested I visit this evening when they would be out, but they were worried that that wouldn't give us long enough to talk over our differences—'

'I don't believe this...Mum and Dad didn't breathe a word to me!' Holly gasped.

'It was spelt out to me that I was going to have a battle persuading you to come back to me, so I came up with the hotel idea—'

'Putting them out of their own home?' Holly exclaimed in dismay. 'They've never stayed in a hotel in their lives!'

'I know...they told me.' Rio smiled down at her with considerable amusement. 'And your mother was thrilled at the prospect.'

'You are *so* sneaky. You got them on your side—'

'We're quits. You've got *my* mother on *yours*.' Rio traded wryly.

'Like heck I have—'

'Is this your bedroom? Oh, I *love* all the flowers and the frills,' Rio teased, grasping her hand and tugging her inch by inch over the threshold and closing the door.

He meshed his fingers slowly into her bronze ringlets, beautiful dark golden eyes bright with adoring intensity as he gazed down her. He brought his mouth down with immense tenderness on hers and she trembled. Less patient, she pushed forward into the sleek, hard, familiar strength of his muscular frame. It felt so good just to be held but even more glorious to know that she was truly loved and to feel the unmistakable shudder of response that went through him as she kissed him back.

'You are so beautiful and I love you so much it hurts,' he husked against her reddened lips, his breath fanning her cheekbone. 'And every time I think that I might never have met you it terrifies the life out of me, *amore*.'

'I love you too,' she moaned, shamelessly eager to express that love, hands sliding beneath his sweater to glide over his hard ribcage, making him jerk against her and haul her even closer.

And then the excitement took over and clothes were shed with breathless energy between frantic bouts of kissing. There was a whole extra dimension to their loving, for they had spent three utterly miserable weeks apart, and being together again felt like a very special gift. In the aftermath of the passion, they lay locked together, full of peace and contentment.

Holly struggled to recall what they had been talking about earlier and blushed at the ease with which she had forgotten that conversation. 'What was that you said about your mother being on my side?' she whispered curiously.

'She came up to London because she was upset about the way she'd treated you, and that's how I found out that you'd met Christabel,' Rio explained lazily, propping himself up on one elbow to gaze down at her. 'So, when my parent discovered that you'd already walked out on me, all I got was a very humiliating lecture about how she wasn't at all surprised. How *could* you tell her that I said I might get fond of you?'

Helpless amusement filtered through Holly, for she was now remembering that Alice Lombardi had said that the only explanation for her son's behaviour was that he had fallen madly in love with her. 'Serves you right.'

Rio dealt her a rueful scrutiny. 'I never did apologise for letting you go down to the Priory alone. It's just that my mother does rather dramatise events, *bella mia*—'

'You told her nothing about me—'

'I told her *everything* in London. She had the smelling salts out, but you now stand high in her estimation as the female who rescued me from a scarlet woman and saved the family name from scandal,' he told her with a wicked grin. 'When she heard you'd been taking Italian lessons she was even more convinced I didn't deserve you—'

'How did you find out about them?' Holly gasped and then she groaned. 'Oh, no, I forgot to cancel them!'

'Relax. Your teacher phoned and I used the same excuse with her that I used for our nanny's benefit. Family emergency. I couldn't tell anyone that you might not be returning because I couldn't *face* that possibility,' Rio confided.

'If you'd told me the truth about your broken engagement it would never have happened...'

His darkly handsome features tensed. 'I didn't want you thinking less of me,' he muttered tautly.

'Think less of you? *How?*'

Dark colour now scored his superb cheekbones. 'I just thought you'd think less of me if you knew the truth. My fiancée turning to another woman... It may sound stupid to you, but I was afraid it might take the stars out of your eyes when you looked at me,' he finally completed in a distinct tone of embarrassment.

'And you liked the stars?'

Rio nodded in serious and steady confirmation.

'I still have the stars.' Holly linked her arms round him and loved him more than she had ever loved him for admitting that to her. So there he was, totally gorgeous and sexy and everything she had ever dreamt of, and yet he could suffer from insecurity too.

'I'm crazy about you, *tesoro mio*. You be sure to tell me if you ever find those stars blinking out.'

'You'll have to spoil me rotten...'

'No problem. Spoiling you usually means spoiling me too.' Rio gave her his husky, sexy laugh and eased her back into more intimate connection with him again.

Holly was entirely hooked on the message of loving intent in his possessive gaze. Just as well he didn't know how many stars there were...enough to last two lifetimes, she thought happily. And then he kissed her and the stars turned into fireworks again and she thought no more.

Eighteen months later, Holly glanced into the nursery at the town house to see Alice Lombardi literally swamped with young children. Seated between the twins' cots with Timothy on her knee, her mother-in-law was reading a story out loud.

Timothy was almost two and a half years old and, only the day before, Holly and Rio's dearest wish had come true. Jeff had not contested their application and the court had granted the adoption order. Alice had flown over from Florence simply to attend the hearing. Rio was now officially Timothy's adoptive father and Timothy had the same right to the Lombardi name as his baby sisters, Amalia and Battista. They had all celebrated with a special dinner the night before.

Three months earlier, Holly had given birth to the twins. It had been an easy but very tiring pregnancy and Rio had fussed over her to an almost embarrassing degree. He had also fainted dead away in the delivery room on the day of their daughters' birth, a reaction which he was still trying to explain away as the result of over-excitement. With three children in the household, Alice Lombardi was in her element when she visited. She adored children and that had been clear to Holly from the instant Timothy had crawled across the floor into the older woman's eagerly extended arms. Alice made no difference between Timothy and the more recent arrivals in the family, and Holly loved her for that.

Furthermore, although Rio's mother still had bad days with her arthritis, her health had improved a great deal. But then, Holly did not think Rio had ever understood quite how bored and depressed the older woman had been with her life prior to their marriage. But Holly had begun to understand as she watched Alice slowly lose her concept of herself as an invalid to become more active.

Leaving the older woman in peace to enjoy the children, Holly thought about how her own parents had also bene-fited from their marriage. Well aware of how independent his father-in-law was, Rio had not made the mistake of offering direct financial help, which would have been re-fused. Instead, her husband had invested in the farm, en-abling her father to hire a worker to help out. Holly had had the pleasure of seeing her own father take on a new lease of life, no longer stressed by worry about how he would cope as he got older.

Yes, there was no doubt about it, Holly reflected as she changed into an elegant blue shift dress. Rio was one very special bloke, who went to endless trouble to help those he loved.

She respected him for what he had done for Christabel as well. Feeling that his former fiancée was having enough of a struggle getting her life back on track after leaving the rehabilitation clinic, he had asked Holly if she would mind if he simply signed that apartment of his over to Christabel. And no, she hadn't minded, and she had even been pleased when the blonde spoke to her months later at a charity function.

'Rio's a really great guy,' Christabel had proclaimed with genuine warmth and had then lowered her voice to groan, 'But, to be honest, he was way too good-living for me!'

Christabel's life had moved on too and she certainly seemed content. Having set up a successful modelling school, she had then caused a great stir with the announcement that she was bi-sexual and a reformed addict. That confessional session in front of the cameras had gained her enormous publicity but she had recently started dating men again.

Holly went to say goodnight to her children. Timothy was almost asleep and she straightened the bedclothes and removed half a dozen toy cars from the spread before dropping a kiss down on his smooth brow.

'Night...night,' Timothy mumbled and then revived slightly as he focused on the tall dark male who had appeared in his bedroom doorway. 'Hug...Dad.'

During the hug, a whispered exchange took place. The toy Ferrari that Holly had removed from the bed was slid back under the covers but she turned a blind eye to that evidence of male complicity. Timothy was such a happy toddler, full of affection and little-boy liveliness.

'One down, two to go, *cara*,' Rio quipped as he curved an arm round her and accompanied her into the nursery. 'After having you around yesterday, I missed you at the office today.'

'I missed you too.' Holly smiled at the thought of how much her outlook on life had changed over the past eighteen months. She had never dreamt that she might end up doing a basic business course just to see what it was like and that she might enjoy it and want to learn more, but that was what had happened.

Right now, of course, with the children all so young, it

wasn't possible for her to do much more than study part-time. That week, however, she had spent a morning with Rio at Lombardi Industries, actually seeing how the business world operated, and she had been fascinated by that insight into an average day in his life.

'If you were there the whole time I probably couldn't concentrate,' Rio confided, smiling appreciatively down into Amalia's cot. 'She's just beautiful when she's sleeping, isn't she?'

Holly tried not to laugh, but there was no denying that their eldest daughter had caused a lot of disruption in her first weeks of life by flatly refusing to sleep at almost any stage of the night. Holly had been darned grateful to have both a husband and a nanny. Mercifully, Amalia had recently settled into a more reasonable routine.

'And Battista...' Rio studied his younger daughter with touching pride. She had the same curly dark hair as Amalia, for their daughters were identical twins, but there the resemblance ended, since Battista slept like a log and seemed to have a more philosophical attitude to life.

Leaving the nursery, they went into their bedroom because Rio said he needed a shower before dinner.

'Same old routine. I don't know why I bother putting clothes on for you coming home,' Holly lamented in a long-suffering tone of teasing provocation.

Laughing, Rio threw back his darkly handsome head and then kissed her breathless anyway. 'What happened to those stars in your eyes?'

'Those stars are multiplying at an incredible rate,' Holly swore, gazing up into dark golden eyes that were full of love and appreciation and tenderness. He adored her and she knew it.

'I must be on a real winning streak, then, *tesoro mio*.'

Rio locked her to his lean, powerful body with possessive hands.

'Not this evening, you're not,' Holly told him ruefully, striving not to quiver against him in an inviting way, although it was very difficult when her resistance was nil. 'Have you forgotten Alice is staying until tomorrow?'

'And dining out with friends,' Rio reminded her with a slashing smile of amusement as she let herself quiver and meld to him like a second skin, all restraint vanishing.

Holly gave him her starry-eyed look of love and saw it beautifully reflected in his own gaze. She wound her arms round him, possessive and proud and dizzy with happiness, and it was a very long time before either of them thought of eating.

The Italian's Passionate Proposal

by
Sarah Morgan

Sarah Morgan trained as a nurse and has since worked in a variety of health-related jobs. Married to a gorgeous businessman, who still makes her knees knock, she spends most of her time trying to keep up with their two little boys but manages to sneak off occasionally to indulge her passion for writing romance. Sarah loves outdoor life and is an enthusiastic skier and walker. Whatever she is doing, her head is always full of new characters and she is addicted to happy endings.

Don't miss Sarah Morgan's new novel,
The Magic of Christmas,
out in November 2007
from Mills & Boon® Medical™!

CHAPTER ONE

THE freezing air was thick with softly falling snowflakes and the darkened streets of the East End of London were totally deserted. With less than a week to go until Christmas, most people were at home, decorating trees and wrapping presents.

Carlo Santini was barely aware of the inhospitable nature of his surroundings. He was restless and on edge, frustrated beyond belief by recent developments in his life. A frown on his handsome face, he paced rhythmically along the icy pavement, his footsteps muffled by the thick covering of snow, the collar of his black coat turned up against the cold.

He'd been warned to keep to his apartment and the hospital but he was totally fed up with the warnings.

In fact, he was so disillusioned with his life that when things had finally come to a head and he'd been ordered to leave Italy for a short time, he'd been only too happy to comply.

His old life was starting to feel like a prison.

Having enormous wealth was a fantasy for most people but for Carlo the reality had become an increasing burden over the years and he embraced the chance to pretend that it didn't exist, even for a few precious weeks. Being forced to come to London and work under an assumed name was a gift that he was determined to grab with both hands.

For the first time in his whole life, no one would know who he was.

People would respond to his medical and personal skills

rather than his reputation as a billionaire playboy or his impressive connections.

Suddenly aware of just how quiet the streets were, Carlo narrowed his eyes and took a brief look around. He'd always refused to have a personal bodyguard and the recent threats to his life hadn't changed that. He preferred to look out for himself.

He gave a slight smile. Matteo Parini, his father's chief of security, was probably in their London apartment biting his nails at this very moment, wondering where he was.

And Carlo was under no illusions about his safety. Even hidden in the East End of London under an assumed name, he wasn't safe. Not until they caught the men who were threatening his life. But at least for a few hours he could pretend that nothing was wrong.

Suddenly aware that two men had appeared in the street ahead of him, he tensed his broad shoulders slightly. They were walking slowly and Carlo's eyes narrowed suspiciously as he watched them.

Why would they be dawdling when it was below freezing? It was hardly the night for a winter stroll.

Then he saw one of them glance across the street and for the first time noticed a young boy, slight in build, hurrying along the pavement, clutching a stuffed bin bag, his eyes down as he struggled against the snow.

Guessing their intention before they'd even acted, Carlo removed his hands from his pockets, his lean features suddenly showing a strength of purpose. Without drawing attention to himself, he increased his pace, every sense on alert as he closed the distance between them.

With no warning they suddenly turned and sprinted across the snowy street, attacking the young boy viciously, grabbing the bin bag that he was carrying and pushing him roughly to the ground.

Carlo's eyes gleamed and adrenaline rushed through his

veins, but before he could reach them the young boy was back on his feet, lithe and agile. He grabbed one of the men in a classic judo hold and threw him heavily onto the pavement.

Carlo winced at the sickening thud and gave a surprised smile.

Maybe the lad didn't need his help after all. He seemed to be doing pretty well by himself.

Or maybe not…

As the man lay groaning on the ground, his accomplice grabbed the boy round the throat and Carlo saw a flash of steel.

His blood heating, he moved swiftly, using the element of surprise to his advantage, attacking the man from behind and enclosing his wrist in a deadly grip until the knife fell to the ground.

'Let him go…' He couldn't think of a suitable word in English so he switched to Italian, twisting the man's arm behind his back in a ruthless hold that forced him to release the boy.

The other attacker scrambled to his feet, winded by the fall, bracing himself for a fight.

Breathing heavily, he caught the cold, dangerous look in Carlo's eyes and backed away, his change of heart evident.

'Hey, it wasn't my idea…'

He glared at his friend, still held captive by Carlo's deadly hold, and then turned and ran for it, sprinting away as fast as he could, slipping and sliding on the snowy street in his haste to put distance between them.

Swearing fluently, the other man whimpered with the pain in his arm and Carlo reluctantly let him go, kicking the knife out of reach, cold fury erupting inside him. Why were they attacking a kid?

Rubbing his arm, the man gave an angry snarl, landed

a final vicious kick in the boy's stomach and then turned and ran after his friend.

Carlo was itching to chase them but he was aware that the young boy was doubled up in pain from the kick. He reached out a hand to offer support and found himself flat on his back on the pavement, staring up at the stars.

How the hell had that happened?

He was an expert in several martial arts and had spent his entire life prepared to defend himself. He just hadn't expected to have to defend himself from someone who didn't even reach his chin and whom he'd just rescued.

But clearly the boy didn't realise he was being rescued.

Grunting with pain, every muscle in his body protesting, Carlo struggled to sit up and then ducked as a booted foot flew in the direction of his face.

'Stay away from me, you scum!'

Deciding that this was becoming dangerous, he grabbed the foot and brought the boy down as gently as he could, rolling on top of him so that he could hold him securely.

'I'm not trying to hurt you,' he gritted, grabbing both arms and pinning the boy to the pavement. Finally the boy stopped wriggling and glared up at him defiantly and Carlo felt something shift in his stomach.

He'd never seen a boy with eyes that beautiful.

They were an amazing shade of green, fringed with thick lashes that were inky black.

Following through on a totally male instinct, he released the boy's hands and jerked off the woolly hat, sucking in his breath as soft dark hair tumbled down and trailed in the snow.

Not a boy...

His last coherent thought was that she was the most beautiful girl he'd ever seen in his life.

And then she hit him.

Carlo winced as her small fist made contact with his

cheekbone, pain splitting the side of his face. He swore fluently in Italian and moved his jaw gingerly, testing for fractures.

He'd say this for the girl, she certainly knew how to fight. Why had he ever thought she needed his protection?

Careful not to hurt her, he shifted himself so that he pinned her more securely and caught hold of her hands as she struggled.

'*Porca miseria*, I'm not attacking you,' he growled impatiently. 'I'm rescuing you!'

Her eyes were blazing up into his, her chest rising and falling as she tried to catch her breath.

'Rescuing me? You're not rescuing me, you're suffocating me! And ranting at me in a strange language. Let me go!'

She was gorgeous.

Utterly captivated, Carlo gave her a lazy smile but didn't move an inch. He was enjoying it far too much to move. The feel of her soft, womanly body under his was fantastic. How could he ever have thought she was a boy?

He must be losing it...

Her outraged glare faded and she stared up at him, her stunning green eyes locking with his. 'Are you going to lie on top of me all night?'

Given the chance, yes.

'Is that an invitation?' Carlo knew he ought to move and help her up, but all he wanted to do was bend his head and kiss her.

So he did.

As his mouth came down on hers he hung onto her hands, fully expecting her to take another swipe at him, but after the briefest hesitation her soft lips parted and she kissed him back, sighing slightly as he used all the skill of his thirty-four years to seduce a response from her.

When he finally dragged his mouth away from hers he

felt drugged. It had only been a taste but it had been enough to make him want the whole meal.

'Wh-what did you do that for?' Those amazing green eyes were still staring up at him, and for the first time in his life Carlo found it difficult to string a coherent sentence together. His body and brain felt disconnected.

'Kiss of life,' he murmured huskily, his mind and body still focused on her mouth. 'They were pretty rough with you—I thought maybe…'

'I don't think it worked.' Her expression was slightly dazed and her voice was smoky and feminine. 'Want to try it again?'

Carlo lowered his head and kissed her thoroughly, this time releasing his grip so that he could use his hands to haul her body even closer to his.

He felt her shudder under him, felt her slim arms slide round his neck, and for endless moments he was lost in the soft, sweet wonder of her mouth.

Then he heard a shout from the pavement opposite and rolled to his feet, instantly alert.

Be discreet, his father and brother had said.

Lying on a snowy pavement kissing a gorgeous female in full view of anyone who happened to pass probably didn't qualify, he admitted ruefully, reaching down a hand to pull her up.

She staggered to her feet and then jerked her hand away as if his touch had singed her.

'I can't believe we just did that.' She backed away from him and lifted her fingers to her lips, her expression stunned. 'I can't believe I let you kiss me. You're a stranger. I don't kiss strangers.'

She looked confused and wary, and he forced himself to stand still and give her some space. He could hardly blame her for being nervous of him. After all, she'd just been mugged.

Carlo searched for the words to reassure her, but before he could speak she stooped to pick up the bin bag and winced in pain.

'Are you hurt?' He frowned, surprised and confused by the rush of possessiveness that swamped him. He didn't even know her name, but the thought that they'd hurt her filled him with red-hot anger. 'That was a nasty kick.'

He searched his brain for a non-sexual way of suggesting that he take a look at her stomach. He was a doctor after all.

'I'm OK.' She brushed her snowy dark hair away from her exquisite face. 'I suppose I've got you to thank for that.' She gave him a cautious look, still keeping herself at a safe distance. 'If you hadn't intervened he probably would have used that knife. I'm sorry I floored you. It all happened so fast I panicked. I thought you were with them.'

She still looked wary, and every muscle in her body was tense, but at least she hadn't run off.

'Don't apologise. I'm glad you floored me.' Remembering the feel of her soft body under his, he was more than glad. If she hadn't done that, he probably wouldn't have kissed her. *And, having kissed her...*

His eyes dropped hungrily to her mouth again and he wrestled with the instinct to act like a caveman and drag her somewhere quiet, where he could make love to her until she couldn't stand up.

But she was visibly nervous and he wasn't going to blow his chances by rushing her. So, instead of grabbing her, he pushed his hands firmly into his pockets and kept his distance.

'Do you always kiss people who knock you to the ground?' She was watching him carefully with those incredible eyes, as if she hadn't quite decided whether she should run or not.

'Never.'

Her fingers tightened on the bin bag. 'So why did you kiss *me*, then?'

Carlo was finding it harder and harder to breathe normally. 'Because you're stunning.'

The wariness left her face and she threw back her head and laughed aloud. 'Dressed in torn jeans and an ancient coat with a woollen hat on my head? Very sexy, I'm sure.'

'Kissing is a good way of distracting an attacker,' he drawled, unable to drag his gaze away from her gorgeous face. 'It's the element of surprise.'

'Well, I've done judo since I was six but that's a move I've never used,' she confessed, still smiling. Suddenly she seemed more relaxed. Her eyes sparkled and snow stuck to her lashes and shiny dark hair, and it occurred to him that if he could have anything he wanted for Christmas then it would be her.

Preferably unwrapped.

'Are you saying that you've never been kissed by your opponent before?' His words and eyes teased her but his body and brain were deadly serious as he moved closer. 'You've been missing out.'

Their eyes locked and she smiled hesitantly. 'It certainly takes your mind off fighting.' Suddenly her smile faded and she stared at his cheekbone in dismay. 'Oh, no! Did I do that? Have I given you a black eye?'

He didn't care about his eye. At the moment he was more concerned about other parts of his anatomy that he was finding distinctly uncomfortable. His jeans were just too tight to accommodate such an extreme reaction.

She stood on tiptoe and touched his bruised cheekbone gingerly, her voice contrite. 'We ought to get some ice on that.'

Ice. He gritted his teeth. Maybe if he thought about ice

it would help him out of his dilemma. He was reacting like a hormonal teenager.

He looked down at her. 'Are you sure you're all right? They were pretty rough with you.'

It occurred to him that, apart from being wary of him, she didn't seem particularly shaken up. He tried to think of one other woman of his acquaintance who would have fought like that and still been smiling afterwards. He failed dismally. All the women he knew panicked if they so much as chipped a nail.

'I'm OK, thanks to you. Apart from ripping my favourite jeans. I was thinking about something else or they wouldn't have taken me by surprise.' She peered at his face again, her expression guilty. 'You saved my life and in return I hit you. That never happens in the movies. I should have been sobbing with relief and gratitude, instead of which I may have given you a black eye.'

'I love a dominant woman,' Carlo drawled lightly, and she laughed.

'Next time I'll try not to panic.'

'I'm not surprised you panicked.' His expression was serious. 'But I don't think he would have used the knife.'

He said it to reassure her, in case part of her was still scared. Or maybe it was himself that he was reassuring. The thought of what might have happened if that creep had done what he'd threatened was too horrific to contemplate.

She pulled a face. 'If it hadn't been for you, he probably would.' Her tone was matter-of-fact. 'This area is notorious for muggings and other unsavoury acts. I'm lucky you were passing and bothered to help. Do you think we should call the police?'

Carlo froze. The last thing he needed was to draw attention to himself.

'I think they're long gone,' he said carefully, his expression guarded. 'And I didn't really get a good look at them, did you?'

'No.' She shook her head and he changed the subject neatly.

'What are you doing out on your own on a night like this?'

She altered her grip on the bin bag. 'I'm working.'

Working?

What sort of work required her to walk the streets at ten o'clock at night wearing worn jeans, a woolly hat and carrying a bin liner?

Surely she wasn't...

She looked up at him and started to laugh. 'I wish you could see your face! I can assure you I don't do what you're thinking! Actually, I'm a midwife,' she said, as if it was perfectly obvious to anyone but a complete idiot.

A midwife?

He'd worked with midwives for most of his adult life, but none of them had looked like her.

Carlo tried to ask her something intelligent but all he could see was that gorgeous smile that seemed to take over her whole face. Suddenly his brain and his body seemed to be ruled by a vicious rush of male hormones. He'd dated some of the most beautiful women in the world, but he couldn't remember a single one who had threatened his ability to walk in a straight line. Until now.

'Do all English midwives walk around in the dark, carrying bin liners?'

'I was trying *not* to attract attention,' she confided, and he gave a wry smile.

'I think you need more practice.'

'You might be right.' She looked sorrowfully at her torn jeans. 'They must have thought I had something exciting in my bin bag.'

'And have you?'

'Well, I haven't robbed a bank, if that's what you mean.' She chuckled and hoisted the bag towards her, twisting the neck so that the contents were safe. 'Actually, I'm on my way to see a patient. So, if you're sure your face is all right, I suppose this is where we say goodbye.'

No way!

'I'll come with you,' he said immediately. 'There's no way I should be allowed to walk these streets on my own. It's not safe.'

She looked up at him, her cheeks dimpling. 'You need my protection?'

'Absolutely.' His voice was husky and he saw her breath catch in her throat.

'You're at least six foot three and you've got more muscles than I've ever seen on one body,' she pointed out, appreciation in her eyes as they wandered over his broad shoulders. 'You tackled those guys without a second thought and you certainly don't look like a man who's afraid of much.'

Up until five minutes ago he would have agreed with her, but since the moment she'd thrown him to the floor everything had changed.

'I'm afraid of never seeing you again.'

The only sound was the soft whisper of snow as it floated past her stunned face and settled on the black wool jacket she was wearing.

When she finally spoke her voice was shaky. 'I suppose I'm meant to say that you're being ridiculous.'

He stepped closer to her, aware of just how delicate she was. Suddenly he felt fiercely protective. 'Say it, then.'

She stared up at him and he could see that she'd stopped breathing. 'I—I can't.' A look of confusion crossed her face. 'Oh, help! What are you doing to me?'

Their eyes held, the heat and tension between them almost melting the snow.

Without shifting his gaze, Carlo held out a hand, and after endless seconds she stepped towards him and took it.

He pulled her against him and stroked her snowy dark hair away from her face, thinking how beautiful she was.

She stared up at him and he could see her breathing quicken. 'I—This is crazy. I really ought to be going...'

'Me, too. Do you think we should kiss each other goodbye?' He was only a breath away from touching her mouth with his when she dipped her head and gave him a gentle push.

'What is it that you do to me? I don't behave like this! I don't even know you.'

Carlo stared down at her thoughtfully, a warm feeling spreading through his body.

He never met people who didn't know him.

In Italy, everyone knew him. His picture appeared regularly in the newspapers and gossip columns and he hated it. He hated being public property.

But to this girl he was a stranger and it was a totally novel experience.

'Everyone is a stranger the first time you meet them,' he pointed out gently, and she gave him a half-smile that betrayed her confusion.

'That's true, I suppose, but I don't usually kiss men I've only known for five minutes.'

'So I'll hang around until you've known me for longer,' Carlo said, and she rolled her eyes in exasperation.

'Are you always this persistent?'

No. He never usually needed to be. He was one of the richest men in Italy and he was usually the one tactfully keeping women at a distance.

'Look, why don't we go somewhere warm and grab a coffee or something?'

'I can't. At least, not right now.' She glanced at her watch and pulled a face. 'There's somewhere I have to be and I don't want to be too late. It's not the best of places in the middle of the day, but at night it's horrid. I meant to go earlier but I had to stay late at the hospital. I need to go and do my visit and you ought to go home and get some ice on your cheek,' she said, touching it with gentle fingers, guilt in her eyes. 'I'm really, really sorry. I wasn't thinking straight.'

'Forget it.' Carlo gave a lopsided smile, wondering where all his smooth chat-up lines had gone when he needed them. He could think of a dozen things to say to her in Italian but none at all in English. 'Just remind me never to get on the wrong side of you.'

She lifted an arm and pretended to flex her biceps. 'Scary, that's me.'

Carlo looked deep into those green eyes and decided that she definitely was scary, but not for any of the reasons she imagined.

The scariest thing of all was that even though he'd only known her for five minutes, there was no way he was letting this woman out of his sight. Part of him knew that he should walk away from her. He was involved in something nasty and he certainly didn't want her dragged into it. But he wasn't prepared to let her go even for a moment. He was going to see where this led and deal with the consequences later.

'All right, if you won't come with me then I'll have to come with you on your call, and then we can both put ice on my face together.'

As a pick-up line it was novel, but he was past caring.

He was a desperate man.

If she turned and walked away, he'd have to consider kidnapping her.

'You can't come with me on my call.' She clutched the bin bag more tightly. 'It's a professional visit. I can't just take a man I picked up on the street.'

'*I* picked *you* up,' he pointed out, and she rolled her eyes.

'Details. Details.'

He gave a lopsided smile. 'Would it help if I confessed that I'm an obstetrician?'

Her eyes widened in disbelief and she started to laugh.

He frowned at her. 'What's so funny?'

'I'm just trying to imagine any of the obstetricians I know fighting like you did.' She shook her head slightly, still laughing. 'I'm failing dismally. They're all very puny and academic. They'd have trouble wrestling with a microscope.'

He lifted an eyebrow, pretending to be offended. 'You don't think I'm academic?'

'You mean you've got all that muscle *and* a brain?' She batted her eyelids and he grinned appreciatively.

'I certainly have.' He adored her sense of humour. 'So, now do you believe I'm an obstetrician?'

'No.' Her cheeks were rosy from the cold. 'I've worked with loads of obstetricians and none of them look like you.'

Was that good or bad?

'So what's wrong with me?'

Her smile faded and he saw the uncertainty in her eyes, and something else that had a serious effect on the fit of his jeans. 'Oh, there's nothing wrong with you at all. That's what I mean.'

His blood heated and he had to stop himself grabbing her again. 'Well, until you see me in action you're just going to have to take my word for it. So, can I come?'

She tipped her head to one side. 'Well, if you're truly an obstetrician, then tell me where you work.'

'I'm doing a locum job at St Catherine's from tomorrow.'

Using a false surname that only he, his security team

and the most senior member of the hospital were aware of.

Her eyes widened. 'That's spooky! I work there, too.'

Did she, now? That was the best news he'd had for months.

'Which definitely means I can come on your visit,' he said smoothly. 'We're colleagues. And after that I'm walking you home and we can heal each other's bruises.'

Her lips parted slightly and he held his breath. If she said no, he was in big trouble.

'I—I don't know...'

The wary look was back and he gave her a smile that he hoped was non-threatening.

'Look, I know this was an unconventional meeting, but you don't need to be scared of me. If I step out of line you can always black my other eye.'

Maybe he was playing dirty by appealing to her conscience but he didn't care. He wasn't going to let her walk out of his life.

'All right.' She hauled the bag onto her shoulder and jerked her head towards a high-rise building in the next street. 'Come with me to see Kelly and then we'll go back to my place and sort your face out. It's the least I can do after having tried to half kill you.'

Resisting the impulse to punch the air in triumph, Carlo shortened his stride to match hers and followed her up seemingly endless flight of soulless concrete steps that intersected the flats.

He glanced around with a deepening frown.

No wonder she didn't like coming here at night. The place was menacing and rough. Definitely not somewhere to be after dark. Especially for a woman on her own. The walls were covered in graffiti, there were smashed windows and boarded-up doors and, even this close to Christmas, there was very little evidence of festive cheer.

The girl came to a halt in front of a door, tugged the woollen hat back on her head and stuffed her hair back underneath it.

'All part of the disguise.' She tossed him a smile that made his whole body ache, and tapped on the door.

'Kelly?' She leaned closer to the door. 'Kelly, it's Zan. Let me in.'

Zan? Carlo blinked in surprise.

What sort of a name was Zan?

He was still trying to work it out when the door jerked open and a burly man stood there.

If ever a man was looking for a fight it was this one, and instinctively Carlo straightened his shoulders and prepared himself for trouble.

What the hell was the girl doing in a place like this? This certainly wasn't his idea of midwifery.

'Hi, Mike.' Zan didn't seem remotely nervous. Instead, she just gave the man the same warm smile she'd used on him earlier and peeped round him into the flat. 'Can I see Kelly? I brought some stuff…'

She jiggled the black bin back temptingly and Mike's face darkened.

'We ain't taking no charity!'

Zan shook her head. 'Of course you're not. It isn't charity,' she said easily, her tone relaxed and friendly. 'Mothers swap clothes all the time. Someone I look after was having a clear-out—I just thought you might find it useful, but I can offer it to someone else if you prefer…'

Mike glowered at her and then opened the door wider. 'And while we're at it Kelly ain't going to hospital, so don't even think about suggesting it.' He looked over her shoulder and his eyes narrowed as they fixed on Carlo. He looked at him man to man, his eyes resting on the width of Carlo's shoulders. 'Who's he?'

Zan opened her mouth but Carlo spoke first.

'I'm a doctor. Carlo Bennett.'

He almost stumbled over the surname, because it wasn't his and he wasn't used to it yet, but it was the name that everyone had agreed he should use while he was hiding out in London. As a qualified surgeon he was actually entitled to call himself Mr, but he didn't think this was the time to worry about the finer points of titles. 'I'm going to be working in this area and Zan said I could come with her on some visits.'

Aware that Zan was staring at him, Carlo gave the other man a friendly smile and reached out a hand.

There was a moment's hesitation and then Mike shook it briefly, but his expression was still unfriendly.

'You don't look English and you don't sound English.'

'Part Italian,' Carlo lied smoothly, denying some of his heritage in the interests of discretion. Mike pulled a face, leaving no one in any doubt of what he thought of foreign doctors.

'Well, you can come in as you're here, but you might as well know that I hate doctors and I'm not having one of them near my woman. Zan's the only one I'll let look at her.'

'No problem.' Careful to be non-confrontational, Carlo strolled into the flat after Zan, trying not to show his shock as they walked into the tiny sitting room.

The room was filthy and stacked high with old newspapers and half-eaten plates of food. In the middle of the carpet a German shepherd dog lay with its head on one paw, eyes fixed warily on Carlo.

The place was damp and freezing, and in the corner was a thin wisp of a girl with a rounded stomach and skinny legs.

'Hi, Kelly.' Clearing a space on the sofa, Zan sat down and opened the bin bag. 'How are you feeling?'

Kelly glanced nervously at Mike, who gave a nod. 'I'm

doing OK,' she said in a low voice, 'but I'm pretty tired. Well, very tired, actually.'

And he would have bet half his fortune that she was anaemic, Carlo thought, running a professional eye over the patient and her surroundings. Judging from the remains of the food on the plate, she wasn't eating properly.

'I think it's possible that you may be anaemic,' Zan was saying as she delved into the bag for a blood-pressure cuff. 'That basically means that your blood isn't carrying enough oxygen. It can happen very easily when you're pregnant, especially if you don't eat properly.'

Carlo blinked with admiration. So she'd homed in on the same problem immediately.

She checked Kelly's blood pressure and then glanced at Mike. 'I really want to take a blood sample, Mike.'

'No way.' His tone was unfriendly. 'I'm not having you sticking needles in her. Just do what you have to do and leave.'

Zan's expression was understanding. 'I'm just trying to help her, Mike. She's thirty-four weeks pregnant. If she is anaemic then that could be the reason she's so tired, and we need to get it sorted out before she has the baby. I want to check the iron levels in her blood.'

'No needles.' Mike moved towards Zan and Carlo took a step forward, ready to intervene.

No way was that thug going any nearer to Zan.

'If you've got iron in your bag then just give it to her,' Carlo said smoothly, and three pairs of eyes turned to look at him.

'There's a strong chance that you are anaemic, and obviously we'd like to check that out.' He spoke directly to Kelly. 'But if you'd rather we didn't then the next best thing is to just give you the iron.'

'Will it hurt the baby?'

'It could hurt you if you don't have it,' Carlo said

gently. 'Being pregnant and giving birth to a child place huge demands on your body. We need to correct it or you could have problems during your delivery and you'll be exhausted afterwards. When you come into the hospital we—'

'She ain't coming into the hospital!' Mike growled, and Zan cleared her throat.

'Don't let's worry about that now. You've got my number, and you know that I'll deliver Kelly any time you want me to, anywhere you want me to, but we really do need her to take some iron.' She reached into her bag and pulled out a bottle of tablets. 'Will you take one a day for me?'

Kelly glanced at Mike for approval before taking the bottle, and he gave a brief nod.

'And now can I just check the position of the baby?'

'Not with him in the room.' Mike glared at Carlo, who strolled towards the living-room door immediately.

'I'll wait in the hallway.'

Whatever had happened to the man to make him so suspicious?

Five minutes later Zan called him back in.

Her eyes were troubled as they met his. 'I don't think the baby is growing quite as fast as it should—She's small for thirty-four weeks.'

Carlo lifted his eyes to Mike. 'Can I examine her?'

'No!'

'Mike, please?' Zan's voice was soft and reassuring and Mike hesitated, his jaw set.

Finally he nodded. 'All right.' He glared at Carlo. 'But I'm watching you.'

'That's fine.' Carlo moved his hands skilfully over the mother's abdomen, thinking that he'd never seen such a half-starved waif in his life. Normally he dealt with the pampered wives of the hideously wealthy, and the contrast was extreme. As he examined the girl he realised just how bored he'd become, working in his world-famous Women's Unit in Milan. The case he was seeing now presented so much more of a challenge, both medically and socially.

'Well?'

Mike was looking at him threateningly and Carlo picked up the tape measure that Zan had used and measured Kelly from the top of the bump to her pelvic bone. The measurement was supposed to correlate roughly to the number of weeks of pregnancy, but in this case Zan was right. The baby seemed small.

'Do you smoke?'

Kelly shook her head, but her eyes slid nervously to Mike and Carlo deduced that the man probably smoked heavily and that she was therefore subjecting the baby to passive smoking.

'The baby does seem slightly smaller than we would like,' he said gently, talking directly to Kelly. 'Ideally I'd like to get you to come to the hospital for a series of scans. Nothing scary. We just slide a clever device that's basically a camera over your stomach and we're able to measure the size of the baby's head. That gives us an indication of what size the baby should be, and we can then take a look at the rest of him.'

Kelly glanced at Mike, who shook his head.

'She's not going to hospital.'

Carlo frowned. 'But—'

'That's fine,' Zan interrupted quickly, shooting Carlo a warning look. 'But if you change your mind then come and see us any time. I brought you some clothes, Kelly.'

She delved into the bin bag again and pulled out another bag full of tiny baby clothes, vests and a gorgeous blanket.

Carlo's eyes narrowed.

If those clothes were second-hand then he was an Englishman.

Kelly gave a gasp and her face suddenly shone like the sun coming out from behind a cloud.

'Someone was giving this away?' She fingered one of the outfits in disbelief and Zan smiled.

'They were no use to her.'

Oh, sure.

'But they're like new.' Kelly looked at Mike, her expression pleading. 'Can I keep them—please?'

Carlo found himself holding his breath and finally Mike nodded. 'I suppose so,' he muttered.

'Oh, and I've had a word with the council,' Zan said casually, 'and they're trying to rehouse you in a flat on the first floor.'

Kelly looked at her with hope in her eyes. 'Really?' Her slim shoulders sagged slightly. 'I just can't let myself get excited in case it doesn't happen.'

'It will happen, Kelly,' Zan said firmly. 'There's no way you can stay here. The weather is getting colder, the flat is damp and there's fourteen flights of stairs between you and the ground floor. How are you going to manage that with a baby when the lift's out of order? I've been talking to Social Services about rehousing you and they're doing their best.'

Carlo listened to her and wondered if the couple had any idea how lucky they were to have Zan to fight their corner.

'She can take the tablets, but she ain't coming to hospital for that scan thing,' Mike said, and Zan looked him in the eye.

'The baby isn't big enough, Mike. We really need to—'

'Get out!'

Kelly flinched and shrank back into her chair.

Carlo's eyes narrowed slightly and he drew himself up to his full height, preparing himself for trouble.

'We're leaving,' Zan said calmly, smiling at Mike as though he hadn't just yelled at her in the rudest way possible. 'We'll talk about it again next time.'

'She ain't going to the hospital and that's final.'

Zan stood up. 'That's fine, Mike.' She turned to look at Kelly, her gaze direct. 'Any problems, call me.'

With that she looked meaningfully at Carlo and walked out of the flat with him following close behind.

CHAPTER TWO

'DOES he hit her?' Carlo followed her down the dark staircase and back onto the streets.

'I don't think so.' Zan turned sharp left and then right down a wide road that stretched along the river. 'I think he's just very controlling.'

'And why does he hate hospitals so much?'

'He's never told me, and I don't push it or I won't get to see Kelly at all.' She glanced sideways and tried not to stare.

She'd never met anyone as strikingly good-looking as Carlo before. Tall, dark-haired and loaded with sex appeal, he exuded a strength and confidence that was magnetic. If she'd had to pick one word to describe him, it would have been *male*. Carlo was very, *very* male.

And he had good shoulders.

She remembered the weight of his body when he'd lain on top of her and smiled slightly. For once she could walk home without worrying.

Who in their right mind would pick a fight with him?

Carlo was frowning. 'Do you have to visit them?'

'Well, if I don't then she gets no antenatal care whatsoever,' Zan told him, crossing over the road so that they could walk next to the river. Fairy lights had been strung between the trees and their reflection danced over the surface of the water. 'Social Services first told me that she was pregnant, but she hasn't seen a doctor once in her whole pregnancy. To start with Mike wouldn't let me in, but I've worked on him and now I get to see her. I'm hoping that if she sees enough of me I'll be able to get her to trust me.'

'She needs a biophysical assessment,' Carlo said, and Zan nodded.

He was referring to an established technique using ultrasound to look at the baby and to measure the heart-rate.

'I know. The truth is she needs a lot of things she isn't getting. It's very worrying, but we can only do the best we can. It's hard enough getting access at all.'

She felt his eyes slide over her. 'Presumably that's why you dress like that? Because they're suspicious of authority?'

He was smart; she'd give him that.

'That's true, but I also hate walking around this area at night,' she confessed. 'I might be a black belt in judo but I'm not stupid. If I have to do it then I dress down and I wear trainers. If anyone suspected I was medical they'd be attacking me for drugs.'

'It isn't a suitable place for a woman to be working.' His gaze darkened ominously and she chuckled.

'Are you always this macho?'

'Of course.' Carlo's arrogant dark head lifted and a wry smile touched his handsome face. 'I'm Italian, remember? Despite our efforts to be politically correct, deep down we still expect our women to stay at home and warm the bed for us.'

The mention of bed brought a faint colour to her cheeks. Whoever warmed his bed would be a *very* lucky woman, but she wasn't telling him that. 'Someone must have forgotten to tell you that this is the twenty-first century.'

He didn't smile, his gaze disturbingly direct. 'It's not a safe area for you to work in.'

He was breathtakingly good-looking and Zan was finding it hard to peel her eyes away from him.

'I work here because it's challenging and I'm really doing some good.' She looked at him curiously. 'This isn't what you're used to, is it? You looked pretty shocked when you saw the flat.'

He pulled a face and rubbed a hand across the back of his neck. 'Was it that obvious?'

'Only to me. Don't worry about it. I was pretty shocked myself when I first came here after twenty years of middle-class upbringing. It's a real eye-opener. Lots of teenage pregnancies, lots of unmarried mothers with several children by different men, and every flat you visit has a German shepherd dog the size of a wolf.' She stepped gingerly over a patch of ice. 'I suppose I'd have one, too, if I lived in this area. The dogs used to be the worst part of the job for me, but generally I've got used to them. Do you have dogs at home?'

He hesitated and then nodded. 'Yes, dogs don't bother me. So, why did you learn judo?'

Zan smiled and huddled more deeply into her coat to keep out the cold. 'I have four older brothers. My father was going for a five-a-side rugby team but then they had me.' She shrugged. 'Anyway, they all decided that I needed to know how to take care of myself just in case they weren't around to do it for me.'

'Sensible.'

'No, massively over-protective,' she said dryly. 'They've scared off every boyfriend I've ever had.'

Carlo looked at her curiously. 'But you're close?'

'I adore them,' she said simply. 'Growing up with four big brothers was just the best thing in the world. We had such fun.'

'But they've taught you to be wary of men?'

She hesitated for a moment and then nodded. 'Yes. Yes, they have. I may love my brothers but I'd hate to be anything other than their baby sister. They're rogues, and when they were growing up they treated women appallingly. I've learned lots about men by watching them. And because they know exactly how men think and act, they scare off anyone male who shows an interest in me.'

'Ouch.' Carlo gave a rueful smile and glanced around him at the dark shadows. 'So can I expect to be pounced on any moment?'

Zan looked at his shoulders and laughed. 'I don't think you've got much to worry about. So, now you know about me, how about you? All I know is that you're part-Italian. What I want to know is, which part?'

He shot her a suggestive smile that was so sexy she almost stopped breathing.

'If you're good, I'll show you later.'

His teasing drawl made her blush, but she couldn't help smiling. There was something so good-humoured and honest about him.

'Well, judging from your slight accent and the fact that you were muttering something incomprehensible when you were lying on top of me, I assume that Italian is your first language. Which must mean that you live over there usually. So what are you doing in London?'

'Having a change from Italy.' His answer was so smooth and glib that she looked at him closely, wondering if he was hiding something. He caught her look and smiled. 'Plenty of doctors from EC countries come and work in England. It isn't unusual.'

'So where were you working last?'

'In a private clinic outside Milan.' He gave a rueful smile. 'Most of my patients were nothing like Kelly, I'm afraid.'

'Too posh to push?'

He smiled in appreciation. 'Something like that.'

'Well, it was decent of you to take a look at Kelly for me.' She glanced at him. 'Don't think I don't know that most doctors would have refused. Too worried about litigation.'

Carlo looked unconcerned. 'I'm well insured.'

And very experienced and self-confident. She also suspected that he would never refuse to help a patient. He was that type of man.

'This is where I live.' Zan stopped outside a block of flats and Carlo leaned against the wall, his eyes watchful.

'So…' he drawled softly. 'Are you going to invite me up?'

She stared at him, caught by the intensity of his gaze. Excitement curled in the pit of her stomach and she struggled to be sensible.

'I don't usually invite strangers up to my flat.'

His smile had a peculiar effect on her knees and she felt them wobble alarmingly. 'I'm very glad to hear that.' He moved fractionally closer to her, his eyes never leaving hers. 'But we've already kissed twice and spent an evening together so we're not exactly strangers.'

She laughed to disguise her awareness of him.

'We spent the evening in a filthy flat with a man who wanted to hit both of us. Is that your idea of a perfect first date?'

'It was different,' he admitted, his gaze dropping to her mouth and lingering there. 'You can trust me, Zan.'

She hesitated, common sense wrestling with temptation.

'I don't know anything about you.'

Except that he was strong, clever and stunningly good-looking.

'What do you want to know?' He smiled down at her. 'I'm Italian, I'm an obstetrician, I have one older brother and one younger sister. I also have a black eye.'

She smiled back and then looked at him cautiously. 'You're not married?'

His gaze didn't shift from hers. 'No wife. No kids.'

She bit her lip. Would it be such a big mistake to invite him up?

She paused a moment longer and then made up her mind. She pushed open the swing doors and led him into the deserted entrance hall. 'I'm on the top floor.'

They walked towards the lift and she pressed the button, watching the lift doors close and wondering what on earth she was doing, taking a total stranger back to her flat.

Was she mad?

Her brothers would have thrown a fit.

But then she'd spent most of the past twenty-four years being cautious, and frankly she was getting impatient with herself. It was time she lived a little. Time she trusted her own instincts.

And her instincts about Carlo were all good.

She loved his wicked sense of humour, the way the corners of his eyes creased when he smiled, and she loved his easy confidence. There was something about him that was tough and kind and, no matter how much she tried to pretend otherwise, the fact that he'd stepped in and rescued her made her insides squishy. It might not be politically correct to have a tough man looking after you but the truth was it had felt good.

Better than good.

It would be a long time before she forgot the feel of that hard muscle pressing her down onto the snowy pavement or the taste of his warm lips as he'd kissed her.

She shivered slightly with nerves and excitement as she remembered that kiss. Until tonight she'd always thought that kissing was a very overrated pastime.

She'd obviously been kissing the wrong men.

She sneaked a sideways look at him, still finding it hard to believe that he was a doctor. All the doctors she'd ever met were mild-mannered and academic or just plain arrogant. Carlo was none of those things. He was all muscle and strength, mixed with a wickedly sexy sense of humour.

He intercepted her look and gave her a smile that reminded her of his kiss. Hot and exciting.

She dragged some air into her lungs and leaned against the wall of the lift for support. If all Italian men looked like him she was moving to Italy.

The lift pinged as it arrived at her floor and she made an effort to stand upright.

'You'd better prepare yourself,' she warned him as she scrabbled in her pocket for the key. 'I call it the penthouse because it's on the top floor and the view are great, but trust me when I say that the resemblance ends there. When I win the Lottery I'm buying something bigger. You can't swing a cat in here...'

She pushed the key in the lock and then paused, aware that he was staring at her oddly. 'What? What have I said?'

'Why would you want to *swing* a cat?' His accent was marked as he repeated her words. 'I thought you English were supposed to like animals?'

'We do. Well, some of us do.' Zan grinned. 'It's just an expression.'

His eyes gleamed. 'Totally incomprehensible language. I thought my English was good, but evidently I still have a lot to learn.'

Carlo had gorgeous eyes—very dark brown and fringed with sinfully thick, dark lashes that he used to hide his expression when it suited him. And it suited him often. She suspected that he wasn't an easy man to read.

'Don't worry—I'll teach you.' Zan opened the door and walked into her flat, flicking on the light.

The pale wooden floor was covered in plastic packets and bags from various shops, and she shot him an embarrassed look as she started to scoop them all up.

'You needn't hide the packaging from me,' he said, his

tone amused. 'I was well aware that all that baby stuff you gave her was brand-new.'

She clutched the evidence to her chest and looked at him in dismay. 'Oh, no! I tried to rumple them and make them look old. Do you think they guessed?'

'I think Kelly was too pleased to notice.' He moved closer to her and removed one of the plastic wrappers from her grasp, lifting an eyebrow as he saw the price. 'Do you always spend your money on your patients?'

She blushed and snatched the wrapper back. 'No. Well, sometimes. I like Kelly and I feel sorry for her.'

He looked at her for a long moment and she felt the breath jam in her throat. Just looking at him made her legs shaky.

As if he'd guessed her thoughts, he gave a lopsided smile and strolled over to the huge windows that made up one wall of her tiny flat.

'Fantastic view.'

'Thanks.' She tugged the hat off her head and shook her dark hair like a kitten in a rainstorm. *Typical. She had a man to die for in her flat and she looked as though she'd been dunked in a puddle.* 'I've never bothered with curtains. No one can see in so it didn't seem worth it.'

'It's a nice flat.'

She smiled. 'Well, like I said, it's the penthouse, but when I win the Lottery I'm buying a bigger version.'

For a moment he didn't respond, and then he turned, a strange light in his eyes. 'You do the Lottery? Is money important to you?'

'No.' She tossed the rubbish into the bin and smiled cheerfully. 'Just what it buys. I love to dream, don't you?'

He sucked in a breath and looked taken aback. 'Well, I...'

'Oh, come on!' She tugged off her boots and coat and dropped onto the sofa, cross-legged. 'Everyone dreams of winning the Lottery. Even people who never remember to do it!'

He was looking at her curiously, arms folded across his broad chest. 'So what would you buy?'

'I don't know, the usual things…' She shrugged. 'A house in a better area, a car so that I don't have to walk around at night.'

'Would you give up your job?'

'Oh, no!' Her expression was horrified. 'I love my job. And just think, if I won money I'd be able to rehouse Kelly and Mike without having to bow and scrape to Social Services all the time.'

Carlo turned back to the window. 'You'd have a job to beat this view.'

'Nice, isn't it? They've converted so much of the Docklands area into housing and it's a pretty good place to live.' She glanced round her with satisfaction. She liked her flat. It was small, but it was cosy and homely and all hers. 'Make the most of it. It's pretty small now, but after tomorrow it's going to get even smaller.'

'What's happening tomorrow?' He moved away from the window and strolled towards her.

'I'm buying my Christmas tree,' she said proudly, 'and it's going to be *big*.'

'Ah.' He folded his arms across his chest and his sexy dark eyes twinkled at her. 'So size matters to you?'

'In Christmas trees, definitely.' Zan was laughing at the innuendo and trying to control the frantic fluttering in her stomach. 'I love everything about Christmas. I used to buy my tree on the first day of December, but the needles always fell off by Christmas Day and I got fed up with staring at decorated twigs so now I make myself wait. It's an exercise in self-discipline. What about you? Do you like Christmas?'

He hesitated and then nodded. 'I suppose so.'

'But you're sad because you won't be at home this year?' She tilted her head on one side and looked at him. 'I know the feeling. I'm working this Christmas so I won't be able to get home until New Year. But I've written my letter to Santa and he knows I'm here so all my presents should still arrive.'

He leaned broad shoulders against the wall and watched her, and she was breathlessly aware of how big he seemed in her tiny flat.

Big and male.

'You've written to Santa?'

'Of course! I've sent him my list. How else will he know what I want?' She ticked them off on her fingers. 'Diamond earrings, cashmere jumper, silky underwear—you know the sort of thing.'

'Diamond earrings?' His gaze slid down to her torn jeans. 'You don't strike me as a diamond earrings sort of girl.'

'Don't judge by appearances. I've never been given the chance,' she told him gloomily. 'With four brothers my childhood was all rugby boots and Action Man. Every single Christmas I'd get the same stuff as them. Don't get me wrong. My parents are great and I love them. But somewhere along the line they forgot I was a girl. I would have given anything for something pink and girly.'

He blinked. 'Pink and girly?'

'You know, something feminine. What about you? What do you want for Christmas?'

There was a long silence, and when he finally spoke his gaze was disturbingly direct. 'You.' He spoke the word softly and then paused, his dark eyes holding hers. 'I want you, Zan.'

There was a hot, pulsing silence and she stared at him, her heart in her mouth and her palms damp.

His words shocked and excited her and for a moment

she had no idea how to respond. The truth was she wanted him too, but the feeling scared her.

She'd only known him for one evening.

'I don't do one-night stands.'

'Good.' His dark eyes didn't shift from hers. 'I'm not interested in just one night.'

She looked into those stunning dark eyes and felt her insides tumble. Suddenly overwhelmed by his directness and the intensity of her own feelings, she jumped to her feet and looked at him nervously.

He was so different from the men she normally mixed with. They seemed younger somehow. More boyish. But there was nothing boyish about Carlo. He was all man. A man who knew exactly what he wanted and went straight for it.

And she couldn't forget the way he kissed.

'Where did you come from?' She wrapped her arms around her middle defensively. 'I mean, one minute my life is thoroughly predictable and full of men who bore me to tears and then the next...'

He lifted a dark eyebrow and prompted her gently, his Italian accent suddenly pronounced, 'The next?'

Her heart was hammering in her chest. She didn't know which was sexier, the tone of his voice or the look in his eyes. 'The next I find myself lying on the pavement, kissing a total stranger.'

'Is that a complaint?' His dark eyes teased her and her breath came in little pants.

'Not exactly. I'm just not used to kissing in the street in front of an audience.'

'But now we have no audience.' He gave a smile that sent her pulse racing and she lost her nerve and took a step backwards.

'Do you want coffee?'

'No.' He moved towards her, standing so close she could feel the warmth from his body against hers.

Zan's heart was pounding frantically. Just remembering what his kiss had felt like was enough to make her knees start to tremble. He was breathtakingly attractive.

But she shouldn't be kissing men she didn't know.

Her eyes dropped to his mouth and her lips parted in breathless anticipation.

Or maybe she should.

Still unsure, she gave him a nervous smile. 'I still haven't put ice on your eye.'

'Right now it isn't my eye that needs the ice.' He pulled her against him and lowered his head, their breath mingling as his mouth hovered above hers.

She shivered with expectation, waiting for him to kiss her, the excitement and anticipation stealing every breath from her body. His lips brushed hers, teasing her lightly, and he gave her a wicked smile, fully aware of the tension he was creating between them.

And then finally he kissed her properly.

And this time the kiss was different.

What they'd shared on the pavement had been exploratory and fun, but this—this was a purposeful seduction, and Zan realised immediately that if this was how kissing could feel then she'd never been kissed before.

Carlo kissed as though he'd invented excitement. The touch of his mouth was a wholly sexual experience that swamped her inexperienced body with unfamiliar sensations of such intensity that she squirmed against him in a purely female plea for satisfaction.

His mouth still on hers, he lifted her arms and wrapped them around his neck and then pulled her hard against him, his tongue delving into her mouth with devastating thoroughness, encouraging her more hesitant response.

It was the most intimate experience of her life. The

skilled sweep of his tongue, the hard ridge of his erection pressed against her and the pounding of her heart against her breastbone.

She breathed in his scent, felt the roughness of his jaw against her, tasted his maleness and felt overwhelmed by a fevered desperation that defied logic.

His touch was totally addictive and when he finally dragged his mouth away from hers she sucked in some air, so shaken by her own reaction that she couldn't bring herself to look him in the eye.

She'd never been kissed by anyone as skilled as him before.

He slid his strong fingers through her hair and tilted her head so that she was forced to look at him.

His dark eyes shimmered with raw hunger, but he veiled it quickly and gave a lopsided smile.

'I don't think we'd better do that for too long, *cara mia*,' he said dryly. 'We might both explode.'

Totally blown away by his kiss, Zan tried to speak and failed.

He touched her cheek with a gentle finger. 'You know what?' He was totally relaxed and easy with himself. 'I could really do with taking a shower. My jeans are soaked because someone threw me on my back in a puddle.'

She loved the way he took the seriousness out of every situation. 'You're joking! Who would do an evil thing like that?'

'I can't imagine, but when I track them down they're going to be punished.' He pulled her against him and gave her another lingering kiss. 'Maybe we should get out of these wet clothes before we both freeze. Can I put my jeans in your tumble-drier and take a shower?'

She nodded and gestured towards the kitchen. 'It's through there. Help yourself.'

His eyes were very dark. 'Are you going to join me?'

No.

Resolving to be more daring was all very well, but you couldn't change the habit of a lifetime in an hour!

It was all too fast.

Zan shook her head and he gave her a warm smile and strolled into her kitchen, emerging moments later with an apologetic look on his face and his jeans dangling from one hand.

'I don't know how to use a tumble-drier.'

Carlo's humble confession broke the ice and she laughed, trying not to look at his tanned, strong legs. He had an incredible physique—athletic and powerful.

No wonder the muggers had run.

'More of the macho Italian guy stuff, I suppose? Who does your washing at home? Or maybe I shouldn't ask that question.'

'I have a housekeeper,' he told her, and she walked over to him and took the wet jeans out of his hand, still keeping her eyes averted.

'Well, she hasn't trained you very well.' She popped them into the tumble-drier, turned the dial and started the machine. 'I assume you know how the shower works, or does your housekeeper do that bit, too?'

His midnight-dark eyes gleamed wickedly. 'I'm OK with the shower, but I've never really got the hang of undressing myself.'

No man should be allowed to have a smile that sexy. It had a lethal effect on her pulse-rate.

'Well, if you don't want another black eye you'd better learn quickly,' she said, ignoring his laughter and hurrying past him. 'I'll fetch you a towel.'

The shower was running by the time she returned with the towel and she half opened the door and talked through the crack.

'I'll leave the towel on the floor.'

'Pardon?' His voice was muffled from the water and she leaned in slightly further, averting her eyes from the shower cubicle.

'I said I'll leave the towel on the floor.'

'I can't hear you.'

She sidled in a bit further and strong arms grabbed her and hauled her under the steaming jet of water.

'You pig!' Laughing and squealing, she thumped him hard, spluttering and screwing up her eyes against the water. 'What are you *doing*?'

'Economising on water.' He was laughing, too, and she gasped as he pulled her close and kissed her, ignoring the water that was raining down on both of them.

She leaned into him and kissed him back, and suddenly the laughter stopped and the kissing intensified until their mouths fused hungrily, the chemistry a living, powerful force between them.

Her whole body was singing with excitement and suddenly she was breathlessly aware of his arousal and the fact that he was totally naked.

An unbearable ache was building between her thighs, but when she felt his fingers on the zip of her soaked jeans she reached down and grabbed his hands, stopping him.

What was she doing?

His skill and experience had her at flashpoint in seconds, but the speed with which he could reduce her to a shivering mass of desperation made her nervous. She'd only ever kissed boys before and Carlo certainly wasn't that. He was a fully adult male and he wasn't playing games.

'Wait—it's too fast...' The water was streaming over her hair and down her back and he reached out a hand to stem the flow, speaking softly to her in Italian as he held her against him.

'You want me to stop?' He switched to English and she struggled to control her response.

'Yes— No…' She was shaking against him and he gave a groan and slid a warm hand over her back.

'Have you any idea how much I want you?'

Zan gave him a shaky smile, breathlessly aware of his masculinity. *He had a fantastic body.* His confidence with his own sexuality was in complete contrast to her own inexperience and she felt completely out of her depth.

From the moment she'd stared into his eyes in the snowy street she'd decided that even if she only had sex once in her whole life, she wanted it to be with this man. But now that the moment had come she felt hideously unsure.

Carlo probably thought that any woman who was prepared to kiss him in a public place was equally experienced and relaxed about sex.

She was still panicking when she felt a warm, soft towel draped around her shoulders.

'Take off your wet jeans and go and put on your least provocative outfit,' Carlo said, his voice infinitely gentle as he stepped back and let her step out of the shower.

She bit her lip and looked at him anxiously. 'I…thought we were going to…'

'Well, we're not,' he said softly. 'At least, not yet. You're not totally sure and I *want* you to be totally sure.'

She hesitated and shook her head, painfully self-conscious. 'It's just a bit fast. I don't know you— I can't—'

'So we slow it down.'

He made it sound perfectly simple and she looked at him shyly, surprised that he wasn't more annoyed with her. 'And you're OK with that?'

'Well, I'll need a lot of cold showers,' he admitted ruefully, 'but we've already agreed that if I step out of line you can black my other eye, so I'll do my best to hold back as long as I can. Now, go and get dressed quickly.'

When Zan arrived back in the sitting room Carlo had the towel wrapped around his hips, his black hair damp and tousled from the shower as he flicked through her CD collection.

'Carlo.' She came to a halt in front of him, her smile hesitant. 'Are you angry?'

He glanced up. 'Of course not.' He seemed surprised by the question. 'Why would I be?'

Zan thought of all the conversations she'd overheard when her brothers hadn't known she was listening, and bit her lip.

'Because I made you think that I... I'm sorry if you thought I... I didn't mean to lead you on...'

Ebony brows came together in a frown. 'You are always entitled to say no, *cara mia*.'

'But I didn't want to say no,' she said quickly, a blush touching her cheek. 'Not exactly. But it all seemed a bit quick and— I know you're very confident, but, you see, I've never actually done it before.'

She broke off, painfully aware of the stunned expression in his gorgeous eyes.

She should never have told him.

The silence seemed to stretch for ever, and when he finally spoke his voice was rough.

'Then I'm doubly pleased that your first time wasn't in a shower, *tesoro*. We can do a great deal better than that when the time comes.'

She looked at him, her heart missing a beat as the warmth in his eyes and the full implication of his words hit her.

'You still want to?'

'What do you think?' Carlo moved towards her and cupped her face in his hands. 'I'm sorry if I moved too fast. It never occurred to me that—'

'I didn't want to tell you. I thought it might put you off,' she muttered, and he laughed.

'In that case, you have a great deal to learn about Italian men, *cara mia*.' He looked into her face, smug male satisfaction reflected in his dark eyes. 'We are a hideously jealous, possessive race. We are not good at sharing. We like a woman to be ours and ours alone.'

His alone.

The thought sent heat flaring through Zan and she pulled away from him. 'I'll see if your trousers are dry.'

He followed her to the kitchen, leaning broad shoulders against the doorway as he watched her.

'I cannot believe that you're still a virgin,' he observed, lush dark lashes shielding his gorgeous eyes. 'Your brothers obviously did a good job at protecting you.'

She reached into the tumble-drier and dragged out his trousers. 'Every time a boy became remotely interested in me they worked really hard to scare him off. Amazing teamwork and family unity. They succeeded every time.'

He lifted an eyebrow. 'And the men in question were willing to be scared off?'

She handed him the trousers and their fingers brushed together. 'I suppose they were boys, really, and my brothers must have been pretty daunting.'

'And what about now you're grown-up?'

'Now they just rely on my natural wariness to keep me out of mischief.' She looked at him anxiously, suddenly aware that she'd only known him for a few hours. How had she ever let him so close to her so quickly?

'It's OK, Zan.' His voice was incredibly gentle. 'I don't go off with women I've just met either. We'll take this slowly and see where it ends up.'

The thought of where it might end up sent her stomach dropping to the floor.

'Do you want some coffee?'

Maybe caffeine would clear her mind.

'What sort of coffee?' His gorgeous eyes narrowed and he looked at her suspiciously. 'At home we clean floors with what you English call coffee.'

She stuck her chin in the air and gave him a superior look. 'I'll have you know I make the best cappuccino in London—'

'Well, that isn't saying much— Ouch!' He winced as she thumped him and his eyes creased with humour. 'In that case, I'll put my jeans on while you make it.'

She made two steaming mugs of cappuccino, tipped some home-made shortbread onto a plate and walked back into the living room.

Carlo sprawled on the cushions by the floor-to-ceiling window, staring down at the Thames.

There was something peaceful and Christmassy about the lights sparkling along the bank, and he relished the fact that for a rare moment in time no one actually knew where he was.

There was going to be hell to pay later.

'I always love London at night.' Zan knelt down next to him and handed him the coffee. 'It's magical, isn't it? And you can't see the grime.'

'All cities are grimy in the day. You should see Milan— smoggy and noisy.' Carlo took a sip of coffee and looked at her in surprise. 'Mmm. You're right, you do make good coffee. This is excellent.'

He'd given up trying to find a decent cup of coffee in England, but she'd managed to produce one.

Maybe it was an omen.

She'd changed into another pair of jeans and a soft cream jumper that just seemed to make her more huggable. She was soft and womanly and so *alive* that everything about her made him smile.

And her shy confession had affected him deeply.

He'd never been with anyone as inexperienced as her before.

'Come here.' He put his coffee down and reached for her, trying to keep his tone neutral and unthreatening. Inside he was a raging mass of male hormones but he had no intention of letting her see that.

He was already feeling guilty that he'd pushed her too far in the shower.

Without the slightest hesitation she snuggled into his arms and they lay together on the cushions, staring out of the window.

She was so trusting.

Carlo felt an uncomfortable twist of guilt at the knowledge that he was deceiving her. On the other hand he couldn't deny that he was enjoying the fact that she didn't know who he was.

She lifted her head and looked at him, a touch of shyness in her twinkling eyes.

'You like my coffee?'

He liked everything about her.

Unable to resist her, he gave a groan and rolled her back onto the cushions, shifting so that he was lying on top of her. Careful to keep his weight off her, he lowered his head and took her mouth, exploring its sweetness, trying to keep the kiss light and teasing.

He failed.

Zan's response to his kiss was so hot and eager that desire ripped through him and he took the kiss a stage further. With every skilled stroke of his tongue he felt her trembling increase and the hand resting on her ribcage felt the rapid pounding of her heart.

The knowledge that she wanted him as badly as he wanted her did nothing for his self-control and he slid his hand under the hem of her jumper and felt her skin, warm and soft under the tips of his fingers. She gasped against his mouth as his fingers found her nipples and he felt his erection throb within the confines of his jeans.

Next time he met up with Zan, he *definitely* wouldn't be wearing jeans.

Aware that he was testing his self-control to its limits, he dragged his mouth away from hers, moved his hand and sucked in some air.

If kissing her drove him this wild then what was going to happen when he finally made love to her?

Out of breath, and shaken by the whole experience of kissing Zan, he rolled onto his back, taking her with him, trying to make sense of the way he felt.

She burrowed into his chest and then finally she lifted her head and looked at him, shyness and question mingling in her green eyes.

'Why did you stop?'

Was she really that innocent?

Carlo gave a wry smile. 'Why do you think?'

Her eyes widened and her cheeks flushed pink. 'You wanted me?'

'You could say that.'

But it would have been an understatement.

'You're an amazing kisser.'

He was tempted to suggest that she sample the rest of his skills, but he didn't want to hear her say no a second time that night.

'You're incredibly good to kiss.'

'Do you know that you talk in Italian when you kiss? You sort of murmur against my mouth and it's so sexy.'

She was all tousled and warm from his kiss and he wondered if his erection was ever going to subside.

'It's my first language,' he reminded her, grateful that she didn't speak it. He'd said some things that would have probably have made her run a mile.

'I love your accent,' she said dreamily, putting her chin

on her palm and staring at him with those huge green eyes. 'Say something to me in Italian now. Go on—anything.'

He kept his face serious. 'Cappuccino.'

'Oh, very funny.' She rested a hand on his chest and he reached for her and pulled her on top of him.

'*Io voglio te,*' he said softly, and she looked at him curiously.

'What does that mean?'

I want you.

But he shouldn't be telling her that. He wasn't in a position to offer her anything except trouble and hurt.

Suddenly feeling hideously guilty for taking advantage of her, Carlo pulled her close, his voice gruff as he spoke. 'It means you're a pretty sexy chick.'

'Does it?' She chuckled and leaned forward to kiss him. 'I'm obviously going to have to learn Italian. Will you teach me?'

'I can think of other things I'd rather teach you.' He smiled at her, thinking that she was the most gorgeous woman he'd ever seen.

Flushed and sparkly-eyed and full of humour and warmth.

He never, ever wanted to give her up.

He frowned at his own thoughts. Of course he'd want to give her up eventually. Commitment was the very last thing on his agenda. Circumstances meant that he'd ceased to trust women long ago and he was incredibly wary of relationships.

But this was different because she didn't know who he was.

'You look serious all of a sudden.' Zan looked up at him, her eyes concerned.

He forced a smile. 'I was just thinking that I start a new job in six hours.'

And his security people would be out there combing the streets for him.

She gasped and glanced at the clock. 'I'd forgotten about work. You'd better go!'

He bent his head and kissed her gently. 'Maybe I don't want to go.'

'Well, you can't turn up at the hospital wearing my clothes,' she teased, her eyes slightly shy as she looked at him. 'Even if you don't sleep, surely you need to go home and get changed. Where is home, by the way?'

He hesitated and then rolled away from her. 'I'm staying somewhere temporary at the moment—nowhere special.'

His brother's three-million-pound penthouse apartment overlooking Hyde Park.

'Right.' She gave him a sympathetic look. 'Well, that's not very nice over Christmas. You need a home, not somewhere temporary.'

He pulled his jumper over his head and stared at her. 'What are you suggesting?'

She gave a nervous shrug. 'You could stay here.' The minute the words had left her mouth she wrapped her arms around herself and bit her lip. 'Forget I said that.'

'What if I don't want to forget it?'

She covered her face with her hands and shook her head. 'I don't know myself when I'm with you. I'm doing really strange things. Like inviting you up to my flat when you're a total stranger and inviting you for Christmas. I've gone crazy.'

He couldn't think of a better way to spend Christmas than moving in with Zan and being surrounded by her warmth and laughter and her incredible body.

But he couldn't do it.

His life was just too complicated at the moment. Complicated and dangerous and he wouldn't put her at risk.

And he could see that she was really confused about the strength of her own feelings.

Carlo stepped forward and gently pulled her hands away from her face. 'As you said earlier, we probably need to slow the pace a little. Let's see how it goes, shall we?'

She hesitated, and then gave a smile that was just a little too bright. 'Good idea.'

He sighed and covered her soft lips with a finger. 'I know what you're thinking and you're wrong. You're thinking that when I walk out of this door that's going to be it.'

Colour touched her cheekbones. 'I've got four brothers,' she muttered. 'I know all the lines they use.'

Zan was incredibly brave and dignified, but he had enough experience with women to know that she was as attracted to him as he was to her.

'I'm not using any of those lines,' Carlo said firmly, ignoring the flash of guilt that exploded inside him.

He *was* deceiving her.

And he probably ought to walk away from her and never see her again because he wasn't in a position to give this woman anything but grief.

But he wasn't going to do that.

He had to see her again.

'Where the hell have you been?'

Carlo glanced at Matteo Parini, his long-time friend and his father's chief of security. 'I went for a walk.'

He shrugged his shoulders out of his coat.

'For five hours?'

'Calm down, Matt, or you'll have a stroke,' Carlo said mildly. 'I left a message on your mobile.'

'Five hours ago!!'

'So?' Carlo gave a shrug. 'I met a girl.'

A girl who had no idea who he was.

For possibly the first time in his life Carlo was sure that a woman was interested in him for himself alone, and he found the knowledge oddly satisfying. Zan didn't know anything about his money.

There was an ominous silence and Matt stiffened with disbelief. '*A girl?* You've been in London for one evening and already you've met someone? That's fast, even for you.'

Not just someone.

The one.

Carlo frowned at his own thoughts. Women had been trying to trap him into a serious relationship for years but he'd never been remotely tempted.

Until tonight.

'Do you believe in love at first sight?'

Matt stared at him with naked incredulity. 'I can't believe you just asked me that.'

Carlo grinned. He couldn't believe it either. 'Well?'

'Only when I've had several drinks,' Matt responded wryly, shaking his head as he scrutinised Carlo's face. 'Tell me you're not serious. You've only just met her.'

'I know that.'

But she'd affected him in a way that no other woman had before.

Matt let out a long breath and tried to reason with him. 'You can't do this. Not now. You're supposed to be keeping a low profile. What if she goes to the press? The whole idea of the false name was to fool the press.'

'She won't go to the press,' Carlo said easily. 'She doesn't know who I am.'

'Yet.' Matt lifted an eyebrow meaningfully but Carlo refused to lose his cool.

'Relax. This isn't Italy. And I don't think she's the type to read glitzy magazines.'

Matt sighed. 'Well, at least take me with you next time.'

It was Carlo's turn to lift an eyebrow. 'I never thought you were kinky.'

'I'll wait outside,' Matt growled, and Carlo gave a grudging smile.

'You're a good friend, but I don't need a watchdog.'

'Really?' Matt looked at his cheek. 'So how did you get that?'

Carlo lifted a hand and touched the bruise with the tips of his fingers, a soft smile touching his mouth. 'I was attacked.'

'Attacked?' Matt stared at him in growing dismay and Carlo's grin widened.

'By the woman. I tried to rescue her—'

'And she hit you?' Matt looked stunned and Carlo started to laugh.

'We had a misunderstanding. She didn't realise I was rescuing her.'

Matt laughed too. 'No wonder you think you're in love with her. There's something very sexy about a confident woman.'

Carlo gave a half-smile, knowing that only part of Zan was confident and feisty. The other part was feminine and shy, and the combination was mind-blowing.

Matt's smile faded. 'Look, you feel this way because she doesn't know who you are. It's just the novelty.'

Carlo thought about it. 'It isn't that.'

Matt shot him a frustrated look. 'This is a really, really bad time for you to get involved with someone, Carlo. You don't know anything about her.'

Carlo's expression darkened. 'And she doesn't know anything about me. There is no way she'd be involved in all this, if that's what you're suggesting. She's totally innocent.'

Completely innocent.

The thought made his insides tighten and he gave a smile of pure male possession.

He was going to make her his.

All his.

Matt wasn't so easily distracted. 'Let's be honest about this for a moment. You left Italy to draw those lunatics away from your family—to tempt them into following you. I still think it was a bad idea, especially as you're so careless about security.'

'Careless?' Carlo's eyes gleamed. 'Oh, believe me, I'm not careless.'

He was totally alert and more than ready to face the threat.

'Well, even if she doesn't shop you to the press, associating with this girl could put *her* at risk. They could use her to get to you,' Matt growled, obviously totally frustrated by Carlo's lack of co-operation. 'Don't think the false name is going to fool them. We did that to lose the press as much as anything. The men behind the threats are pros. I'm willing to bet they already know who you are and where you are.'

Carlo's smiled. 'Of course they do.'

He was under no illusions about his current position.

Matt frowned. 'You can't see her again. At least, not until this mess is sorted out.'

'I know that, too.' Carlo's smile faded and he rubbed long fingers over his forehead.

Everything Matt said was true. He had left Italy to draw the men who were threatening him away from his family.

To see Zan again could be risky for her. But he knew he couldn't give her up.

Maybe he could stall her and hope that the guys who were threatening him came out into the open quickly.

On the other hand, if he was honest, he was enjoying

living his life as someone else for the time being. He liked the fact that Zan didn't know about his true circumstances.

For the first time in his life he was able to have a normal relationship with a woman without his money getting in the way. There was no way he was letting that go.

'There's another thing to consider.' Matt's tone was cautious. 'Even if she doesn't know who you are now, it's bound to come out soon. And she'll be hurt that you didn't tell her. And a hurt woman—'

'Is dangerous,' Carlo finished flatly, pacing across the apartment and staring down at the snow-covered trees.

'She could go to the papers.'

Carlo frowned, knowing that it was true. His family had been hurt on numerous occasions when girls he and his brother had dated had later sold their stories to the newspapers. It was one of the reasons he was extremely careful in his relationships with the opposite sex.

He couldn't believe that Zan would do a thing like that.

But he'd been burned before. Badly.

He stirred and looked at his friend. 'She isn't the type. She's special.'

'Special enough to forgive you when she discovers that you've lied?'

Carlo let out a long breath. 'I certainly hope so.'

If she wasn't, then his life had just become even more complicated.

CHAPTER THREE

'ALL right, what's going on?' Kim, Zan's best friend and the sister in charge of the antenatal clinic, glanced up curiously as they prepared for the morning clinic. 'I've just told you we've got a full clinic, a locum doctor who doesn't know the ropes and two off sick. Why are you grinning? Did I miss the joke?'

Zan picked up a stack of notes and hugged them to her chest. Her insides were so churned up with excitement that she hadn't even managed breakfast. All she could think about was Carlo.

'I'm just happy.'

'That's what worries me,' Kim said dryly. 'Why would you be happy, given that by the end of the day you'll have blisters on both feet and a headache bigger than Africa?'

'I don't care about blisters. I met someone.' She tried to sound nonchalant and then wondered why she was even bothering. Kim was her best friend and they told each other everything.

'You met someone? *When?* We worked together yesterday and your smile was normal-sized then.' Kim looked at her, stunned, and Zan laughed.

'I met him last night.'

'Last night? So it wasn't quick or anything?' Kim shook her head in disbelief. 'Zan, I hate to be the one to point this out, but falling for men in one night isn't your style. In fact, correct me if I'm wrong, but you've never fallen for anyone, no matter how many nights were involved. You invented the word "cautious". I'm the reckless one in this friendship.'

Zan shrugged. 'So maybe it's time I changed.'

Kim glanced around to check that no one was within earshot and lowered her voice. 'So did you...*you know*?'

'Kim!' Zan pretended to look shocked and then grinned. 'No. We didn't. But I've made up my mind I'm going to. He's going to be my Christmas present to myself. I'm fed up with being cautious and he's gorgeous.'

'Obviously.' Kim sounded faint. 'He's managed to achieve in one night what the whole male race has been struggling with for years. I can't wait to meet him.'

Zan dipped her head, deciding not to mention that the locum and her new man were one and the same. Her relationship was too new to expose it to one of Kim's indiscreet comments.

'Anyway, if you could pull yourself down off the cloud you're sitting on, we need to get this clinic started,' Kim said brightly. 'And when we've finished that, we've got a tree to decorate.'

'That's OK.' Zan smiled. She loved decorating Christmas trees and she wasn't afraid of hard work. 'So where do you want me to start?'

'Here in clinic, keeping an eye on my locum, who's in Room 1,' Kim told her, and Zan fought to control her expression. If the new locum was the person she thought he was then she intended to keep much more than an eye on him.

Her heart banging against her ribcage and her hands suddenly shaking, she picked up a pile of notes and walked towards her room.

It connected with the room next door, and through the open door she could see Carlo sitting at the desk, stethoscope looped around his neck, reading through a set of notes.

It was the first time she'd seen him in daylight and her heart missed a beat.

Her first thought was that he was stunningly good-looking. Dressed in a dark suit, he had an air of strength and authority that made her catch her breath.

Her second thought was that he didn't look English.

Her eyes slid over his short, cropped hair, rested for a moment on his olive skin and dark jaw and then dropped down to those powerful shoulders.

He looked completely and thoroughly Italian.

She knew she was staring but she couldn't help herself, and when he glanced up and saw her standing there his face broke into a smile that made her remember why she'd ended up semi-naked in the shower with him after only a few hours' acquaintance.

He was the sexiest man she'd ever met.

He rose to his feet in a fluid movement and strolled across to her, his gaze heating as he looked at her.

'*Buongiorno*—good morning.'

'Good morning.' Suddenly she felt ridiculously shy and lifted a hand to smooth her dark hair behind her ear.

He gave a low groan and glanced over his shoulder to make sure that no one was listening. 'Don't do that or I'll never get any work done this morning.'

Before she could answer, Kim walked into the room, clutching a pile of notes.

'Mr Bennett?'

At first Carlo didn't react, but he must have seen something in Zan's eyes because he suddenly shook himself and turned to the other woman.

'Yes. Sorry, sister.' He cleared his throat. 'I was miles away.'

Zan frowned, puzzled. It was as if he hadn't heard his own name. Was she really that distracting?

Kim beamed at him. 'I just came to say that you're very welcome, and if there's anything at all you need while you're working here, you can ask one of us. We're very informal here. Do call me Kim. And this is Suzannah Wilde, but we call her Zan. She'll be working in the room next door so that you can see patients together when the need arises.'

'Well, that's good to know.' Carlo's eyes gleamed slightly and Zan turned away so that Kim wouldn't see her blushing.

Kim was chattering away to both of them, oblivious to the tension between the two of them. 'We've got Mrs Hughes in the waiting room; she's expecting twins. We try not to keep her waiting too long for obvious reasons.' Kim handed Carlo the notes. 'Have you had much experience with multiple pregnancies, Mr Bennett?'

'Call me Carlo, and the answer to your question is, yes, plenty.' Carlo stretched out a lean brown hand and took the notes from her. 'One of my special interests is infertility, and I'm afraid one of the consequences of infertility treatment is an increase in multiple pregnancies, even though we do try to avoid that happening. I delivered several sets of twins and two sets of triplets last year.'

'Mrs Hughes is thirty-seven weeks pregnant and has two more children at home, both under five,' Zan told him, trying to keep her tone professional. 'It's pretty hard for her to get enough rest. Her blood pressure was borderline last time.'

Carlo nodded and flicked his eyes over the notes. 'Let's get her in. Do Zan and I see her together or separately?'

'Together. Zan is her midwife,' Kim said immediately. 'Has she explained how we work here?'

Carlo shook his head and looked at Zan expectantly.

'We try and give continuity of care whenever we can,' Zan explained, 'so, instead of working in one place, we all rotate. One day I might be in clinic and the next I might be on the labour ward. Basically we try and follow the patient, at least up until they have their baby. After that I'm afraid they get whoever is on the ward.'

Carlo listened carefully. 'So you see them in clinic and you deliver them?'

'That's the idea. We divide the midwives into teams, so the woman should at least be familiar with someone from the team. It means that they don't go into labour and find themselves being delivered by someone they've never met before,' Zan explained, and then gave a gasp and turned to Kim. 'I forgot to tell you—I saw Kelly Turner last night.'

Kim sighed. 'I hardly dare ask. And?'

'Well, she wasn't great,' Zan confessed, deciding not to mention that Carlo had been there, too. 'She's thirty-four weeks pregnant now, she looks tired and her uterus isn't the size it should be. I tried to get her to come in for a scan but Mike wasn't having it.'

'If we're not careful there's going to be a tragedy there,' Kim muttered. 'I'll have a word with the bosses and let them know what's going on and I'll speak to Social Services again. Any luck with the housing?'

'Not yet.' Zan's eyes twinkled. 'But I'm working on it.'

Kim grinned. 'They have my sympathies. What I want to know is how did you find time to see Kelly *and* meet a man?' She glanced at Carlo and winked. 'You'd better watch her concentration this morning. She met someone last night and now she's in love.'

Oh, thank you, Kim!

Zan closed her eyes and stifled a groan. Why, oh, why had she been so stupid as to tell her friend?

Carlo cleared his throat. 'Well, that's nice.'

Even without looking at him Zan could sense his amusement, and she backed towards the door.

'I'll go and tell Mrs Hughes she can come in, if you're ready.'

'Oh, I'll do that,' Kim said immediately. 'You and Carlo had better have a quick chat before you start seeing patients. By the way, what happened to your eye?'

Carlo lifted a hand to his cheek. 'Oh. I, er, had an accident.'

'Right.' Kim grinned and as soon as she'd left the room Carlo lifted his eyes to Zan's, the laughter in them unmistakable.

'A very interesting accident. So, who's this man you're in love with?'

'I never said I was in love,' she said hastily. 'Kim has a vivid imagination, that's all.'

'So you're *not* in love?'

She knew he was teasing her and her face flamed. 'I don't fall in love with men I've only just met.'

'Ouch. Is that a put-down?'

She looked at him and smiled shyly. 'I'm buying my tree tonight. If you'll lend me those muscles again, I'll cook you supper.'

His smile faded and there was no missing the sudden tension in his frame. 'Zan, about tonight…'

She saw the hesitation and felt the colour rush to her cheeks.

He'd had second thoughts.

Oh, damn, damn, damn. How could she have been so stupid?

A man as experienced as him certainly wouldn't want to be bothered with a virgin.

'Don't worry, I'm strong enough to carry the tree myself,' she said quickly, looking away and missing the frown that touched his brows. 'We'd better get going. This clinic sometimes runs until early afternoon if we dawdle. I'll call Mrs Hughes.' Without giving him a chance to speak, Zan left the room and sought sanctuary in the waiting area. She saw her patient immediately and managed to produce a smile.

'We're ready for you, Mrs Hughes.'

Carlo closed his eyes and cursed softly in Italian.

Zan thought he didn't want to see her again.

He was in an impossible situation. He'd promised Matt that he wouldn't see her again, at least for the time being, but that was going to hurt her badly and frankly *he* didn't feel too great about it either. But if he carried on then eventually he was going to have to confess that he'd been withholding significant information about himself, and additionally he could be putting her at risk.

Whichever route he took, he was going to hurt her.

She walked into the room at that moment, the twinkle missing from her gorgeous green eyes.

'This is Helen Hughes.' She smiled at the lady with her and helped her up onto the examination couch. 'You might as well see us both at the same time, Helen. It will save us asking the same questions.'

Carlo introduced himself and tried to drag his mind back to the job in hand. He gave the patient a warm smile and walked over to the couch. 'How are you feeling?'

'Pretty awful,' Helen Hughes confessed immediately. 'I've got terrible backache and indigestion which keeps me awake at night.'

Carlo nodded. 'Because you are carrying two babies, your uterus is that much larger than that of a mother who is pregnant with one child. I'm afraid that all the normal problems of pregnancy are often worse when you are expecting twins.'

Helen pulled a face and rubbed her back. 'Tell me about it. And it doesn't help that I already have two children to look after.' She exchanged a wry smile with Zan. 'We thought we'd have one more baby and look what happened.'

Carlo smiled. 'Is there a history of twins in your family?'

Helen nodded. 'I'm a twin and my aunt and my sister both had twins. I suppose I'm lucky I only had one set!'

Zan checked Helen's blood pressure and tested her urine sample for evidence of protein.

'That's all fine, Helen.' She showed the results to Carlo, who nodded.

'I'd like to feel your stomach, if that's all right.' He helped Helen wriggle down on the examining couch and then assessed the size of the uterus and the way the babies were lying.

Helen looked at him curiously. 'Can you tell which is which?'

'The first twin is lying head down in what we call a longitudinal position,' Carlo said immediately, and Helen's eyes widened.

'That's very impressive. The last doctor I had didn't have a clue! He had to scan me.'

'It can be hard when there are two babies,' Carlo admitted. 'Sometimes we need a scan to assess precisely how they are lying, but twins and triplets are a special interest of mine. Where I work in Italy, we also run an infertility clinic and, as you probably know, one of the consequences of infertility treatment is sometimes multiple births. We try to avoid it wherever we can, but I have more experience than most in delivering twins and triplets.'

'Oh.' Helen looked at him with a new respect. 'The doctor I saw here last time had never even delivered twins before. I have to confess it didn't fill me with confidence. Will you deliver me?'

Carlo smiled. 'That depends on when you have the babies. I will try to.'

'Well, I certainly hope you do, and that leads me to my next question,' Helen said promptly. 'When do you think they're coming? I'm going to need help with the other two and I daren't invite my mother too far in advance or my husband will leave home, especially at Christmas. I've already wrapped the children's presents and frozen enough food for an army.'

'So it's a wonder that your blood pressure isn't higher,' Carlo said dryly, finishing his examination and helping her to sit up. 'The answer to your question is that it is unusual for a twin pregnancy to last for the full forty weeks. Most women go into labour at about thirty-seven weeks, which is where you are now.'

Helen stared at him. 'So do you think it will be soon?'

Carlo smiled. 'In all probability, yes, but you might last until after Christmas.'

'I hope I do.' Helen looked worried. 'There's no way my husband could cope with two children under five, my mother *and* a raw turkey.'

Zan laughed and helped her off the couch. 'Perhaps he'll surprise you.'

'Perhaps.' Helen looked doubtful. 'So what happens now?'

'Everything is fine at the moment,' Carlo told her. 'I want you to go home and do as little as possible, which I realise is asking a great deal when you have two small children. If nothing happens then we see you again next week, but I have a suspicion that you might not be around to cook that turkey.'

'Well, I hope you're wrong.' Helen walked slowly to the door, one hand on her back to relieve the pressure.

Zan followed her out to the waiting room and Helen turned to her with a wicked smile.

'Where did you find him? He's totally gorgeous.' She buttoned up her coat and wound a scarf around her neck.

'I tell you this much, if he delivers my babies then I'll definitely know it's Christmas. I didn't think doctors could be that sexy.'

Zan managed a smile and walked with her towards the door. 'You shouldn't be thinking about sex at your stage, Helen.'

'Well, thinking is just about my only option,' Helen said gloomily, opening the door and shivering as the freezing air hit them both. 'And once these are born that'll be the end of it for ever.'

Zan laughed and gave her arm a squeeze. 'Have a good Christmas if I don't see you before.'

She walked back into the waiting room and gave herself a sharp talking-to. She'd known Carlo for less than twenty-four hours so she couldn't really feel anything for him. Not really. It was just because he was so different from the doctors she usually worked with.

Exotic, exciting—*Italian*.

It wasn't anything special about him.

Then she remembered the sexy look in his eyes, his gentle touch and the way he teased her, and she knew that her feelings had nothing to do with his nationality and everything to do with the man himself.

Carlo Bennett was special.

But he didn't want her.

She'd had her chance to spend the night with him and she'd blown it.

The clinic was hideously busy, and it was past two o'clock when Kim asked Zan to go to the labour ward.

'Vicky Morris has just come in and they reckon it's going to be the fastest delivery on record.'

Vicky was one of Zan's mothers and her face brightened. 'Oh, that's wonderful. She was desperate to be home before Christmas.'

Carlo frowned slightly. 'You haven't eaten lunch.'

'This is the NHS, Carlo,' Kim said dryly. 'What's lunch?'

'I'm not hungry anyway,' Zan said quickly, handing the last set of notes to Kim and making for the door. She was glad to get away from Carlo. 'I'll see you later.'

Up on the labour ward it was organised chaos, as usual.

'We've got two women labouring on the antenatal ward at the moment because we're full up here,' Diane told her as she gave Zan a quick hand-over. 'It looks as though your Vicky might deliver quickly, and frankly I hope she does because we need the space.'

'Always nice to work in such a relaxed environment,' Zan quipped, making her way along to Room 6.

She pushed open the door. 'Vicky, this is great—just what you wanted.'

'It doesn't feel great at the moment,' Vicky panted, her face white with pain. 'One minute I was Christmas shopping in town, minding my own business, and the next my waters break and suddenly I'm standing in a puddle in agony. I thought labour was supposed to be slow, but the midwife who admitted me told me that I'm already seven centimetres dilated.'

'And how are you coping?' Zan washed her hands and checked the CTG machine which provided a read-out of the baby's heartbeat and the mother's contractions.

'Well, all things considered, I'd rather be having lunch with the girls,' Vicky confessed, groaning as another pain hit her.

'Use the gas and air,' Zan instructed, encouraging Vicky to lift the mouthpiece. 'That's it. Well done.'

She put a hand on Vicky's abdomen and felt the strength of the contraction.

When it finally passed Vicky sagged back against the cushions, limp with exhaustion.

'OK, that's it. I've had enough. When can I go home?'

'Soon.' Zan gave her hand a squeeze. 'You need to start breathing in the gas and air at the beginning of the contraction. If you wait until it's really taken hold then there's no chance of it working.'

Vicky sighed. 'Nag, nag.'

'That's me.' Zan checked the foetal heart-rate and gave a nod. 'It's all looking good. Is the gas and air enough for you?'

'Well, I'd actually like a general anaesthetic,' Vicky said dryly, 'but I don't suppose that's on offer, is it?'

'Not today. Where's Andrew?'

Zan had met Vicky's husband at the last group of antenatal classes she'd run and knew that he was keen to be at the birth.

'He's on his way in. Oh, here we go again…' Vicky screwed up her face and started to breathe in the gas and air, her eyes tightly shut.

Zan encouraged her gently, watching the monitor to check that the baby's heart-rate wasn't affected by the contraction.

'I really, really want to push,' Vicky gasped, dropping the mouthpiece and grabbing the sides of the bed.

Zan frowned. Could she possibly have dilated that quickly?

'I just need to examine you again,' she said, washing her hands and dragging on a pair of sterile gloves. 'I don't want you pushing unless you're fully dilated.'

Two minutes later she looked at Vicky with a stunned expression on her face. 'Push away. You're obviously trying to do this in record time.'

She pressed the buzzer to summon some help and at that moment Andrew hurried into the room, looking out of breath and worried. Diane followed close behind him.

Vicky gave a sob of relief. 'I thought you weren't going to make it.'

'I didn't know you were planning to do it so quickly,' Andrew said, the strain evident in his face as he dropped his parcels by the door and went straight to his wife. 'You told me first labours always took hours.'

'Well, you know I like to be different.' Vicky gave another groan as another contraction hit her.

Zan encouraged her quietly and after several pushes the baby's head was delivered.

'The head's out now, Vicky,' Zan told her as she waited for the shoulders to rotate. 'Your baby will be born any minute.'

But the shoulders didn't rotate.

Feeling cold fingers of panic down her spine, Zan looked at Diane. 'I can't deliver the shoulders.' Zan kept her voice calm but both she and Diane understood the seriousness of the situation. Impacted shoulders were an obstetric emergency.

Vicky was breathing rapidly, dread showing in her eyes. 'What's the matter with the shoulders? Why can't you deliver them?'

'I'll fast-bleep the obstetrician,' Diane said immediately, and Zan turned her attention back to Vicky and her unborn baby.

'It will be all right,' she said quickly, praying that it was true. 'Sometimes the shoulders don't move into the right position and we have to give the baby some help.'

Diane reappeared only seconds later, accompanied by Carlo.

In the meantime Zan had made another attempt to deliver the shoulders and failed.

Zan looked at Carlo, her heart thumping in her chest. She knew just how serious the situation was. 'The anterior shoulder has failed to rotate. I've tried doing it manually, and I've checked that the hand isn't alongside the head.'

'So we'll try and deliver the posterior shoulder first.' He was amazingly calm, talking quietly to Vicky as he washed his hands and tugged on sterile gloves. 'Vicky, I need to change your position. The baby is stuck and we need to give him more room to be born.'

With Zan's help he adjusted Vicky's position and then he slipped his fingers behind the posterior shoulder and rotated it into the hollow of the sacrum.

Still talking quietly to Vicky, he did something magical with his fingers and the baby slithered out into his waiting hands. He lifted it straight onto Vicky's tummy.

Zan gave a gulp of relief and exchanged amazed looks with Diane, who grinned.

'Now I know it's Christmas. The time for miracles. Done that before, have you, Mr Bennett?'

'Not too often, fortunately.' Carlo smiled, his eyes on Vicky and the baby just as the paediatrician rushed in.

'Problems?'

Diane let out a long breath, not bothering to hide how thankful she was. 'Not any more—but now you're here you might as well check the baby.'

Carlo grabbed his coat and sprinted down the stairs to the front of the hospital.

Had he missed her?

He slammed through the main door and into the freezing air and then looked left and right, cursing the call from the ward that had slowed him down.

'Looking for someone?'

Her voice came from behind him and he turned, sighing with relief as he saw her standing there, dark hair pushed up inside her woolly hat again, her green eyes wary.

'I've been looking for you.'

For most of his adult life.

'Why's that?' Zan tried to sound casual but he could see the hurt in her eyes and he didn't blame her. He was only too aware that he was giving her mixed messages.

'I thought you were going to buy your tree.' He smiled down at her, remembering what she'd said the night before about getting a tree that would fill her flat. 'The *big* tree.'

'I am.' She stuffed her hands in her pockets and looked at him. 'Did I mention that you were great back there, by the way?' She rubbed her boot in the snow and avoided his eyes. 'You saved that baby's life. I'm impressed.'

So was he. He'd hurt her feelings but she was still generous enough to offer praise.

He took instant advantage. 'Impressed enough to cook me that dinner you promised me?'

He knew he shouldn't see her again, and he knew Matt was going to kill him, but he couldn't help himself. If Zan was a drug then he was well and truly hooked.

There was no way he was giving this girl up. He'd worry about the consequences later.

'I don't think so.' She turned to walk away from him and he grabbed her arm, his grip hard through the wool of her coat.

'If that Christmas tree is as big as you say then you're going to need help carrying it.'

She stared at him and shook her head. 'I'll be fine.'

'Zan.' He suddenly sounded very Italian and very frustrated. 'I meant what I said last night.'

She gave him a wan smile. 'You also made it perfectly clear in clinic this morning that you'd had second thoughts.'

He sucked in a deep breath but he didn't let her go. 'That isn't true.'

He'd been trying to do the right thing but he knew now

that he couldn't do that. He had to be with this woman and somehow he'd make sure that she was kept safe.

'I can read body language, Carlo.' She lifted her chin. 'So what did you want to talk about?'

'A relationship between us isn't straightforward.' He almost laughed as he listened to himself. That had to be the understatement of the year.

'You mean because you'll be going back to Italy?'

No. Because he was deceiving her about who he was. Because some crazed lunatic was out to get him.

'Zan—'

'I don't expect commitment,' she said, her head tipped to one side, her cheeks pink from the cold. 'All I want is for you to be honest with me.'

Carlo rubbed a hand over the back of his neck, her words creating an unbearable tension in his body.

Honest.

That was the one thing he wasn't being.

In many ways their whole relationship was a charade. She had absolutely no idea who she was involved with. What his life was like back in Italy.

And he ought to walk away from her but there was no way he could do it.

'Decorating a tree is no fun on your own.' *He'd make sure that she was kept safe,* he told himself. And he'd find a way to tell her the truth about himself when the time was right.

She looked at him for a long moment and he could see the question in her eyes.

She was trying to decide whether she could trust him.

'Should I buy a Scotch pine or a blue spruce?'

He grinned. 'Blue spruce. It's the best.'

CHAPTER FOUR

'IT's too big.' Carlo gazed up at the top of the Christmas tree and then back at Zan, who was winding the lights around the branches.

'It's not too big.' She crawled out from under the branches, eyes shining, humming along to the Christmas carols that were playing in the background.

'It's touching the ceiling,' Carlo pointed out, and she grinned.

'It's supposed to. Now we just have to decorate it.'

'We?' Carlo lifted an eyebrow and she nodded and handed him a box.

'Might as well make use of your superior height. These go on the top.'

He followed her instructions, trying not to be distracted by the way her jeans hugged her rounded bottom as she leaned over to hang things on the bottom of the tree.

He'd rushed things the night before and he'd made up his mind that he was going to control himself and slow the pace as he'd promised.

He just hoped he didn't die in the attempt.

He finished the top of the tree and then crouched down next to her to look through the rest of the decorations.

'We need to hang these at the front because they're so pretty.' She handed him a box of delicate silver baubles and he took them carefully, his fingers brushing against hers, their heads close together as they inspected the decorations.

'These *are* pretty.'

And so was she. Completely gorgeous. He was fascinated by those thick black lashes and the soft fullness of her mouth.

Carlo tilted his head so that their mouths were tantalisingly close and fought the urge to kiss her. He watched her lips part in anticipation and bit back a groan.

She wanted him to kiss her.

But he wasn't going to. He wanted to make sure that she was comfortable with him before he touched her again. And in the meantime he was going to make her want him as much as he wanted her.

Deliberately cranking up the heat, he hesitated just long enough to see her breathing quicken and then dragged his attention back to the baubles.

Every nerve ending in his body was tingling with frustration and he was grateful that he was wearing tailored trousers this time. At least they were slightly more forgiving than his jeans.

'So these go at the front?' Trying to keep his tone casual, he straightened up, still holding the box, and started hanging the baubles on the branches.

'Yes—just there—' she sounded breathless and he gritted his teeth, forcing himself not to turn round.

If he turned round he was going to kiss her, and he was determined not to kiss her again yet.

She wasn't touching him and yet every sense in his body alerted him to how close she was.

It occurred to him that he'd never been in this position before. He'd never had to hold back with a woman. But, then, the women he usually mixed with were experienced and sophisticated whereas Zan... He dragged in a breath and tried to ignore the way her subtle perfume wrapped itself around him. Zan was sweet and natural and she'd confessed that she had virtually no experience when it came to men.

The knowledge satisfied everything that was male in

him. She was going to be his and there was no way he was rushing her.

'Can you reach the plug to switch on the lights?' Her voice was husky and feminine and he clenched his fists and decided that he'd never known temptation before he'd met Zan.

'*Sì.*' He bent down and flicked the switch.

The tree lit up, throwing sparkling silver lights across her living room.

Zan gasped and clapped her hands. 'Oh, that's so pretty!' She smiled at him, her green eyes reflecting the glitter of a hundred tiny Christmas tree lights. 'Merry Christmas, Mr Bennett.'

The stark reminder that she didn't actually know who he was stabbed at his conscience. *She trusted him and he wasn't being honest with her.*

'It's very pretty.'

'Isn't it just?' She scrabbled in her bag and pulled out a piece of paper. 'I've just remembered. Lottery numbers for tomorrow. You can help me choose.'

He stared at her. She was expecting him to choose lottery numbers? He rubbed a hand over his jaw. 'Do you really want to do the lottery?'

In a few weeks, when all this was sorted out, he'd be able to buy her anything she wanted.

'Of course I want to do it. The jackpot is eleven million. *Eleven million.* Imagine how amazing it would be to win a bit of that at Christmas.' She grinned and sat cross-legged on the cushions which were always piled by the huge window. 'Go on, if you had all the money in the world what would you want from me as a present? It's got to be a car, right? You look like a man who likes fast cars.'

She was spot on. He did like fast cars. He already had three at home.

'Let me guess.' Zan tipped her head on one side and looked at him thoughtfully. 'Ferrari? Red?'

This was ridiculous.

'Ferrari, definitely.' He played along with her game, thinking how nice it was going to be to be able to buy her whatever she wanted.

'What else would you buy?'

Carlo stared at her, finding the whole situation surreal. Here was he, trying to pretend that he didn't have money, and she was asking him what he'd do if he did. It was enough to give a guy a headache.

Suddenly he realised just how much he took his life for granted. True, he was fed up with all the complications that went with wealth, but the benefits outweighed the disadvantages and he'd started to forget that.

'I'd buy a ski lodge,' he said slowly, thinking of their family home in Cortina, 'and a villa in Sardinia.'

In fact, all the things he already had. *And loved.*

'Sardinia?' She tipped her head on one side. 'Is that a nice place?'

'Fabulous.'

'Well, if we win, you're taking me there.' She sucked the pen and squinted at the numbers. 'I'll choose three and you choose three.'

Carlo suppressed a groan. He could just imagine the newspaper headlines if he won the lottery. They'd have a field day.

'You do it,' he suggested lightly. 'I don't want to bring you bad luck.'

Or at least he didn't want to bring her any more than he might already be bringing her.

She filled out the form, stuffed it back in her pocket and smiled at him. 'Remind me to take it to the newsagents later. Now, then, time for dinner.'

She cooked a fabulous chicken dish, bursting with flavour, and Carlo decided that he needed to find a way of getting her to ask him to stay at Christmas again. This time he'd say yes.

They dined by candlelight and Christmas tree lights and Carlo was just thinking that he couldn't remember a time when he'd been happier when she asked the question he'd been dreading.

'Tell me about your family.'

Carlo tensed. 'My family live in Milan,' he said carefully. 'My father owns his own business.'

And he was the richest man in Italy.

Zan tipped her head on one side and looked interested. 'What does he do?'

'Sort of medical supplies—technology,' Carlo hedged, hoping she wouldn't delve too deeply. His father's company was a household name in Europe and the States.

'But you weren't tempted to join him?'

'My brother and I wanted to carve our own way in the world,' Carlo told her, suddenly filled with an overwhelming desire to tell her just how hard it was to be the son of a billionaire. It was pretty hard to see yourself as successful when your father had success all sewn up.

'So your brother's a doctor, too? Where?'

'He works in Milan. He's a surgeon.' A famous children's heart surgeon, and she might even recognise the name if he mentioned it because he'd worked in her hospital for a while. Carlo chose not to mention it. 'He lives with his wife and their daughter, who's two now. They're expecting another baby any day. You're an amazing cook.'

'Well, someone had to help my mum and it certainly wasn't my brothers,' Zan said dryly, standing up and clearing the plates.

Carlo stood up, too, relieved that he appeared to have successfully changed the subject away from his family.

'I'll help you wash up.'

'No need; I've got a dishwasher.' She walked into the kitchen and opened a cupboard. 'This flat may be small but it's very well equipped. Can I ask you something?'

'Of course.' Carlo braced himself. Now what? More questions about his family that he was going to have to dodge?

She hesitated slightly. 'The children's ward is looking for someone to be Father Christmas. Usually the Chief Exec does it, because he's tall and broad and looks good in the outfit, but he's off sick with flu at the moment and...' She broke off and looked at him hopefully.

He grinned. She was *so* sweet. 'You want me to dress as Father Christmas?'

Her cheeks dimpled wickedly. 'I've always fancied men in uniform.'

'You have a fetish for men with white beards?'

They were both laughing and Carlo had to stop himself grabbing her. 'And where and when does all this take place?'

'The day after next. Christmas Eve. The children's ward opens onto a huge lawn so you arrive that way.'

'In my sledge?'

'Nothing so fancy, I'm afraid. This is the NHS. No sledges.' She closed the door of the dishwasher and pressed the button. 'You get to walk with a few elves as helpers to give out presents.'

Carlo looked at her thoughtfully, an idea forming in his mind.

'I'll do it,' he said immediately, and she gave him a wide smile that hit him straight in the solar plexus.

'That's great. You'll get to see my elf costume.'

If her elf costume was anywhere near as attractive as her tight jeans then the Father Christmas outfit had better be baggy.

Deciding that he'd stretched his self-control to the limits

for one night, he glanced at his watch and gave her a rueful smile.

'I'd better be going. Thanks for supper.'

'Thanks for helping with the tree.' She looked at him wistfully and then looked away quickly, but not before he'd caught the blush on her cheek.

He knew exactly what she wanted because he wanted the same thing and it was starting to drive him crazy.

'Zan…' His voice low, he reached out a hand and turned her face towards him, sliding his fingers around the back of her neck, feeling the softness of her dark hair teasing the back of his hand. 'So, after I've been Father Christmas, what happens then? Do the elves invite me home?'

She laughed. 'I think you spend the rest of the night squeezing yourself down chimneys.' Her laughter died and she looked at him warily. 'Alternatively, you could spend Christmas Eve here.' She gave a hesitant smile. 'But you didn't seem too wild about that idea when I mentioned it last night.'

Carlo stuck his hands in his pockets to stop himself grabbing her.

'Trust me, I'm wild about it.'

'Really?' She looked at him doubtfully and then smiled. 'In that case, we can come back here after our visit to the children's ward and then open presents on Christmas morning before we go to the hospital.'

Which meant that she was inviting him to stay the night.

His eyes gleamed in anticipation. 'Does that mean I get to hang my stocking next to yours?'

'That depends.' Zan gave a shy grin. 'Will it behave itself?'

'Probably not.' Carlo bent his head and brushed his mouth against hers in a kiss designed to tease and frustrate them both.

He had absolutely no intention of behaving himself.

Which meant that he had forty-eight hours to make sure she felt the same way.

'You're going to carry on seeing her?' Matt stared at him in dismay but Carlo merely grinned.

'I'm going to carry on seeing her, and you're going to protect her.' He almost laughed at the expression on Matt's face. 'Don't look like that. You're always dying to do your macho bodyguard act and here I am giving you permission. Be as macho as you like. Just don't let her see you.'

Matt exhaled sharply. 'Let's get this straight. You're asking me to follow the girl?'

'Absolutely,' Carlo said pleasantly. 'And her name is Zan.'

'I'm supposed to be protecting *you*.'

Carlo frowned impatiently. 'I protect myself. And anyway, apart from when I'm working I'm going to be with her, so protecting her will be protecting me.'

'You could be putting her in danger.'

'But you're the best,' Carlo said softly, 'and so am I. Between us we can stop anything happening to her. We have to, Matt, because there's no way I'm letting her go.'

'I can't believe you're doing this.' Matt raked long fingers through his cropped hair and his jaw tensed. 'Have you really thought this through? You're a multi-millionaire, Carlo. This can't be anything but a short-term relationship.'

'Why?' Carlo's tone was noticeably cooler and Matt glanced at him warily.

'You really need me to tell you that? You've got a life in Italy—your clinic is one of the most famous in the world. People pay huge sums of money to see you personally because you're so damn talented.'

'So maybe I want to use those talents with the less fortunate for a while,' Carlo replied smoothly, remembering what Zan had said about visiting Kelly. She made a difference.

'But sooner or later you'll be going back,' Matt pointed out logically. 'And then what?'

Carlo pushed the thought away. He didn't want to think about going back.

'I'll worry about that later. At the moment I just care about keeping her safe.'

And waking up next to her in bed on Christmas morning.

'And what if they use her to get to you?'

Carlo looked him in the eye. 'They're not going to do that.'

Matt frowned. 'And how can you be so sure?'

'Because we're going to be protecting her,' Carlo said smoothly. 'I don't want her to go anywhere without one of us within hugging distance of her.'

Matt blinked. 'You seriously want me to tail your girlfriend?'

'I want you to do whatever it takes to keep her safe,' Carlo said gruffly. 'You're the best. We both know that. No one gets past you.'

'Which is why I'm supposed to be looking after you,' Matt said dryly, his frustration obvious. 'What's it going to do for my professional reputation if they get you?'

'They won't,' Carlo said calmly. 'You know as well as I do that I can take care of myself. We also both know that I shouldn't be dragging Zan into this, but I have, so now it's my responsibility to keep her safe. I want you on her tail every time she leaves that flat of hers and I want you or one of the team parked outside her apartment every night. No one enters or leaves without your knowledge. Oh, and by the way...' Carlo gave a smug grin. 'She's invited me to spend Christmas with her so I'll be staying with her on Christmas Eve.'

Matt shook his head. 'You've lost your marbles.'

'You only think that because you haven't seen her,' Carlo drawled, shrugging out of his coat and walking towards his bedroom.

'And are you going to tell her the truth?'

Carlo stopped walking. 'No. Not yet.'

He was enjoying the simplicity of their relationship.

'And what if she goes to the press once she finds out who you are?'

Carlo's fingers tightened on his coat. 'Then I'll have made a serious error of judgement.'

Carlo hadn't laid a finger on her.

Zan pulled her coat over her uniform the next morning and tried to squash the feelings of disappointment.

They'd spent the whole evening together and he hadn't even kissed her properly. About a dozen times she'd thought he was going to—at one point he'd seemed to be within kissing distance every time she'd turned around—but he hadn't made that final move. Obviously he wasn't as frustrated as she was. She was beginning to wish she hadn't said no on the first night.

She'd wanted him to slow down, not stop altogether!

She stepped out of the lift and through the door that led to the street, gasping as the cold hit her. It had stopped snowing but the air was freezing and her breath made smoky clouds ahead of her as she hurried along the pavement towards the hospital.

It was still fairly early but the roads were already busy and there were several other people walking to work, heads down against the cold.

Uneasy after her experience with the muggers, Zan glanced briefly over her shoulder, checking that no one was following her. The only person behind her was an elderly woman with a stick and on the other side of the road a broad-shouldered man in a long coat strode briskly, paying no attention to her whatsoever.

She relaxed slightly but still felt considerable relief when she reached the hospital gates and hurried inside.

The unit was as busy as ever and Zan made her way to the antenatal clinic.

Kim was looking harassed. 'Just tell me, what happened nine months ago?'

Zan dragged the scarf off her neck and raised an eyebrow. 'Frankly, I have trouble remembering what happened yesterday. Why are you asking about nine months ago?'

'Because I want to know why there are so many women delivering this week,' Kim muttered, staggering under the weight of a pile of notes that she was carrying back to the desk. 'Did I miss a wild party or something? I'm trying to count back and work it out.'

Zan laughed. 'Don't be a misery. Christmas babies are always really special. I'm still hoping that Helen will have her twins on Christmas Day.'

Kim gave her an incredulous look. 'Don't you want to eat your turkey in peace?'

Zan gave a wistful smile. 'I just think it would be really exciting if the twins were born on Christmas Day.'

'You need your head examined.' Kim glanced up with a smile as a very pregnant woman approached the desk. 'Hello, Millie. How have you been?'

Zan picked up the first set of notes and walked through to her consulting room to begin the clinic.

She saw a steady stream of patients and it was lunchtime before she caught up with Kim again.

'Are you joining me in the canteen for lunch?' Kim's eyes gleamed with curiosity. 'I want to hear episode two of your story.'

Episode two had been decidedly non-eventful, Zan reflected gloomily. Lots of tension but absolutely no action. Carlo hadn't even kissed her. Apart from the brief touch of his lips when he'd left her for the night. And that hadn't really been a kiss. More a tease.

She gave a slow smile as a suspicion grew in her mind.

Was he playing games with her?

Was he trying to drive her wild?

Maybe that was exactly what he was trying to do.

Suddenly cheered, she smiled at Kim. 'I'm popping out at lunchtime to buy a present for my brother.' It was true. She still had a couple more things to buy. 'But I'm still free tonight for that pizza.'

She and Kim had arranged to go out the previous week and she'd been looking forward to it.

Having arranged the details, she wrapped up warmly, slipped out of the hospital and walked towards the shops.

The streets were crowded with Christmas shoppers loaded with bags and she fought her way into a small boutique that sold unusual knitwear and chose a chunky ribbed jumper for her brother.

Then she remembered Carlo. If he was spending Christmas with her then she'd need to buy him something.

Thinking back to their conversation, she smiled.

She knew exactly what to buy him and she knew just the shop.

She was hovering by the till, waiting to pay, when she glanced up and noticed a man buying chestnuts across the road.

It was the same man that she'd seen that morning.

Frowning slightly, Zan paid for the jumper, trying to convince herself that it was perfectly possible to bump into the same person twice in one morning. He probably worked locally.

She was just jumpy after the attack the night before.

Still feeling edgy, she left the shop and went back to

the hospital, telling herself that there was nothing to worry about.

Kim grabbed her as soon as she arrived back in the clinic.

'Someone called for you but they didn't leave their name. It was a woman and she sounded frantic.'

Zan dumped her parcels and frowned. Who would have called her?

Her eyes widened as a thought struck her. 'Kelly?'

'Possibly.' Kim gave a sigh. 'I did ask her, but she hung up at that point.'

'Oh, help.' Zan glanced round the packed clinic and bit her lip. 'Do you think...?'

'Maybe. You'd better check it out,' Kim said immediately. 'I'll call the agency and see if I can get some extra help here. If you need anything, call us. Not that she's likely to let anyone help but you.'

Without waiting to argue, Zan sprinted off and found the bag she used for community visits. She checked the contents, added some extra equipment and then made her way to the door.

For a brief moment she contemplated telling Carlo where she was going and then she thought better of it.

He was busy in the clinic and she didn't want to interrupt him.

Carlo had just finished seeing a patient when his mobile rang.

It was Matt.

Carlo listened in silence and then closed his eyes briefly, his broad shoulders suddenly tense. 'She's gone into the flat?'

He listened to Matt's response and then let out a long breath. 'Hang around outside. I'll be there in ten minutes.'

He made two more phone calls and then snapped the

phone shut and went to find Kim, who was placating a woman who'd been waiting for two hours.

'We have a problem.' He took her to one side and glanced around to check that no one was within earshot. 'Zan's with Kelly and I think she needs help.'

Kim's eyes widened. 'She's called you?'

'I…er…yes.'

No. His bodyguard had been following her. And he'd heard a woman screaming from inside the flat.

Had it been Kelly or Zan?

Sweat broke out on his brow.

The temptation to order Matt to break the door down had been overwhelming.

'Oh, hell.' Kim raked fingers through her blonde hair, visibly panicking. 'I shouldn't have let Zan go on her own, but the problem is that the husband won't let anyone else near her.'

'I'm going to see if I can help her.'

Kim shook her head. 'They won't let you in.'

'They might.' *They'd let him in before.* Just. 'The registrar can cover the rest of the clinic. If he has a problem he can call me.'

Kim nodded and looked at him helplessly. 'What can I do to help?'

'Nothing for now.' Carlo dragged on his coat and picked up his bag. Then he paused. 'On second thoughts, maybe you can. Do you have a portable oxygen cylinder?'

'I'll fetch it.' Obviously thinking along the same lines, they hurried to the equipment room.

Carlo stuffed a bag full of equipment while Kim helped.

'I really, really hope you don't need any of this,' she said fervently, and he nodded agreement.

'Let's hope not. But if that baby is arriving six weeks prematurely, in a freezing flat, we could have a problem on our hands.'

It was an understatement, and they both knew it.

Kim walked with him to the door. 'I'll alert Social Services and the ambulance service. If necessary, we can put an incubator in the ambulance.'

'Good. I'll call you.' Carlo strode out of the door and made for the car park.

Slumped in a car at the far end of the car park, two men watched as Carlo walked towards his car. The bigger of the two men sat up slightly, suddenly alert, checking a photograph that lay in his lap.

'That's him.'

His partner nodded agreement and both of them watched while Carlo slid into the driver's seat and drove away.

'So we've finally tracked him down. Now what?'

'Nothing yet.' The man gave an unpleasant smile. 'We wait. But Carlo Santini is about to have a memorable Christmas.'

CHAPTER FIVE

ZAN finished examining Kelly for the second time and tried to stay calm.

It was the hardest thing she'd ever done.

The flat was freezing and she was delivering a premature baby at home.

This was a midwife's equivalent of a bad hair day.

'Kelly, you have to let me call an ambulance,' she said quietly as she listened to the foetal heart again. So far it had been steady and strong, but it was starting to dip with contractions and Zan was feeling vulnerable and exposed with so little equipment and no medical back-up.

Mike stepped forward, his eyes cold. 'She has the baby here.'

Zan glanced at Kelly but she just stared at the floor, her face white with pain, her long hair straggly as it hung past her thin shoulders.

For a wild moment Zan wondered whether she could floor Mike and drag Kelly bodily to hospital.

But that wasn't an option, of course.

She was just going to have to do the best she could in the circumstances.

'Just as long as you realise that this baby is going to be very small when it's born,' Zan told him. 'Babies born this early often need to go to our intensive care unit to help them breathe.'

Kelly gave a little sob and bent double as another pain hit her.

Zan talked to her quietly, reminding her how to breathe,

almost wishing that Kelly had bonded with another midwife.

Why her?

Kelly gave a sharp scream and even though the room was freezing Zan felt sweat break out on her forehead.

'Try and remember your breathing, Kelly,' she murmured gently, rubbing the other girl's back, horrified by how thin she was.

'I want to push,' Kelly sobbed, and Zan examined her again to check that her cervix was fully dilated.

'You're right,' she said finally, 'you are ready to push. Let's get you into a better position.'

She glanced at Mike, but before she could speak there was a loud knocking at the door.

Mike glared at her threateningly. 'Did you call someone?'

'You've been in the room with me the whole time,' Zan pointed out logically, 'so you know I haven't.'

'Then who—?'

'Mike, it's Carlo Bennett.' Carlo's deep voice penetrated the door and Zan closed her eyes in relief.

Kim must have told him.

Mike's mouth tightened. 'I'll get rid of him.'

'No!' Zan's sharp tone stopped him as he strode towards the door, shoulders braced for conflict.

'He ain't coming near my Kelly!'

Zan took a deep breath. 'Mike, ideally Kelly should be in hospital, but if you won't allow that then at least let the doctor come to her. *Please.*'

Mike's jaw was set. 'No way.'

'Mike, *please.*' Kelly spoke in a quivering voice and then gave a groan as she pushed again.

Mike looked at her uncertainly. 'No…'

'Let him in,' Kelly whispered, her eyes squeezed tightly shut and her hand gripping Zan's.

Without another word Mike dragged open the door and Zan felt the tension drain out of her as she saw Carlo, broad-shouldered and powerful, standing in the doorway with an impressive array of equipment tucked under his arm.

'Thank goodness.' Zan shot him a look of pure relief and he gave her a reassuring smile.

'It'll be OK.' He put a hand on Mike's shoulder, ignoring the frosty look that the other man gave him. 'Can I take a look at her?'

Mike hesitated, but then glanced at Kelly again and stood to one side.

Carlo found the bathroom, washed his hands and then crouched down beside Zan.

'How are you doing, Kelly?'

'Not too good.' The girl was deathly pale and clearly exhausted.

'Her waters broke in the night but she didn't call until lunchtime,' Zan told him. 'I've tried to persuade them to go to the hospital but they won't. She's fully dilated and ready to push.'

'So hospital isn't an option for the moment,' Carlo muttered, glancing around him with a frown. 'This place is too cold for a premature baby.'

Without waiting for an answer from anyone, he reached into his pocket for his mobile phone, leaving Zan to deal with Kelly.

'I'm just calling a friend,' he told Mike, and proceeded to dial a number and speak in rapid Italian.

Zan had no idea what he was doing. She was too busy delivering the baby.

She'd brought clean sheets and blankets from the hospital, and she laid them out now and fished the mucus extractor out of her bag.

Then she prepared an injection to give Kelly to help her uterus contract once the baby had been born.

'I'll give that.' Slipping the phone back into his pocket, Carlo took the syringe from her and watched while Zan delivered the baby's head.

'Gently now, Kelly,' she said quietly as she controlled the delivery. 'That's great...'

As the head slid out Zan felt her heart start to pound. The baby was so tiny. It should have been born in hospital, with a team of paediatricians handy and a warm intensive-care cot ready.

Instead, it was about to be born in a filthy flat which was freezing cold, while snow fell outside.

Kelly gasped as another contraction hit her and Zan delivered the anterior shoulder, aware that Carlo had swiftly given the necessary injection and was now preparing himself to take the baby.

'You see to the mother,' he ordered quietly, and as the baby slithered into her waiting hands she found herself praying.

'You have a little boy, Kelly,' she said softly, passing the limp body to Carlo, who wrapped the baby in a towel.

Please, let him cry.

The baby lay still, showing no signs of life. His skin was tinged a sickly blue colour and he made no effort to breathe.

Kelly struggled upright and then gave a sob of desperation. 'Why isn't he crying? *Why isn't he crying?*'

Zan bit her lip and tried to keep her voice steady. 'Mr Bennett's just examining him, Kelly.'

Kelly's eyes were wild and she shook her head. 'No! Oh, my God, no—tell me he isn't—'

'We're working on it, Kelly,' Carlo was using the mucus extractor to clear the airway but he glanced up when he heard the knock on the door.

'Open it,' he ordered harshly. Mike heard the command in his tone and for once responded without argument.

Zan's eyes widened as he came back into the room carrying two heaters.

Following Carlo's instructions, Mike plugged the heaters in and positioned them.

Heat belted into the room and Carlo dried the baby carefully and reached for the oxygen. Then he directed a low flow of oxygen over the baby's face to try and stimulate a gasp reflex.

Meanwhile Zan turned her attention back to Kelly and delivered the placenta.

Despite her weakened state, Kelly seemed to be doing remarkably well, but she was obviously beside herself with worry about the baby.

'Please, don't let him die—*please*. Oh, Mike—do something.'

Tearing sobs shook her slight frame and Zan put her arms around her, praying for a miracle.

It was Christmas. Didn't miracles happen at Christmas? Obviously not.

The baby was limp and unresponsive and Mike gave a moan of anguish, the fight draining out of him.

Zan felt her eyes fill.

It was so unfair.

The baby was so tiny and helpless.

It deserved to live.

Finally Carlo bent his head and covered the baby's mouth and nose with his mouth, breathing gently. Then he started cardiac massage, using his index and middle fingers to depress the sternum.

The tears spilled out of Zan's eyes and trickled down her cheeks. Maybe it was unprofessional to cry but she just couldn't help it.

She could see that Carlo was using every trick at his disposal but the baby was showing no signs of responding.

He was just too little.

'What's happening—?' Mike's voice was rough with panic and Zan looked at him pleadingly, trying to appeal to the father in him.

'He's very, very sick. We have to get the baby to hospital. Please, let me call an ambulance. *Please*, Mike...' She choked slightly and saw Mike hesitate, but before he could speak the baby gave a little cough and a feeble cry.

Kelly gasped in delight. 'He's alive! You've done it. Oh, thank you.' She burst into tears again and Mike frowned and went to put his arms around her.

Carlo was still working on the baby.

'He isn't out of the woods yet,' he said grimly, wrapping the baby warmly and covering his head to prevent further heat loss. 'This baby is tiny, Kelly, and he's grunting. That means that he's having trouble with his lungs. Babies that are born early can suffer from something called respiratory distress syndrome. They need help with their breathing.'

'And what happens if they don't get it?' Kelly's voice shook and Carlo looked directly at Mike.

'Sometimes they die.'

Zan flinched at the brutality of his words but she knew what he was trying to do. He was trying to make Mike understand the seriousness of the situation. Carlo had produced a miracle but this baby was desperately in need of hospital care, and without it...

Kelly turned to Mike, her eyes terrified. 'We have to let them take him into hospital. *We have to!*'

Mike was breathing heavily. 'You know how I feel about hospitals.'

'I know.' Tears were streaming down Kelly's face as she watched Carlo working to save her son. 'And I wanted to stay at home, too. But that's before it all went wrong.

He's ill, Mike. If he stays at home he might die, and we'll always blame ourselves and I don't think I can live with that. They're trying to help. They *care*. They're not like the others.'

'What others?' Carlo asked the question, still monitoring the baby's breathing.

Zan held her breath. In the few months she'd been coming to visit them she'd never got to the bottom of Kelly's story. All she knew was what the social worker had told her. That Kelly and Mike hated doctors and hospitals.

No one knew why.

'If you can tell us what happened, what you're so afraid of, then maybe we can help,' she said softly, and Kelly swallowed hard.

'Mike lost his brother...' She glanced nervously at Mike, obviously expecting her confession to provoke an angry reaction, but Mike was slouched against the wall, his face drawn.

Carlo looked up, his gaze suddenly intent. 'I'm sorry. That must have been terrible for you. What happened?'

'Doctors. That's what happened,' Mike answered bitterly. 'Eddie found a lump in his testicle but his GP kept telling him it was nothing. By the time he found out how serious it was he had just a few weeks to live.'

Kelly reached out a hand but Mike turned away and strode into the kitchen, slamming the door behind him.

Kelly flinched and looked at them helplessly. 'He adored Eddie. They were twins. When he lost him I thought...' She broke off and looked at the closed door with something close to desperation in her eyes. 'I thought I'd lose Mike, too. We've been going through a terrible patch. He never lets me out of his sight. He says I'm all he has now and he doesn't want to put me in anyone's care.'

Carlo let out a breath, visibly moved.

'I can understand that. In the same circumstances I wouldn't be that eager to trust the medical profession either.' Carlo rose to his feet and glanced at Zan. 'Try and get the baby on the breast. His blood sugar is low and he needs food. If his breathing changes, call me. I'm going to talk to Mike.'

He opened the kitchen door and closed it behind him, and Zan lifted the baby, positioning him against Kelly's breast, trying to encourage him to feed.

The baby played idly with the nipple but showed no inclination to suck.

Kelly gave a sob of desperation. 'He can't do it,' she wailed, and Zan frowned, determined not to give up.

'He's very little,' she said quietly. 'His suck reflex may not be fully developed yet. We'll just persevere.'

She also suspected that Kelly's poor physical condition might limit her supply of milk, but now wasn't the time to discuss that.

There was no other way of getting food into the baby in this tiny flat. He desperately needed to be in Special Care, with high-tech equipment and a specialised medical team.

At least Carlo's heaters had warmed the place up.

Even as she held the baby in place for another try, Carlo and Mike came out of the kitchen and Carlo reached for his phone.

'We're taking you both to hospital,' he said gruffly, his voice heavily accented and lines of strain visible around his dark eyes. 'Mike's agreed it's the best thing.'

'Oh, Mike…' Kelly burst into tears again and Zan gave a sigh of relief.

She just hoped it wouldn't be too late for the baby.

Carlo was talking into his phone and within minutes an ambulance crew were at the door.

Only moments later the baby was in the warm incubator

inside the ambulance and Mike and Kelly were seated next to her.

Zan looked at Carlo in amazement. 'How did you arrange all that so quickly?'

'I didn't.' He flashed her a smile and sprang into the ambulance after the crew. 'I arranged it all before I left. They've been parked at the end of the road, waiting for my call.'

Zan was stunned. 'But Mike might have refused…'

'I have amazing powers of persuasion.' He lowered his voice and gave her a sexy smile. 'You'd do well to remember that, Suzannah.'

Zan followed the ambulance in her car and once back at the hospital the whole team moved into action.

The baby was taken to the special care baby unit and Kelly was taken to the ward for a check-up and a rest.

'But I want to see the baby,' she fretted, as they examined her again.

'As soon as the paediatric staff ring us, we'll take you up to the special care baby unit,' Zan promised. 'They're just taking a good look at him and deciding what he needs.'

Mike was hovering nearby, not knowing whether to worry more about his wife or his son.

Carlo had gone straight up with the baby and the ambulance crew and was supervising the hand-over.

Zan was only too aware that the baby was alive only because of him and she was totally in awe of his skills as a doctor.

He was incredible.

She didn't know a single other doctor who would have coped in that situation. The flat had been filthy and freezing and he'd had next to no equipment. But he'd managed to resuscitate the baby and keep it alive until he could talk sense into the father and transfer the family to hospital.

And he'd been *so* cool.

Finally SCBU rang to say that they were ready for the parents, and Zan took Kelly and Mike up to see their son.

'It can seem a bit scary when you first see him,' she warned, knowing that the baby would be having a lot of help. 'He might have tubes in to help him breathe and things.'

'I don't care.' Kelly gave a gulp and clung to Mike's hand. 'As long as he's alive, I don't care.'

Mike was white with the strain and there was no sign of his usually tough approach to life.

It was much later, after mother and baby had been re-united and she was back on the labour ward, that Zan suddenly remembered that she'd caught a glimpse of a man watching her before she'd knocked on Kelly's door.

He was the same man she'd seen on her way to work and then again when she'd been shopping for Christmas presents.

Zan shifted uneasily.

Was she imagining it?

'Why are you frowning?' Carlo's deep voice came from directly in front of her and she gave a start.

She'd been so deep in thought that she hadn't even seen him approach.

'Oh—hi.' She smiled at him. 'Have you finished on SCBU?'

He nodded, his smile weary. 'Now we just have to hope the little chap makes it.'

'You were amazing.' Her voice was soft. 'I don't know what I would have done if you hadn't arrived. The baby would have died, Carlo.'

'Maybe not.'

He seemed oblivious to his accomplishment but Zan was under no illusions. She knew that he'd saved that baby.

'So, come on, why were you looking so worried a minute ago?' His eyes narrowed and he looked at her searchingly. 'Tell me.'

She blushed. What if she'd imagined it all? 'I'm probably being stupid…'

'But?' he prompted her gently, and she bit her lip.

'I think someone is following me. I saw this man this morning on my way to work, and then again at lunchtime when I did some shopping, and when I arrived at Kelly's flat—' She broke off, aware that Carlo was suddenly looking tense.

'Can you describe him?'

Zan looked at him, surprised by the urgency in his tone. 'I don't know…' She racked her brains. 'Tall, broad, dark hair—he wore a fawn coat with a black scarf…'

Carlo seemed to relax. 'I'm sure it was your imagination,' he said lightly, and she gave him an odd look.

'I saw him, Carlo.'

'I don't doubt that you saw him,' he replied smoothly, 'but I'm sure it was your imagination that he was following you. Maybe he was just going to the same places as you.'

Zan frowned. That might explain the first two encounters, but what would he have been doing outside Kelly's flat?

Still, Carlo obviously didn't think there was anything to worry about, and maybe he was right. It wasn't as if the man had shown any interest in her after all. He hadn't even been looking in her direction.

'It's been a long day.' Carlo seemed keen to change the subject. 'I'm on call but everything seems quiet at the moment so can I buy you supper?'

Zan smiled. 'I'm meeting Kim for a pizza at our favourite Italian restaurant. I didn't think you'd be free.'

'I'm free until I get called out.' Carlo said immediately. 'I'm feeling hideously homesick and I could do with some Italian cooking. You have to invite me.'

'Invite you where?' Kim bounced up to them, a brightly coloured scarf wrapped around her neck. 'Are you joining us?'

'Is that OK?'

'Of course.' Kim grinned at him and then glanced at Zan, who was bright pink. Her mouth fell open. 'Oh, my goodness—how could I be so slow? You're the one who—'

'Kim!' Zan interrupted her before she could say something indiscreet, and Carlo smiled.

'Why don't we go and eat? I'm starving.'

The restaurant was tucked away in a back street and the welcoming heat hit them as soon as they opened the door.

The owner greeted them in Italian and almost dropped the plates he was carrying when Carlo replied equally fluently.

Delighted to have a customer who spoke his language, the owner was immediately distracted and talked for several minutes before finding them a table.

Carlo ordered some wine and sat back in his chair while they all looked at the menu.

'So how did you two meet?' Kim was showing no interest in the idea of food.

Zan shrank into her chair in embarrassment. 'Kim, we're not—'

'Yes, we are.' Carlo's voice was firm and he flashed her a reassuring smile before turning his attention to Kim. 'We fell over each other in the street while she was on her way to visit Kelly. I didn't think it was a great place for a girl to be wandering on her own so I went with her. Then we had dinner last night.'

Zan's face heated under the look he gave her. She couldn't quite believe that this man wanted her.

She didn't need to notice that all the women in the restaurant were sneaking looks at him to be aware of his attractions. He was gorgeous. Warm and charismatic, but incredibly strong, too.

It was a combination that left her breathless.

'Well, you've definitely got the touch,' Kim said dryly, picking up the bottle of wine and helping herself. 'Have you any idea how many men Zan's chased away over the years?'

Zan flushed with embarrassment. 'Carlo's agreed to be Father Christmas,' she said quickly, changing the subject before Kim said something to embarrass her further.

Kim grinned. 'Really? You wait until you see Zan in her elf costume. Father Christmas usually has trouble with his blood pressure from the moment she takes off her coat. I keep a supply of suitable drugs at the ready.'

Their order arrived and they ate their meal, talking and laughing, and it was only when she glanced up to order coffee that Zan noticed the man sitting on his own at a table in the corner of the restaurant.

She gave a gasp and the colour drained from her face.

'What?' Kim looked at her in alarm. 'What's the matter?'

Carlo frowned. 'Zan?'

She reached across the table and grabbed his hand. 'It's the same man I saw earlier,' she whispered urgently. 'He's sitting at the table by the window. It can't be a coincidence. Every where I go, he's there, too.'

Carlo glanced around and then turned his attention back to the table as the waiter brought the coffee.

'Just ignore him,' he advised, but his fingers tightened on hers reassuringly.

Zan bit her lip. What was the matter with her? She was behaving like a real baby.

'Sorry.' She gave him a wan smile. 'I'm being stupid, aren't I? I've never really been nervous of anything before. But after the other night I'm a bit jumpy.'

Kim frowned. 'What happened the other night?'

Carlo was looking at Zan, his expression reassuring. 'There's no need to be jumpy, *cara mia*. No one is going to hurt you.' There was a hint of steel under his warm, male tones. 'We will drink our coffee and then I will take you back to your flat myself.'

She loved the fact that he was so protective.

Glancing at his powerful shoulders, she suddenly had a disturbing memory of him naked in the shower and, remembering his raw, male sexuality, she felt excitement spiral up through her body. He had an incredible physique. It was hardly surprising that he wasn't intimidated by anyone.

'Will someone please tell me what's going on?' Kim glanced between them with a mixture of concern and frustration.

'Someone attacked me the other night,' Zan said flatly. 'Carlo rescued me. It's how we met.'

Kim stared at her in horror. 'Someone *attacked* you?' She lifted a hand to her mouth. 'Oh, my God! Were you hurt?'

Zan shrugged and shook her head. 'Not really.'

Kim looked at Carlo in dismay. 'And your eye—is that how...?'

Carlo laughed. 'No. That was Zan. She was fighting like a wildcat when I got to her. She mixed me up with the attackers.'

Kim blinked in disbelief. 'And what were you saying about someone following you?'

Zan put down her coffee-cup and glanced across the

restaurant again. 'Every time I turn around, that man is behind me.' She lifted her chin and frowned. 'In fact, I'm going to stop being so pathetic and confront him. I want to know why he's following me.'

She rose to her feet but Carlo put a hand on her arm.

'Sit down.' His voice was calm but firm. 'Finish your coffee. I'll deal with it.'

She opened her mouth to argue and then closed it again, seeing the sense in his suggestion.

After all, if the man following her realised that she was with Carlo then he might think twice about following her.

Carlo strode over to Matt and sat down in a vacant seat, his back to the two women.

'You're losing your touch,' Carlo told Matt grimly, his brows locked together in a frown. 'She knows you're following her.'

'I guessed as much.' Matt rubbed a hand over his jaw and looked apologetic. 'Sorry. I underestimated her. The girl's been looking over her shoulder every two minutes and frankly I didn't expect her to be so jumpy.'

'Nor me.' Carlo felt his insides twist. He hated to think that Zan was frightened. She'd successfully concealed the fact from him.

'Whatever happened the other night obviously freaked her out,' Matt said thoughtfully. 'On her way to work this morning she looked over her shoulder at least eight times and she didn't slow down until she walked inside those hospital gates. She was better at lunchtime but she was still keeping an eye on her surroundings. She dashed to Kelly's house so quickly I didn't realise she'd seen me.'

'Damn.' Carlo was frowning but Matt gave a shrug.

'Actually, I think it's probably a good thing that she's alert in the circumstances.'

'Alert, maybe, but I don't want her frightened,' Carlo growled. 'I hadn't even noticed that she was nervous.'

Matt shrugged. 'She probably isn't when she's with you. It's just when she's on her own.'

'Well, you're going to have to keep a low profile now,' Carlo pointed out, dragging his fingers through his hair and letting out a long sigh. 'Maybe we'd better get one of the other guys to follow her.'

Matt lifted an eyebrow and Carlo shook his head. 'No, you're right. Bad idea. At least I know that if she's with you nothing's going to happen to her. Maybe I should tell her the truth.'

The longer it went on, the worse he felt about the fact he was deceiving her and he knew he was going to be faced with a major dilemma soon.

Could he make love to a woman who didn't know who he was?

'You can't tell her!' Matt glared at him. 'Not until we've caught those lunatics. You don't know that you can trust her.'

'But if she sees you again…'

'She won't. I'll be invisible and I'll change my image tomorrow.'

'All right.' Carlo was still disturbed by the news that Zan was so nervous. Why hadn't she told him? 'Oh, and by the way, while we're working in the hospital and you're kicking your heels, I need you to do something for me.'

Matt's eyes narrowed warily. 'I hardly dare ask.'

'I need you to find me a team of reindeer and a sleigh.'

Matt blinked. 'Reindeer.' His tone was faint. 'And a *sleigh*?'

'That's right. I'm going to be Father Christmas.'

And he was going to give Zan a Christmas to remember.

He walked back to the table and gestured to the waiter to bring the bill.

'It's fine, *tesoro*,' he said easily, paying the waiter in cash and reaching for his coat. 'If you saw him earlier then I'm sure it was just coincidence. He's Italian and he lives around here.'

She accepted what he said without argument and he felt a pang of guilt as he saw the trusting look in her eyes.

Whatever happened, he was going to keep her safe.

They said goodnight to Kim and then made their way back to Zan's flat.

'Only two more days until Christmas.' She smiled at him, her cheeks pink from the cold. 'Do you want to come up?'

Yes. He wanted to check that her flat was safe.

'I'll just see you into your flat and then I'd better go home.' He followed her into the lift and waited while she found her keys, his senses constantly alert to danger.

'Why do you keep looking around you?' She looked at him anxiously and this time he sensed her nerves. 'I thought you said that man wasn't following me.'

Damn. She was amazingly observant.

'He's not,' he said smoothly, cursing the fact that Matt hadn't been more discreet. It was going to be harder to keep a careful watch on Zan from now on.

Carlo took her keys and unlocked the door, hoping that she'd think he was chivalrous by nature. The truth was he wanted to enter her flat first.

He wasn't taking any chances.

He flicked on the lights and glanced swiftly around the room. Everything was neat and ordered. No sign of problems.

She tilted her head to one side and smiled. 'Coffee?'

'I shouldn't.' He walked towards her window and gazed

down at the river below with a frown. The view was great but he wished she had curtains. From the outside this room would be lit up like a stage. 'I've got to go home and practise being Father Christmas in front of my mirror.'

And tighten the security arrangements so that she was kept safe.

He wanted someone to check the opposite bank of the river to see just how visible her flat was.

'I haven't had a chance to thank you for this afternoon,' Zan blurted out. 'If it hadn't been for you, I dread to think what would have happened to Kelly and the baby. It's lucky Kim told you I was there.'

Kim hadn't told him, but he wasn't in a position to correct her.

'Resuscitating a baby in those surroundings was certainly a new experience,' he admitted dryly, and she shook her head in admiration.

'So you mostly dealt with infertility in your last job?'

'Actually, we offered a total care package,' he explained. 'From conception to discharge home after delivery.'

'Do you think the baby will be all right?'

He pulled a face and shrugged. 'Who can say? He's in the right place now—all we can do is wait and see. I'm just glad they agreed to go to hospital in the end. It made life a lot easier.'

She nodded agreement and smiled up at him. Suddenly the smile faltered and her green eyes locked with his, anticipation heating her gaze.

She wanted him to kiss her.

The silence thickened around them and he sucked in a breath.

'I'd better go.' His voice came out in a croak and he

almost laughed at himself. He'd never been so clumsy around a woman before.

But, then, he'd never known chemistry like this before either. The sexual tension between them was so powerful that it was a living force, drawing them together.

She stepped closer to him, her eyes never leaving his.

'Do you want to go?' Her question was loaded with meaning and he closed his eyes briefly.

How had he ever got himself in this mess?

He couldn't make love to her when she didn't even know who he was. He just couldn't do it.

'Zan, I don't think—'

She reached up and touched a finger to his mouth, silencing him.

'That first night, when you wanted to make love, it just felt a bit fast.' Her slim fingers were locked on the front of his jumper, hanging onto him, her eyes incredibly shy. 'But you're not a stranger any more and I— I mean, if you still want to…'

Her meaning was clear and he felt desire slam through his body.

She wanted him to make love to her because she felt that she was beginning to know him.

But she didn't know him.

He wasn't who he said he was. In fact, she knew virtually nothing about him.

Conscience ripped through him and he muttered a curse and stepped back from her.

Having a secret identity had been great at the beginning, but it had gone from being the solution to the problem.

Her hands fell to her sides and she wrapped her arms around her middle self-consciously. 'You've changed your mind.' She kept her tone light and her brave smile made him want to thump the wall.

'I haven't changed my mind.' His voice was husky and he fought the urge to reach for her again. 'I promised you I'd slow the pace.'

'Oh.' Zan's eyes brightened and the smile that followed his confession was pure sexual invitation.

Heat engulfed his body.

For a woman with no experience she certainly knew how to make a man sweat.

She licked her lips. 'You need to learn the difference between slow and stop.' Her eyes dropped to his mouth and then lifted to his eyes.

Drawn in by the expression in her green eyes, Carlo forgot about going slow. In fact, he forgot about everything.

He closed his fingers around her wrists and backed her against the wall, his mouth capturing her soft gasp of excitement. Her lips were soft and warm and she opened her mouth for him, tempting him inside.

He accepted the invitation, tasting her sweetness, showing her with every intimate touch of his mouth and tongue just what he wanted to do to the rest of her body.

Desire exploded inside him and he released her hands and cupped her face, sliding his hands through the silky mass of hair as he kissed her until the heat between them reached an intolerable level.

He lifted his head briefly, their foreheads touching, his expression dazed as he stared down into her eyes.

She looked as stunned as he felt, her green eyes cloudy, her soft lips bruised and damp from his kiss.

'Carlo.' She whispered his name with a reverence that made him groan and lower his mouth again.

He knew he ought to stop now, before stopping ceased to be an option, but he couldn't drag his mouth away from hers.

Her tongue teased his and he wondered how on earth he was going to keep it slow and gentle when the time came to make love to her. She drove him so wild he didn't know himself.

He felt her small hand slide under his jumper and then rest on the warm muscle of his chest, finding his heartbeat.

Muttering in Italian against her mouth, he dealt with the zip of her jeans and slid a hand inside, over the soft curve of her bottom.

'You feel incredible.' He moved his hand lower and found what he was looking for, his fingers touching her with a deliberate intimacy that brought a sob to her lips.

She moved against his hand and dragged her mouth away from his, her eyes glazed with desire and her cheeks fevered.

'Carlo, it feels so... I didn't know...'

'Shh—' He moved his hand and hugged her against him, trying to lower the temperature a notch.

He didn't succeed.

His whole body burned for this woman.

And he wasn't being honest with her.

The thought was like a shower of cold water and he released her and stepped away, raking a hand through his dark hair as he struggled with his conscience.

She leaned against the wall for support, looking at him in confusion.

Her dark hair was tangled from his touch and her cheeks were flushed. She looked like a girl who'd been thoroughly kissed and he felt desire slam through his body with a force that left him breathless.

'It's getting late. I'd better go...'

He worked on his will-power. If she asked him to stay he was in trouble.

But she didn't.

In fact, she didn't speak at all. She just stood there, supported by the wall, staring at him.

He picked up his jacket from the floor and walked back to her. He locked their hands together and bent his head to give her a gentle kiss.

'Goodnight, Zan—I'll see you tomorrow.'

And by then he would have worked out how to tell her the truth.

CHAPTER SIX

CARLO stared at the ultrasound scan and tried to forget about Zan.

She was dominating his every thought and it was starting to drive him mad.

He'd already decided that the first opportunity that he had he was going to tell her the truth and risk the consequences.

'Mr Bennett?' A young student nurse cleared her throat nervously to attract his attention. 'The labour ward has been calling. They need you up there urgently.'

Despite the fact it was Christmas Eve, the day was frantically busy and they barely saw one another as they coped with the huge workload.

Fortunately by five o'clock labour ward had calmed down and the clinic was empty.

In the nurses' locker room, Zan dragged on green tights and a figure-hugging tunic and pulled a face in the mirror. 'Are you sure this is an elf costume? I look more like Peter Pan.'

'Definitely elf,' Kim murmured as she pushed her feet into a pair of black boots. 'Next year I'm coming as something warm and furry, like a reindeer. There's something to be said for being Father Christmas. At least you can wear a thick jumper underneath. Talking of which, what's happening with that gorgeous man of yours?'

Zan blushed and tucked her dark hair under a green hat. 'He's finished on Labour Ward and he's gone to change.'

'That wasn't what I meant,' Kim said dryly, and Zan smiled.

'Nothing's happening exactly…' *Not yet anyway.* 'But we get on well. And he's such a brilliant doctor, Kim.' Her eyes shone. 'You should have seen him with Kelly. He was so calm and he just wouldn't give up on that baby. And then he managed to talk Mike round and persuade him into going to the hospital, and he'd arranged heaters and an ambulance…' She broke off, breathless, and Kim grinned.

'So you're not in love, or anything like that, then?'

Zan sucked in a breath and her eyes widened.

Love?

It had been so fast she hadn't even examined her feelings in any depth, but now she did and the result shocked her. She sat down with a thump on one of the hard chairs.

'It's only been a few days,' she croaked. 'How do I know if it's love?'

Kim shrugged. 'I don't know. Try and imagine him walking down the aisle with someone else. How do you feel?'

Zan thought about it. 'Sick?'

'That could be love or too many mince pies,' Kim said sagely. 'Do you want to punch her on the nose?'

'I think I've done enough punching in this relationship,' Zan muttered, remembering Carlo's bruised cheek. 'And I'm not kidding myself it's marriage he has in mind.'

Carlo was a red-blooded Italian male who certainly didn't need to get married to have an active sex life.

Kim shrugged. 'I wouldn't be so sure about that. He must be early thirties. All Italian men want babies at some point. They're very into the family thing. It's got to be on his agenda.'

Zan bit her lip. Did he want to get married? The thought of Carlo smiling at another woman, kissing another woman, making love to another woman, made her utterly miserable.

'OK.' She lifted her palms and gave a resigned smile. 'To answer your original question—I'd definitely want to punch her on the nose. Hard.'

Kim grinned. 'I knew it. You're in love.'

'I think I might be.' Zan's expression was gloomy. 'Bad news, huh?'

'Why bad news?' Kim straightened her costume and reached for her coat. 'He seems pretty keen on you, too.'

'Bed keen,' Zan said wistfully. 'Not marriage keen.'

'You don't know that.'

'I've only known him for four days,' Zan pointed out, and Kim shrugged.

'Well, it's been long enough for you.'

Zan thought about everything Carlo had done since she'd met him. Waded in and rescued her from being mugged, made her laugh, intervened in a difficult delivery, kissed her breathless and saved the life of a baby. She'd learned a lot about him in four days.

'He'd be a brilliant father. Oh, help!' Zan sighed. 'What's happened to me? I used to be cautious and rational. Now I want to have his babies.'

'Love is never rational,' Kim said dryly. 'When are you seeing him again?'

'Tonight.' Zan blushed slightly. 'He's staying the night so that we can open our presents together tomorrow morning. He's on call tomorrow.'

'So tonight's the night.' Kim looked at her curiously. 'Spending Christmas together sounds pretty romantic to me.'

'Well, his family is all in Italy and I can't get home so it seemed like a good idea.' Zan shrugged dismissively and Kim laughed.

'Stop making it sound like a business arrangement. You're not fooling me. What have you got planned?'

Nothing she could share with her friend.

Fortunately, before she could answer there was a knock on the door and one of the other elves stuck her head round, her eyes twinkling with fun.

'Message from Father Christmas—the reindeer are playing up and he needs some elves desperately. He's waiting for us by the main entrance.'

'Reindeer?' Kim and Zan exchanged baffled looks and made their way to the hospital entrance.

Zan pushed open the revolving doors and then stopped with a gasp of amazement.

Immediately in front of the hospital was a sleigh straight out of a fairy-tale, decorated with delicate silver chains and tiny lights and pulled by six brown reindeer with knobbly antlers and velvety noses, their breath producing clouds of steam in the frosty air.

Carlo sat holding the reins, a huge sack bulging on the seat behind him.

He was dressed as Father Christmas, most of his face concealed under a ridiculous white beard. 'Hurry up, elves. I'm never going to get down all the chimneys at this rate.'

Zan gave a laugh of delight and jumped into the sleigh next to him. 'I can't believe you found a sleigh. Did you arrange this?'

'What use is Santa without his reindeer?' His face was barely visible under the white beard that he was wearing. Then he smiled at her and bent his head for a kiss.

A laughing Kim jumped up next to them. 'Hey, this is a family show!'

They broke apart reluctantly and Carlo ran a gentle finger down Zan's flushed cheek.

'What exactly are an elf's duties?' His voice was husky with passion and Zan smiled.

'We're here to service your every need, Father Christmas.'

'Glad to hear it.' He gave her a sexy wink.

The other nurse jumped onto the sleigh and for the first time Zan noticed a girl standing next to the reindeer, holding their reins.

Once everyone was settled on the sleigh, the girl led the first pair of reindeer forward and the others followed, pulling the sleigh down the path and onto the lawn behind the children's ward.

Despite the cold and the snow, the doors had been flung open and excited children gathered in the doorway, their faces pink with delight. Those who were confined to bed had been pushed as close as possible to the window so that everyone could have a look.

Carlo said something to the girl who was helping him and she leaned forward and untied one of the reindeer, leading him carefully towards the children.

Carlo followed, leaping down from the sleigh and grabbing the bag of presents.

'Ho, ho, ho, children,' he bellowed, and Zan burst into a fit of giggles. He was the most convincing Father Christmas she'd ever seen.

He walked onto the ward and the children were soon clambering all over him, hugging him and trying to tell him what they wanted for Christmas.

Carlo listened intently and nodded and then indicated to the elves that they should give out presents.

Kim, Zan and the other nurse dipped into the enormous sack and pulled out boxes wrapped in blue and pink, passing them into eager little hands.

Several of the children were stroking the reindeer, totally enraptured by the soft covering on its antlers. It was totally docile, standing quietly while they swarmed all around it.

'I have to confess that I never knew reindeer were so small,' Kim muttered as she delved into the sack for another present.

'Does size matter in a reindeer?' Carlo's eyes twinkled suggestively and Zan laughed.

She couldn't believe he'd arranged real reindeer. When she'd asked him to be Father Christmas she'd never thought for a moment that he'd enter into the spirit of things to quite this extent.

But the children were loving every minute of it.

And as they sat on the floor, ripping open their presents, the hospital choir arrived at the entrance of the ward and started to sing carols.

The moment was so magical that Zan felt her eyes grow hot.

'I feel really Christmassy,' Kim said happily, and then she glanced across at Carlo and lowered her voice. 'He's fantastic, Zan. After tonight, I'd have his babies, too.'

Zan watched as Carlo hugged a little girl who had her leg in plaster, his dark eyes warm and kind as he listened to her breathless requests for presents.

Kim was right. He was fantastic.

And then he looked up and caught her looking at him. The benign, fatherly look in his eyes vanished, to be replaced by a look of such sexual intensity that her insides burned with excitement.

She could hardly breathe for wanting him, and she wondered how she was going to show him that she didn't want him to slow the pace any more.

It was obviously going to be up to her to take the initiative.

Finally the reindeer were loaded back into their trailer and the children were settled into bed.

'Not that I expect them to sleep much,' the ward sister admitted with a sigh as she tried to calm the excited children.

Zan moved closer to Carlo. 'How's Kelly's baby doing?'

'I've been too busy to go up and check.' He looked at her quizzically. 'Shall we go up now?'

'Dressed like this?' Zan glanced down at herself doubtfully and he laughed.

'Why not? It's Christmas Eve after all.'

So they took the lift to the labour ward and walked through to SCBU. The ward was warm and festive and the staff greeted them with amusement as they strolled onto the ward in their costumes.

'How's baby Turner?' Carlo walked over to the incubator and gazed down at the baby lying attached to tubes and monitors.

'Actually, he's doing pretty well.' The doctor looking after the baby glanced at the machines with a frown and twiddled a knob. 'They're scanning him later because they're worried about the risk of intraventricular haemorrhage.'

'Oh.' Zan looked shocked. 'Why are they worried about that?'

'It's a fairly routine procedure in premature babies,' Carlo assured her, picking up the chart and scanning it. 'Brain haemorrhage can occur in up to forty per cent of babies who weigh under 1500 grammes. How's everything else?'

The doctor adjusted her glasses. 'His blood gases deteriorated so we had to ventilate him overnight but he's stabilised now.'

She and Carlo proceeded to have a detailed conversation about the baby's progress and then Zan looked up and saw Kelly and Mike hovering in the doorway, looking out of place and uncomfortable.

'Hi.' Zan moved towards them, waving an apologetic hand over her costume. 'Sorry about the way we look—

we dressed up for the children's ward earlier and we haven't had time to change. How are you?'

'We're fine.' Kelly looked pale and thin and she was gazing longingly at the baby. 'He's being fed through a tube and I so wanted to breast-feed.'

'You can still breast-feed him,' Zan assured her, taking her arm and walking with her towards the incubator. Machines beeped and the lights sent a glow over the dark ward. 'Have you talked to the nurses about it?'

Kelly shook her head. 'They're so busy.'

'Not too busy to help you breast-feed,' Zan said firmly. 'What you need to do is express milk to begin with and they can give that down his tube.'

The doctor looking after the baby glanced up and smiled. 'In fact, that would be brilliant. He's actually not tolerating our formula milk very well. I think it's a bit too rich for his little tummy. Any time you want to give us some breast milk, please, feel free.'

Kelly glanced nervously at Zan, who smiled reassuringly.

'How about now?' She sensed that Kelly was out of her depth on this ward full of strangers. 'I could help you. They've got a special room here where you can sit quietly. Providing the staff don't mind me butting in, I can show you the ropes.'

Carlo lifted an eyebrow. 'There's no end to what an elf can do.'

Zan glanced down at herself and pulled a face. 'I'd forgotten I'm an elf.'

'I'll lend you a white coat if you'll stay and help,' one of the nurses said dryly as she walked past and heard the exchange.

Zan looked at Carlo. 'Is it OK?'

'Of course.' He smiled easily, as relaxed as ever. 'Give me a shout when you're ready to go.'

He made no secret of their relationship and Zan blushed slightly.

'OK, Kelly, come with me and I'll introduce you to Daisy.'

They left Carlo talking quietly to Mike and walked down the corridor and into a small but comfortable room. Kelly hovered on the threshold.

'Who's Daisy?'

Zan laughed and waved a hand towards the machine on the table. 'Meet Daisy the cow. So called because of her role in milk production. Let me show you what to do.' She picked out various items of equipment and ripped open the packets. 'These are sterile and you need a fresh one of these every time.'

She showed Kelly what to connect where and then helped her get the pressure right on the machine.

A few drops of milk-like fluid trickled into the bottle and Kelly looked at Zan anxiously. 'It isn't very much.'

Zan sat down next to her. 'It takes a few days for your milk to come in properly. This is what we call colostrum. It's not high volume but it's very high in calories and full of antibodies.' Zan hesitated. 'You've been anaemic, Kelly, and you're pretty underweight. It's possible that you won't be able to produce enough milk to feed him completely on your own. We might need to top her up.'

Kelly's eyes filled but she nodded. 'I see.'

'It's important that you eat a good diet from now on—plenty of protein,' Zan told her, 'and keep expressing because that will stimulate your milk supply.'

Kelly looked at her. 'And will he ever be able to feed from me?'

'I'm sure he will.' Zan was quick to reassure her. 'As soon as he's a bit stronger, we'll start putting him to the breast to get him used to the idea.'

'What if he doesn't get used to the idea?'

'He will.' Zan gave her a warm smile. 'You're going to be a great mum, Kelly. How are you feeling in yourself?'

'Tired,' Kelly admitted, and Zan made a mental note to mention it to Carlo. She still needed to have her blood checked for anaemia.

'How's Mike coping?'

Kelly pulled a face. 'Pretty well, really, considering how much he hates hospitals. It brings back horrible memories for him.'

They walked back onto SCBU to find Carlo still in conversation with Mike and the doctor.

He smiled at Kelly. 'Has this little boy got a name yet?'

Kelly nodded and looked at Mike. 'Eddie,' she said softly. 'We're calling him Eddie after Mike's brother.'

There was a silence and Carlo cleared his throat. 'Good name,' he said gruffly, and Mike looked at him and rubbed a hand across the back of his neck.

'I don't know how to say this, Doc,' he mumbled, and Carlo put a hand on his shoulder, his dark eyes warm with understanding.

'There's nothing to say,' he said quietly. 'You had a difficult choice to make, but you did the right thing. You were brave.'

Mike shook his head. 'It was you who did the right thing and don't think I don't know that,' he said hoarsely. He grabbed Carlo's arm. 'You need anything—*anything at all*—you come to me.'

Carlo was visibly moved and Zan leaned forward to give Kelly a hug.

'Merry Christmas,' she said softly, looking at Eddie Turner and deciding that miracles did happen after all.

It was much later when they walked towards Zan's flat, both still dressed in costume.

'That was fun,' Carlo said, a laugh in his voice as he

reached up to rub his dark jaw. 'Apart from the beard. The beard made me itch.'

'You were brilliant.' Zan glanced over her shoulder, still nervous that someone might be following her. 'Where did you find the reindeer?'

'They came down from Scotland,' he told her, following her gaze and looking at her quizzically. 'Why do you keep looking over your shoulder?'

'Because I'm paranoid about being followed,' she confessed, moving a little closer to him. 'I thought I saw a man watching me again this morning.'

Carlo glanced at her. 'The same man from the restaurant?'

'No.' Zan shook her head. 'Someone different. Well, actually, there were two of them. I'm sure it was my imagination. I'm seeing men on every corner.'

Either way, she didn't really care at the moment. No one was going to hurt her while she was with Carlo. No one in their right mind would attack someone of his build.

They arrived back at her flat and Zan flicked on the Christmas-tree lights and lit a few candles.

She needed subtle lighting for what she had in mind.

'I put some champagne in the fridge earlier,' she murmured, moving through to the kitchen and fetching two glasses.

By the time she moved back to the sitting room Carlo had removed his hat and was wearing a snug pair of jeans and a thick jumper.

Zan's eyes twinkled. 'So this is what Father Christmas does in his spare time.'

'Consorts with elves, you mean?' He moved towards her and took the bottle, popping the cork and catching the bubbling liquid in the glasses that she held out. 'You're shivering.'

'Yes, well, elves are obviously tougher than me,' she

admitted, a plan forming in her mind. 'This outfit is freezing. I'm just going to take a shower and change into something warmer.'

Carlo tensed slightly. 'OK.'

She walked through to her bedroom, stripped off the elf costume and showered quickly.

Her heart banging against her chest, she opened a drawer and removed a bag. Did she dare?

Taking a deep breath, Zan gave a womanly smile and started to dress.

Carlo glanced towards the bedroom as he dialled, hoping that she was going to take some time.

He'd managed not to react when she'd announced that someone was still following her, but a nasty suspicion was growing in his mind.

'Matt?' He spoke in Italian, talking in a low voice as he briefly outlined the situation to the chief of security.

'I'm staying here tonight.' Carlo kept his eye on the bedroom door as he talked. 'I'm on call from eight o'clock tomorrow morning, so I could get called into the hospital then, but if I do I'll find some way of taking her with me. I don't want her left alone.'

Having agreed a plan with Matt, he ended the conversation as quickly as possible, flicking the phone shut and slipping it back into his pocket.

If there was going to be trouble, at least they were prepared.

The bedroom door opened and as he glanced up, all thoughts of danger vanished from his mind.

In fact, all rational thought vanished from his mind.

Zan was standing in the doorway looking like something straight out of a bad boy's dreams.

She was wearing skimpy briefs, sheer stockings that

made her long legs shimmer temptingly and the highest heels he'd ever seen.

Struggling to breathe, he dragged his eyes upwards, past the smooth curve of her waist and the swell of her breasts to the blatant invitation in her green eyes.

'Zan.' His voice was a tortured croak and she smiled as she walked towards him, her legs endless as she closed the gap between them.

'The other night I told you that we were going too fast.' She sounded breathy and feminine and decidedly nervous. 'I know you've been holding back, but you don't need to any more. I didn't know how to tell you…'

The draw of her smooth, creamy skin was too much, and he slid a hand around her waist, feeling the silky warmth of her skin under his fingers.

'I think I get the message.'

She trembled slightly under his touch but her gaze didn't falter. 'I want you, Carlo—if you still want me, that is.'

What a question.

Carlo almost groaned aloud. Of course he wanted her, but he needed to talk to her first. *He needed to tell her who he was.*

'Zan, I—'

He saw the uncertainty flicker in her eyes. 'Have you changed your mind?'

Zan pressed closer and his senses were swamped by her. That special scent that drove him wild, the touch of her warm skin, the feel of her breath against his cheek.

'I haven't changed my mind, but—'

'Good.' She slid her small hands under his jumper and he shuddered as he felt her fingers slide over his skin.

Part of him jerked back to reality. *He had to tell her who he was.*

'Zan, I just…'

'What?' Her voice was low and husky and she stood on tiptoe and licked at his lips in a provocative gesture that made every male hormone in his body work overtime.

He tried to capture her mouth, but she moved away with a tantalising smile that made him groan with frustration. She continued to tease him, pressing light, fluttery kisses against his mouth and cheek but dodging him when he tried to deepen the connection.

Then she tugged lightly at his jumper and he yanked it over his head and dropped it on the floor, aware that his erection was blatantly evident through the fabric of his jeans.

Her lips parted and her breathing shallow, Zan ran a finger through the dark hair on his chest, following the line downwards to where it vanished into the waistband of his jeans. She lifted her eyes to his, her gaze hot and inviting as her fingers dealt with the fastening and then the zip.

Still holding his gaze, she touched him intimately and he saw a hint of uncertainty in her eyes.

And he decided that it was time he took over.

He dispensed with his jeans and scooped her up into his arms, carrying her though to the bedroom and kicking the door closed behind them.

Her silky dark hair brushed his cheek and he lowered his head and kissed her hungrily before laying her on the bed and coming down on top of her.

She stroked a hand over the muscles of his shoulders and the trust in her eyes made something twist inside him.

He knew that they ought to be talking, not making love, but the moment for talking was long past.

All he could do now was make sure that her first time was the best time she'd ever have.

The talking would have to come later.

* * *

Zan lay trembling on the bed, both hands holding onto Carlo as he kissed her.

She loved the feel of solid muscle under her fingers, loved his combination of strength and gentleness.

The truth was, she loved *him*.

He lifted his head, his breathing ragged as he looked down at her, his dark eyes unbelievably sexy. Then he murmured something in Italian and the tone of his voice made her heart thump against her chest.

'You're doing it again,' she pointed out huskily. 'You're talking in Italian and I don't understand a word.'

His smile was intimate. 'I said that you are very, very beautiful, *cara mia*.'

His hand moved slowly but deliberately down her body and suddenly she found it hard to breathe. He lowered his head and kissed her slowly and the excitement he roused was so intense that it frightened her.

She pulled away slightly, stunned by how out of control she felt.

Carlo's eyes searched hers and then he gave a very male smile that showed that he understood. 'I know…'

He kissed her again, this time teasing her tongue into an erotic dance with his, arousing feelings so powerful that she pressed against him in an unspoken demand for more.

Without lifting his head, he moved his hand lower and curved it over her breast, the rough pad of his thumb teasing her hard nipple.

Sensation stabbed low in her abdomen and she gasped against his mouth and instinctively parted her legs.

He lifted his head and stroked her dark hair away from her face with a hand that wasn't quite steady.

'You are incredibly responsive, *tesoro*, and you have a disastrous effect on my self-control.' His eyes smiled into hers and he kept their gazes locked together as his hand moved lower.

Zan felt his hand on the soft skin of her thigh and then

his fingers slid inside her flimsy panties, his eyes never leaving hers as he found what he was looking for.

Her fingers tightened on the muscles of his shoulders and she tensed slightly.

'Don't be shy with me.' He murmured the words against her mouth, kissing her gently as he removed her panties. Reassuring her as his skilled fingers worked their magic. Excitement exploded inside her and she slid her hands over his skin, touching his warmth and maleness, moving her hips in an instinctive quest for satisfaction.

Carlo slid down her body, using his mouth in an exploration so thorough and intimate that by the time he finally slid back up and settled himself on top of her she was a seething, uncontrollable mass of sensation.

Desperate to know him as he knew her, she reached down to touch him, but he caught her hand and shook his head.

'No way, *tesoro*, I'm too close.'

'But—'

'There'll be time for that later.'

She felt his weight on top of her, his strength as he parted her thighs, and suddenly a flash of trepidation penetrated her consciousness.

Totally attuned to every response her body made, he slowed the pace, his dark eyes suddenly gentle as he looked down at her.

'Relax, *cara mia*. You can still change your mind.'

She didn't want to change her mind.

She wanted him to make love to her—now!

'I don't want to,' she said urgently, pulling him towards her. 'Please...'

He stared down at her, his breathing unsteady, and she could see the conflict in his dark eyes.

'If you stop now, I'll black your other eye,' she joked, her voice unsteady as she slid a hand over his smooth back.

She tugged his head down to hers and kissed him, coaxing his tongue into a game with hers.

But it was clear that he wasn't going to be rushed. His kiss was slow and leisurely, and he trailed a finger down her body, exploring her with an expert touch that drove her to fever pitch.

Finally, when she was writhing and gasping underneath him, when every part of her body ached for him, he lifted his head and looked down at her.

His gaze hot, he shifted his position slightly and entered her slowly, holding back with a visible effort, checking that she was all right.

She was more than all right.

She was in heaven.

Feeling his pulsing strength inside her, she wrapped her legs around him, her eyes locked with the heat of his as she raised her hips to meet him.

With a low groan Carlo pushed deep, driving into the heart of her, setting their bodies on fire with each skilful thrust.

Zan gasped as excitement consumed her, clutching at his hard shoulders with her fingers, feeling the strength of his body against hers.

He shifted his position slightly, his gaze locking with hers as he moved, his eyes fierce with need.

He was no longer gentle but Zan didn't even notice.

Their love-making had a wild, primitive edge to it, and she trembled beneath him as he moved inside her, deeper, harder, surrounding and filling her with his strength.

It was the most intense and intimate experience of her life.

Her climax hit without warning and she felt him shudder above her as he drove them both to a peak of excitement that consumed them both in its explosive intensity.

She clung to him, breathless and stunned, her eyes locked with his as she struggled to come back to earth.

He stroked her damp hair away from her face with a gentle hand and bent his head to kiss her again. Then he rolled over, taking her with him.

She held him tightly, relieved that he didn't seem to want to lose the physical contact.

A soft smile of satisfaction touched her lips.

She might have missed this.

If she'd been sensible and cautious she never would have invited him back to her flat on that first night, and then she never would have known what love could feel like.

He held her tightly, one arm clamping her against him, one leg slung over hers. Then he moved slightly so that he could look at her. He looked very sexy and very, very male.

'Are you OK?'

His voice was deep and accented and she gave him a shy smile.

'Are you kidding? If I'd known it was that good I would have done it years ago.'

He glowered at her and his grip tightened possessively. 'Don't say that. Ever.' His tone was raw. 'You're mine and no one else's.'

She chuckled and her eyes teased him. 'I love it when you're macho.'

He grinned and rolled her onto her back. 'I'll show you macho.'

His voice was a sexy rumble and she sighed against his mouth as he kissed her thoroughly, stoking the fire again.

'I never knew that Father Christmas had so many talents.' She lifted a hand to touch his dark jaw, loving his rough masculinity. 'I love you, Carlo.'

He stilled above her and his dark eyes narrowed slightly, revealing nothing of his thoughts.

Zan felt her cheeks warm.

She shouldn't have said anything.

Embarrassed by her declaration, and by the lengthening silence, she tried to roll away from him but his hold tightened and he used his weight to keep her still while he slid a hand into her hair, forcing her to look at him.

'I love you too.' His voice was hoarse. 'I want you to remember that, Zan. Whatever happens, I want you to remember that.'

His thumb moved gently over her cheek and she stared into his eyes, wondering what he'd meant by that remark.

Why would she need to remember that he loved her?

Something jarred inside her brain, but before she could explore the source of her unease he lowered his head and kissed her again, making her head spin and sending all rational thought from her head.

CHAPTER SEVEN

CARLO watched Zan as she slept and wondered how he'd got himself into this situation.

He'd just made love to a woman who didn't know who he was.

Shaken by the depth of his feelings, he held onto her tightly, as if keeping her close physically could prevent anything driving them apart.

He'd made love before but he realised now that it had always been a purely physical act. With Zan it had been totally different. She'd seduced his emotions as well as his body.

And when she woke up he was going to tell her the truth.

Zan smelt coffee and opened her eyes.

'Merry Christmas.' Carlo placed a tray by the bed and bent to kiss her. 'He's been.'

She sat up and rubbed her eyes, still drugged from sleep. 'Who's been?'

'Father Christmas, of course.'

Without giving her a chance to protest, he dropped an elegantly wrapped parcel into her lap and she woke up rapidly.

Her eyes widened. 'For me?'

He nodded. 'Open it.'

She tugged at the ribbon, ripped the paper and then gasped as she saw the oyster silk wrap and pyjamas.

'Oh—they're beautiful.'

She fingered them gingerly, almost afraid to touch the delicate fabric.

'Put them on.' His eyes burned into hers. 'If you don't get dressed now, I won't be able to undress you later.'

She blushed at the reminder that she was still naked, and slipped her arms into the pyjama top, loving the way the silk slithered over her skin.

'They're gorgeous.' She gazed down at herself and then up at him. 'I've never worn anything so beautiful.'

'Good.'

He smiled with satisfaction and waited for her to finish dressing. 'Now come with me.'

Still fingering the pyjamas with awe, she followed him through to the living room and gave a smile of delight when she saw the stocking stuffed full of presents lying under the tree.

'More?'

He bent his head and kissed her gently. 'Much, much more.'

She stood on tiptoe and wrapped her arms around his neck, loving the feel of his rough jaw against her skin.

'What did I do to deserve you?'

Something flickered across his face, but it was gone in an instant and he waved a hand at the bulging stocking.

'Get started. I'll fetch the coffee.'

Zan knelt down on the cushions and reached for the stocking, squeezing it as she had as a child.

'Very lumpy and bumpy.' She laughed. 'This used to be my favourite game as a child. Guessing the present. I used to break half of them before Christmas Day because I'd poked them so much.'

He sprawled alongside her and handed her a coffee. 'Drink this. It will wake you up.'

'I'm awake.' She was tugging the first present out of the stocking and ripping at the paper. 'Oh!' She picked up the pretty doll and smiled at him. 'You certainly pay attention, I'll give you that.'

'You said you'd never had one.'

'I know.' She stroked the doll's hair wistfully. 'She's beautiful.'

She worked her way down the stocking, touched by the thought that he'd put into each present. There was a book, a beautiful pen, a soft cashmere jumper in a shade of green that she knew would suit her and beautiful, feminine underwear.

'You bought me so much.' She glanced at him, embarrassed, knowing that she'd only bought him a few things and hadn't spent nearly so much.

'Put your hand in the bottom of the stocking,' he suggested, leaning forward to see what she was doing. 'There should be one more parcel.'

Zan did as she was told and withdrew a small, flat box wrapped in silver paper and bows.

'Gosh, this is elaborate.' She undid the bow, removed the paper and flipped open the box, and her face broke into a smile. 'My diamonds!'

Lying in the box were a pair of the prettiest earrings she'd ever seen.

'Do you like them?' He sounded strangely uncertain and she leaned forward to kiss him.

'I love them. They're perfect.' She lifted them out of the box and held them up to the light, watching as they twinkled and shone. 'They're *huge*! Imagine if they were real.'

There was a long silence and Carlo cleared his throat, sounding distinctly uncomfortable.

'Zan, listen—'

Suddenly aware that she might have sounded rude, Zan interrupted him.

'They're gorgeous, Carlo, and I'd hate to have real

ones,' she assured him hastily. 'I'd be terrified to wear them. Now it's my turn.' She moved over to the Christmas tree and rummaged underneath for his presents.

'This is my main present to you.' She handed him a small box, hugely pleased with herself.

The man in the shop had assured her that it was the perfect present for an Italian male. Or any male, for that matter.

Carlo ripped off the paper and stared down at the toy car in his hand.

'It's a Ferrari,' Zan said breathlessly. 'Apparently it's called an Enzo Ferrari and there aren't very many and they cost almost half a million pounds. So I thought I'd get you one for Christmas.'

Carlo was very still, staring down at the car with a strange expression on his face.

Zan's smile faded and she looked at him anxiously. 'Do you hate it? Have you already got one?'

Carlo seemed to shake himself. 'No. Not like this.'

'Good.' He seemed totally distracted and Zan looked at him in confusion. 'When I win the Lottery I'll buy you the real one.'

His eyes met hers.

'Zan, there's something I have to tell you.' His voice sounded strange and his expression was deadly serious. He put the car on the floor and reached for her hand. 'I should have told you before, but I—'

The shrill tone of his mobile phone interrupted them and he said something in Italian that she was sure wasn't polite.

'We'll talk in a moment.' He flipped open the phone. 'Carlo Bennett.' He listened, frowning slightly as the person on the other end spoke briefly. 'OK—I'll come in. Yes, she's coming, too.'

He closed the phone, his expression grim. 'Helen Hughes has gone into labour.'

'Well, what's the problem with that? Oh, no.' Zan clamped a hand over her mouth and started to giggle. 'I'd forgotten about her mother staying. She won't even have had time to put the turkey in the oven yet. Why are you looking so tense?'

Carlo hesitated. 'Because I wanted to talk to you.'

'You can talk to me while we get dressed.' Zan scrambled to her feet and dashed into the bedroom. 'What stage is she at?'

'Her waters have just broken and she's been having regular contractions for the past two hours so they've told her to come straight to Labour Ward. They wanted to let me know and I said I'll go in and check on her. I know you're not officially working until lunchtime but I thought you'd like to do the same as you're her named midwife.'

'Of course I'll come with you.' Zan dragged a uniform out of the wardrobe. 'Try keeping me away! Would you believe, I've never delivered twins? I'm really excited. This is the best Christmas ever!'

Carlo looked oddly tense as he pulled on a pair of tailored trousers and dug a roll-neck jumper out of his bag.

She reached for her coat and glanced across at him. 'What did you want to talk to me about?'

He hesitated briefly and then shrugged. 'It can wait.'

She smiled. 'We can talk tonight, after we've delivered these twins.'

Whatever it was couldn't be that important.

The two men in the car watched them leave.

'I'll say this for Santini—he's got taste,' one of the men muttered. 'That girl is gorgeous.'

His friend frowned at him. 'You shouldn't be looking at the girl. You should be looking for the bodyguard.'

'Parini?'

'He's the best there is. I'm not going near that apartment until I know he's out of the way. I value my life.'

They sat in silence for several minutes and then the larger of the two men gave a sigh of satisfaction.

'There he goes. He's not letting Santini out of his sight.'

'Which means that he's not watching the apartment. Now what?'

His friend gave a nasty smile. 'We go upstairs and leave Carlo Santini a message.'

Helen Hughes was waiting for them on the labour ward.

'How did you know?' She glared at Carlo and then screwed up her face as another contraction hit her. It was half a minute before she could finish the conversation. 'You said that I wasn't going to cook Christmas dinner. How did you know?'

'Experience. And instinct.' Carlo gave her a sympathetic smile. 'Tell me what happened.'

'I had a lousy night. Backache, leg-ache, headache—you name it, it ached. Then I got up to make a cup of tea and my waters broke so I started Christmas morning by cleaning the floor. I've been getting regular contractions ever since.'

Carlo nodded. 'OK. This is what we're going to do. I'm going to examine you to check what's happening and then, providing your cervix has dilated sufficiently, I'm going to put a scalp electrode on the first baby's head to help us monitor his heart-rate.'

Helen looked worried. 'What about the other twin?'

'We'll monitor that one externally,' Zan assured her, helping her onto the bed while Carlo washed his hands and pulled on a pair of gloves.

She opened the pack for him and got everything ready.

'You're three centimetres dilated, Helen,' he said eventually, reaching to pick up the electrode. 'I'm just going to attach this to his scalp.'

His fingers moved swiftly and skilfully and he attached the electrode with the minimum of fuss. Then he connected it to the machine.

Helen looked at it doubtfully. 'What on earth does that thing measure?'

Carlo ripped off his gloves and tossed them into the bin. 'It allows us to watch the baby's heart and how it responds during each contraction. Zan will put an external monitor on the other twin now, so that we can measure his heartbeat, too.'

Zan strapped the ultrasound transducer to Helen's abdomen and checked that she had a heart trace.

'That seems fine.' She glanced up at Carlo. 'Do you want to get a line in?'

She knew that it was important to have intravenous access in twin delivery because of the risk of complications.

'Definitely.'

He explained what they were doing to Helen and then waited until another contraction had passed before he found a vein and inserted a venflon.

'Are the babies in the right position?' Helen looked worried, but Carlo gave her a reassuring smile.

'The first baby is fine, and we don't worry about the second one until the first is safely born. Once he has room to move he might change position,' Carlo explained. 'After delivery of the first twin we will scan you to check on how the second one is lying.'

'You always call the baby *him*,' Helen pointed out tartly, and Carlo gave a sheepish grin.

'Because all Italian men are chauvinists. We always call babies *him* until proved otherwise.'

'So what happens if it's a girl?' Helen teased. 'Do you refuse to deliver it?'

'Of course not.' Carlo gave her a wink. 'I love girls.'

'I can imagine.' Helen's tone was dry and Zan changed the subject. She didn't want to think about the fact that Carlo loved girls.

'What's happening at home, Helen?' Zan handed her a drink of water and waited while she took a few sips. 'Is your husband coming in?'

Helen handed the cup back and tried to make herself more comfortable. 'Later. The children were ripping open their stockings when my waters broke, so we thought we'd try and give them as normal a Christmas as possible.' She gave a short laugh. 'I even managed to get the turkey into the oven between contractions and I did all the veg last night.'

'Sounds incredibly relaxing.' Carlo glanced up from the notes, his tone dry. 'No wonder you went into labour.'

'Well, Christmas is not the ideal time to have a baby,' Helen agreed, biting her lip and sucking in her breath as another contraction hit her. 'Ouch—this is really starting to hurt.'

'When we talked about pain relief in antenatal classes, you wanted to try and stick to gas and air,' Zan said quietly, 'but you know that you can change your mind, don't you?'

Helen breathed carefully. 'I don't know what to do any more,' she confessed. 'I read somewhere that if I have an epidural it means you can operate in an emergency.'

'I don't foresee an emergency,' Carlo said calmly. 'You do what's right for you. If we need to intervene at any stage then we'll tell you.'

Helen gave him a grateful smile. 'In that case, I'll stick to gas and air for now and see how it goes.' She looked at Zan. 'Will you be with me the whole time? It helps just to have people I trust around me.'

'I promise I'll be with you all the way,' Zan said quietly, giving her hand a squeeze.

Helen bit her lip. 'I've ruined your Christmas,' she muttered, and Zan grinned.

Ruined her Christmas?

She thought back to the night before and everything that had happened between her and Carlo.

'Are you kidding? I'm having the best Christmas I can ever remember, and delivering twins will be the highlight.' Her green eyes sparkled and she glanced up to find Carlo watching her with a heat in his eyes that made her draw breath.

He was *so* sexy.

And he loved her.

She was so happy she could barely keep it to herself.

'The labour ward staff were telling me that you weren't even supposed to be working this morning,' Helen said, clearly fretting that she'd made Zan give up her Christmas.

'I'm on a late,' Zan told her, 'which means that officially I start at lunchtime, but this is fine. I had time to open my presents.'

She looked at Carlo again, remembering the pretty earrings and the doll. He'd chosen her great presents. He wasn't just a fantastic lover and a great doctor, he was thoughtful and caring as well.

She couldn't believe she'd known him for less than a week.

Satisfied that Helen was doing well, Carlo made his excuses. 'I have to go and see some other patients now, but I'll be checking up on you and I'll be here for the delivery.'

Helen watched him go with a sigh. 'Gorgeous.'

Zan spent the rest of the morning by her side, monitoring the baby's heart and the strength of the contractions, satisfied that everything was going well.

At lunchtime she examined Helen again and found that she was seven centimetres dilated.

'This is going well, Helen,' she said, dropping her gloves in the bin and helping Helen into a more comfortable position. 'Are you sure that the gas and air is enough?'

'Just as long as you keep telling me funny stories to distract me,' Helen said, sucking in a breath as another contraction started.

Zan held her hand and encouraged her. At the end of the contraction there was a tap on the door and Kim walked in, a rope of silver tinsel wrapped around her neck and reindeer antlers on her head.

Zan looked at her. 'Something's stuck in your hair.'

Kim glared. 'Oh, very funny.' She smiled at Helen. 'I'm so sorry that Zan's your midwife today. She was all we could get on Christmas Day.'

Helen laughed. 'She's great. My favourite person, as you know.'

'Well, if you need a real midwife just press the buzzer.' Kim adjusted her antlers and grinned at her friend. 'Go and grab a coffee and a mince pie from the staffroom. I'll stay on twin watch.'

Suddenly desperate for a cup of coffee, Zan did as Kim had suggested and had just poured herself a strong cup of coffee when Carlo strolled into the room.

He looked sexy and dangerous and the look in his eyes made her heart-rate take off. Last night it had been as if they were in a separate world where reality would never intrude. Seeing him now in the staff-room, looking overwhelmingly male and very, very real, she felt suddenly shy.

'This wasn't exactly how I planned to spend the morning,' he said huskily, stepping closer to her and curving a warm hand around the back of her neck.

She glanced nervously at the door. 'We can't—not here.'

He chuckled. 'I was only planning to kiss you. If Kim can get away with wearing antlers to work, then I can certainly kiss you under the mistletoe.'

With that he lowered his head and took her mouth, exploring her fully, his free hand pulling her against his hard body.

When he finally lifted his head she was flushed and breathless and desperate for more.

More of what they'd shared last night.

'Carlo—'

He put a finger on her lips, a wry smile touching his mouth. 'I know—I feel the same way. Let's hope these twins are delivered soon so that we can both go home.'

She looked into his dark eyes, wondering what he was thinking.

He'd said that he loved her but did he really mean it?

And what did the future hold?

Did they have any sort of future?

Just after lunch Helen's husband John arrived, clutching a huge box of food, including a pile of turkey sandwiches.

'I managed to cook the lunch,' John Hughes said proudly, and Helen grinned.

'Has anyone been sick yet?'

'Charming.' He smiled at Zan. 'Have you eaten? I brought you a box of goodies for the staffroom.'

Zan thanked him and left them alone for a few minutes while she took the food to the staff room.

When she arrived back Helen was having another contraction and her husband was looking anxious.

'She says she wants to push.'

'Really?' Zan washed her hands and pulled on a pair of sterile gloves. She examined Helen carefully and then gave a smile. 'You're fully dilated, Helen, and the first head is already descending nicely. Let's try and get you a bit more upright and then I need to call in the cavalry.'

Helen gave a grunt. 'Why do we need cavalry?'

'I need to call Mr Bennett and the anaesthetist and we need to have two paediatricians—one for each twin,' Zan told her as she hit the buzzer.

Kim's antlers appeared round the door. 'Do we have lift-off?'

Zan nodded. 'Can you call the team, please?'

Kim vanished and Zan grabbed a bean bag. 'Let's try putting this behind you for a moment. It might help if you have something to push against.'

Minutes later Carlo strolled into the room dressed in theatre scrubs. His shoulders looked impossibly broad and Zan struggled to keep her attention on Helen.

He examined her quickly, checked the foetal heart trace and glanced up as one of the paediatricians entered the room.

'Just one of you?' He was frowning slightly but the doctor shook her head.

'My colleague is on her way.'

The second paediatrician arrived with the anaesthetist and from then on there was an air of anticipation and excitement as they waited for Carlo to deliver the first twin.

With the minimum of fuss and bother he delivered the head and then the shoulders and finally the first twin slipped into his hands.

'A little boy, Helen,' Carlo said quietly, letting the paediatrician check the baby carefully before putting him to the breast. 'I want him to feed if he can, because it will stimulate your contractions. In the meantime, I'm going to scan you to assess the lie of the second twin.'

Zan noted the time of delivery and carefully labelled the baby 'Twin One' so that there was no confusion.

'The second twin is lying head down, Helen,' Carlo told her finally, pressing on the top of Helen's uterus. 'I'm just moving him down a bit.'

Helen stroked the first baby's downy head and looked up at her husband in wonder. 'He's so tiny.'

Zan was concentrating on the second twin with Carlo. She glanced at the machine and placed a hand on Helen's uterus.

'She's stopped contracting.'

Carlo nodded. 'We'll put up an oxytocin infusion and wait for the head to descend.'

They did that and Zan kept monitoring the contractions. 'That's better—will you rupture the membrane?'

Carlo shook his head. 'Not yet. The baby isn't distressed, so I'd rather leave nature to take its course if we can.'

Zan looked at him with a new respect. She'd come across so many obstetricians who couldn't wait to intervene and hurry everything along, but Carlo was completely relaxed and confident, happy to let the mother's body do the work if it was possible.

Helen looked at him anxiously. 'Is it taking too long?'

'Everything's fine.' Carlo put a hand on her abdomen to feel the contraction and checked the monitor. 'We're waiting for the baby's head to come down and for the waters to break. If necessary I can speed things up, but for the moment you're doing well.'

Even as he spoke the waters broke, and when Carlo examined her again he was satisfied that the second twin's head was engaged.

'You're doing really well,' he said, encouraging Helen, who was now looking exhausted. 'Push with the next contraction.'

He shot a meaningful glance at the second paediatrician who gave a brief nod of understanding.

The second twin was born in a slippery rush and lay still in Carlo's hands. Immediately the paediatrician took the baby and cleared the airways. The baby coughed and spluttered and gave a thin wail of protest.

Zan breathed a sigh of relief and gave Helen a hug. 'Congratulations,' she said hoarsely. 'A little girl. One of each.'

'Is she all right?' Helen was straining to see the second twin, but the paediatrician was taking no chances and was giving the baby a full examination.

'She's fine,' Zan assured her. 'We're just giving her a whiff of oxygen and then you can give her a cuddle.'

Carlo delivered the second placenta, checked that it was intact and glanced at Helen. 'No tears, no stitches needed. You did brilliantly.'

Zan hid a smile. One of the main reasons that Helen hadn't encountered a problem was because Carlo was so skilled. He was undoubtedly the best doctor she'd ever worked with.

He exchanged a brief smile with Zan and then had a conversation with the paediatricians while Zan made Helen more comfortable.

The first twin was feeding happily now, firmly attached to Helen's breast, his eyes wide as he sucked.

'He's so gorgeous.' Zan touched his cheek gently.

Suddenly she had a mental picture of Carlo's babies—dark-haired and dark-eyed with seductive smiles, just like their father.

She shook herself quickly.

What was the matter with her?

She'd known him for less than a week, for goodness' sake, and here she was imagining having his babies.

She'd been spending too much time with Kim.

After they'd transferred Helen to the ward Zan grabbed her coat and went in search of Carlo.

She found him by the ward desk, finishing off some notes.

'I'm off home.'

'Wait for me!' His rough command surprised her, but she settled herself in a chair next to him and waited for him to finish writing.

Finally he closed the notes and sat back with a sigh. 'Done. Let's go. If they need me again they can call.'

They walked the short distance to her flat, and Zan was still busy chatting about the twins and the excitement of the day when the lift doors opened and she caught sight of the door of her flat.

It was splintered and torn off its hinges.

'Oh, my God.' Her face lost its colour and she made a movement towards her flat, but Carlo grabbed her and pulled her backwards.

'No!'

He thrust her behind him and reached into his pocket for his mobile phone. He keyed in a number, said a few words of Italian, his eyes never leaving the open door, and then flipped the phone shut and put it back into his pocket.

'Stay behind me.'

His harsh order made her flinch and she looked at him, startled, seeing a side of him that she hadn't encountered before.

His eyes were cold and dangerous and she swallowed hard.

'I— It's probably just kids.'

But the uneasy feeling inside her was growing.

She'd never seen Carlo this tense before. Even while delivering Kelly's baby he'd been relaxed and amazingly cool.

Something was very wrong.

He walked softly to the door and looked inside, his jaw tightening as he saw the mess in her flat.

'Oh, no!' She peeped around his shoulder and gave a groan as she saw the Christmas tree lying on its side, the presents scattered around the living room. 'My tree! My things...'

Her favourite blue sofa had been torn apart and glasses had been smashed on the wooden floor.

'Who would want to do this?' Distressed by the mess, she pushed past him and dropped to her knees, tears filling her eyes as she picked up some of the presents. 'Who would want to rob someone on Christmas Day?'

It seemed so unfair that she stifled a sob, aware that Carlo was prowling around her flat, checking every room, his face dark and dangerous.

She stared at him, puzzled by his behaviour. 'What are you doing? They're not likely to still be here. It was just children.'

Zan brushed the tears away from her face and scrambled to her feet, frowning slightly as her eyes rested on the television and the stereo.

'That's odd.'

'What's odd?' Carlo's tone was clipped as he moved towards the doorway of her flat, obviously waiting for someone.

'They don't seem to have taken anything.' Zan glanced around the room and then bent down and picked up the earrings that Carlo had given her for Christmas. 'Why would anyone break in and not take anything?'

Carlo's sucked in a breath. 'Zan—'

Before he could finish what he was going to say the lift doors opened and a man stepped out.

Zan's eyes widened. It was the same man who'd been following her and who Carlo had spoken to in the restaurant.

She looked at him in confusion and then back at Carlo, who was speaking in rapid Italian.

Then she heard footsteps on the stairs and armed police swarmed into her flat.

'What the hell is going on?' She backed away, intimidated by the sight of guns and bulletproof vests. She stared at Carlo in shock and then looked at one of the policeman.

'They've broken in and trashed the place but they don't seem to have taken anything.' Her voice tailed off as she watched them comb the flat, suddenly aware that they weren't interested in her. It was like something out of the movies and a chill spread over her body.

Why were they turning up with guns?

She didn't fool herself that the police took breaking and entering that seriously.

Something else was going on.

One of the policemen was talking to Carlo, his manner respectful. 'We've had them under surveillance since they entered the country but they gave us all the slip last night. They were obviously hiding out somewhere, waiting for you to go to the hospital.'

Zan stared. Who? Who had been hiding out?

Carlo's mouth was grim. 'How did they find me?'

The policeman gave a wry smile. 'It's hard for anyone as well known as you to hide anywhere for long. Someone somewhere would have spotted you and passed on the information. We've had calls from the press, too, so I think it's safe to assume that your secret is well and truly out.'

Well known? Secret?

Why were the police treating Carlo as if he were royalty?

Zan had had enough. She stalked up to Carlo, her face pale. 'Would someone mind telling me what's happening?'

The policeman was still looking at Carlo. 'This was probably a warning. They want you to know that they've discovered your identity and that they're on to you.'

'I realise that.' Carlo let out a long breath as he turned

to Zan. 'I need to get you away from here. I never should have dragged you into this.'

'Dragged me into what?' Zan looked round at the armed police and shivered with cold. Then she looked back at Carlo, but suddenly he seemed like a stranger. Gone was the warmth and good humour that she'd come to expect from him. In its place was a tough, ruthless detachment which she found intimidating. 'What's all this about discovering your identity? Just who the hell are you?'

Her voice rose and Carlo stiffened. 'Zan, listen—let me sort this out and then we'll talk.'

'No way.' She shook her head and planted herself firmly in front of him, ignoring the police and the other man who clearly knew Carlo well. 'We talk now.'

'All right.' He ran a hand over his dark hair and let out a long breath. 'My surname isn't Bennett.'

There was a long silence while Zan digested that piece of information. *Not Bennett.* She remembered that first day when Kim had spoken to him and he hadn't reacted to his name. No wonder. He hadn't recognised it.

He'd been lying to her. Suddenly she found it difficult to breathe. *He'd been lying to her from the first evening they'd met.*

How could she have been so gullible?

It had all been too good to be true.

Her eyes were hurt and accusing. 'So, what *is* your name?'

'It's Santini,' he said quietly, and she stared at him in silence, wondering why the name was familiar.

Santini.

Suddenly her eyes widened. 'As in SMS? Santini Medical Supplies?'

SMS was a huge multinational corporation. Massive. Everyone had heard of it.

Somehow she found her voice. *'That's you?'*

A muscle worked in his dark jaw. 'It's my father,' he admitted. 'I don't get involved. I really do run a women's clinic in Milan. I left Italy to get away from some men who were threatening me. The authorities arranged for me to work under a different surname.'

She licked dry lips. 'You lied to me?'

'I tried to tell you last night.'

'But you didn't try that hard, did you?' She closed her eyes briefly, remembering just what had happened the night before. Just what she'd let him do. *Just how much she'd trusted him.*

Oh, God, how could she have been so stupid?

She'd made love to a stranger.

A stranger who had been deceiving her all the time.

'I trusted you...' Her voice was little more than a whisper as her mind ran over all the intimacies she'd allowed him. *'I trusted you.'*

Oblivious to the curious stares of the policemen, she backed away, looking at him with such pain in her eyes that he sucked in a breath.

'And you can still trust me.' His tone was urgent. 'We'll sort this out, Zan, I promise.' He reached out and grabbed her hands. 'But for the time being we just need to get you somewhere safe.'

She jerked her hands away and looked at him, her eyes glistening with tears. 'I was safe before I met you.'

He flinched visibly and she knew that he'd understood the depth of meaning behind her words.

It wasn't just the criminals who had rocked her life; it was *him.* By deceiving her.

'Why are they after you?'

Carlo was tense, rattled out of his usual cool. 'One of my patients had a stillborn baby. There was absolutely no way my staff could have prevented it. It was one of those sad cases that just happen. But the father blamed me.'

'And he's trying to *kill* you?' She stared at him, aghast. 'Don't Italian people ever communicate? Don't they have things like counselling in Italy?'

'He was past counselling,' Carlo said wearily. 'When a child dies the parents often look for someone to blame; you know that. It's normal.'

'And you just accept that?'

'No, of course not. But I can't help him if I can't find him. So far I've received nothing but threats. We were hoping that by leaving Italy we might be able to lure him out into the open.'

She gave an incredulous laugh. 'So you're saying you *wanted* him to follow you?'

Carlo dragged long fingers through his dark hair and nodded. 'Yes. He was threatening my family. We thought that if I left Italy it might be safer for everyone.'

'Except you.'

'I can take care of myself.'

'And what about me?' Her eyes were bright. 'It's *my* flat they've trashed Carlo. *Mine*.'

'I can put that right.' His jaw tightened. 'And as for you personally you've been watched every minute of the day since we met. I would never put you in danger—'

One of the policemen cleared his throat. 'We need to fingerprint this place.'

Carlo nodded and moved out into the corridor, taking Zan by the arm. 'Listen, I'm going to take you somewhere safe until this is over.'

She shook his arm off and turned to look at the man who'd been following her. 'And who's he? One of your henchmen?'

Carlo frowned at her description. 'He's my father's chief of security and he's the best there is. He's had you in his sight from the day after you met me.'

'Well, if that's supposed to make me feel better then

I'm afraid it doesn't.' Zan stared at him, her mind working overtime. 'Was he the reason you knew I went to Kelly's?'

Carlo hesitated and then nodded, and she turned to Matt, tears glistening in her eyes.

'So if you're so good, why didn't you stop them trashing my flat?'

'I wasn't watching your flat. I was watching you,' Matt said quietly, his eyes sympathetic. 'Look, I can understand why you're upset, but Carlo wasn't in a position to tell you. Try and understand. He'd only just met you—he didn't know you well enough to trust you.'

'Is that so?' She planted herself in front of Carlo, brushing away the tears that trickled down her cheek. 'You knew me well enough to go to bed with me and say that you loved me, just not well enough to be honest and tell me who you really were.'

Carlo tensed. 'Zan, listen, we—'

'I don't want to listen. I just want you to answer me something honestly.' Her voice was hoarse as she interrupted him. 'Clearly everyone knows who you are, and I suppose I should have recognised you, too. I've seen your picture often enough in those stupid glossy magazines. But I didn't. And what I want to know is why a multimillionaire would be interested in me. What were you doing, Carlo? Slumming it?' She stepped closer to him, her small fists clenched by her sides, her green eyes on fire. 'Were you finding out how the other half live? Using me as a distraction for your brief spell in exile?'

'*Dio*, it wasn't like that.' His words were heavily accented and she could tell that he was longing to break into Italian. 'It's true that it was a refreshing change, being with someone who didn't know who I was, but that had nothing to do with our relationship.'

'It had everything to do with it,' she said flatly, the anger suddenly subsiding. In its place was a numbness that slowly worked its way through her whole body. 'You could have told me who you were if you'd wanted to. But you didn't trust me enough. I was good enough to sleep with, but not good enough to confide in.'

He frowned. 'That isn't true.'

'Yes, it is. You didn't trust me, did you, Carlo?'

He hesitated a fraction too long. 'You have to understand something—'

'I understand everything. Our whole relationship has been based on a lie, hasn't it? So tell me one more thing.' She tilted her head on one side, her green eyes challenging him. 'Just how much money *have* you got, Carlo?'

He sucked in a breath. 'Enough.'

'Which, roughly translated, means that you're loaded,' she said. 'That toy Ferrari I gave you this morning—you gave it a really odd look. You've got the grown-up version at home, haven't you?'

He had the grace to look uncomfortable. 'Yes, but—'

Half a million pounds' worth of car.

'And the earrings...' A thought occurred to her and she stuck her hand in her pocket and removed them. She stared down at them, sparkling in her palm, a vivid and cruel reminder of what they'd shared only that morning. 'Oh, my God...'

How could she have been so naïve?

She studied them, speechless. Then she thrust them into his hand.

'They're real, aren't they?'

'Yes.' Carlo met her gaze head-on and she shook her head in disbelief.

'You did the Lottery with me, you helped me plan how you'd spend the money, and all the time you've got more money than you know what to do with.'

'Zan, you're not making any sense.' His tone held a hint of exasperation. 'So I've got money. Why does that matter? You're always planning how you'd spend money—well, now you *can* spend it.'

She shook her head, her expression incredulous. 'You just don't get it, do you? We laughed together, we shared things, but none of it was real. You lied to me. *I don't know who you are.*'

His jaw tightened. 'I'm the same man who made love to you last night.'

She lifted a hand and slapped him hard across the face, wounded by his blunt reminder.

'And I hate you for that!' Her voice rang with passion and she glared at him. 'And I don't want your babies any more—and if you'd married someone else I *would* have punched her on the nose, but now she can have you!!'

With that she turned on her heel and made for the stairs, ignoring the lift which was still standing open.

She'd wanted to have his babies?

Carlo blinked, trying to make sense of her tumbled speech. Punched who on the nose? Who was she saying could have him?

He was still pondering the answer as he sprinted after her, with Matt close behind. 'Zan, wait!'

He heard her footsteps clattering on the stairs as she fled from him and cursed fluently under his breath.

He didn't want her out there alone.

Finally they reached street level and he slammed through the doors and stared around, looking for her.

Everything was quiet. She'd vanished.

Carlo whirled around and paced up to Matt. 'We've got to find her,' he growled ominously. 'Before *they* do.'

CHAPTER EIGHT

'LET me get this straight.' Kim reached for a second box of tissues. 'You found out that he's a millionaire—no, sorry, a *multimillionaire*—and you slapped his face and walked away from him?'

Sitting cross-legged on the bed, Zan helped herself to a bunch of tissues and blew her nose hard. 'Basically, yes.'

'Right.' Kim gave her a look of total incomprehension. 'But you love the guy, yes?'

'Yes. No. I don't know any more.' Zan's eyes filled again and Kim gave a sigh.

'You love him. I recognise the signs. And frankly I'm missing something here. You love him, you slept with him, but now you've found out he's rich you're walking away from him.' She pulled a face. 'Sorry, but it doesn't make sense.'

'It isn't the money,' Zan sniffed. 'It's because he *lied* to me. He didn't tell me who he really was.'

Kim spread her hands. 'Well, the guy was obviously in a spot of bother.'

A spot of bother.

Zan remembered the police, the guns and the mess in her flat.

'I think he was in more than a spot.'

'Well, then, you can hardly blame him for keeping his identity a secret,' Kim reasoned. 'He had a bunch of thugs after him.'

'He should have told me.' Zan blew her nose again and settled herself more comfortably on the bed. 'I feel totally humiliated. As though I slept with a stranger.'

'Well, you did in a way. But that's OK,' Kim added hastily. 'I mean, you liked him. A lot. More than you've ever liked a man before.'

'That was when I thought he was a normal person.'

'He is a normal person.'

Zan shook her head. 'He's super-rich, Kim. Bodyguards, private planes, homes around the world. Where do I fit into all that?' She jettisoned the tissues and stood up, padding over to the mirror. 'You've seen the magazines. The guy dates models and actresses. What's he doing with me?'

She stared gloomily at her blotched reflection and Kim sighed.

'Well, when you're not howling you don't look too bad. He was having a good time. Zan, you're gorgeous. You just don't see it yourself and you never have.'

Zan shook her head. 'The truth is, he was with me because it was a refreshing change to be with someone who didn't know who he was.'

Kim shrugged. 'Well what's wrong with that? It must be pretty tough, being a multimillionaire. How can you trust anyone's motives? At least he knew you wanted to be with him for himself.'

'But what about *me*? Didn't he think about me? He should have told me.'

'Yes, well, maybe he should,' Kim conceded, 'but look on the bright side. You've got a *very* rich boyfriend. At the very least you should get some decent Christmas presents.'

Zan sniffed. 'He gave me diamond earrings.'

'Really?' Kim's eyes widened and she gave a slow smile of approval. 'Good for him.'

'I gave them back.'

Kim stared at her in disbelief. 'Are you mad?'

'No.' Zan looked at her, trying to make her understand.

'He let me believe they were fake, just like he let me believe that what we had together meant something. Once I found that the earrings were real I couldn't keep them. They were part of the deception.'

'You gave diamond earrings back because they *weren't* fake?' Kim stared at her in obvious confusion. 'You're a disgrace to women. And you're making no sense whatsoever.'

Zan struggled to explain. 'I thought I knew what they were but then they turned out to be something different. Like Carlo.'

'I wish I could say that I understand,' Kim muttered, lifting a hand and scratching her head. 'But, frankly, I don't.'

Zan took a deep breath, her expression bleak. 'I don't know who he is.'

Kim stood up and gave her a hug. 'Of course you do. The money doesn't change anything.'

'It changes *everything*,' Zan said flatly, pulling away from her and walking across the room. 'Can't you see that? He isn't the man he pretended to be. His lifestyle is totally different. He's only here for a short time and once they've caught the idiots who are threatening him he'll be back in Italy, running his exclusive clinic and jetting between his different homes. I was just a temporary distraction and I was a fool to have trusted him.'

'Whoa!' Kim held up a hand. 'You're making lots of assumptions here. Have you tried discussing this with him?'

'Only long enough for me to make a total fool of myself in front of half the police force.' Zan turned and walked back again. 'I told him I didn't want his babies, that I wouldn't punch the woman who married him on the nose and to finish it all off I've probably blacked his other eye.'

'Really?' Kim looked intrigued. 'Did the police arrest you for bodily harm?'

Zan gave a groan and lifted a hand to her aching head. 'Don't even joke about it. I was angry. He lied to me!'

'Don't worry about the punch. Men love a feisty woman,' Kim assured her, frowning as Zan turned and walked again.

'Can you stop pacing for a moment?' She glared at her in exasperation. 'You're wearing out a perfectly good carpet.'

'Pacing helps me to think.'

Kim sighed. 'OK, so what happens next?'

Zan paced again. 'I redecorate my flat and get on with my life. And next time try not to be so gullible.'

Kim looked doubtful. 'You think he'll leave it at that?'

'Of course he will.'

'I wouldn't be so sure. He's a pretty confident guy,' Kim said. 'He's going to go after what he wants.'

'But he didn't want me,' Zan said in a choked voice. 'Not really. I was just a novelty. Someone who didn't know who he was.'

But now she knew the truth.

Their whole relationship had been false.

Zan awoke on Boxing Day with a terrible headache and a hollow feeling in her stomach. Nursing a cup of coffee in Kim's sitting room, it seemed as if the Christmas decorations had somehow lost their sparkle.

Like her life.

She'd never experienced such extremes of emotion in such a short space of time. She'd gone from being ecstatically happy to utterly miserable in less time than it took to say 'mistletoe'.

Deciding that the only way forward was to just get on

with her life, she borrowed one of Kim's uniforms and went to work with her head held high.

She wasn't going to cry.

Fortunately no one but Kim knew about her relationship with Carlo, so there wouldn't be any pitying glances.

There was no clinic because it was Boxing Day, so she was sent to work on the labour ward, which was frantically busy.

'Can someone go out and look for a warm stable?' one of the midwives quipped. 'There's no more room at the hospital.'

'I feel sorry for all these babies born at Christmas,' Kim said as she fixed her antlers in place for the second day running. 'Imagine—they're facing a lifetime of joint presents. Talk about cruel.'

Despite her smile, Kim was looking tired and worried, and every now and then she gave Zan a searching look, checking that she was OK.

Zan tried to smile back, telling herself not to be so pathetic.

A week ago she hadn't even met Carlo and she'd been happy enough then. Surely it wouldn't take long to get back to normal?

But a week ago she hadn't been in love.

The sister in charge took her to one side. 'There's a patient in Room 3 who's requesting that you take care of her. She wasn't registered with us, so I suppose she must be a friend or something.'

Zan frowned. She didn't have any pregnant friends.

'Her name is Abby Santini. Ring any bells?'

Zan sucked in a breath. A relative of Carlo's? But why would she be asking for her?

'Her husband is a top paediatric cardiac surgeon,' the sister told her. 'He actually worked here for a short while and I remember him vaguely. Scarily brilliant and doesn't suffer fools—you know the type.'

My brother is a doctor.

Zan racked her brains to remember what Carlo had told her about his family and didn't come up with much.

He'd hardly told her anything, she realised dully. He'd managed to dodge most of her questions and she really knew next to nothing about him.

'I don't know them.'

The sister frowned slightly. 'Well, they asked for you by name, and they need someone good, so unless you've got a problem with it you can be their midwife.'

She had a big problem.

Spending a day with Carlo's family wasn't part of her rehabilitation. And if his brother's wife *was* in the unit then that must mean that Carlo would turn up at some point, and when that happened she didn't want to be near the place.

Reminding herself never to go off with strangers again, she walked down the corridor, tapped on the door of Room 3 and walked in, determined to persuade them to choose another midwife.

A broad-shouldered man had his arm round a very pretty young blonde woman who was gasping in pain.

Zan frowned, forgetting her problems for a moment as she hurried across to her. 'Is it bad?'

'Terrible.' The young woman could hardly speak, her eyes closed in agony.

'Breathe in through your nose, out through your mouth—slowly,' Zan instructed. 'That's better. And again…'

She helped Abby with her breathing until the contraction had ended and then moved her across to the bed.

'Slip your shoes off and pop up on there. I'll need to

examine you and then we'll have a conversation about pain relief.'

Abby caught her breath and then looked at her curiously. 'Are you Zan?'

Zan reached for the blood-pressure cuff and nodded, trying not to look at the dark-haired man hovering next to them. He was breathtakingly handsome.

And he looked like Carlo.

'I'm Abby.' The young woman gave her a friendly smile. 'We've heard lots about you—Carlo said you're the best midwife he's ever worked with. This is my husband, Nico.'

'Nice to meet you.' Zan felt a lump building in her throat and concentrated on taking her patient's blood pressure.

'That's fine.' She removed the stethoscope from her ears and sat down on the bed with a blank set of notes. 'You're not booked in with us so I don't know your medical history.'

Abby smiled. 'I'm booked at Carlo's clinic in Milan, but then he had to come here so I followed him. I've been staying in London for the past few weeks. I wanted him nearby when I delivered.'

She obviously thought that Carlo walked on water.

Zan tried to smile. 'So…' The words stuck in her throat. 'Does Carlo know you're here?'

'Of course.' It was his brother who spoke this time, his English perfect. 'He's joining us shortly.'

And at that moment the door opened and Carlo strode in, his face strained.

'*Ciao, bella.*' He embraced Abby and his brother and proceeded to conduct a conversation in rapid Italian while Zan tried not to look at him.

That one quick glance when he'd walked through the

door had been more than enough to remind her of why she'd behaved so recklessly.

He was stunningly good-looking and had an air of calm authority that transmitted itself to those around him. No wonder she'd fallen so hard. What woman wouldn't? What she needed to know was how she was going to get up again.

Finally he ended the conversation and gave Abby a reassuring smile. 'It will be fine, *angelo*. Trust me.'

Unable to stand any more, Zan gritted her teeth and left the room to fetch the CTG machine that would measure Abby's contractions and the baby's heart-rate.

Trust him.

She'd done that once and look where it had led her.

Carlo followed her out of the room and walked purposefully across to where she was standing.

She tensed, painfully conscious of his close proximity.

'Her blood pressure is fine,' she said formally. 'I haven't examined her yet, but I'm going to do that next. She seems to be having quite strong contractions so I need to talk to her about pain relief and—'

'Zan,' he interrupted her, his voice low. 'Abby can wait for one more minute. We need to talk about last night.'

Zan froze and her fingers tightened on the machine.

'No, we don't.' She took several breaths and then lifted her chin. 'Frankly, I didn't even expect you to be at work. I assumed you would have gone back to your old life. Tell me, what name are you using today? Santini or Bennett?'

He flinched visibly and muttered something under his breath. 'I asked you to trust me, Zan. I would have told you who I was. I would have explained everything if you hadn't run away.'

Easy enough to say that now.

'So, did they catch them?'

He shook his head, his dark eyes weary. 'Not yet. Which

is another thing we need to talk about. The police don't think you should return to your flat for the time being. It isn't safe. I want you to come and stay at my apartment.'

No way. It would be torture.

'I've found my own accommodation.'

'With Kim.'

Her eyes widened. 'Are you still having me followed?'

He nodded. 'And don't expect me to apologise for it. I put you in danger, the least I can do now is keep you safe. I'm just sorry it ruined your Christmas.'

She felt tears prick her eyes. Oddly enough, it wasn't the trauma of the break-in that had ruined her Christmas as much as his betrayal.

'You should have told me the truth right at the beginning.' Her voice shook with emotion. '*You* should have trusted *me*.'

'I can understand why you think that.' His voice was soft, his dark eyes holding hers, refusing to let her look away. 'But maybe if I tell you a little bit about my life you might understand why I didn't tell you straight away. And I *was* going to tell you, Zan. You have to believe that.'

She took a step backwards, unnerved by the way he made her feel.

'Women get involved with me for all sorts of reasons, none of them the usual ones.' Carlo's tone was resigned. 'Usually it's because they find my wallet attractive, sometimes it's the so-called status of being seen with me. I admit it's been a long time since I trusted a woman. Not since someone I thought I was close to sold intimate details about my family to the press for a great deal of money.'

Zan winced. 'That's awful. But you know I wouldn't do that.'

'I think it's unlikely, but you'd be amazed what people will do when they're offered money.' He sounded tired.

'The truth is that part of me is still wary, and I wanted our relationship to develop before I revealed the reality. I admit that I really, really enjoyed the fact that you didn't know who I was.'

Zan felt totally confused. 'But what we shared wasn't real.'

'It was real, Zan. For me it was even more real because you didn't know who I was.' He moved closer to her, his voice low and urgent. 'You spent time with *me*, away from the money and the crazy lifestyle. I always knew that we couldn't live in a cocoon for ever, that sooner or later I'd have to tell you, but I hoped that by then what we had together would be strong enough to withstand the realities of my life. Unfortunately they intruded sooner than I'd planned and I didn't have time to tell you the truth myself.'

She looked at him uncertainly, trying to think objectively and failing dismally. When he was this close she couldn't think at all. She was breathlessly aware of his overwhelming physical presence, his masculinity and the unexpectedly gentle look in his eyes.

But he'd fooled her before. 'Without trust there can be no relationship.'

'I do trust you, Zan.' His eyes were steady on hers. 'Because you didn't know who I was, I can be totally sure that what you felt was for me alone, not for my name or my connections. I trust you completely. Now it's up to you to decide whether you can trust me.'

Could she?

'How will I know that you're not keeping more secrets?' Zan's voice was choked and he cursed under his breath and pulled her towards him.

'Because from now on whatever I tell you will be the truth.' His fingers tightened on hers. 'The press print something different about me almost every day, just because of my name. Some of it is total fabrication, and some of it comes from people with a grudge. It doesn't matter where it comes from; the press are constantly digging for dirt. No relationship of mine has ever survived the intense scrutiny that I'm subjected to on a daily basis. I swear that from now on I won't hold anything back from you, but in return you have to be able to ignore all the things that people say about me. If you can't trust me, Zan, we don't stand a chance.'

Did he really believe that they might still have a future together?

Zan stared at him in confusion, but before she could answer the door opened and Nico walked out, looking tense. He said something to his brother in Italian and Carlo nodded.

'We need to get back to Abby.'

Suddenly aware that they'd been having an intensely personal conversation in the middle of the corridor, Zan glanced around self-consciously and started to push the machine to Abby's room.

Ten minutes earlier she'd been totally sure that she could never forgive him. But now nothing seemed clear.

Could she trust a man who hadn't been entirely honest with her, even if he'd had good reason for the deception?

She walked back to the bedside, trying to hide her feelings, but then she met Abby's searching gaze and felt her eyes fill.

Abby said something in Italian to the two men and then took Zan's hand. 'If you're going to examine me then I'd rather they went and had a coffee. I don't need an audience.'

Carlo frowned. 'I ought to examine you.'

Abby smiled calmly. 'This is my second baby, Carlo. I need you around for emergencies but so far there isn't one and Zan and I can manage fine on our own. Take Nico to find some coffee. He's a nervous wreck.'

Carlo hesitated and then caught his brother's eye and nodded briefly. 'All right. We'll be back in ten minutes.'

They left the room and Abby screwed up her face as another contraction hit her.

'Oh, help—my first delivery was nothing like this. I'm trying not to be a baby but I'm in agony.'

Zan slid an arm around Abby's shoulder and helped her with her breathing until the contraction passed.

Abby flopped back against the pillow. 'OK. We need to talk fast before the next one hits me. What's going on with you and Carlo?'

Zan flushed. 'Nothing—we're just colleagues.'

'Then why do the pair of you look so miserable? There's one thing you should know about Italian families,' Abby said gently, 'and that's that they're very close. Carlo's been talking to his brother regularly. Nico has known about you from the first. We were all getting excited that Carlo might finally have found someone he could be happy with.'

Zan bit her lip. 'He told you about me? But he's known me for less than a week.'

'And you made a real impact,' Abby said. 'I've never known him seriously smitten before. So what went wrong?'

Zan bit her lip. 'He lied to me. He told me nothing about himself and he used a false name.'

Abby sucked in a breath and put a hand on her stomach. 'Hold that thought—I've got another contraction coming.'

Zan took her hand and coached her through it, reminding her how to breathe.

The contraction passed but Abby held onto her hand. 'He had to use a false name,' she said, struggling to get her breath back. 'The press have been hounding him in Italy. After that baby was stillborn he started to receive death threats and there's been a massive security operation ever since. It's been awful for him.'

Zan gave a wan smile. 'I still think he could have trusted me.'

'Perhaps he could, but if you knew the attention that the Santini family attracts in Italy you'd understand why he didn't,' Abby said. 'It's pretty hard for them to trust anyone. Carlo really liked the fact that you didn't know who he was. For once in his life he was able to have a normal relationship with someone.'

'But it wasn't normal, was it? I didn't know who he was.'

Abby looked at her thoughtfully. 'Tell me what you love about Carlo.'

Zan sat down on the edge of the bed, not even bothering to deny her love. It was obvious. 'I love his sense of humour. I love the way he's so relaxed and confident. I love his strength, and I even love the fact that he doesn't know how to be politically correct about women.'

Abby laughed. 'All Italian men are like that. Carry on. What else do you love?'

Zan shrugged. 'I love the fact that he's such a great doctor and I love the fact that he has such a strong bond with his family.'

Abby nodded with satisfaction. 'And all those things that you love about him are still there, no matter what his name is. Having a different name doesn't change the person.'

Which was basically what Carlo had said.

'It hurts that he didn't trust me enough to tell me his name,' Zan muttered, and Abby sighed.

'That's true, but he's trusting you now. You've got plenty of information which you could take to the press. 'They'd probably pay quite a lot of money for your story.'

Zan frowned. 'I wouldn't do that.'

'I know. But he's been so badly burned in the past that trust doesn't happen overnight for him.'

Zan gave a short laugh. 'And I thought *I* was the one who has problems trusting.'

'One of the reasons that the Santini family is so close is because outsiders have let them down so badly. They've learned to trust their own and no one else.'

Zan nodded. 'I'm beginning to see that.'

'You know, if you talk to him you can still sort this out.'

Zan shook her head. 'I don't know.' She swallowed back a lump in her throat. 'He needs me to trust him unconditionally and I don't know if I can do that.'

What if he hurt her again?

'But you didn't understand anything about his background until he explained who he was,' Abby pointed out. 'And now you do, so surely you can forgive him. You both love each other and that has to count for something.'

Did it? Zan wasn't sure anymore.

She stood up and washed her hands. 'I really ought to examine you. They'll be back any minute and all we've done is talk.'

'Nothing wrong with that.'

Zan looked at her curiously. 'You're not Italian, are you?'

'English.' Abby wriggled down the bed so that Zan could feel her abdomen. 'I first met Nico when I was at school with his sister, and then we met up again years later. It's a pretty complicated story.'

Zan lifted Abby's jumper and ran her hands skilfully over her bump, feeling for the baby's position. 'I'm starting to expect nothing less from the Santini family. Their whole lives are obviously very complicated. So this is your second child?'

'We have a little girl who's just two. She's called Rosa.'

'And you live in Italy?' Zan's hands kept moving and she frowned slightly as she palpated one part of the abdomen and looked at the shape of Abby's stomach.

'Well, Nico works mostly in a hospital in Milan, but he's brilliant at his work and gets invited to all sorts of places to teach.' She smiled proudly as she spoke. 'And wherever he goes, Rosa and I go with him.'

'So where's Rosa now?'

'Nico owns an apartment in Knightsbridge,' Abby said. 'She's there with our nanny. Why are you frowning?'

Zan finished her examination. 'Abby, your baby is in what we call an occipitoposterior position, which basically means that his back is lying along your back.'

'Is that why I'm in so much pain?'

Zan nodded. 'Let me just examine you internally and then we'll talk about a plan of action.'

She washed her hands and pulled on a pair of sterile gloves. 'OK, this might be a bit uncomfortable but hopefully not too much…'

She was as quick as she could be. 'You're four centimetres dilated, Abby.'

Abby gave a groan and wriggled upright again. 'Is that all? Another six centimetres to go? I'll die.' She gasped as another pain hit her and this time the gasp turned to a sob. 'This is agony. I don't think I can stand it.'

'It's because of the way the baby is lying,' Zan explained. 'I think you should seriously consider having an epidural.'

Abby pulled a face. 'Nico doesn't really want me to.'

Zan smiled sympathetically. 'That's because he doesn't know the details and because he's a doctor. They're always the worst when their wives are in labour. I'll talk to him when he comes back. I think Carlo will agree with me in the circumstances.'

At that moment the door opened and Nico strolled back into the room, deep in conversation with his brother.

Zan walked up to him and came straight to the point. 'Abby needs some pain control. The baby's OP. She's four centimetres dilated and she's starting to get distressed with each contraction. She's still got a long way to go.'

Carlo frowned. 'You're sure it's OP?'

Zan nodded. 'She's got a saucer-shaped depression just below the umbilicus, the head is high and I just examined her and the anterior fontanelle is in the anterior part of the pelvis.'

Nico tensed and looked at his brother. 'What does all that mean?'

'Let me examine her and then we'll talk.'

Carlo sat down on the edge of the bed and kissed his sister-in-law on both cheeks, his affection obvious.

'Is it bad, *angelo*?'

Abby nodded, her face white and drawn. 'I thought second births were supposed to be easier, but this is much, much worse than Rosa.'

Carlo ran a hand over the top of her abdomen, feeling the contraction as it hit, holding Abby's hand as she gasped.

Carlo talked to her quietly, encouraging and supporting her, his calm tone totally reassuring. Zan watched him, realising with a sick feeling that she loved him as much as ever.

Once the contraction had passed Carlo stood up and examined Abby, his eyes clashing with Zan's.

'You were right. She's OP.' He frowned. 'When were you last checked by a doctor?'

Abby blushed. 'A while ago.'

Nico was looking tense. 'Is someone going to tell me what's wrong?'

Finally Carlo stood up. 'Nothing's wrong. The baby is

lying in the occipitoposterior position,' he told his brother. 'We call it OP.'

'What does that mean?'

Nico wanted medical facts and Carlo gave them willingly.

'It means that labour will probably be prolonged. The head isn't flexed and doesn't fit well onto the cervix. Because of that, it doesn't stimulate effective contractions. The head has to flex and rotate into the right position so that delivery can occur normally.'

Nico's eyes narrowed and his gaze was sharp. 'And if it doesn't?'

'She may need forceps or a Caesarean section. Either way it will be easier and safer if she has an epidural in place. It will also be less distressing for her. Zan's right that she still has a long way to go.'

Nico sucked in a breath. 'I don't want someone poking her in the back.'

'I understand your concern but the anaesthetist is excellent.' Carlo put a hand on his brother's shoulder and took a deep breath. 'If I had a baby with a heart defect I would put it in your hands because you're my brother and I trust you. You have to do the same with me. You have to think about what's best for Abby.'

Nico hesitated and then gave a sigh. 'You're right, of course.' He walked over to Abby and hugged her. 'I'm sorry. I don't mean to be overprotective. I just hate seeing you in pain.'

'I love the fact that you're overprotective,' Abby said huskily. 'You think I want a man who doesn't give a damn about me?'

Zan blinked back tears and went to call the anaesthetist. When she came back, Carlo had already set up an intravenous infusion.

'Let's give her 500 mils of Hartmann's solution,' he

instructed, and Zan did as he asked, attaching the giving set to the bag and hanging it from the pole.

'Why do I need that?'

Abby was looking slightly nervous but Carlo was quick to reassure her.

'An epidural can drop your blood pressure so we put up a drip to prevent that happening.'

Half an hour later Abby was sitting up and smiling, the pain a distant memory.

'This is like magic!'

Nico was looking slightly more relaxed. 'It was a good idea. I should have let you have it sooner.'

'We wouldn't have given it much earlier,' Zan told him, 'because it can switch off the contractions. The cervix has to be more than three centimetres dilated.'

She checked Abby's pulse, blood pressure and breathing, as well as monitoring her contractions and the foetal heart.

'Can you check every fifteen minutes?' The anaesthetist gave her some instructions and talked to her about topping up the epidural.

Carlo was checking the foetal heart. 'The baby is doing fine,' he said quietly.

Nico raked a hand through his hair. 'So what happens now?'

'We wait,' Carlo said. 'But don't expect this to be quick.'

Abby sighed. 'I feel guilty. You two should be at home, celebrating Christmas.'

Remembering how special Christmas Eve had been, Zan briefly met Carlo's eyes and then looked away.

Was it too late for them?

Did she trust him?

She was suddenly frustrated that they were surrounded by people. She didn't know when she was going to get the chance to talk to him again. She didn't know what his plans were.

And why was he still at the hospital when those men were on the loose?

Carlo seemed unconcerned, concentrating his attention on Abby and the baby, checking the foetal heart-rate with each contraction.

'The baby seems fine but your bladder isn't emptying properly,' Zan said, having examined Abby again. 'We need to put a catheter in.'

Abby pulled a face. 'That didn't happen to me when I had Rosa.'

Carlo gave a rueful smile. 'This baby is in a different position, I'm afraid.'

Zan washed her hands and fetched a catheter pack, aware that Nico was looking more and more tense.

By contrast Carlo was relaxed and in control, nothing about his manner betraying his concern. In fact, Zan was surprised that he hadn't interfered more, but he seemed content to let her manage the labour.

They made Abby more comfortable and continued to stay with her. Nico left once more to get some coffee and breathe some fresh air, but apart from that he was by his wife's side for the whole time.

It was growing dark outside when Abby screwed up her face. 'I want to push.'

Zan examined her again and shook her head. 'Not yet. You're not fully dilated.'

Abby gave a sob. 'So why do I have the need to push?'

'Because of the way the baby is lying,' Carlo said quietly, sitting on the side of the bed and taking her hand. 'If you push now you will bruise your cervix.'

They helped Abby to breathe gently, encouraging her not to push, and then finally Zan was satisfied that the cervix was fully dilated.

Nico looked at Carlo, his jaw tense. 'At what point do you operate?'

Carlo smiled and put a hand on his shoulder. 'She's doing very well. I have no intention of operating.'

'But?'

Carlo shook his head, his expression exasperated. 'Have I ever told you that you make a very bad relative?'

Nico sucked in a breath and paced across the room. 'You wait until you're in this position.'

Zan felt a shaft of pain shoot through her. She didn't want to think of Carlo having children with anyone but her. He'd be a great father.

Suddenly aware that he was looking at her with a keen expression on his face, she dropped her eyes and forced her attention back to the job at hand.

'I can see the head,' she said quietly. 'The baby's rotated well so you shouldn't have any problems.'

She opened the delivery pack and got everything ready, then helped move Abby into a more comfortable position.

'I want to go home now,' Abby groaned. 'I've had enough.'

Nico slipped an arm around Abby's shoulders and looked at Zan. 'How much longer?'

'Not long, but babies tend to do things at their own pace.'

'I don't know how you do this every day.' Nico ran a hand through his hair and shook his head. 'I couldn't stand the stress.'

'The stress is because you're the father,' Carlo pointed out, his eyes flickering to the monitor to check on the baby's heart-rate. 'Believe me, it's different when you're the doctor.'

'I never realised how helpless it feels to be the patient,' Nico muttered, dragging both hands through his hair. 'I'm never going to be unsympathetic again.'

'You're the most sympathetic doctor I know,' Abby said, touching his face lovingly, her face drawn and tired from pushing. 'And I love you.'

Nico gave a groan and bent to kiss her. 'I love you too, *tesoro*. More than life.'

Envying their close relationship, Zan concentrated on delivering the head, aware that Carlo was watching her closely.

She was grateful that he was there. It was a far from straightforward delivery and if she had problems she had every confidence that he would be able to solve them.

She checked that the cord wasn't around the neck and then waited for the next contraction to deliver the shoulders.

'Little boy, Abby,' she said gruffly, as the baby slithered into her hands. She lifted him onto Abby's stomach.

'A boy?' Nico couldn't hide his delight and Carlo gave him a hug.

'Congratulations.'

An hour later Abby and the baby were washed and installed comfortably in bed, so Zan slipped up to the SCBU to look at Eddie.

Kelly was sitting by the side of a normal cot, gazing wistfully at the sleeping child.

Zan tiptoed up to her, delighted to see that Eddie was no longer in the intensive-care cot. 'They've taken him out of the incubator?'

Kelly nodded. 'Apparently he's doing a lot better. His brain scan was normal and his breathing is good, although they're still having to watch his sats, whatever that means.'

Zan smiled. 'It's medical-speak for the amount of oxygen in the blood.'

'Oh, right.' Kelly gave her a grateful smile. 'And they're

still tube-feeding him, although we're giving him a go at breast-feeding every time he has a feed.'

'Well done.'

Zan turned to see Mike coming up behind them, his arms full of soft toys, a huge smile on his face.

'How is he?'

'He's great.' Kelly smiled at him and Zan was relieved and delighted to see them so happy together.

The death of Mike's brother had obviously been the cause of many problems between the couple. It was fortunate that things with the baby had turned out so well.

She wished them goodnight and then glanced at her watch. Time to go back to Kim's.

On the way past the nurses' station she stopped and spoke to the sister.

'Eddie is doing well.'

The sister nodded. 'Unbelievably well.' She gave a gentle smile and looked across at the couple who were bent over the cot. 'Nice to have a happy story at Christmas.'

Zan walked back to the staffroom, pulled on her coat and made her way down the stairs to the front of the hospital. A huge Christmas tree dominated the foyer and she looked at it briefly, wondering why Christmas Eve seemed so long ago.

She was longing to go home, but as they still hadn't caught the men who were threatening Carlo she wasn't allowed to.

She slipped a hand into her pocket to check that she still had Kim's keys safe and then pushed through the revolving doors and into the cold night air.

Lights exploded in her face and she blinked and lifted a hand to shield her eyes, trying to work out what was happening.

A group of people swarmed around her, most of them with cameras, some with recording equipment. There was a furious sound of camera shutters and blinding flashes and suddenly everyone seemed to be calling her name, jostling for her attention.

'Miss Wilde?'

How did they know who she was?

Bemused by the attention, she backed away slightly but they closed in tightly, pelting her with questions before she could escape.

'Is it true that you're having a relationship with Carlo Santini?'

'Did you see the men that broke into your flat?'

Zan looked round, desperate for some help, but there was no one around. How had this gaggle of press managed to congregate outside the hospital without anyone noticing?

One reporter, a small man with a nasty expression on his face, elbowed his way past the others. 'Is it true that they're after him because he let a baby die?'

Outrage exploded inside her. 'Mr Santini is the best obstetrician I've ever worked with,' she said, her voice shaking. 'There are all sorts of reasons why babies are stillborn but I know that Carlo wasn't responsible for that death.'

'How long have you known him?'

The questions came all at once and she shook her head, looking for an escape.

Poor Carlo.

If this was the sort of hassle that he encountered then no wonder he found it hard to lead a normal life.

Another reporter wriggled to the front of the crowd. 'Did you know that a woman in Italy has filed a paternity suit against Carlo?'

Zan froze.

Carlo had a child?

For a moment she felt numb, and then snatches of conversation came back to her.

The press print something different about me almost every day. Some of it is total fabrication, and some of it comes from people with a grudge.

And she remembered what he'd said to her the first night they'd met. *No wife. No kids.*

They might have heard the rumours but she knew Carlo well enough to know that he wouldn't lie to her about that.

She lifted her chin. 'Carlo Santini doesn't have a child.'

They all started shouting questions and another journalist waved something under her nose. 'Don't you read newspapers? It's been in the Italian press for months.'

'I'm not interested in what you print in your newspapers,' Zan said quietly. 'I'm only interested in what Carlo tells me.'

She broke off as she realised what she'd just said. *What Carlo tells me.*

'And you trust him?' The journalist gave her an incredulous look and Zan smiled.

'Oh, yes, I trust him. I trust him completely.'

It had just taken some wild accusations to make her realise the truth.

Abby was right. His name didn't matter.

She'd spent time with the man himself and she *knew* him. Knew him well enough to know that he wasn't guilty of what these people were accusing him of.

She didn't need to hear him tell her because she loved him. She loved him with all her heart. And now she needed to try and find him so that she could tell him to his face.

Hoping that he hadn't left the hospital, she pushed through the pack of journalists and sprinted up the emergency stairs to the labour ward.

One of the midwives was sitting at the desk, sorting out notes.

Zan paused, flushed and breathless. 'Has Carlo gone?'

Suddenly she was desperate to see him.

The midwife looked up, surprised. 'Oh, there you are—I thought you'd gone. I had a call from him five minutes ago. He said to tell you that he'd see you at your flat.'

Zan frowned briefly. Surely he'd told her to stay away from her flat?

There'd obviously been a new development.

Relieved and excited, longing for the opportunity to tell him how much she loved him, she sprinted back down the stairs and took the back way out of the hospital to avoid the journalists.

Carlo gave his nephew a final cuddle and handed him back to Abby.

'He's totally beautiful.'

Abby beamed at him. 'Time you had one of your own.'

Carlo's mouth twisted. 'I don't get that lucky.'

Abby stretched out a hand. 'She loves you, Carlo.'

'Does she?' Carlo's expression was bleak and he glanced up with a frown as Nico flicked through a series of channels on the television. 'Hold it!' He snatched his hand away from Abby's, his voice ragged. 'Go back one!'

Nico did as he'd been instructed and all three of them watched in silence as the television cameras zoomed in close to Zan's shocked face.

Carlo cursed under his breath as he saw her lift her arm as protection against the flash bulbs.

'Where the hell did they come from? And where the hell were the security guys?'

'Hush.' Nico held up a hand and turned up the volume so that they could hear what was being said.

'I'm not interested in what you print in your newspapers,' Zan was saying quietly. 'I'm only interested in what Carlo tells me.'

'And you trust him?' The journalist gave her an incredulous look and Zan smiled.

'Oh, yes, I trust him. I trust him completely.'

Abby gave a womanly smile that bordered on the smug. 'I told you so. I think it's time that the pair of you had a conversation. Don't let her go, Carlo.'

'I don't intend to.' With a brief smile to his brother Carlo strode out of the room and hurried to the labour ward. 'Where's Zan?'

'Oh!' The midwife looked at him in surprise. 'She was here a minute ago and I gave her your message.'

Carlo frowned. 'What message?'

The midwife looked confused. 'You called and left a message that she was to meet you at her flat.'

Carlo felt the blood drain from his face. 'I didn't call.'

'But he sounded Italian and he used your name.' The midwife looked distressed and Carlo shook his head.

'It isn't your fault.' Carlo hit a key on his phone and called Matt, then turned back to the midwife. 'Call the police and tell them to meet me at Zan's flat.'

Without waiting for her answer, he sprinted along the corridor and down the stairs as if he was being chased by demons.

Someone had used his name to lure Zan to the flat and he knew exactly who it was.

And he knew that she was in danger.

Zan went up in the lift, thinking only of Carlo.

What should she say to him?

Was it really possible that they had a future together, despite the differences in their backgrounds?

The lift doors opened and she walked towards her flat, noticing that she had a brand-new door, which was standing half-open.

A light was shining inside, which must mean that Carlo was already there.

She paused on the threshold, slightly uncertain about how she'd feel once she was inside.

The last time she'd walked into her flat all her personal belongings had been strewn over the floor. She hadn't really had time to think about the break-in. All she'd thought about was her relationship with Carlo.

Lifting a hand to touch the solid wood of her new door, she bit her lip. Would it still feel like a safe place to live? Would it still feel like home?

Of course it would.

Zan took a deep breath and pushed open the door, expecting to see Carlo standing in the living room.

It was empty.

'Carlo?'

Her voice sounded tentative and she scolded herself silently. She was behaving like a real wimp.

'Are you in the kitchen?'

She stepped further into the flat, noticing that the Christmas tree was back upright and the whole flat looked completely undisturbed.

She smiled slightly. Everything looked fine. Just like home.

And she didn't feel strange.

She felt safe.

And then she heard the door slam behind her and knew that she wasn't safe at all.

Carlo sprinted out of the hospital straight into the car that Matt had waiting. Journalists swarmed towards them but Matt slammed his foot on the accelerator and they scattered nervously.

'She's at the flat.' Carlo's voice was ragged and he flexed his fingers, preparing for a fight.

Matt kept his eyes on the road. 'I lost her. She didn't go where I expected her to. Fire me.'

'It isn't your fault. This whole situation has been too damned complicated.' Carlo shifted in his seat, anxious to arrive. 'Can't you go any faster?'

Within minutes they shrieked to a halt outside the flats and Carlo was out of the car.

They took the stairs at a run and paused outside the flat to draw breath.

The door to Zan's flat was shut and Carlo flung himself at it, intending to break it down.

'Hold on.' Matt grabbed him before his shoulder made contact and shoved him to one side, reaching into his pocket for a small implement. 'We replaced it with a solid wood door, remember? You'll put your shoulder out. I've got a better way.'

He did something to the lock and within seconds the door swung open.

Carlo stared at him. 'How did you…?'

Matt gave a sheepish grin. 'It's what you pay me for.'

Carlo strode into the flat and stopped dead.

One man lay groaning on the floor. The other had an arm around Zan's neck and a knife at her throat.

She looked at him with relief in her eyes. 'What took you so long?' Her voice was croaky. 'I've used all my moves except the kissing one.'

'Shut up.' The man jerked his arm and Zan gave a cry of pain.

Matt growled angrily and took a step forward, but Carlo held up a hand to stop him. 'No.' He looked at the man, his gaze steady. 'Drop the knife. Now.'

The man replied in Italian. 'I'm going to kill her, Santini. You're about to find out how it feels to lose someone you love.'

'I know that you're hurting,' Carlo said, trying to keep his voice steady, 'and I'm sorry about your baby. But this isn't going to help. Let her go.'

'*You should have saved her.*' The man's voice was hoarse and his arm tightened around Zan's throat. 'You should have saved my little girl.'

'I'm flattered by your faith in me,' Carlo said, taking a step forward, 'but no one could have saved your child. It's not always possible to find a reason for a stillborn child. Let her go and we can talk about it.'

'Don't come any closer!' The man's eyes were wild and Carlo paused, choosing his words carefully.

'Where's your wife, Signor Agnelli?'

The man breathed heavily. 'At home with her mother.'

'But the person she needs is you.' Carlo held his gaze and moved another step closer, gesturing behind his back for Matt to move to the right. 'She needs you with her. This is something you need to work through together for the sake of the family and there are people who can help you.'

'I shouldn't need to work it through.' The man's voice was ragged. 'I should have a healthy child.'

Carlo nodded, his eyes warm and sympathetic but watchful. So far Zan was being her usual brave self but he saw the fear in her eyes.

He also saw the trust and he felt his gut twist.

She was trusting him to sort it out.

His eyes narrowed slightly, measuring the distance. He still wasn't close enough.

'Everyone should have a healthy child,' he said, taking another step forward, 'but sadly that isn't always the way. However skilled we become at medicine, there will always be unanswered questions. There will always be children who die.'

'*You could have saved my baby.*'

'No.' Carlo shook his head and moved again, making a final gesture to Matt and praying that he'd understand.

He did.

Matt moved in from the right, providing a distraction, and in that split second Carlo plunged forward and grabbed the hand that held the knife, twisting it away from Zan's throat.

The man snarled in anger and turned on Carlo, hurling his body towards him.

Thrusting Zan out of the way, Carlo sidestepped neatly, but the man regained his balance and came back again, this time aiming for Zan.

With a growl of fury Carlo stepped in front of him and punched him hard, wincing as pain exploded through his hand.

The man staggered slightly and Carlo grabbed him by the throat, powering him against the wall.

'Don't you *ever* threaten a member of my family again!'

Under the relentless pressure of Carlo's fingers the man dropped the knife, his face contorted in pain.

Carlo's muscles bunched as he held the man captive and he said something in Italian, his words making the man blanch.

Matt frowned and took a step forward, prepared to intervene, but Zan's warning shout turned his attention to another threat.

The man on the floor was up on his feet and ready to defend his friend. Zan shouted another warning but Matt was already there.

'I've got him.' With no visible effort he lifted the man off his feet and half carried him to the wall. 'Stand there and shut up. This has got nothing to do with you.'

Carlo turned his attention back to the man he was holding, trying to contain his anger.

'Let him go, Carlo.' Zan was suddenly next to him, her voice soft. 'He needs help. He's devastated.'

'Devastated enough to want to kill a member of my

family.' Carlo's grip tightened and he felt a murderous rage tear through him.

He'd never thought of himself as violent before, but if anything had happened to Zan...

'I'm sorry.' Suddenly all the fight went out of him and the man went limp and started to cry. Great tearing sobs that shook his whole body. 'I don't even know what I'm doing any more. I just wanted to blame someone.'

Carlo's mouth was still tight but he relaxed his grip slightly.

'Of course you did.' Zan reached out a hand, her touch gentle. 'That's a normal part of grieving for someone you love. It's easier to blame someone than believe that something so awful just couldn't be avoided.'

Sensing that the man was no longer a danger to them, Carlo let him go and took a step backwards. Even making allowances for the man's loss, he couldn't be as forgiving as Zan.

The man had threatened his mother, his sister and the woman he loved.

'Nothing will ever take the pain away,' Zan said quietly, 'but time will make it less acute. But Carlo's right—your family needs you. You've already lost a child. Don't lose your family, too.'

Before the man could reply the police stormed into the room and Carlo dragged Zan against him possessively.

He wasn't letting her out of his sight ever again.

He spoke briefly to the police and they handcuffed the two men and marched them out of the door.

Zan watched them go with sadness in her eyes. 'Poor man.'

Matt stared at Carlo. 'The man had a knife to her throat and she thinks he's a poor man.'

Carlo gave a twisted smile. 'I'm afraid I find it hard to be so forgiving.'

Zan sighed and touched his cheek gently. 'I'm not really that forgiving. He frightened the life out of me and he's made your life hell, I know. But he lost a child and grief does odd things to people.' She gave a wan smile. 'I thought you were never going to come. How did you get in?'

'Matt's good with locks.' Carlo moved towards her and she looked at him warily.

'And where did you learn to fight like that?'

Carlo shrugged. 'I always refused to have a bodyguard so Dad made sure I had the right training—a bit like your brothers and your judo, I suppose.'

Her eyes were wide. 'You were scary.'

'I'm Italian. We know how to protect our own and he threatened the most important person in my life,' Carlo said softly.

Matt cleared his throat. 'I'll go and sort things out with the police and ring the family. Nico will want to know that it's all sorted.'

An hour later Zan was curled up on the sofa, snug and warm in Carlo's arms. Judging from the way he was holding her, he was never going to let her go.

And it was a really good feeling.

'Usually all that happens on Boxing Day is that I get to eat the remains of the turkey and the mince pies,' she said lightly, tilting her head so that she could look at him. 'Life with you is certainly exciting; I'll give you that.'

Carlo pulled her against him with a groan. 'When that midwife told me you'd gone to your flat to meet me, I almost had a heart attack.'

'I wasn't thinking straight or I would have realised that it wasn't you,' Zan confessed sheepishly. 'But I was so excited about seeing you that I just dashed off and walked right into their trap.'

Carlo's grip tightened and his eyes darkened in anger. 'They were waiting inside the flat?'

She nodded. 'The moment I walked inside they shut the door and attacked me. I managed to floor one of them.'

Carlo gave a wry smile. 'I wish I could have seen that. I bet you gave him a shock.'

'Well, he hit his head when he fell so I don't think he thought about it too much. Unfortunately the other guy grabbed me from behind and I couldn't shift him. He said he was going to wait until you arrived and then kill me.'

She gave a shudder and Carlo frowned. 'How did he know I was coming?'

'Don't ask me. I can't read men's minds. I just know he wanted to kill me with you watching.'

'Nice guy,' Carlo drawled, and she gave a sad smile.

'Hurt guy.' She let out a breath. 'How did you know I was here?'

'I saw you on television, announcing to the world that you loved me and trusted me,' Carlo said smugly. 'Naturally I tried to find you to compliment you on your taste in men.'

Zan laughed. 'Is your ego as large as your fortune, Mr Santini?'

'Larger,' Carlo said proudly. 'I'm Italian, remember. And size matters when it comes to egos. Egos, Christmas trees and—'

'Yes, yes, I know,' Zan interrupted him quickly, her eyes twinkling and her cheeks pink. 'You still haven't explained how you found me.'

'I asked the midwife where you were. The same midwife who'd told you to meet me at the flat. I put two and two together, as you say in this country.'

'I was starting to get worried.'

Carlo hugged her against him. 'You don't know worried,' he groaned. 'Worried is what I felt when I saw that lunatic holding a knife to your throat.'

She hugged him back and then saw him wince. 'Your hand! I forgot about your hand. Show me.'

Carlo wiggled his fingers. 'I'll live.'

'It's bruising already.' She looked up at him. 'You hit him hard, Carlo.'

She'd never forget the raw fury in his eyes when he'd looked at her attacker and the skill with which he'd freed her. It was no wonder he didn't use a bodyguard.

'He threatened the woman I love.' Carlo's voice was soft and Zan bit her lip shyly.

'You're sure you love me?'

A strange expression crossed his face. 'Could you fetch me some ice for this hand, *tesoro*?'

So his hand was hurting more than he'd let on.

Slightly disappointed that he hadn't declared his love more emphatically, she stood up and hurried into the kitchen.

Maybe he didn't love her that much.

She pulled the ice tray out of the freezer compartment and then gasped.

Inside one of the squares was a stunning diamond ring. *Was he proposing?*

'I love you, Suzannah, and I want you to marry me.' His velvety male tones came from behind her and she turned quickly, still clutching the tray of ice cubes with the ring inside.

'How long has this been in here?'

'Since this morning when we finished tidying up your flat. It's a good job those thugs didn't want ice in their drinks,' he drawled, lifting the ring out of the ice tray and holding it in his palm. It sparkled and winked temptingly and she gazed at it in astonishment.

'You bought it this morning? But it's Boxing Day. You can't buy a ring on Boxing Day. The shops are shut.'

Carlo smiled. 'Not if your name is Santini.'

She shook her head in wonder as he reached forward and took her hand.

'I can't believe you mean this,' she whispered, her lips parting in a sigh as he slipped the ring onto her finger. 'You seriously want me to marry you?'

'Oh, yes.' His dark gaze was fixed on her possessively. 'I've never been more serious about anything in my whole life.'

'B-but you date models and film stars,' she stammered, twisting the ring on her finger and looking at him doubtfully. 'I'm just me.'

'And I love everything about you,' he said softly, pulling her closer. 'I think I loved you from the moment you knocked me onto the wet street. You were brave and funny and dedicated to your patients and you were nothing like the women I've ever known before. I love your green eyes and your dimples and your amazing legs. I love the fact that you care about everyone—I even love the fact that you can give me a black eye if I ever step out of line.'

Zan put a hand on his chest. 'But we're so different. I haven't got money.'

Carlo looked amused. 'But I have more than enough for both of us.'

'Aren't you worried I'd be a threat to your bank balance?'

'Fortunately my bank balance is *big*.' He laughed. 'It would take quite a lot to threaten it.'

Zan looked at him, her eyes twinkling. 'So, if I marry you, do I get to spend your money?'

'You do indeed, *tesoro*.' He was still smiling. 'What did you have in mind?'

'Nothing. I was just teasing.' She looked at him and

smiled shyly. 'I don't care about the money. All I want is you.'

'You're sure?' He sucked in a breath and his arms tightened around her. 'I thought what we had was special but then, after last night, I wasn't sure you felt the same way. I thought I'd blown it totally.'

'I was so angry with you.' She bit her lip guiltily. 'I'm sorry.'

'Don't be.' His voice was gentle. 'You had every right to be angry and, believe me, I felt very bad about not telling you the truth. But everything else about us was real.'

'I know.' She stared into his eyes. 'I realised that when those journalists started spouting lies about you. I suddenly realised just how well I knew you.'

He stroked a thumb over her cheek. 'Do you think what you feel for me is strong enough to withstand the dirt that journalists throw at me?'

'Yes.'

He took a deep breath. 'And how do you feel about living in Italy with me?'

'Excited.'

She couldn't believe that it was really happening. That he really wanted to marry her.

He lowered his head and took her mouth, his kiss hot and demanding, and when they finally broke apart she was flushed and breathless.

'When you were shouting at me last night, you said you didn't want my babies and that you weren't going to punch the woman I married. Frankly, I had trouble keeping up. What did you mean?'

'Oh…' Zan went pink and rubbed her toe on the wooden floor. 'It was a conversation I had with Kim.'

'Which was?'

He wasn't letting her be evasive and she gave a sigh.

'She asked how I'd feel if you married someone else and I said I'd want to punch her on the nose.'

Carlo threw back his head and laughed. 'Good job I'm marrying you, then.' He hesitated slightly and there was an odd gleam in his eye. 'And the baby bit?'

She blushed shyly. 'I looked at you on Christmas Eve when you were Father Christmas and I knew I wanted to have your children.'

His smile faded. 'And do you still feel that way?' His voice was hoarse. 'Do you still want my babies, *tesoro*?'

She sucked in a breath. 'More than anything.'

'And you've forgiven me for keeping my identity a secret?'

'Providing you never keep a secret from me again.' She reached up to kiss him. 'Otherwise I might just give you a black eye.'

He hugged her close. 'No more secrets. I promise you that. From now on we share everything. And you need to stop doing the Lottery. It would be embarrassing if we won.'

Zan smiled. 'I've already won,' she said softly, standing on tiptoe to kiss him. 'I found you.'

Mediterranean Men

Let them sweep you off your feet!

Gorgeous Greeks
The Greek Bridegroom by Helen Bianchin
The Greek Tycoon's Mistress by Julia James

Seductive Spaniards
At the Spaniard's Pleasure by Jacqueline Baird
The Spaniard's Woman by Diana Hamilton

Irresistible Italians
The Italian's Wife by Lynne Graham
The Italian's Passionate Proposal by Sarah Morgan